D1253918

SOMEONE TO SAVE YOU

ALSO BY PAUL PILKINGTON

The One You Love (Emma Holden trilogy, book 1)
The One You Fear (Emma Holden trilogy, book 2)
The One You Trust (Emma Holden trilogy, book 3)
Be Careful What You Hear

PAUL PILKINGTON

SOMEONE TO SAVE YOU

This is a work of fiction. Names, characters, organizations, places, events, and incidents are either products of the author's imagination or are used fictitiously.

Text copyright © 2015 Paul Pilkington

All rights reserved.

No part of this book may be reproduced, or stored in a retrieval system, or transmitted in any form or by any means, electronic, mechanical, photocopying, recording, or otherwise, without express written permission of the publisher.

Published by Thomas & Mercer, Seattle

www.apub.com

Amazon, the Amazon logo, and Thomas & Mercer are trademarks of Amazon.com, Inc., or its affiliates.

ISBN-13: 978-1503948471
ISBN-10: 1503948471

Cover design by bürosüd° München, www.buerosued.de

Printed in the United States of America

For my family

PART ONE

Chapter One

The teenage girl came from nowhere, running straight out into the middle of the country road from behind a line of trees.

Sam Becker slammed on the brakes and wrenched the wheel hard right, feeling the seat belt lock as he was thrown forward at speed. The car jerked before losing control, spinning on its axis while throwing up an ear-piercing screech. Everything was a blur until suddenly the spinning came to a violent stop, sending Sam's head flying back into the headrest.

Shaking off his dizziness, he twisted anxiously left, then right, looking for the girl, but he couldn't see her. 'Please, no.'

He staggered out of the car and was about to look underneath the vehicle when he spotted her standing across the road, several yards down a dirt track that ran off to the left.

'Please, help us!' she shouted, crying. 'Please!'

He moved towards her as she ran in the opposite direction, heading farther back down the lane. 'Wait,' Sam shouted after her. 'Are you okay?'

He followed her around the corner and found her standing by a smashed-down fence. 'Down there – you've got to help us,' she pleaded. 'Please, help us – quick.'

As Sam moved closer, he could see down the embankment to the railway line below.

'Oh my God.'

The car was astride the railway line, and someone was sitting motionless in the driver's seat.

'Please, help us!' the girl repeated, standing there at the edge of the embankment, sobbing.

Sam nodded, trying to take in the situation. His eyes traced the journey of the car, from the point where they stood, through the smashed wooden fence and down the steep, grassy embankment onto the track. 'What's your name?'

'Alison.'

'My name's Sam.' He placed a hand on the girl's shoulder while trying to think. His body was on overdrive. As a cardiothoracic surgeon he was used to dealing with emergency situations, but nothing like this. He looked left, then right, down the line. No trains. But he would have to be quick. 'Is that your mum down there?'

Alison nodded, sniffling. 'She said she wants to die. I didn't know she was going to drive on there. Please, help.'

'It's going to be okay,' he promised, hurriedly picking his way through the broken fence. Alison began to follow, but he gestured at her to stop. 'You'll be safer staying here.'

'Jessica's in the back,' she sobbed.

'Right,' he replied, turning back to the car. Now he looked more closely, he could see something in the back seat. 'Just wait there. Everything will be okay, I promise.'

Alison nodded, but already Sam was scrambling down the bank, his hands brushing against stinging nettles as he tried to keep his balance. He raced onto the track and up to the car. Now he too was in the impact zone for any approaching train. He would have to act quickly. He pulled at the door handle.

Locked.

'Open the door,' he shouted at the woman inside. She appeared slightly older than him, maybe late thirties. She looked utterly vacant, staring straight ahead at the track, not even acknowledging his presence. He banged on the glass. Without her co-operation, this could end very badly. 'Open the door, please.'

He peered through the back window. There were two young children in the rear, a boy and a girl, about a year old, strapped into booster seats. The child nearer him met his gaze. They'd both been crying; their reddened faces were tear-stained, but they seemed calm now.

Sam looked back at the woman. Then he noticed the handcuffs attached to the steering wheel. What the hell? This hadn't been a spur-of-the-moment suicide attempt; this was well planned. It would make things so much harder. 'Christ.'

He looked down the track, which turned off at an angle a few hundred yards ahead. This was no longer just a matter of coaxing her out of the car. Blood was pulsing in his head as his heart raced. He thrust his hand into his pocket for his mobile, but it wasn't there. It was in his jacket, on the front seat of his car.

'So stupid,' he said, chastising himself for not picking it up at the time. There was no time to go back.

He tried to push the car, straining until his body felt like it was about to explode with the effort. But the handbrake was on, and his feet slid on the stones between the tracks, denying him any grip. The vehicle just rocked back and forwards. Sam turned back to the woman. 'I know how you must be feeling,' he pleaded, 'but you don't want to kill your children, do you?'

She never flinched.

'Look,' Sam shouted, throwing another nervous glance down the track. 'Any minute a train could come, and we'll all be dead. Your daughter up there,' he said, pointing to Alison, 'you don't want her to see this, do you? What will she do without you, without her brothers and sisters?'

Nothing.

Sam looked at the two children, then at the window. There was no other way.

He searched between the rails and found a sharp-edged stone, about the size of a tennis ball. 'Close your eyes,' he ordered, already hammering on the bottom right-hand corner of the passenger front window. He increased the force, until cracks appeared. After four more hits the window shattered, but being safety glass, held itself in place. The children in the back seat began crying, shocked and scared by the drama. 'Close your eyes,' Sam shouted again as he elbowed away the glass as gently as he could. Cubes of glass flew onto the front seat, some hitting the woman, who remained wide-eyed and motionless. Finally, the way was clear for Sam to reach the inside door handle. Undoing the lock, he ripped open the passenger door and grabbed for the handbrake. Once more, he tried to push the car, straining with the effort. 'For God's sake, please move.' This time the car did move forward a little, but the wheels were jammed in between the tracks, and there was no way it could be pushed any further.

Another glance down the line – still no train.

He needed to try something different. Stay calm, stay focused. He reached back in the car and thrust the spare passenger seat forward, giving him access to the children.

'Come on,' he said, undoing the children's seat belts with shaking hands. He grabbed at the little boy. 'Come with me.' He pulled him close to his chest and placed him carefully on the grass bank, just a couple of yards away. Rushing back to the car, he brought out the little girl. Then, as carefully as possible, he scooped up the two children, one under each arm. They were heavier than he expected, weighing him down as he fought his way up the embankment. The steep incline was hard going, but this was the safest place. He passed the children to Alison, peeling them away from him as they clung onto his shirt. 'Look after your brother and sister.'

And that's when he heard the ominous hiss, reverberating across the overhead power lines.

A train was approaching.

'My mum, please help my mum!' Alison screamed.

He slid back down towards the car, burning his hands against the dry scrubland, momentum slamming him into the car's side. Still no train. But the hiss was getting louder.

His chest felt volcanic, and he struggled to catch his breath. The woman was still silent, still staring dead ahead. 'The keys to the handcuffs,' he gasped. 'Where are the keys?'

No answer.

'The keys!' he shouted. 'Tell me where they are.'

He thrust his hands into her coat pockets and then the rest of her clothing, desperately searching every possible place where the keys might be. There was no reaction from her, even when he forced his hands into her tight jeans pockets. The keys were nowhere.

What was he going to do now? Maybe he should have told Alison to retrieve his mobile phone. He looked up at her, watching from the top with the children in her arms.

And then the train appeared around the top of the bend, travelling fast. A horn blared and the emergency brakes screeched. 'Please, God, no,' Sam cried, stepping back from the car as the train sped towards them. 'Look away!' he shouted to Alison, through the deafening scream of the brakes. 'Don't look!' The horn blared again, but the train didn't seem to slow. Sam tried to push the car again, in one last desperate effort.

It was still held fast.

'Please, help Jessica!' Alison screamed hysterically from the top of the embankment. 'She's in the back! Jessica's in the back!'

7

Sam looked up at her, then back towards the car. What did she mean? Then a sickening realisation hit him.

The boot.

He thrust his head in the car, scrambling to find the boot release lever. As with his vehicle, it was on the far side, near the accelerator pedal. He threw himself across the still motionless woman and strained to reach the lever, pulling it upwards, knowing that any second the train would hit. Hauling himself out of the car he rushed to the back. The train was bearing down on them, brakes still screeching, no more than a hundred yards away. He had only seconds before impact. He threw open the boot. A tiny baby, wrapped in a pure white shawl, looked up at him with watery blue eyes. He grabbed it as a thunderous noise enveloped him, instinctively sprinting off to his left and diving for cover, shielding the baby from the impact as he hit the ground.

And then everything went black.

Chapter Two

Sam's head was pounding with the sound of sirens, shouts and screams, piercing the darkness. Then a soft Irish voice sliced through the gloom.

'Sam? Mr Becker?'

He opened his eyes, the harsh, artificial hospital light blasting him like a full-on torch beam. For that first moment he didn't know where on earth he was; his bearings were all over the place. And then, with shocking suddenness, he remembered – the train crash. His dry lips peeled apart as he tried to speak.

'Sorry to disturb you,' the sister said, smiling warmly, 'but there's someone here that I'm sure you'll want to see.'

Sam shifted in the bed, his eyes still adjusting to the conditions. He saw his wife, Anna, approach. For a second, watching her standing there with her face full of concern, he wondered if the blow to his head was causing him to hallucinate.

She shouldn't be here.

'I'll leave you be,' the sister said, exiting with a smile.

Anna moved anxiously towards the bed. 'Thank God, you're okay.'

Sam raised himself from his pillows to meet her, trying to reassure her with the movement that things weren't as bad as they seemed. 'How did you . . . you should be on a plane to Bangladesh.'

As co-ordinator for Hope Springs, an emergency relief charity based in London, Anna had been called out to respond to severe flooding in the delta region of the south of the country. A water and sanitation specialist, she had spent years working abroad, mostly in India, where Sam had first met her six years ago during his placement in the paediatric department at the Christian Medical Hospital in Vellore. And although she now spent most of her time working out of the London offices, occasionally her technical and organisational skills would be required on site.

'The hospital called me just as I was about to leave for the airport,' Anna explained, taking his hand. Her skin was warm and smooth, and as she kissed his cheek, Sam breathed in her familiar, comforting perfume. She'd bought the scent on a romantic break in Rome three years ago, and it always reminded him of that magical weekend in the Eternal City. 'Louisa and I drove up here as quickly as we could,' said Anna.

'But what about the trip? The emergency.'

'Don't worry about that,' she replied, examining his face with concern. 'Anyway, I'm pretty sure this classes as an emergency. Let me deal with one at a time, eh?'

She placed a comforting hand on his head, gently brushing away some stray hair.

'It only comes in black and blue,' Sam noted, referring to the nasty-looking bruising around his left eye that was throbbing to its own pulse.

'Looks sore. Are you sure you're okay?'

'I'm fine, honestly. Just minor bruising – nothing broken, no lasting damage. They've done all the obs. Said they might let me go in a couple of hours. Feel like I could sleep forever, though.'

He twisted to read his wristwatch by the bedside, wincing at the short stab of pain from his side. He'd been asleep for just over an hour, and it was now three hours since the crash. He'd slept most of the time since that horrific event, and everything was a bit of a blur. There were snippets of memories – the acrid smell of burning, the shouts and the moans, the wail of sirens and flash of blue lights, the squawk of radios, the young female paramedic talking him back to consciousness and then struggling to keep him awake, the first few minutes in the ambulance as it rocked and rolled away from the scene over the uneven ground.

He slumped back onto his pillow. 'Did they tell you what happened?'

'Not much,' Anna said, perching on the edge of the bed. 'There was a crash involving a train, a car and you. I was so scared when they called,' she added, squeezing his hand as her green eyes glistened with tears. 'What the hell happened?'

Sam shook his head, thinking back to the events. 'I was driving home and a girl ran straight out in front of the car. Somehow – I really don't know how – I managed to avoid hitting her, and then she led me to her mother. She'd driven her car onto the railway track, with her kids strapped in the back. Her baby was in the boot.'

'My God,' Anna said, aghast. 'You think it was a suicide attempt?'

'Her daughter told me she drove the car straight onto the track and that she wanted to kill herself,' Sam replied. 'I tried to talk to her, convince her to move, but it was like she was in a trance, just staring straight ahead. I tried to move the car, but it wouldn't budge. I got the children out, but I couldn't get her before the train came.' He thought of the woman in the driving seat, the emotional shutdown that he'd seen too many times before in the eyes of mothers and fathers, brothers and sisters, who had just lost a loved one on the operating table. 'Did they say anything about the children and the mother? They wouldn't tell me anything.'

Anna shook her head.

'The people on the train?'

'They didn't tell me anything else.'

'Who spoke to you? The hospital?'

'The police. They're waiting outside to see you. I think the nurses have been holding them back until they think you're ready.'

'I should speak to them.'

'Only if you're ready,' Anna replied. 'If you're not, I'll tell them to wait.'

Sam smiled – Anna was always ready to defend people in their hour of need, and now it was his turn. 'I'm okay. Where's Louisa?'

'Getting some coffee – it was a busy, stressful drive. It took us two hours to travel the twenty miles from home. Louisa said she's never going to travel through London at rush hour ever again.'

Louisa was a childhood friend of Sam and now a good friend to Anna also. She was considered more like family. Probably the only aspect concerning her that Sam didn't trust completely was her driving skills – her car, a rusting old-style mini, had had more bumps and scrapes than a dodgem.

'You didn't have to ruin your trip for me you know,' he said. 'The people in Bangladesh need you more.'

Anna kissed his forehead tenderly.

Sam smiled. 'But I'm glad you're here. That's all the treatment I need.'

The two plain-clothes officers strode in, led by the Irish sister. As the sister left them, she exchanged a glance with the officers that

Sam could tell was a warning to take it slowly with her patient. After twelve years on hospital wards, he was adept at interpreting the body language and expressions of staff.

'Mr Becker,' the taller of the two began as Anna reluctantly stepped back from the bed and took up a place a few feet away, her arms folded across her chest. The policeman was pushing six foot four, and built like a rugby front row forward. His dark hair was shaved short, and his face was strong and sculpted. Sam placed him in his late thirties. His partner, the scribe, was round-faced, noticeably shorter and older, maybe in his fifties. He sported a greying moustache. 'How are you?'

'I'm okay,' Sam replied, sitting up straighter. He could smell diesel and smoke, and noted that their white shirts were holding black dust.

'That's good,' the officer said. His accent wasn't too dissimilar from Sam's own: somewhere around Manchester. 'I hear you're a doctor yourself.'

Sam nodded.

'What speciality?'

'Paediatric heart surgery.'

The officer unfurled a lip, impressed. 'Must be strange to be on the other side, being the patient rather than the one doing the looking after.'

'It is,' Sam agreed. And it was. Sam, like most doctors, was a terrible patient, as Anna had commented on the previous year during a bout of heavy flu. It felt completely wrong to be in the bed rather than the one standing over it. Maybe it had something to do with the loss of control: placing yourself in someone else's care. When it came to it, most doctors were control freaks. 'I don't intend to be a patient for much longer,' he added.

The officer suppressed a smile, getting back to the task at hand. 'Mr Becker . . .' He hesitated. 'It is Mr, isn't it?'

Sam nodded. He had successfully completed his training and Royal College of Surgery exams six months ago, and in the ironic world of medicine, the seventy-hour weeks, the nights sleeping on the ward while on call, the years of study, all those personal sacrifices, had resulted in the dropping of the doctor title he'd worked so hard for in the first place.

'Well, Mr Becker – Sam – I'm Detective Inspector Paul Cullen, of the British Transport Police, and this is my partner, Detective Sergeant Tony Beswick. We're part of the accident investigation team examining this afternoon's crash. We have a few questions, if that's okay with you.'

'Sure,' Sam replied. 'But can I ask a question first?'

Cullen nodded.

'How are the children and their mother?'

'The children are all fine.'

'Even the baby?'

'Yes.'

'And the mother?'

'I'm sorry,' said Cullen.

Sam wasn't surprised, but it still saddened him greatly. He nodded his understanding.

DI Cullen continued. 'No one could have survived a head-on impact at that speed. The train was travelling at fifty miles an hour when it hit. She would have died instantly.'

Sam took in the news. The woman had got part of what she wanted, but she hadn't taken the children with her. Had she really wanted them to die too? And what about the other people who were affected? Did she think about them when she'd made the decision to crash through the fence and drive onto the track?

'The passengers on the train?'

'All okay,' said Cullen. 'A few walking wounded – half a dozen or so cases of whiplash, minor injuries to arms and legs, and some

14

people with shock. The driver is being counselled. As you can imagine, he's pretty shook up about the whole thing. Thankfully, the train stayed on the tracks. If the thing had derailed, the situation would have been very different.'

Sam pondered that thought. It was still hard to believe that he'd been a matter of yards from a head-on, high-speed train collision, yet had survived with nothing more than a black eye and slight bruising. And for the baby to have been unharmed too – it was nothing short of miraculous.

'Are you okay to answer some of our questions now, Mr Becker?' the officer asked, his voice revealing a touch of impatience. 'We'll be as quick as we can.'

'Fire away,' Sam said.

'Great. We need to piece together what happened. How you became involved, what you did, what you saw, right up until the impact.'

Just then Sam heard a commotion outside and saw a flash of light up against the window of his private room.

Cullen spun round and pointed at the door. 'Get that photographer ejected from the premises,' he barked at his colleague. 'And if they resist, arrest them. I told them, no one is allowed up here.'

His colleague nodded and exited the room.

'Sorry about that,' said Cullen, regaining his composure. 'We tried to keep the media away from this, but there's a swarm of them down at reception. Somehow they must have found out which ward you were on.'

'It's okay.' Sam exchanged glances with Anna, who was looking out towards the melee. DS Beswick could be heard directing the photographer back downstairs in no uncertain terms.

'Right,' Cullen said. 'First of all, what brought you to the location of the crash?'

'I was driving back home from a family event in the North West,' Sam explained.

'Family event?'

'My sister's birthday.'

'So you were with your sister over the weekend?'

'Not exactly,' Sam replied.

'I don't understand.'

Sam hesitated and Anna, who had been listening intently, picked up the baton. 'Cathy, Sam's sister, died when she was young. Yesterday would have been her thirtieth birthday.'

'Oh, right,' Cullen said, his brow creasing. 'Sorry to hear that. So, it was a commemoration . . .'

'Celebration,' Sam corrected. 'At least that was the plan.'

'Okay.' Cullen made some more notes. 'So can you just talk me through what happened as you were driving back home?'

'I was driving back – it was about five o'clock – when something ran straight out in front of me. It came from my left, and my first thought was that it was a deer or something. But I realised it was a girl, a teenage girl. I swerved to miss her, and then I followed her down to the—'

'You were led to the scene by a teenage girl?' interrupted Cullen, his face expressing surprise and possibly disbelief.

'Yes, Alison,' Sam confirmed, noting Cullen's reaction. 'The woman's daughter. What's the matter?'

Cullen didn't answer, simply raising a hand as he brought a police radio receiver up to his mouth. 'Hi. DI Cullen here. We've got a problem.'

Chapter Three

The morning following the train crash, Sam prepared the breakfast, handling the knife with a surgeon's skill as he buttered the toast and skimmed off the top of the boiled eggs. He'd been up for three hours now, since just before five, unable to stop his mind from racing and his body aching. For a time he'd just sat up in bed, staring at the wall while Anna slept, before tuning in to the early morning news. The main news items that had been replayed several times in the ensuing hours – a hurricane slamming into the Caribbean, and yet more killing in the Middle East – weren't a recipe for sound sleeping.

Anna appeared, and Sam smiled as she approached. Her slender, almost fragile frame belied an inner toughness, and her youthful face disguised a wealth of life experience. She was wearing her pyjamas, with her chocolate brown hair tied back from her lightly tanned skin in a loose ponytail – a style that always reminded him of the first time they had met, when a feisty, determined twenty-four-year-old Anna had burst into his sweltering corrugated-iron outreach theatre room in the tiny rural Indian village, cradling a young girl whom she had found lying by the side of the road after the child had been hit by a motorcycle. Bypassing the security on the door, who had told her to wait, Anna had taken it upon herself to bring the child, Grace, to Sam's attention. And for good reason – ten minutes later and the girl might not have survived her internal injuries. That meeting had sparked an instant and lasting mutual attraction between Sam and Anna. They grew closer throughout Sam's year elective at the Vellore Christian University Medical School; and for the next two years, when Sam returned home, inspired to train in paediatric surgery following his experiences in India, and Anna continued her work abroad, they stayed in contact by email and phone. Then one day Anna turned up at his flat. She'd been promoted, and her time would now be split between co-ordinating projects in countries around the world from the London offices, with occasional travel abroad to oversee the work. A year later they were engaged, and eighteen months after that, married. It was only then Anna admitted that, with her father being a successful but work-addicted consultant neurologist who always put medicine before family, she had initially been extremely hesitant about getting into a relationship with a doctor.

'Couldn't sleep?' asked Anna, rubbing her eyes as she watched Sam pour the tea.

'Not much,' he admitted, turning to face her.

'Bad dreams?'

Sam shook his head, stirring the tea. 'I just keep seeing the look in the eyes of that woman. And I keep thinking – how can you do that to your children?'

Anna shrugged.

'I mean, what could be so bad that you'd lock your baby up in the boot of your car, strap your children in the back seats and drive straight onto a railway track?'

'She can't have known what she was doing.' Anna took the tea that Sam proffered.

'Probably not,' Sam agreed, looking off towards the left.

'What are you thinking?'

'I'm thinking that she must have locked the doors after driving down the embankment. She watched one of her children get away and run for help, and her reaction was to lock the doors, knowing that the other three would probably die as a result.'

'It's impossible for us to understand,' Anna said.

Sam exhaled, taking a sip of tea and grimacing at the singeing heat. 'If only I could have got the car off the tracks. I was nearly there; I could feel the car moving . . .'

'You're bound to think things like that.' Anna cradled her drink. 'But you couldn't have done anything more. You saved three people's lives.'

But he hadn't saved one person's life. And that thought gnawed at him, the same as it did whenever a patient was lost. Yes, he pushed it to the back of his mind – he had to, in order to focus on the next person – but the regret was still there. It was what drove him to improve: he didn't ever want to find such failure acceptable.

'I should have called someone to stop the trains. I should have gone back to get my phone.'

'It's easy to say that now,' Anna countered. 'Hindsight is a wonderful thing. And who's to say the outcome would have been any different?'

Sam nodded. 'You're right – as usual.'

'Come here,' she said, putting down her tea and embracing him. They hugged tightly, and Sam wallowed in the comfort of Anna's body as it moulded to his. He buried his head in her hair, smelling her shampoo.

'I do love you, Sam Becker.'

'I love you too,' he replied over her shoulder, kissing her hair. He pulled back to see Anna's eyes were watering. 'You okay?'

Anna nodded. 'Just a bit emotional after everything that's happened. I don't like the thought of losing you.'

'You won't,' he reassured her, hugging her again. 'I promise. I'll take you to the airport. Seeing as I've now got the day off.'

This time it was Anna who pulled back. 'Are you sure you don't want me to stick around?' she said, searching his eyes for the answer. 'I can call Bob now, and that will be that. They'll just have to make do without me this time.'

Sam shook his head. He had persuaded Anna on the drive home from the hospital that she should make the trip to Bangladesh – they desperately needed her expertise – so she had somewhat reluctantly booked a replacement flight when they got home. 'They need you, Anna. Honestly, I'll be okay. The hospital wouldn't have let me go so soon if they hadn't been satisfied. I just need some rest. Anyway, it's only four days.'

'Okay,' Anna replied, not sounding convinced. 'But on one condition.'

'Go on.'

'That you'll think about seeing that counsellor.'

The hospital had offered Sam an appointment with a counsellor, which was now standard procedure for anyone involved in a traumatic event. It was meant to reduce the likelihood of developing post-traumatic stress disorder, although there were some who believed that it actually increased the chances of suffering after-effects. Sam had politely declined, although Anna had thought it could be a good idea.

'Okay,' he conceded. 'I'll think about it.'

One hour and a hearty breakfast later, Doug McAllister, a consultant anaesthetist who was a good friend and colleague of Sam's, rang to let them know that there was a short piece in the *Telegraph* about the train crash. Anna set off immediately to the local newsagent's, returning ten minutes later.

'I checked all the papers, and the story is in five of them.'

She handed Sam the pile of papers as he sat by the large bay window of their ground-floor flat. It offered a lovely view across to a small but beautiful area of parkland in Clerkenwell, North London. The place, the bottom half of a Georgian property, wasn't the largest, but it was more than adequate for two people, and they were lucky in having the garden. It had also been fortunate that they'd bought when they did – just before the London house price boom. Their long-term upstairs neighbours, a young couple with whom they had become good friends, had recently sold the top-floor flat for just over three hundred thousand. It was no wonder that the new guy to move in was a City banker – you had to be to afford those kinds of prices. Sam had been meaning to return the spare front-door key, which they'd recently found buried in a kitchen drawer.

Sam surveyed the papers on his lap with horror, hardly daring to open them for fear of what was written inside.

'They don't mention you by name,' Anna said, flicking through the top newspaper and pointing at the story on page ten. The headline read; 'GOOD SAMARITAN SAVES TRAIN CRASH FAMILY.' Sam skimmed the article. There was indeed no mention of his name, although the piece documented the identity of the dead woman, Jane Ainsley, from Islington, North London, and her children Alison, Simon, Charlotte and baby Jessica.

'They only live just down the road.' Anna settled down next to Sam, perching on the wide ledge.

Sam nodded. 'It doesn't mention that Alison is missing,' he noted, reading on.

'None of the papers do,' Anna confirmed. 'They're all a little sketchy. I guess they had to go to print before they could get many details. What do you think's happened to her?'

21

'Who knows? Maybe, like Louisa said, she's traumatised and just wanted to get away. I just hope that she's safe, wherever she is. I guess we'll just have to wait to hear from the police.'

Anna nodded. 'They'll probably want to speak with you again.'

'I'd say definitely, especially if Alison isn't found soon,' said Sam, moving on to the next paper. The story was essentially the same. He placed all the papers on the side and looked out across the street outside, watching the people pass by. He watched a stocky man as he crouched down, stroking his dog in front of the flat, before moving on. 'I hope that's the end of the press. I don't want any publicity.'

'You're afraid they'll pick up Cathy's story?'

'They did last time.'

Twelve months ago, in the middle of a transatlantic flight to a conference in Washington, DC, Sam had saved a baby's life. The baby was suffering from a collapsed lung, and Sam used a straw and a needle to reopen the infant's airways. The saving of the baby, who happened to be the child of a high-profile American senator expected to be a future presidential candidate, made headlines around the world. The story brought press attention that Sam found difficult to handle – especially when the press picked up on the story of his sister Cathy's death. Over a decade ago, she had been brutally raped and murdered by Sam's then best friend, Marcus Johnson. The coverage had reopened wounds that even a surgeon of Sam's talent couldn't easily mend.

'Maybe today's stories will be it,' Anna said.

'Hopefully.'

Anna reached for his hand. 'I'm really sorry. With all that's happened we haven't even spoken about what it was like at the weekend. Was it okay?'

'Better than I expected,' Sam replied. 'Mum and Dad seem to be finally moving on with their lives. It's only taken fifteen years.'

'Did anyone mention Marcus Johnson's release?'

Marcus Johnson, the person who had so brutally cut short his little sister's life, was now able to walk the streets and make a new start. Sam was shocked by the strength of hatred he still felt towards the man he used to be so close to. It remained unfathomable to him how Marcus could have betrayed such trust. And during his fifteen years in jail, Marcus had offered no explanation. In fact, he had always protested his innocence, despite the overwhelming evidence against him. It had happened on a camping trip in North Wales. Sam and Marcus, Louisa and Cathy. On the second morning Louisa had woken Sam and Marcus. Cathy had gone. After twenty minutes of frantic searching, her body was found on the nearby sand dunes. Tests revealed later that Cathy's body had been covered with Marcus's DNA. There was hair, skin, semen – it all matched. They had never found the murder weapon, thought to have been a glass bottle, but they hadn't needed to. In the immediate aftermath, Marcus had denied being with Cathy that night. But when it became clear that the evidence was so stacked against him, he'd changed his story. He claimed they had been dating in secret for months and that they had crept out of the tents and walked down to the beach, before drinking vodka under the stars and making love. He had written to Sam, protesting his innocence. He said his last memory was lying down next to Cathy, and although he was unable to remember anything after that, he would never have hurt her.

Sam shook his head. 'No one said a word about it, including me.'

His parents hadn't spoken about Marcus's release, and instead it had hung like a ghost over the Remembrance Day.

'So you don't know how they feel about it – your parents?'

'I can guess,' Sam replied. 'I think they just want to pretend that he's still locked up.'

'And you?'

Sam shrugged his shoulders. 'Pretty much the same, really. I think he should have spent the rest of his life inside. But he's out, and that's it.'

Sam glanced across at Anna, in the front passenger seat, as they crawled through the traffic on the outskirts of Heathrow later that afternoon. She'd been uncharacteristically quiet throughout the journey to the airport and had spent most of the time staring out of the window. 'You're sure you're okay?' he asked.

She shook herself out of her daydream. 'What? Sorry?'

'Just wondering if you're okay,' Sam explained. 'You've been really quiet. If it's about going away, I'll be okay, honestly. And if it's about me risking my life like an idiot, I promise I won't do that again.'

He glanced over at his wife.

'It's something else?' he tried. She was biting on her lip – a sure sign that something was bothering her.

But Anna kept quiet.

Sam brought his attention back to the road as the traffic thinned slightly. He followed the signs for Terminal 3, edging around coaches and cars that were busy unloading luggage irrespective of traffic laws. One car was parked across half a lane, the boot jammed full of cases. Heathrow was always a nightmare to negotiate. Once they were finally parked in a drop-off zone, Sam looked across at Anna, whose eyes were now glistening with tears. She very rarely cried.

Sam placed a hand on her shoulder. 'What's the matter, A?'

Anna surprised him by smiling as she pinched the tears away. 'I've got something to tell you,' she began. 'I was going to tell you last night, but it didn't seem like the right time. And I wanted to be sure, so I did another test just before we left the house.'

Suddenly Sam knew, breaking out into a smile of his own. 'You're . . . ?'

Anna took his hand in hers and smiled broadly. 'We're having a baby.'

Chapter Four

S am Becker watched little Sophie Jackson. She looked so fragile while asleep, like a doll, eyes closed, with alabaster skin. Born with a congenital heart defect, Sophie, now two years old, was clinging to life as her heart failed. But now she had a chance, thanks to the Berlin Heart, a miniature heart pump that acted as a bridge between her own failing heart and a donor one. Five days ago Sam had led the procedure to fit the device. It had all gone to plan; yet it would all come to nothing unless she could get that transplant.

'Your mum and dad love you very much, Sophie. Keep fighting.'

Sam had known Sophie and her parents, Tom and Sarah, since her birth, and they had been in contact ever since. The adorable little girl had been a fighter since her first breath, and she was still fighting, but time was running out. The pump would buy her time, maybe up to twelve months, but in truth there was no telling, and the risk of death was always there. She was, however, in the best place. The Cardiothoracic Centre at St Thomas's Hospital, on the banks of the Thames in Central London, was one of the most advanced treatment centres in the world. With state-of-the-art equipment, a suite of private high-dependency rooms, and some of the best-trained staff in the world, the centre was barely five years old. It was up there with the best in paediatric cardiac surgery, and for Sam, working under one of the world's foremost surgeons, Professor Adil Khan, it was a dream job.

'Thought I'd find you here.'

Sam looked up as Louisa approached and pulled up a chair. Louisa, with her flowing hippy dress, corkscrew curly red hair and freckled face, cut a distinctive figure in the otherwise uniformed, groomed hospital environment. Far from unattractive, she turned heads among both staff and patients. Always jovial, she was a popular clinical psychologist who did a lot of good work with patients and family on the wards. She was a master listener and, where necessary, imparter of advice.

'Hello there,' Sam said.

'I had a few minutes between consultations,' she explained, 'so I thought I'd come up and congratulate the main man in person.'

'Thanks,' Sam said, receiving a hug and peck on the cheek.

Although it would be some weeks before they would make an announcement about Anna's pregnancy to family and friends, Anna had told Sam he could tell Louisa straightaway. She thought he might need someone else to talk to about it while she was away. And Louisa wasn't just any friend. Following Cathy's murder, Sam had cut ties with his childhood friends, moving to London to study medicine. But he had remained in contact with Louisa, who in many ways took on the role of his surrogate little sister. She didn't have any brothers or sisters and, like Sam, was left alone by the tragedy. She had also been a good friend of Marcus's before that fateful trip – they had been next-door neighbours – so she felt the same sense of betrayal. Having trained as a clinical psychologist, she'd worked for a time in Liverpool before a job came up at St Thomas's. Sam was surprised but delighted when she went for it, explaining that she needed a change of scene and a new challenge. And although she was a constant reminder of Cathy, her presence and friendship was a great comfort.

'I bet you're higher than a kite,' she added.

'I am,' Sam replied. 'I'm not sure it's sunk in yet, but it's going to be fantastic.'

Louisa squeezed his arm. 'I was so excited when you told me. You'll make great parents – I just know you will. And I can't believe I'll be an aunty.'

Sam smiled. 'Aunty Louisa has a certain ring to it.'

'And how is the mum-to-be?'

'Emotional. I'm not used to Anna breaking down in tears, but she couldn't stop crying when I said goodbye.'

'Understandable,' Louisa noted. 'It's a massive life-changing moment. Not that I'd know, of course.'

'You will,' Sam said. 'Maybe this new boyfriend of yours will turn out to be The One.'

'Maybe,' Louisa agreed. 'Early days yet, though – it's only been a few weeks.'

'Well, I've never seen you as happy as you've been since you met him, so whoever he is, he must be pretty special.'

'He is – but enough about my love life. How is the little golden girl?'

'She's still doing okay,' Sam replied, watching Sophie sleeping, her small chest rising and falling with each breath. 'She's very tired, sleeping lots, but that's to be expected.'

'You still hopeful?'

'We have to be,' Sam said. 'But it just depends on whether she can hold on until we find a suitable donor.'

'Any news?'

'No,' Sam revealed. 'She's top of the list, but hearts suitable for two-year-olds aren't easy to come by.'

It was a sad truth that more than twenty per cent of paediatric heart transplant candidates died while waiting for an organ to become available.

'I guess not,' Louisa said. 'It's sad that we're here, hoping that a heart becomes available, yet for that to happen another child will have to die. It's really horrible when you think about it, isn't it?'

'Some good comes from tragedy, I suppose.'

Louisa nodded. 'I can't really imagine what it must be like to see your own child like this. I mean, I've spoken to parents who have had sick children, counselled them, but until it's your child, I don't think you can ever really understand.'

'No,' Sam agreed. 'The expression on Tom's and Sarah's faces over the past few days, you can see how much it's hurting.'

'Are they around now?'

'They're taking a rest. It's pretty much the first time they've left her side since she came in here. They're exhausted, mentally and physically.'

For a minute or so they both sat there, watching the fragile-looking little girl.

'And how are you?' Louisa said finally. 'I thought you were going to take some time out to recover from your near-death experience.'

'I was going to,' Sam replied. 'But I wanted to see Sophie and check the latest on the donor situation.'

'I hope you're not working today. You should be taking it easy.'

'Mr Khan gave Miles my list.'

'Bet Miles is happy about that,' Louisa joked. 'I can just imagine his reaction. That guy is a total idiot.'

Miles Churchill and Sam were colleagues – or more accurately rivals. Both thirty-four years old, both senior registrars in the speciality of paediatric surgery, and both in competition for a consultant post at the hospital that had just been advertised. The atmosphere between the two had never been great in their four years of working together – Miles had already been working at the hospital for two years when Sam arrived, and Sam sensed that Miles saw him as an invader on his patch. But last year things had cooled to glacial proportions when one of the junior doctors working under Miles had confided in Sam that she felt bullied by him. Wanting to nip things in the bud, Sam had delicately raised the issue with Miles. But his intervention provoked a furious response, with Miles accusing Sam of trying to undermine him. The junior doctor moved on, but the incident dealt a fatal blow to what was left of their working relationship.

'He probably sees it as a promotion opportunity,' Sam commented, prompting a laugh from Louisa.

'Seriously though, Sam,' Louisa added, 'why don't you get away from this place for a few days? Take a total break. You need time for everything to sink in – the crash, Cathy's commemoration, the baby news.'

'Is that what you'd tell one of your clients?'

'It's something that I'd tell anyone.'

'I'd rather be here, trying to be useful.'

Louisa put up her hands to signal surrender. 'Fair enough. Who I am to argue with my adopted big brother, eh?'

'Now you're talking. And as your big brother, I want to vet this new boyfriend of yours – make sure he's good enough for you.'

Sam was only half-joking. Louisa's track record in relationships wasn't the best, and she'd dated some strange men in recent years, most of whom she'd met via Internet dating websites. Although some had obviously been unsuitable – a bad match, others had been plain weird, like the guy who created scrapbooks with newspaper cuttings from high-profile murder trials (he'd claimed he was just interested in the law). And playing the big brother role, Sam truly did want to see her with someone who was right for her.

'All in good time,' Louisa replied, patting him on the knee. 'So, how are you really coping with yesterday's events? Have you booked that appointment with the counsellor?'

'You're as bad as Anna.'

'You need to talk to someone about what happened,' she insisted. 'We should talk about Cathy too. I'm really sorry I couldn't be there, Sam. I was thinking about you all Saturday, wondering how it went.'

'It was okay. And don't worry; it just wasn't possible for you to be there. Everyone understood.'

'So you'll talk about things?'

'I'm not convinced I need it.'

'It will help. Talk to me about it. Not as a psychologist – as a friend.'

Sam met her hopeful smile and nodded. 'Okay, but not here. Let's go grab some coffee.'

Just as they stood up, his phone started to vibrate. He pulled a guilty face. 'Shouldn't really have this on in here.' He retrieved the mobile from his pocket. It was a text message from an unknown number, and it contained just one word.

'"*Hero*"?'

'You okay?' Louisa asked, leaning in to look at the screen.

'Spam message.' Sam snapped the phone shut. 'Come on, coffee time.'

They got as far as the main doors.

'Damn,' Sam said, glaring at his pager as it beeped an alert.

'What is it?' Louisa said.

'The board want to see me.'

'Now?'

Sam nodded. 'Right now. Said it's urgent.'

He picked up the note and stared at the scrawled writing and accompanying telephone number. Since he received it the previous night, his heart hadn't stopped racing. Had he been stupid to believe that everything would work out? Walking over to the telephone, he grabbed the receiver and dialled the number, his hands shaking as sweat coated the handset. As it started to ring at the other end, he thought his heart was about to burst out of his chest. And then the call went through to the answer service, and he relaxed slightly. It would make it easier.

'I just called to say, the answer's no.'

He put the phone down, and moved into the bathroom to wash his face. His skin was ashen, his eyes red and swollen from lack of quality sleep. He couldn't take much more of this.

But maybe that last call would be enough.

He spent the next two long hours trying to pass time, watching crap daytime TV, on pins that the caller would phone back or, worse, arrive in person. When that didn't happen, he dared to believe that maybe it was all over. But then, before hope could really take hold, the phone rang, breaking through the silence of the flat with a shrill cry for attention.

He moved slowly over to the phone, just watching it for twenty or more seconds, hoping that it would stop ringing. But it continued, so he brought the receiver to his ear.

An hour later, as the clock turned eleven, he sat staring into space, now knowing that he would never be allowed to move on.

Chapter Five

Sam stepped into the waiting lift, but just as the doors were closing, Miles Churchill darted between the shrinking gap.

'Miles,' Sam nodded. The stench of over-liberally applied aftershave filled the space, and for a moment Sam wondered mischievously whether Miles was trying to hide something. Was the alcoholic waft coming only from the cologne?

'Sam,' Miles responded, rearranging his pale pink shirt and tie in the mirrored wall as the lift started its ascent. 'I hear that you were involved in a spot of bother last night.'

'News travels fast,' Sam noted.

'Khan told me.' Miles caught Sam's eye via the reflection. 'Just before he gave me an extra four patients this afternoon.'

'Yeah, sorry about that,' said Sam, for the first time pleased at the Professor's decision to relieve him of his afternoon list. Although he knew it was for the best, he had still found it difficult to relinquish the patients, especially to Miles – not that Professor Khan, or Anna for that matter, had given him any choice. 'I'm sure you'll manage, though.'

'Of course I will,' retorted Miles. 'But it doesn't mean that I'm happy about it.' He started on his hair now, brushing thick, floppy dark strands away from his eyes. He was like a preening bird. 'So,' he said, finishing the makeover by brushing his lapels and addressing Sam to his face, 'if you're not up to operating, what are you doing around here?'

'Couldn't keep away from the place,' Sam replied.

Miles nodded as if that was the answer he expected. 'Afraid that people will forget you.'

Sam kept quiet, not dignifying Miles's jibe with a response. The lift pinged and the doors slid open at the fourth floor – the level for the cardiothoracic centre. Miles stepped out, then turned around, surprised, as Sam stayed in the lift. Sam suppressed a smile as the doors closed between them. That would get Miles wondering.

He took the chance to examine himself. Thankfully, he didn't look as bad as he felt, although the reddish tinge smudging the blue of his eyes betrayed the lack of sleep. Then, of course, there was the angry bruise that circled around his left eye. His blonde stubble, now flecked with white, was deliberately thicker than usual – he'd recently cut his fair hair shorter, and Anna had said it made him look five years younger, so this was a way to counteract that effect. For a doctor to look young wasn't particularly desirable, especially when aiming for a consultant position. He straightened himself to his full six foot three inches, brushed his tie, collar and suit jacket – and looked himself in the eyes. It would have to do.

Glancing at his watch, he thought of Anna. She would be just over two hours into the flight now, somewhere over Southern Europe. He knew exactly what she would be doing: trying to lose herself in one of the in-flight movies. Ironically, for someone who had visited all but one of the planet's continents, she was a reluctant flyer. While Sam would gaze down at the landscapes below, revelling in the bird's-eye vantage point, Anna would use any possible method to try and forget there was thirty thousand feet of fresh air between their seat and the ground. Sam thought of his wife on her important mission, and of the unborn baby developing inside, hitching along for the ride. He still couldn't quite get his head around the news that he was going to be a father, although it felt just as wonderful, exciting and daunting as it did at the moment of Anna's announcement.

The lift pinged again as it reached the top floor. Sam turned around and stepped out onto the plush royal-blue carpet. This was the world of senior management. Perched at the highest level of the hospital, it seemed far removed from the activities below – the smells, the shouts of patients, the non-stop activity. Here, money ruled, or at least that's how it felt. It wasn't an environment in which he was at all comfortable. He strode down the corridor, wondering whether his summoning really was about last night, as he'd assumed. Reaching his destination, he knocked firmly on the oak door and took a step back.

'Come in,' said the voice of Carla Conway, the chief executive of St Thomas's, from inside.

Sam counted out three seconds before pushing at the door. To his surprise, the board table was empty. Carla stood at the window on the opposite side of the room, looking out across the London skyline towards Westminster. She turned around and smiled. Dressed in a figure-hugging black suit, with her jet-black hair pulled tight back in a bun, Carla Conway cut an impressive and imposing figure. She had a reputation for being a tough operator, but Sam knew from first-hand experience that she was also a fair person. Fifty years old, Carla had been at the hospital for three years, following a career in the financial sector, including most recently the position of executive director of the London offices of UGT, the American investment bank. The appointment of someone from the City had caused a stir, especially among the senior clinicians, who feared that a CEO without any public sector background would think only of money and nothing of patient care. But their fears had been largely unfounded. Carla had, in fact, been a champion of patients' rights, a legacy of her own family experience in which two of her three sisters had died from a genetic form of breast cancer. As she had said in her opening statement, she wanted to make a difference after years of just making money.

'Nice to see you, Sam.'

'Carla,' Sam replied. 'You sent for me?'

She nodded, beckoning him over with her eyes. He moved up towards the window and looked out at the Thames. A tourist cruiser passed by, sharing the water with several other boats, including a small coastguard dinghy. The blue light on the back of the dinghy flashed as it skimmed across the tops of the waves, like a polished stone.

'I wanted to congratulate you about yesterday,' said Carla. 'What you did was an amazing thing.'

'Thanks,' Sam replied, thinking back to the whereabouts of Alison. There had still been no word from the police. 'I did what anyone else would have done in the situation.'

Carla raised a disbelieving eyebrow. 'I don't think so, Sam. Not everyone would have risked their life the way you did.'

Sam shrugged, not wanting to dwell on the event.

'How are you? That's a nasty-looking bruise.'

'I'm fine,' he replied. 'A little bit sore, but I was really lucky.'

Carla nodded. 'You're a hero, Sam.'

'Well, I wouldn't say that. I was just in the right place at the right time.'

'Like on board the plane last year?' Carla smiled. 'You're making a habit of being in the right place at the right time.'

'That was different,' Sam replied.

'Different circumstances,' Carla agreed, 'but it still demonstrated something special, Sam. It's something that people wanted to hear about. People should hear about last night too.'

'The story is in today's papers. People already know about what happened.'

'I've seen them.'

'So that's okay,' Sam added. 'People know.'

'The basic story is there, Sam, but not the details. You aren't even mentioned by name in any of the articles, unless I've missed it?'

Sam shook his head.

Carla looked off towards the city. 'Then I think that more does need to be done, Sam. The general public will want to know more about the human story behind what happened.'

'Just because people want something, it doesn't mean you have to give it to them.'

'True,' Carla replied, 'but sometimes it's the best thing to do.'

'I don't want to speak with the media,' Sam said. 'I don't want any more coverage, and I don't want my name mentioned. Surely you can appreciate that, after last time. I didn't run onto the track and save those children because I wanted my name splashed all over the papers.'

Carla turned to face him. 'I do understand, Sam. I really do. And I know that it was difficult last year with some of the coverage, but we've learnt lessons, and this time it will be different.'

Sam shook his head.

'Sam, this is a great opportunity.'

'For who?'

A mother had died. It was a tragedy, not an opportunity.

Carla blinked. 'For you and the hospital.'

Sam smiled and shook his head. 'I'm in surgery, not public relations.'

'I realise that. That's why I called you up here. We can help.'

Sam doubted that. 'Help? In what way?'

'We can draft a press release and put in a quote from you. The press will be happy with that. They can run their story, and they'll leave you alone. And by the day after tomorrow you'll be yesterday's news, free to get on with the rest of your life.'

'I was hoping the press wouldn't be interested after today,' Sam said.

Carla let out a laugh. 'Do you know how many enquiries from the media we've had this morning about you? Twenty – and that was the latest update, an hour ago. We've managed to put them on hold for now, promising them a press release later this afternoon. But if the press release doesn't materialise, they'll come knocking on your door for the story instead.'

Sam gripped the hair on the back of his head, considering his options. This changed things. Carla was right; if the press were so keen, they would track him down, quiz him and then write whatever they wanted. So this way would be better, despite his genuine reticence to engage. He thought for another few seconds, fighting against his instincts. 'Okay,' he conceded. 'I'll do it.'

'Good, that's good.' Carla's relief was evident. 'Sam, I know you probably think that I'm some sort of vulture, taking advantage of this, but the reality is that good news stories for the hospital really matter when it comes to decisions at the highest levels – especially with the kicking we've had in the press during the past eighteen months over the infection rates.'

'You're just doing your job,' Sam replied.

'I'm not sure if that's a veiled criticism, Sam.' Carla smiled. 'But you're right; I am just doing my job – which is to ensure that this hospital is a success. And by being a success, I'm not just talking about money. I mean improving patient care. We're all chasing the same goal here.'

Sam nodded. 'I know.'

'That's good to hear, because I want to ask you one last favour.'

'Go on,' Sam said, wary as to the way this conversation was going.

'We got a call this morning from the BBC. They want to do an interview with you this afternoon on *Radio Five Live*.'

This was a step too far. He had been interviewed on the radio the last time, and it had been a really stressful experience. 'No way.'

'We have people who can help,' said Carla. 'Melanie Grace is our new communications manager. She'll be able to advise you, and she'll also liaise with the BBC to make it clear where the boundaries are.'

'I really don't want to do this.'

'Please, Sam, I would really appreciate it; the board would really appreciate it. You have no idea how much this could help the hospital. Just for fifteen minutes of your time. Your story can make a real difference, believe me.'

What choice did he have? He'd ceded control of the situation, giving Carla a yard, and now she was taking a mile. 'What if I say no?'

Carla shrugged. 'Then it doesn't happen. We call the BBC and tell them we can't do it.'

Sam thought it over. It was a foolish man who went against the wishes of the chief executive, even a fair one. Carla had been highly supportive of the cardiothoracic centre, giving the go-ahead for the expansion of the team and acquisition of several expensive bits of equipment, and they needed to keep that support. And then there was the important fact that she would be on his interview panel. 'Fifteen minutes? And then that's it?'

'A quote for the press release and a fifteen-minute interview,' said Carla, the hope rising in her voice. 'Then that's it.'

'Okay,' he conceded. 'But on one condition. I do this one interview, and then that's it: no more interviews, no more comments. Nothing.'

Carla held out her hand and smiled. 'You have my word, Sam.'

Chapter Six

You're doing *what?*'

'I didn't feel I had a choice,' Sam admitted as Louisa shook her head. They were in a quiet part of the hospital cafeteria, out of earshot from the other staff and patients. 'I know it sounds terrible, but in two weeks I'm going to be facing Carla Conway across an interview table, and I don't want to make an enemy.'

'So you do whatever she says.' Louisa's face was flushed with anger. She didn't often get angry, or at least she hid it well, and the strength of her reaction took Sam by surprise.

'I've got more than just me to think about, Lou,' he explained. 'If everything goes to plan, I'll have a family to support in just under nine months. And it's just fifteen minutes.'

Louisa shook her head again, unconvinced.

'They have helped me today, dealing with the media enquiries. And Carla's right. If I don't go along with this, the press will come right to my door. At least this way there's some control.'

'I'm just worried about you, Sam,' Louisa said, softening.

They paused for a second as someone approached them. The white-haired man, middle-aged or perhaps older, was wearing a distinctive neon-yellow, puffer-style coat, like something you'd expect to see on a roadside worker. He fixed his sights on Louisa.

'Miss Owen, I – I – I'd like to speak to – to . . .'

'Richard, now isn't a good time,' Louisa interrupted with uncharacteristic abruptness. 'We're seeing each other on Friday. Remember what we agreed?'

The man's face pursed as if in heavy contemplation. 'Of c-c-course,' he said, his eyes drifting to the floor. 'Sorry to – to bother you, Miss – Miss Owen.'

He turned, his head lowered, and moved off more quickly than Sam had expected, obviously agitated. They both watched his journey as he weaved around the tables and chairs and then disappeared out of sight through the main exit doors.

'He's a patient?' Sam asked.

Louisa nodded. 'Richard Friedman. I'm having a few problems with him. I really hate being like that with people, but sometimes you have to be quite firm.'

'Want to talk?'

'It's okay,' Louisa said dismissively. 'The guy is struggling to come to terms with a bereavement. He's just a little clingy. I can handle it. Anyway, you're not changing the subject on me, Sam. We're talking about you and this silly radio appearance.'

'Fair enough.'

'I'm worried about you, Sam. I just don't think that this is a very good idea when you're still coming to terms with what happened. Yesterday was a massively traumatic event, even for someone like you who deals with death every day.'

She was right, of course. 'I'll be okay.'

'But will you? You were nearly killed yesterday – *yesterday*, for goodness' sake. And today, instead of speaking to a counsellor about things, or speaking to your friend, who just so happens to be a clinical psychologist, you'll be talking to a DJ on national radio.'

'I know, I know,' Sam admitted, recognising the irony of the situation. He still wasn't at all comfortable with the decision, but he'd made up his mind.

'And after what happened last time, I just don't know how you can even contemplate putting yourself through that again. I know how much it affected you last year when the papers were full of your life story. It affected me too; it affected your parents, and Anna. Journalists dredging through your past, gossiping about Cathy, speculating about what happened. Do you really want to risk that happening again?'

'They've promised that they won't ask me any questions about Cathy.'

'But can you really guarantee that?'

'No, I suppose not.'

'The media might not be able to resist it, Sam. Marcus has just been released from prison; Cathy would have just celebrated her thirtieth. You can see how it might be too tempting?'

Sam nodded; he'd thought the same himself. 'I know, but if they do start asking questions about that, I'll stop the interview there and then.'

'If you say so.'

Sam glanced at his watch. 'I'd better go. They've got a taxi coming to get me in a few minutes.'

Louisa just stared at her coffee.

Sam tried again. 'Look, Lou, I know what you're saying, and I do agree. But I just think that this could be the best way of getting the press attention out of the way in a more controlled fashion. It might backfire – who knows? I don't want this any more than you do, but I've decided it's the best thing to do under the circumstances. Will you support me?'

Louisa looked up. 'Just be careful, Sam.'

During the ten-minute taxi ride over to the BBC radio studios, Sam dwelt on what Louisa had said. He just hoped the station would be true to its word and the interviewer would steer well clear of anything to do with Cathy. Louisa had been right – the media coverage the previous year had hurt Sam terribly. It had also really affected his parents, pushing his father back into depression. After over a decade of them trying to shut out the pain and horror, it had all come crashing back into their lives, as fresh and raw as ever.

By the time he reached the studios, had registered at reception and was waiting on the comfy green sofa, he was full of trepidation. He was close to walking out when a young Asian girl approached, clipboard in hand.

'Hi, it's Sam, isn't it?'

Sam nodded and followed her along a corridor. She talked as she walked, explaining what would happen, but distracted by his own thoughts, Sam only heard bits of it. They went down a flight of stairs, passed through a set of double doors and emerged into one of the main broadcast areas. Three goldfish-bowl-like recording studies, fronted by glass, led off from the central waiting area in which they now stood.

'You'll be interviewed by Simon Saunders,' the girl said, looking over to the only occupied studio. 'He's covering the afternoon slot while Mike is away.'

Sam could see Simon at the control desk, headphones on, talking to the sports reporter sat opposite him. The broadcast was being piped over the speakers. At the moment they were speculating about the latest rumours on the football transfer market. He wasn't familiar with this presenter – he tended to listen to Radio 4 – but Sam was grateful to be spared the confrontational well-known regular host, Mike Bennett.

'You'll be on in a few minutes,' the girl explained. 'Just after the news. Take a seat, and we'll come and get you.'

'We've got time for one more caller. Richard from London, what's your question?'

Sam looked over at Simon and wished he were somewhere else. The presenter had been fine, asking some standard questions about the previous night. But he hadn't reckoned on a full-blown phone-in to follow. For almost ten minutes now, he'd been quizzed by callers about the crash. Some had wanted to know the basic facts of the event. Others had sought to reflect on the nature of what it meant to be a hero. It was like a back-street psychiatry session in front of an invited audience. He should have listened to Louisa. But one more caller, and it would be all over.

'Hi, Simon,' the caller began. 'Hi, Sam, how are you?'

The sentence was slow and deliberate, as if each word were being stretched.

'I'm fine, thanks,' Sam lied, gazing down at the console that curved around him. The headphones were starting to irritate, and he longed to rip them off and end this now.

'But you're not,' the caller replied, in the same slow drawl. 'You're not fine at all, Sam.'

For a few seconds the comment just hung in the air as Sam decided how to respond. But before he could speak, Simon stepped in.

'How do you mean, Richard?' He glanced over at Sam as he spoke, and the excitement in his eyes was clear as he waited for a response.

'I mean that Sam isn't as fine as he's making out. We've not heard the truth.'

Sam shook his head. Louisa had been right. This had been a terrible idea.

Simon moved closer to the microphone, keeping his eyes fixed on Sam. 'You're not accusing Sam of lying?'

'I'm not making any accusations,' the man replied. 'Just an observation, that's all. I'm interested to hear what Sam thinks about it.'

Simon looked over at Sam, giving him an opportunity to respond that Sam felt unable to turn down.

'I've answered the questions as honestly as I could,' he said, trying hard not to sound defensive.

'Ah,' the caller replied, 'but that's different.'

Sam met Simon's gaze as he moved back towards the microphone – the guy was captivated. 'I don't see how.'

'Tell me about what she said, Sam.'

This was getting totally out of order. Couldn't the station just cut this guy off? He looked again at Simon. 'I don't understand what you mean.'

'I think you do,' replied the caller. 'Tell me about what she said to you just before the train hit. That's what I want to hear.'

'Er . . . I think we've heard enough,' Simon said. 'Thanks for your call, Richard—'

'No,' Sam interrupted, putting up a hand and leaning into the microphone. He'd changed his mind and now wanted to challenge this individual. 'I want to know why you think you've got the right to ask that, Richard.'

Simon nodded, taking a symbolic move away from the control console.

'Because I want to be entertained, and you're not giving me the full show.'

Sam laughed in disbelief. 'This isn't a show.'

This time it was the caller's turn to laugh. 'It's entertainment, Sam. And you're the star attraction.'

'I don't have to listen to this.'

'You think you're a hero, Sam, don't you? But you couldn't save your sister from Marcus Johnson.'

Sam just sat there, stunned. It felt like someone out of nowhere had just delivered a sharp blow to his gut.

Simon stepped in. 'Thanks for all your calls. And thanks to our guest in the studio, Sam Becker. It's clear from the vast number of calls we've had, that he's considered a true hero and a testament to the staff of the health service. Thanks for coming in today, Sam, and sharing your experience with us. I know it must be really difficult talking about this. Thank you.'

Sam nodded, the words of the caller lodged in his brain.

'And now time for the traffic and travel with Claire Davies. Over to you, Claire . . .'

'I'm really sorry about that last caller,' Simon said as they both took off their headphones. 'You get those sorts of people sometimes. We try our best to screen out people like that, but every now and again one slips through the net. You'd be amazed by how many crazies there are out there.'

'It's okay,' Sam replied, placing the headphones on the desk in front of him. In truth, he felt anything but okay, but he wasn't about to discuss this with someone from the media. 'Really, it's fine.'

Simon nodded, seemingly unconvinced.

⌣

'Sam. It's Doug. Sorry to call you out of the office.'

'Doug,' Sam said as he emerged from the BBC building onto the busy pavement. The heavens had opened, and the rain was bouncing up from the pavement, so he sheltered in the entrance. 'Did you hear the interview?'

'I caught the end of it. They had the radio on in the staff room, and everyone who could was listening. That last caller was something else. I mean, talk about deranged.'

'Tell me about it.' Sam rested against the wall of the building and watched as taxis and buses splashed by. He'd spent the past few minutes since the interview reflecting on the caller and his words. What sort of person got their kicks out of that sort of thing? 'What's up?'

'It's not good news,' Doug replied. 'I was going to tell you when you got back, but I thought you'd want to know straightaway.'

'Go on,' Sam said, moving out into the heavy rain, already looking for a free taxi. It had to be something at the hospital.

'It's that young patient of yours, Sophie Jackson. She's gone downhill, and they've rushed her into theatre. Sister Keller told me that it's not looking good.'

'No.' Sam scanned the road – all the cabs were taken. 'Who's operating? Mr Khan?'

'Miles,' Doug replied. 'Prof Khan is on his way.'

This was not good. Miles was technically a good surgeon, but not in the Professor's league, and Sam only wanted the best for Sophie. 'I don't believe it.'

'You can see why I called.'

'Sure, thanks, Doug – I appreciate it. I'll be there as quick as I can.'

Chapter Seven

She lay down on the thin, uncomfortable mattress, staring at the ceiling that was flaking and black from damp. The room, bare except for the double bed, smelt like the cellar in her house. One time she had wandered down there, looking for fairies, only to panic in the darkness as the door closed behind her. Her mum had come to the rescue, chastising her for tackling the steep set of stairs at the age of five. Rescued from that total, all-encompassing darkness, she had never been as relieved in all her life.

But this time her mother wasn't here to save her.

She sat up against the limp, stained pillow and held her head in her hands. She didn't know what time it was or how long she had been in the room. They had taken her watch as soon as she had arrived. There were no windows, so she couldn't tell whether it was day or night. It must have been hours and hours since the last meal, and her stomach growled, even though she didn't feel like eating. Her hair, usually kept so pristine, was greasy and unwashed, as was her face.

Then, next door, she heard a noise. A man's voice, muffled, but definitely the deep voice of a man. She put her ear against the wall and recoiled as she heard moans and groans, this time from both a man and a woman. Placing her hands tightly against her ears, she began to cry.

And then a lock clicked, and the door to the room opened.

She scrambled back against the bedstead, like an animal caught in a trap.

'Is okay,' the young woman said, edging into the room, holding out a hand. 'I not hurt you.'

She watched as the woman, wearing a short, tight leather skirt and tightly fitting red top, moved towards her, beckoning her with both hands.

Could this be a trap?

'Come with me,' she said. 'I help you out. Get out.' She reached out her hand to the frightened child. She was pretty but would be prettier without the over-liberal make-up. 'Come. Not afraid. Your name?'

'Amy,' she said without hesitation. It was the name of her best friend in school, Amy Long. They'd been friends since playschool, meeting for the first time on a swing set.

'Come, Amy. My name is Yvette. We go. But quick.'

She took Yvette's hand. It was rougher than she expected.

'Good,' Yvette said as they made their way for the door. 'Quiet. No noise, please.'

She nodded as they left the room and emerged into a narrow corridor flanked with doors. It was the first time she had seen it, having been blindfolded on her arrival. As they passed the door to the adjoining room, she heard the man inside let out a loud moan.

'Come, in here,' Yvette whispered, passing through a door into what looked like a large store cupboard. But at the back of the room, past the bed sheets and boxes, was another door. 'Stairs,' she said, pointing at the door. 'Lead outside. Please, go – go now, quick. Otherwise they come.'

'Aren't you coming too?' she asked.

Yvette shook her head. 'Please, go quick,' she repeated.

She nodded and pushed at the door, emerging into a dimly lit stairwell. The metal stairs wound around a central post, like a helter-skelter. She looked back just as the door closed, then turned and began running as fast as was safe down the steps.

She neared the bottom, but on the last turn she realised too late that he was waiting for her. She tried to turn back, but he thrust out a powerful arm and grabbed her ankle. She tried to kick out, but instead she slid down the steps, smacking her head against the handrail. He pulled her up, held her firmly and smiled.

———

Never get too emotionally involved in your patients. Always keep a distance, for your own sanity. As a doctor you can't afford to get too attached. Sam had always struggled to follow the rules that had been outlined to the class at medical school by their course leader on that first day of undergraduate studies. From those first days on the wards, he realised that emotional attachment was a double-edged sword. Yes, it gave him sleepless nights, worrying about how a patient was doing. There had been times when he'd travelled back to the hospital late at night to check on their progress. It also increased the pain of losing people. But it made the job more fulfilling, more human, to feel something for the people under his care. They and their families put so much trust in him, so the least he could do was give something of his emotional self in return.

But the way he felt about little Sophie Jackson was on another level. He knew he had got too close, closer than ever before, and that for this reason the stakes felt so very high. She was more than a patient. He searched frantically, left, then right, looking for an available taxi. It should take about ten minutes to get back to the hospital and another five or so to get prepped for theatre. Maybe he could get back in time. But with the deluge of rain, there wasn't a free taxi in sight. Then, just down the road, on the opposite side, he saw a black cab pull up, having been flagged down. He raced diagonally across the road, darting between the traffic, narrowly missing a moped that had to swerve to avoid him. Car horns blared as he weaved in between two cars that had stopped, stunned by his presence in the middle of the road.

'Hey!' he shouted at the suited man who was just getting into the back of the cab. 'Wait!'

The man saw him approach but ignored his cries and closed the door.

'Wait!'

Without thinking of the implications, Sam raced up to the cab and stood in front of the vehicle, his palms flat against the warm, wet bonnet. The driver stared back at him with a look of bemusement.

'I'm a doctor,' Sam explained through the windscreen. 'I need to get to St Thomas's hospital. It's an emergency.'

The driver just looked back at him.

'A little girl might die if I don't get there right now.'

The driver turned around and said something to the man in the back. He turned back to face the front, then put his head through the open window.

'You'd better get in then, Doctor,' he said.

Despite the driver's heroic efforts, taking back streets, speeding around tailbacks, the drive back to the hospital was agonisingly slow in the choked late-afternoon London traffic. Sam watched the time and the meter tick by, with growing frustration and concern.

They came to a standstill just north of Westminster Bridge.

'Looks like an accident up ahead,' the cabbie observed, glancing at him in the rear-view mirror. 'Sorry, Doc, no way around this.'

Sam looked up ahead. A bus had collided with a lorry. It didn't look serious, but it was enough to block the road completely. The police were on the scene.

They were so close to the hospital.

Sam paid the driver and jumped out, splashing through oily puddles as the rain continued to fall, dodging and weaving through the umbrella-wielding crowds. He skirted past the Palace of Westminster, with Big Ben his reminder that time was not on his side. Thankfully, he was physically fit, having been in training for months for a half marathon that Doug had persuaded him to run in, which was taking place in eight weeks' time, so he traversed the busy Westminster Bridge as quickly as the crowds would allow him, taking to the road in places. Sprinting up to the hospital's front entrance, he drew glances from patients and staff who were milling around outside as he raced into the main lobby towards the lifts. He pressed the buttons hard several times but then decided to head for the stairs, taking them two by two. Sweat was pouring from him, and he felt a burn inside his chest as he burst onto the fourth floor, nearly knocking over a cleaning trolley.

'Sorry!'

He continued running down the corridor to the surgical ward, dodging surprised nurses and other healthcare staff. Reaching the doors, he flung them open.

Doug was waiting for him on the other side, his arms crossed tightly across his chest.

Sam knew straightaway that the news wasn't good.

'No,' he said, shaking his head, looking for a miracle in Doug's eyes. 'Please say she isn't—'

'She's still alive.' Doug placed a hand on Sam's shoulder. 'But she's critical. It's not looking hopeful.'

'What happened?' Sam felt an equal sense of relief that she was still alive and concern about her condition.

'I don't know,' Doug admitted. 'I've only just had word from one of the nurses. She's on life support up on ICU.'

'Where's Miles?'

'In his office. But I don't think it's a good idea . . .'

'I need to find out what happened.' Sam brushed off Doug's attempt to stop him.

'Sam, don't.'

He strode past the front desk and headed for the office. He didn't bother knocking. Miles looked up from the paperwork that lay on the table.

'Sam,' he said, seeming inconvenienced by his appearance.

'What happened?'

'To who?'

'You know who. Sophie Jackson. What happened?'

'She suffered internal bleeding as a result of a ruptured artery,' explained Miles, putting down his pen. 'I managed to stem the flow and patch her up, but the next few hours will be crucial.'

Sam tried to take in the news. Having got past the first few crucial post-operative days, Sophie should have settled down. The setback highlighted the perilous state of her cardiovascular system. It was an extremely worrisome development. 'How do you rate her chances?'

'Not good. Maybe ten, fifteen per cent, but I did my best.' Miles picked up his pen again and looked down at the paperwork. 'Sam. I really have to deal with this, and I've got to prepare for another operation that starts in twenty minutes. So if you wouldn't mind.'

Sam ignored the hint. 'Where are Tom and Sarah?'

Miles looked confused. 'Tom and . . . ?'

'Sophie's parents, are they here?'

'Right. They're in the family room across the corridor. I've already spoken with them and explained the situation.'

'I want to talk with them too,' Sam said.

'Always competing,' Miles muttered, shaking his head.

'Excuse me?'

Miles looked up. 'Sam, I've already spoken with the parents. I know you're upset that you missed out on things, but you made your choice.'

'What's that supposed to mean?'

'I hope you enjoyed your radio appearance.'

Sam felt an upwelling of anger. 'Do you know, Miles, you're a real—'

'Sam, walk away.' Doug was standing at the open door. 'Come with me and we can talk about it.'

'It's good advice,' Miles said. 'You allow yourself to get too emotionally involved with your patients. You just can't afford to do that in this profession.'

'Whereas you just don't give a damn,' Sam replied.

'You shouldn't have come back into work so soon, Sam,' Miles said, getting back to his notes. 'Give yourself a break.'

'C'mon, Sam,' Doug said, steering him out of the room. He let himself be led, feeling detached from the situation, as if he'd been possessed and things were only now coming back into focus. He didn't know whether it was grief, shock or just pure anger, but something had really taken hold.

'Sam,' Miles began just before they exited the door. Sam stopped but didn't turn around. 'I don't expect you to listen to my advice, but really, ask yourself whether you should be here.'

Chapter Eight

Sam peered through the glass of the door to the family room, steeling himself for the conversation to come. Tom Jackson was in the corner, alone. He was staring straight at the facing wall, his face blank and emotionless. Sam had seen that face a thousand times before in his years as a doctor – a face of total emotional shutdown in response to extreme grief. It was a sight he never got used to.

He took a deep breath and opened the door. Tom looked across at him, and Sam nodded a hello as he pulled up a chair. He didn't say anything. Experience had taught him that this part of medicine wasn't about making people better – they didn't want to feel better in the immediate aftermath – it was about listening.

For around half a minute, the two men just sat there. Sam glanced across at Tom. Tom and Sam were the same age; Tom's wife, Sarah, three years younger. But the years of heartache and chronic worry had taken its toll, ageing the couple prematurely. Their daughter's fight was sucking the life out of them, mentally and physically. Both Tom and Sarah had had spells on antidepressants, and their as yet unsuccessful attempts to produce a brother or sister for Sophie had added to the strain. Sam looked down at the toy rabbit Tom was holding. His fingers were stroking the fur of what was Sophie's favourite toy.

'I really believed everything was going to be okay,' Tom said finally, still looking straight ahead at the wall. 'I never doubted it – not for a second. Ever since she was born, since the first time the doctors told us that she had problems. Something deep down inside made me believe that it was all going to be all right.'

Again they sat in silence and Sam waited.

Tom shook his head, still absentmindedly stroking the rabbit. There were no tears. His face was a mask, hiding the torment. 'I can't believe this is happening. I can't believe that our little Sophie – that she – she might not make it. Our Sophie, we might never see her smile again. Never look her in the eyes. I just can't get my head around it. It won't sink in.'

'I'm so sorry, Tom,' Sam offered.

Tom pinched his eyes to stem a single tear. He looked at Sam. 'Was I just deluded, believing that it would all be okay?'

'No,' Sam replied.

'You believed it too? You thought she'd be okay, didn't you? You really believed.'

Sam nodded. 'There's still hope.'

'She's a fighter, Sam,' continued Tom, almost pleading. 'You could see it from the very beginning. That first look she gave me in the delivery room, when I held her for the first time. She's strong, isn't she?'

Again Sam nodded.

Now the tears were really falling, dripping down onto Tom's lap. 'She's a fighter, Sam – she wants to live. She wants to grow up, go to school, get married, have children – she wants that, I know she does. She'll battle for it. We all will.'

Sam brought a comforting arm around Tom's back. 'We've got to stay positive, but there's also a chance that it might just be too much for her. You have to prepare yourself for that.'

'If only a heart had become available last week, last year, maybe she'd be okay now, living a normal life, like she should be living.'

'I know,' Sam agreed.

'Will we have more of a chance now, now that her situation's worse?'

'I don't understand . . .'

'Will we have a better chance of finding a heart quicker, now that it's critical?'

Sam shook his head, reluctantly puncturing Tom's hope. But he knew it could do untold damage to raise expectations. 'Sophie was already at the top of the list.'

'What are the chances that a heart might become available in time?'

'I can't say,' Sam admitted. 'But if Sophie is too ill, we might not be able to operate even if a heart is there.'

'I just can't understand what happened,' lamented Tom. 'I can't understand it. She was doing well, wasn't she?'

'She was,' Sam confirmed. 'But her heart is weak, and there's always a possibility that something like this could happen at any time.'

'I don't know what went wrong.'

'What did Mr Churchill tell you?'

Tom put a shaking hand to his head, clinging to his greying hair. 'I can't really remember. Something about — oh, I don't know – something about internal bleeding. You weren't in there, were you, in the theatre?'

'No. I'm sorry . . . really sorry I couldn't be there.'

'Could you have done better — I mean, if you'd been there? You know her better – you know her case. Would you have done anything differently?'

'Dr Churchill is a highly skilled surgeon,' Sam replied. 'I wouldn't have done anything differently. It wouldn't have made a difference. I'm sorry, Tom.'

And that was true. Even if Mr Khan had been there himself, it would have probably ended in the same result. So why did he still feel so bad? Why did a part of him, deep down, truly believe that if only he'd been around, that wonderful little girl would now have a better chance of surviving? Was it just the surgeon's mindset that you could always do better, or was it guilt?

'It's not your fault,' Tom said, as if reading Sam's mind. 'You've always done your best for us, Sam. You've always been there for us. We couldn't have asked for more from you.'

Sam felt like shouting out that he was a fraud. He had failed Sophie. While she had been fighting for her life, he had been doing a radio interview. But instead he just said nothing.

Tom shook his head again. 'Sophie means everything to us. Four years we'd been trying for a baby – the doctors said we'd probably never have children. You know we've tried for another since – Sophie said she wants a brother or sister. But we've not been able to. This will destroy us if she dies. I'm not sure that we'll survive this.'

'You and Sarah are the closest couple I have ever met,' Sam said. 'You need each other.'

'I've seen it before,' Tom continued. 'People think that they'll get through this, but sometimes they don't.'

'It won't happen with you and Sarah,' Sam insisted. 'Where is she?'

Tom turned to him, his eyes red and swollen with grief. 'I don't know. She said that she had to be on her own.'

'She just needs time. Do you want me to get one of the nurses to find her?'

'No,' Tom said, 'it's all right.'

Again more silence.

'Do you think Sophie will be okay?' Tom asked.

'I don't know.' It was an honest, if not altogether comforting, answer. 'But you're right, Tom – she is a fighter. She's the strongest little girl I've ever known, and if anyone can come through this, Sophie can. And I'll do whatever it takes to give her every chance. I'll be there for her, I promise.'

'Thanks,' Tom said, 'that means a lot, really.'

'But you and Sarah need to stick together, no matter what happens. It's what Sophie would want. She needs you to be strong, as a couple.'

Tom nodded, wiping his nose with a clean tissue Sam produced from his pocket. 'When will we be able to see Sophie?'

'I'll call intensive care now,' Sam promised, 'and then you can both be with your daughter.'

Sam bit down hard on his emotions until he emerged from the main entrance of the hospital. He turned left, heading through the grounds, keeping his head down as he passed a group of nurses who were sipping coffee, laughing and joking. He recognised a couple of them, but they gave him only a cursory glance. By the time he reached the bench in a quiet corner around the back of the building, the dam holding back his emotions ruptured and burst. He sat there, with his head in his hands, sobbing. He hadn't even cried like this at Cathy's funeral. A mix of thoughts tumbled around in his head: the vacant stare of the woman in the car just before the train hit; Sophie, giggling uncontrollably in that way she always did, as her proud parents Tom and Sarah looked on; the pained faces of his mother and father at Cathy's birthday memorial, and then the words of the caller: 'You couldn't save your sister from Marcus Johnson.'

'Mr Becker?'

Sam was shocked by the voice. He looked up to see Maria Hennessey, a young nurse from the surgical ward. She was an enthusiastic member of staff, being only six months into her job.

'Oh, hi, Maria.'

'Sorry to bother you,' she said, noticeably taken aback by the sight of Sam in tears. She reddened at the uncomfortable and unexpected situation. 'I just saw you out here, and I – I wanted to say I'm really sorry about what happened to Sophie. I just heard. We all hope she pulls through.'

Sam smiled sadly. 'Me too.'

Maria nodded. 'I have to go back in now; my break was over a few minutes ago. Do you think she'll be okay?'

'I hope so,' Sam replied, his composure now recovered.

'I hope so too.' Maria looked down at her feet. 'She's such a great little girl. I'd better go back in.'

As she walked away almost apologetically, Sam shouted after her. 'Maria!' She stopped and moved back towards him. 'Can you try and find Sarah Jackson? Her husband's looking for her. They need to be together. He's up on ICU with Sophie.'

Maria nodded and continued walking back towards the hospital.

Sam watched her walk away, reflecting on what had just happened. As much as he hated to admit it, maybe Miles was right, and he should go home. He could lock himself away and watch a couple of films or read a book. It might just give him space to digest recent events. First, though, he would go up to ICU and check on Tom and Sophie.

But halfway back towards the hospital entrance, he received a text message that stopped him dead. It was from Louisa.

Meet me by the London Eye – it's about Cathy.

Chapter Nine

Sam hurried across the grounds and out onto the main road running up towards Westminster Bridge. The Houses of Parliament towered up ahead, and then off to the right the London Eye came into view. He crossed the road, waiting for a gap between the black taxis and open-topped tourist buses. The rain shower had passed, and ahead a swath of tourists meandered by the banks of the Thames in the bright late afternoon sunshine, many pointing their cameras towards the Eye. By the time Sam reached the base of the Eye, the crowds had increased. Hundreds queued for their turn on the big wheel, while others were content to look up and marvel at the sight of the four-hundred-foot structure as it turned slowly, almost imperceptibly. Sam looked around, trying to spot Louisa, but had no luck. He reached for his mobile and was about to punch in her number, when the phone sprang to life.

The caller ID read 'Louisa'.

He brought the phone to his ear. 'Louisa, where are you?'

There was no answer.

'Louisa?'

Again, there was no answer.

Sam moved through the crowds, looking out for her, still not hearing any response. He stopped on the grass area next to the Eye, where it was quieter. 'Louisa, I can't hear anything. Can you hear me?'

'I hear you,' a male voice replied.

Sam froze. 'Who's this? Where's Louisa?'

'Do you think you're a hero, Sam?'

He thought he recognised the voice. It sounded like the caller from the radio interview. But could that be possible? 'Who is this?'

'Is that why you became a doctor?'

'Where's Louisa?' Sam scanned the crowd.

'To make up for what happened,' the voice continued. 'I'm perceptive, Sam. I can see everything from where I am.'

Sam looked up at the Eye. Each pod was filled with people. He stepped back several paces, scanning the pods. It was difficult to make out individuals. And he couldn't see anyone talking on a phone. 'Who are you?'

There was no reply.

Just then Sam spotted a man on a mobile. He was in a pod that was just descending towards the disembarkation point. The guy was about thirty and seemed deep in concentration. Sam moved closer, fixing him in his sights as the pod opened and its occupants dispersed towards the exit.

'How have you got Louisa's phone?' Sam was weaving his way through the crowds towards the man. He wanted to see if the guy replied, but he had his back towards him. Sam reached for his shoulder and spun the man around.

'Hey?' the guy said, seeming taken aback by Sam's intervention.

'Is it you?' Sam demanded. The man just stared back. And then a small girl appeared from behind, wrapping herself around the man's leg.

'Hey, Daddy,' she asked in an American accent, 'can I have an ice pop?'

Sam looked down at her, then back up at the man. 'Sorry, I thought you were someone else. Sorry.'

The man nodded. 'Sure, honey,' he said to his daughter while eyeing Sam suspiciously.

Sam looked around again, seeing another group disembarking the Eye. It was no use – there were just too many people. 'Tell me who you are,' he ordered into the phone.

'Wouldn't you rather know how Louisa is?' the man replied.

And then the line went dead.

Sam raced through the crowds along the banks of the Thames, towards the hospital. He tried to call Louisa on her office number, but there was no answer. He called her mobile back, but it just cut straight through to the answer service. By the time he reached the hospital entrance, he had run through all manner of scenarios in his head – none of them good. He made for the stairs, sprinting up them for a second time that day. But this time he emerged onto the second floor, forcing himself to slow to a brisk walk as he passed colleagues and patients. Louisa's office was towards the end of a winding corridor. He peered through the glass section of the door. The room was empty. He turned and headed towards the suite of consulting rooms at the far end. Louisa spent most of the day in those rooms, and he prayed she would be safely in one of them right now.

The doors to all four rooms were closed. On the front of two doors, the sign had been slid from vacant to busy. Trying to listen for Louisa's voice, he pressed his ear up against the doors, one then another. But the door was too thick, specially designed to maintain privacy. He looked from one to the other, knowing that it was considered extremely bad form to disturb a consultation. But this was an emergency. He went for the door on the right, knocking gently.

He couldn't hear any response, so he opened the door anyway. This wasn't a time to obey normal conventions.

'Sorry, really sorry,' he said as he interrupted a conversation between a guy he recognised as being one of Louisa's colleagues and a small woman who appeared to physically shrink into the chair at his appearance. 'I was looking for—'

'Louisa,' the bearded man said, rather tersely. 'She should be next door.'

'Thanks,' Sam replied, closing the door, feeling simultaneously embarrassed and elated that Louisa was here. He went for the second door, knocked and entered.

'Sam?'

Louisa was mid-conversation with a young man. Like the woman next door, the young man seemed shocked by the intrusion, as if he'd been caught red-handed doing something illicit. Sam turned his eyes away, recognising the patient's need for privacy. He understood the delicateness of these consultations and the potential damage his intrusion, if handled badly, could cause – Louisa had explained how you had to be so careful to build and keep patients' trust, to get them to the point where they could truly open up and release the emotions that had been slowly choking the life out of them.

'Sorry to disturb,' Sam said, hiding his relief that Louisa was safe and well, 'but can I have a word?'

Louisa hesitated as her professional persona fought against her natural instincts.

'It's urgent, Lou.'

Her eyebrows creased, and then she nodded. 'I'm really sorry about this,' she said to the patient. 'I'll just be a second.'

The man nodded, his head down, angled away from Sam.

'What's the matter?' Louisa asked as she closed the door behind her, her face full of concern.

'Where's your phone,' Sam said. 'Have you lost it?'

She frowned. 'My phone? You mean my mobile?'

'Yeah.' Sam nodded. 'Do you know where it is?'

'In my locker. I always leave it there during the day. Why?'

'Someone just called me using your mobile.'

Louisa looked confused. 'What?'

'A man phoned me, using your phone,' Sam repeated. 'He talked about the train crash and about Cathy.'

'Cathy?' she said, aghast. 'But, who would—'

'The same person also called the radio station. Did you hear it?'

'No,' Louisa said absentmindedly, as if deep in thought. She snapped back. 'I had a consultation, so I couldn't listen. I was going to listen to it later on the Internet. Are you sure it's the same person?'

'Pretty sure. Same voice saying the same sort of things. He knows who you are, Louisa. He made it sound like something had happened to you.'

'My God,' Louisa muttered, looking down.

'Have you got any idea who this person might be?'

'Maybe,' she replied.

'Who?'

'Go to my locker,' she said, evading the question. 'Find out if my mobile is missing. Here's the key. I'll be finished here in five minutes.'

Sam made his way quickly to the locker room, which was located just down the corridor. The room, which also doubled as a kitchen, was empty, and at first glance it didn't look as if anything was wrong. But as he approached Louisa's locker it was clear that it had been forced open – the door was ajar, and the metal lock was bent at a right angle. He looked inside, and the first thing that hit him was the piece of paper that was blu-tacked onto the back of the door. It was a photocopy of a newspaper article that Sam knew well. The headline read: 'BEST FRIEND MURDERED SCHOOLGIRL AFTER RAPE ATTACK.' Sam pulled the paper off the metal, and stared at the photograph of himself and Marcus Johnson, standing side by side, smiling for the camera. The mystery of how the photograph had made its way to the press had never been solved – no one was going to admit betraying the family so callously. But the betrayal had caused tensions among friends and family at a time when emotions were already fraught. It still hurt him to look at that photograph – to see Marcus's face – to think of how things were before that night.

What sick individual was doing this?

Sam slipped the article into his pocket and began searching through the jumble of multicoloured scarves that made up most of the locker's contents. And there, right at the bottom of the locker, wedged against a pair of trainers, was an envelope addressed to Sam. He looked at it for a moment before tearing it open. It had to be from the man who had stolen Louisa's phone. But it wasn't; it was a typed note from Louisa:

> *Dear Sam, I hope you will understand what I did. The last thing I ever want to do is hurt you. Love always, Lou xxx*

Sam sat outside the consulting room for the next few minutes, waiting impatiently for Louisa to emerge. The caller, whoever he was, wasn't just an anonymous sicko who had picked them at random. He knew Louisa, knew where she worked, knew where she kept her mobile and knew about Cathy.

And then there was the note. But that could wait.

Finally, Louisa emerged, stealing a glance at Sam as she said goodbye to the young man. She waited until the client was out of hearing range. 'Was it there?'

'No,' Sam said, getting to his feet. 'Someone's broken into your locker. The phone's gone. And this was on the inside of the door,' he added, handing her the newspaper cutting.

'What the . . .' she said, scrutinising the article. She looked up. 'What the hell's going on, Sam?'

'You said you might know who this is. Tell me.'

'I might be wrong.'

'You might be right,' Sam countered. 'Whoever this guy is, he's dangerous. He's already gained access to your stuff, Louisa. If you have even the slightest suspicion of who this guy is, you need to say. Is it the client from the cafeteria? The guy with the bright jacket?'

Louisa paused, thinking. 'CCTV. There's that camera just at the top of the stairs, near the lift. Do you think they'd let us have a look at the film?'

'You don't want to contact the police?'

'Not yet. I'd rather check this first.'

He decided not to press her further just yet. Maybe the camera images would clear things up, and then they could go to the police. 'Okay,' he said. 'CCTV is a good idea.' You couldn't get to the locker room without passing the camera, so surely it would have captured the person responsible. 'You free now?'

Louisa nodded. 'My next consultation is in an hour.'

Chapter Ten

Charlie Foggerty, head guard at the high-security prison HM Fairfield, heard the commotion and left his post, heading through the double doors towards the main cell block. He was met by Karen Armstrong, a new officer, just twenty-three years old. She was distraught.

'It's Wayne Cartwright – he's dead. Killed himself.'

Charlie placed a hand on her shoulder as he moved past, heading for the cell. He would need to check on her later, make sure she was okay. A group of guards were milling outside. They straightened as he approached.

'Let me in.'

They parted and he entered the cell. Wayne Cartwright was hanging from the light fitting in the centre of the room. Two guards were struggling to get him down, like trainee butcher boys trying to unhook a piece of meat.

Charlie stepped closer, examining the situation, fighting his instinct to just turn around and go home. He'd seen suicides before, many of them hangings, in his thirty-year career. It didn't get any easier. Every act was a tragedy and a failure of the prison service to protect these often vulnerable young men. Whatever they had done to arrive here, there was no way their departure should be in a box.

He looked at the cord that wrapped itself tightly around Wayne's neck, cutting into the skin. It was thick. Electrical wire possibly. How the hell had he smuggled that into the cell? The other end was tied around the light fitting. The body twisted around, and Charlie looked at the boy's face. His eyes were wide, his mouth set open, as if he'd been frozen at the point of the bone-jarring impact.

Something wasn't right.

'Leave him.'

The two guards looked across, confused.

Charlie waved them away. 'Let go of him.'

Wayne Cartwright was hanging from the centre of the room. You need three things for a successful hanging – a rope or wire, a place to tie it, and something to jump off.

Two out of three meant only one thing.

⌣

The security room was located below ground level, in a subterranean world unseen by most hospital employees and patients – at least those still breathing. The level was also home to the morgue and had an even more pervading clinical smell than the rest of the hospital. Sam rapped on the door, with Louisa silent at his side; he tried to shake off his discomfort. With the nearby presence of the recently dead and the absence of natural light, it was hard not to be spooked, even for a doctor used to staring death in the face.

The door swung open at speed. A moustachioed man of indeterminate middle age, wearing the black uniform of the security team, eyed him with suspicion. 'Yes?' Unlike those in the hospital above, he didn't possess the physical bulk needed to carry out their far too frequent duties of dealing with the violent, mostly drunk visitors who graced Accident and Emergency every day. These days the security guards upstairs resembled nightclub doormen, and some had come from that sector.

Sam explained the situation, half-expecting the guy to cut him dead with a negative response. But the man seemed genuinely excited at being able to help.

'Take a seat,' the man directed, gesturing to two threadbare chairs as he pressed various buttons on the hi-tech unit that was flanked on all sides by television monitors. Sam and Louisa watched live images from the front entrance, the A&E unit and the grounds at the rear. The footage showed the bench where Sam had received the text message directing him to the London Eye. He hadn't known there was a camera there, and he wondered whether the man had been watching him in his moment of weakness. He glanced across at Louisa and smiled hopefully.

'We've just had these new digital cameras fitted,' the guard explained. 'They're great little things, you know. Used to have to search through videotapes, but now we can jump to the exact time we want.'

Sam nodded as the guard looked at him, impatient to find out whether the images would reveal anything.

'Unfortunately, we don't have cameras up on the floor you're interested in.'

Louisa's forehead creased. 'But I've seen it. Right opposite the lifts.'

'Dummy box,' the guard replied. 'We'll be rolling out more working units in the coming months. But we can look at the main entrance.'

Sam nodded as Louisa pursed her lips. It was disappointing that they had been denied their simple solution.

'What time frame would you like to watch?'

Sam looked over at Louisa. 'I went to my locker just before my last consultation,' Louisa said. 'That was about three o'clock.'

'And you noticed the phone was missing at—'

'I got the call from her mobile just after three thirty,' Sam confirmed.

'So a window of thirty minutes or so, from three till three thirty,' said the guard to himself as he pressed buttons again. 'Not to say that the person wasn't already in the hospital before that time, but it's a good place to start.'

They focused on a larger TV screen, scrutinising the images of the main entrance. This was the only entrance into the hospital for visitors and the vast majority of staff. The image quality was excellent, giving a clear side-on picture of each and every person entering and leaving the building. At three fifteen, Sam saw himself walk past the camera, heading outside. Louisa spotted his pained expression and threw a concerned glance in his direction before returning her gaze to the screen so as not to miss anything or anyone. Sam's eyes remained fixed on the screen.

And then, just two minutes after Sam himself had appeared, Louisa spoke. 'There,' she said, pointing. 'Stop it there.' The images continued. 'Can you rewind it and pause?'

'Certainly,' the man said, scrolling back ten seconds. He kept his hand at the console, over the pause button. 'Say when.'

'There,' she said again. This time the screen froze instantaneously, locking the image of a man in its centre as he entered the hospital.

Sam examined the image. It was Richard Friedman, Louisa's patient, the man who had approached them in the café earlier that day. He was still wearing the fluorescent-yellow coat. That matched with the approximate time the phone went missing, but what about later when he'd been called to the Eye? 'What about just before three thirty?'

The guard nodded and whizzed forward through the minutes before letting the recording play on in real time.

'There he is again,' Louisa said.

Again the image was locked into place. Richard Friedman was leaving the building just a few minutes before Sam received the call. And he was holding something in his left hand. It could certainly have been a mobile phone.

Sam turned to Louisa. 'Is there any other reason that could explain why he was here at that time?'

'Not that I know of,' she replied.

'The phone could be his,' Sam suggested.

'No,' Louisa corrected. 'He doesn't have a mobile.'

⌣

'This place always helps me to relax,' Louisa said as they entered the vast atrium of Tate Modern.

Sam looked around at the current exhibition – a towering series of sculptures that were a twisted, warped representation of the London skyline. Unlike Louisa and Anna, he'd never been that keen on art, but this was pretty impressive, even if he could only guess at the meaning.

'I want to show you something,' Louisa explained. 'Up on the next floor.'

They made their way up the stairs, emerging into an exhibition entitled 'Healing Minds'.

'The gallery commissioned people across London with a mental illness to create artistic representations that explained their experiences and state of mind,' Louisa explained. 'Art therapy. Our hospital was one of the places that took part.'

They stood in front of a disturbing black-and-white sketch – an image of a screaming face flanked by what looked like bolts of lightning crossed with daggers.

'Unnerving, isn't it?' Louisa said.

Sam nodded. He looked at it some more. There were what looked like tombstones mixed in with overgrown grass, and a pair of animal-like eyes. Then he moved to the information panel next to the canvas.

It read, 'Richard Friedman – 2010.'

Louisa watched Sam's reaction. 'Richard said he used to draw and paint a lot when his wife was alive – mostly landscapes – but this was the first time he'd produced anything since she died.'

'When was that?'

'Eight years ago. She was killed in a road accident – knocked down on a zebra crossing by an uninsured, speeding driver.'

Sam shook his head as he was drawn in to the tortured face. Now he knew the author, he did recognise the features. It was a self-portrait of sorts. 'He doesn't look like an artist.'

Louisa smiled. 'Why? Because he hasn't got a goatee beard and flowing hair?'

'Point taken,' Sam said. 'Have you spoken to him about this?'

'The sketch? No.'

'How long have you been seeing him?'

'Just over eight months.'

'He's depressed?'

'Depressed, lonely, angry. He's been to see people in the past for counselling, but he was getting worse again, threatening to kill himself, so he was referred to me.'

'Do you think he's capable of doing what we suspect he's doing?'

Louisa shrugged. 'If you'd asked me that a couple of weeks ago, I'd have said no way, definitely not.'

'But now?'

'Maybe.'

'What's changed?'

'I've always been wary of his neediness – like I said, the man's lonely. But it's been getting more sinister.'

'How do you mean?'

'Turning up outside my flat.'

'What? But, how did he know—'

'I have no idea,' Louisa interrupted. 'I never reveal any personal information to patients.'

'What happened?'

'I told him to leave. And he did. But he came back the next night and then again a week later.'

'My God, Louisa, you should have told me,' said Sam, his protective instinct kicking in. 'I thought something was going on, that you were acting a bit strange recently.'

'I'm a big girl, Sam – I can handle things. I don't need to tell you everything.'

Sam thought of the note that he had found in her locker. 'But you should have told me, or the hospital or police.'

'He always just left when I asked him to,' she explained. 'I thought he was harmless.'

'But he's not.'

'Probably not,' Louisa corrected. 'But what I don't really get is why he'd be targeting you. What would he have against you?'

'I haven't got a clue,' Sam said, still perturbed that Louisa had kept this serious situation to herself. What if this guy had done something to her?

'It just makes me wonder whether it is him.'

'Okay,' Sam conceded, 'he might not be responsible. But you've got to let the police investigate. When was the last time he came to your flat?'

'Last night.'

Sam shook his head. This was crazy. 'Louisa, tell the police, please,' he said, trying to hide his anger.

'I will. I'm just worried that it might make things worse.'

'The women you counsel whose husbands are beating them up – they say the same thing, don't they?' He sensed Louisa's reluctance to answer, knowing where this was going.

'Yes,' she admitted.

'And you tell them to go to the police.'

'I do.'

'Then you've got to follow your own advice before things escalate,' he said. It was more an order than a request. 'The guy knows where you live, he's been to your home after you told him not to, he more than likely broke into your locker and stole your phone, and we think he then made me think you were in danger. This has got to end now.'

He watched them from a distance as they left the hospital grounds and walked side by side along the banks of the river. Using the crowds as cover, he followed them as they entered Tate Modern, pausing outside for a second as he surveyed the group of youths on skateboards just off to his right. Entering the building, he ignored the sculptures and instead honed in on the couple as they climbed the staircase. He waited until they had disappeared from view before following.

It was risky, but he would be careful.

He spotted them stood by the painting, deep in conversation, with their backs to him. He moved behind them in a wide arc, longing to interrupt the conversation with his stunning revelation.

But now wasn't the time, so he just watched and waited.

Chapter Eleven

S am got home just after seven, mentally drained from the stress of the day. It was good to be back, and even though the place felt strange without Anna, all around there were comforting reminders of his wife. The flat was filled with gifts from various parts of the world in which Anna had worked; often the locals whom she helped would present her with something as a token of their thanks. She treasured and displayed each and every present, saying that to do otherwise would cause great offence, as if the gift givers might find out if she had instead hidden the things away in a box. Sam walked around the flat, examining the items one by one, connecting to Anna through them. There was the traditional Indian jewellery box on the fireplace, encrusted with pink shell; the tribal African mask hung on the kitchen wall, given to her by an elder in a remote village in Ethiopia; and the Peruvian throw in the bedroom that had been hand-woven for her by the daughter of a local leader high up in the Andes. Finally, there was the portrait of Anna, sketched in charcoal by a talented young schoolboy in Gambia, which was hung in the hallway. It captured her beauty and strength better than a photograph ever could.

Sam returned to the kitchen and cooked his signature meal of tuna pasta, Anna's favourite, before turning his thoughts back to Louisa. He'd gone with her straight from Tate Modern to the police to report the theft of the phone and Richard's behaviour. Defying their expectations, the officer on duty had seemed concerned, promising to get back to them as soon as possible. Sam had invited Louisa to stay at his, but she'd declined, saying that she'd arranged to go out for a drink with a few girls from work. He didn't want to push her, but he had insisted on accompanying her back to her flat, less than a mile away on the other side of Islington.

He was worried about her.

Sam had just finished the meal when the call that he had been longing for came. Anna sounded full of energy, even though it was midnight local time. The flight had run to schedule, and she'd just arrived at the relief centre in the delta region of Bangladesh. From there, she would help to kick-start the efforts to ensure that the displaced population received clean, secure water supplies. Sam could almost feel the adrenalin coursing down the phone line. This was the sort of situation in which Anna thrived, and he wondered how she might adapt to life as a mother, which would have its own but very different adrenalin rushes.

Saying goodbye to his wife, Sam felt an urge to escape the flat. He needed to clear his head for the next day, and he was already behind in his training schedule. As part of a team at the hospital planning to run next year's London Marathon for charity, he had a detailed training schedule that had been designed by Doug, who was also taking part. Doug was a lifelong road runner, and the schedule was punishing.

Changing into his jogging bottoms and a T-shirt, he set off at a pace, heading west towards Regent's Park. Out on the streets, dodging commuters, tourists and assorted vehicles, he felt his head clear. He pressed on, enjoying the mild breeze against his face as he reached the outskirts of the darkening park. The shoulder ached a little, but apart from that he felt better than he had done in a long time. The park was quiet, populated only by a few dog walkers and fellow joggers. Deciding to head for Primrose Hill, he picked up speed, feeling the burn in his legs as the gradient increased. By the time he reached the top, his breath was shallow and his pulse racing. But this was good. He looked out across the city – his favourite view in London – enjoying the world-famous vista. Off to the right the BT Tower thrust skyward, while to the left the dome of St Paul's battled for prominence among the modern financial office structures. He stood there for a while, his mind once again return-ing to the various issues at hand. There really was no running away from them.

He had just set off back down the hill when Louisa called.

'It wasn't him,' she said simply.

Sam stopped against the side of a tree, just off the main path, catching his breath. 'What?'

'Richard Friedman. It wasn't him. The police have just called.'

The police had indeed acted swiftly. 'They've already spoken to him?'

'They went straight round to his house.'

'So what happened?'

'He admitted being at the hospital. But he said he was visiting a friend who's an inpatient over on Geller Ward.'

'He's got to be lying,' Sam said, resting against the tree.

'They checked it out. A patient confirmed that he's a friend of Richard's and that he came to see him today around that time.'

Sam wasn't convinced. 'He could also have stolen the phone while he was there.'

'The police don't have any evidence.'

'Do you really think it was just a coincidence that he was in the hospital at the same time your phone was stolen?'

'I don't know. Maybe I jumped to the wrong conclusion, picked the obvious suspect.'

'But if it wasn't him, who was it?'

'No idea. I've been racking my brain, but I just don't know. How about you? Any suspicions?'

'Someone who holds a grudge against me?'

'The police said the person might be connected to you, not me.'

Sam thought on that. There was one obvious candidate who was impossible to ignore. 'Someone who's recently been released from jail, do you mean?'

'I don't think it would be Marcus,' Louisa replied.

Sam had assumed that was whom Louisa had been alluding to, so he was surprised by her strength of conviction that it wouldn't be him. 'It would explain the references to Cathy.'

'You would have recognised his voice.'

He thought back to the man's voice. Louisa was right. It hadn't been Marcus Johnson. It was fifteen years since he'd last spoken to his one-time best friend, but he knew that voice hadn't been his. 'I still think it could be Richard Friedman. Maybe he's done some digging about your past and made the connection with me and Cathy.'

'I just don't know, Sam. Part of me wants it to be him. At least we'd know who we're dealing with.'

Sam pulled each heel back towards his bottom, stretching his tightening tendons. If he didn't get moving again soon, he'd suffer tomorrow. 'So what else did the police say?'

'They told me to keep records of everything – any phone calls, other communication, if anything else goes missing. They've also warned Richard not to come to my flat any more.'

'At least that's something.'

'You should keep records too. And keep an eye out for anyone following you.'

'Sure,' Sam said, instinctively scanning the nearby vicinity for people. A girl and her dog were some way off up the path. A middle-aged man was jogging off to the left. A young couple were walking hand in hand nearby, leaning playfully into each other.

'And you've spoken to the hospital about allocating him to someone else?'

'Already done,' she said. 'Karl is taking him on. I feel bad, but I know it's the right thing.'

'Definitely. And don't feel bad. You've done your best with him, Lou, but you shouldn't see him again, for both your sakes.'

'I know. Look, I've got to go now,' Louisa said. 'The girls will be waiting. But call me if anything happens.'

'Louisa,' Sam said.

'Yes?'

'Please be careful. And if Richard Friedman comes anywhere near you, call the police straightaway.'

Shirley Ainsley stared at the fading photographs of her daughter. She was three years old, laughing as she played on the beach with a bucket and spade. It had been a wonderful holiday. Shirley looked over to the corner of the room where Charlotte and her brother Simon were sleeping. Charlotte was the exact likeness of her mother at the same age. It upset Shirley even to look at them because it reminded her of what she had lost and what the children would never know. Baby Jessica was asleep in the cot upstairs. Thank God, they were too young to understand what had happened.

How could Jane do that to those little ones? Try to kill them all?

Shirley turned over the page of the photo album and inspected the next set of now-tarnished memories.

How had things gone so wrong? Jane had been such a strong person, such a good, devoted mother. Life had been hard, of course – they didn't have much money, and it was difficult looking after three children ever since the father had left without warning, a year ago. But she seemed happy, and the children had everything they needed. Shirley and her husband Eric had helped out.

But now Jane was dead, by her own hand, and Alison was missing.

Where was she?

Tears splashed onto the album, trickling along the plastic covering and pooling on a photograph of Eric and Shirley, with Eric holding his smiling daughter aloft.

Vincent McGuire. She blamed him for this.

Vincent had come into Jane's life two months ago, sweeping her off her feet and promising her more. Jane had met him when she'd been out shopping at the local arcade. He'd offered to carry her bags, and things progressed quickly from there. But despite Jane's platitudes, Shirley had never been sure of Vincent. He had been fine with them, had eaten at their table and talked politely, said the right things, but there was something about him that made her feel uneasy. Maybe it was just the natural reaction of a protective mother who had seen her daughter hurt once too often by a man. But part of it was the uncomfortable reality that from the very beginning Shirley did not believe that this dangerously good-looking man would really want to settle down with a single mother of four children. And unfortunately, she had been proved right. He had called Jane and coolly ended their relationship the day before her death.

Shirley had tried to tell him the news – that because of him, Jane was dead. But the mobile phone number they had for him was no longer working. That said it all really.

She'd told the police about him. Maybe they could track him down.

Shirley removed her glasses, rubbing her tired, irritated eyes. She hadn't slept properly now for forty-eight hours. Her little girl was gone and she longed to be held by her husband. But Eric was at the pub. He'd been out for hours now, and she could only hope he wasn't getting drunk as he'd done the previous night. He'd taken Jane's death the hardest, but as usual was bottling up his emotions, neither displaying his own turmoil nor offering sufficient sympathy. She broke down, sobbing uncontrollably. These attacks of grief, regular since the police had come knocking, came on like a sudden thunderstorm of despair.

The phone rang.

She nearly didn't answer it, letting it ring five times before dragging herself off the sofa. But then she thought it might be the police. It wasn't.

It was her granddaughter, Alison.

Sam jogged back to the flat, increasingly uneasy at the thought that there was someone out there, unidentified, targeting him and Louisa. Who was this guy? Could it be someone connected with him, like the police had suggested? And if so, were they following him right now? They'd been watching him at the London Eye, taunting him, so why not here too? He slowed as he reached the high street, crossing at the lights opposite the tube station. And then his mobile rang.

The caller ID read unknown.

He snapped his phone open. 'Hello?'

No reply.

'Who is this?'

He stopped against the wall of the tube station as the last of the commuters passed him on their way home. Was this the same person as before? 'Is it you, Richard?'

Still no reply.

'Marcus?'

He watched a businessman just ten or so yards away from him, on the opposite side of the tube station entrance. The man was on the phone. But the call ended, and the man strode across the road towards a waiting bus.

'Hello?' repeated Sam.

The line went dead.

Continuing home, he reflected on the silent call and what it might mean. He reached the flat, glancing back as he pulled out his keys and let himself in. On the mat behind the door was a hand-delivered letter. He recognised the handwriting immediately, and his stomach went into free fall.

Chapter Twelve

S am took a deep breath and knocked on Louisa's office door. He'd spent half the night wondering whether to show her the letter. It wasn't that he wanted to keep secrets, but he worried about the ramifications of opening all this up again.

'Come in.'

Sam met Louisa's gaze as he entered the room. She looked guilty, and the upturned novel on her desk betrayed the reason for it. 'Caught me,' she said, holding the book up. 'It's pretty good, you know – helps me to relax. Well, actually, it's rubbish really, but the relaxing bit is true.'

Sam forced a smile. Louisa had always been a bookworm. That's how she and Cathy had met, at the school book club, all those years ago.

Louisa watched as Sam took the seat opposite, her face changing. 'You okay? Has something happened?'

Sam nodded, bringing the envelope from inside his jacket and placing it on the desk. 'This was waiting for me when I got home last night.'

Louisa took one look at the handwriting and grabbed the envelope, almost tearing out the letter. She read intently, biting on her bottom lip.

'I wondered if he'd contact me,' Sam said as Louisa continued reading, her face full of concentration. 'But it's been so long since the last time that I decided he wouldn't. I thought he might just want to move on.'

Louisa looked up from the letter. 'He still says he's innocent.'

Sam nodded.

'How do you feel about that?'

'Marcus saying he is innocent doesn't change anything,' Sam replied. 'The police had the evidence.'

Louisa nodded. 'I know.'

And yet here he was again, protesting his innocence, just as he had done in the previous three letters of correspondence that Sam had received during the fifteen years of his incarceration. The first letter had arrived a year after the court's verdict. Marcus had sworn that although he couldn't remember what had happened that night because he was so drunk, there was no way he could have hurt Cathy. He just couldn't believe it of himself. But he said that he didn't blame Sam for not believing him. Sam had shown that first letter to his father, who, enraged, promptly threw it in the bin. While the second letter, a year later, reiterated the points from the first, the third mailing took Sam by surprise. Marcus wanted to meet with him. That was three years ago.

Louisa looked back at the letter and then up at Sam. 'He wants to see you.'

Sam shook his head. 'I can't, Louisa. I can't meet with him.'

'It might help,' Louisa offered.

Three years ago Sam had come to that conclusion, if only briefly. He'd even gone as far as contacting the prison and arranging a time to visit. He hadn't told anyone. His parents would have been devastated. And he just didn't know what Louisa would think. But en route to the prison, he changed his mind. What did he expect to gain from sitting face-to-face with Marcus? He'd thought maybe it might help him move on – or at least understand what had happened – but how could it? What could such a meeting ever really achieve? So he had turned around. And that was the last he had heard of Marcus. Sam had never revealed to anyone just how close he had come that morning.

'It won't help,' Sam said. 'I just want to forget about him, Lou.'

'You've got to do what feels right for you,' she acknowledged, handing Sam back the letter. Sam glanced down at the address at the top of the page. Marcus was living in a flat in Rotherhithe, a run-down area of London, just south of the river. Why had he moved down there? He folded the letter and slipped it into his pocket.

'Were things okay last night?' he said, changing the subject. 'No more calls, no visits from Richard Friedman?'

'Everything was fine,' Louisa replied. 'I had a good night, actually – it was nice to go out with the girls and just try and forget about everything. It really helped me to relax for the first time in ages.'

'Good, that's good.' He paused, feeling bad for the bubble-bursting news he was about to deliver. 'I got another call last night when I was out running, just before I found Marcus's letter.'

Louisa's mood immediately darkened. 'From the same person?'

'I assume so. It was a silent call.'

'From my phone?'

'No, not this time. It was from an unknown number.'

She looked troubled. 'You don't really think it could be Marcus, do you?'

'Why not?' Sam replied. 'You asked me to think of someone who might hold a grudge against me. The caller at the London Eye mentioned Cathy's murder; there was the newspaper article in your locker; and all of this only started happening since he's been released from jail. Then there's that note from him, hand delivered. How does he know where I live?'

Louisa shrugged.

'You don't think it could be him?'

'I can't see it, Sam,' Louisa admitted. 'It just doesn't make sense to me. Why would he write to you saying he's innocent and wanting to meet you, but at the same time be doing all this?'

'I don't know. Maybe he's playing some kind of twisted game, wanting to stick the knife in some more.'

'Do you really believe that?'

'I don't know what to believe. But it's a possibility, isn't it?'

'I guess so. But you said it wasn't his voice.'

'Maybe he disguised it.'

'Are you going to tell the police?'

'Not yet,' Sam said. 'What would I tell them? I've got no evidence that Marcus is involved.'

'That's right,' Louisa agreed.

'And then there's still Richard Friedman.'

'I still feel bad, you know, about dropping him as a client.'

'It's for the best.'

'I know it is, but still . . .'

'Even if he didn't steal your phone, and he isn't the one calling me, he still crossed the line in a big way.'

'You're right,' Louisa admitted.

'Maybe this will put an end to it.'

'I hope so. You were right, Sam, it was getting out of hand. Something had to be done. Sometimes I just don't know when to let go of something, admit defeat. I really appreciate your support.'

'No problem.'

'So what are you up to today?'

'Not much,' Sam said. 'I'm off to see Prof Khan in a minute, and then I'll check up on how Sophie's doing. Not sure what I'll do for the rest of the day.'

'So you're still off your list?'

'Sure am.'

'It will be good to have a break,' Louisa said. 'Professor Khan knows what he's doing.'

'Maybe. You know me, though; I like being busy, especially with Anna being away.'

'I know. But it's only for a day or so.'

'I know. And at least the press interest has died out. Carla left a message for me. There've been a few articles in this morning's papers based on the press release, but no one has contacted the hospital today.'

'That's great, Sam. You're yesterday's news.'

She smiled and Sam smiled back.

***

'Sam, my boy, do come in.'

Sam entered Professor Adil Khan's office. The room was an oasis of calm in the hectic world of the hospital. It reminded Sam of the rooms of the Colonial Empire that he'd seen in films – deep brown, ornate mahogany furniture; carved wooden lamps; and decorative rugs. Professor Khan had brought all the furniture himself, flown over from Pakistan on his appointment eighteen years ago. It wasn't hospital policy to allow such a thing, but for one of the world's leading surgeons, the request had met no resistance. The room was also a temple to what was arguably Adil Khan's greatest love – cricket. He'd combined his medical training with a passion for the sport. A gifted batsman, he had represented the national side at the under twenty-one level before suffering a serious leg injury following a car accident. Damage to the tendons in his left leg had put paid to his cricket career but left him free to focus his energy and passion on medicine.

'Do sit down,' he said, gesturing to the impressive carved wooden chair. As ever, his jet-black hair and beard were neatly trimmed, and his styling immaculate around his broad physique. His suits were made to measure by his good friend and personal tailor in Islamabad. 'Why pay for Savile Row when you could have the best?' he would say. 'You like it?' he said, noticing that Sam had spotted a new addition to the wall behind his desk – a signed photograph of Imran Khan, the legendary Pakistani cricketer (no relation). The conversation often turned to cricket, with Professor Khan knowing that Sam too had played the sport for Lancashire schools.

'Impressive. You got that last week?'

Professor Khan nodded, looking back at the photo. 'I was speaking at a charity dinner he arranged in Karachi. The photo was a thank-you present.'

He turned back to face Sam, examining him with those intense deep brown eyes, his hands steepled on the desk. It was down to business. 'And how are you, Sam.'

'Good, good,' Sam replied. 'Well, as good as can be expected.'

'Are you enjoying your time off?'

'Not really.'

Adil Khan smiled. 'I imagine you're not.'

'I understand, though,' Sam added. 'I did need the break.'

Khan nodded slowly, bringing his hands up so that the tips of his fingers touched his bottom lip. 'I've been working in medicine for longer than I can remember. I love my profession, Sam. Maybe I love it too much. There are times when I've worked on when I should have rested. I realise that now.'

Sam stayed quiet. The Professor was teeing him up for unwelcome news.

'You're a very talented surgeon, Sam. Very talented – one of the best young surgeons that I have worked with. And I don't say that lightly. You're also very dedicated. You really care for your patients – don't underestimate the importance of that. One can be technically brilliant with a scalpel, but if he doesn't care for his patients, be cognisant of their human needs, he can never be a truly great surgeon.'

Sam was pleasantly surprised about such open praise. Professor Khan was notoriously coy when it came to his opinion about those working under him. 'Thanks. That means a lot.'

'I'm not looking for thanks. I'm seeking your co-operation.'

'I'm not sure I understand.'

Adil Khan sat back, his hands still joined. 'I would like you to refrain from operating for the next seven days.'

Sam had been right to suspect imminent bad news. He couldn't hide his disappointment.

'I know you wish to work,' said Professor Khan. 'I understand totally. But this is for the best.'

'But the interview, it's less than two weeks away. If I'm—'

Professor Khan held up a hand. 'Trust in me, Sam. And more importantly, trust in yourself, in your own ability and what you have already demonstrated in the years that I have worked with you. You are young, but I believe more than ready to step up to consultant level, of that I am sure. One week without surgery will make no difference, believe me; but one week *with* surgery might.'

'I don't understand.'

Adil Khan leant in. 'You have been through a great trauma, Sam. You are strong, but still, everyone needs time to recover mentally. Do you feel at one hundred per cent?'

Sam fought the urge to lie. 'No.'

Professor Khan opened his palms. 'Then there you are, Sam. You make a mistake in the operating theatre this coming week because you are not one hundred per cent, and your career is jeopardised.

You rest for a week after a major trauma where you are a hero, and you ensure you are ready for the interview. Do you agree?'

Sam nodded. There was nothing else he could do.

'A very wise decision, Mr Becker. Enjoy your recuperation.'

Sam emerged from the office, still smarting from the decision. Professor Khan was right, of course, but it didn't make the thought of seven days without surgery any more bearable. It would be hell. And Miles would be sure to gloat, seeing Sam's absence as a sign of weakness that might sway the interview panel. It might not affect Professor Khan's judgement of who was the best person for the job, but he was only one assessor out of seven.

He made his way across the hospital to ICU. Sophie was still stable and had improved slightly, but the situation remained grim. Sam was glad to see both Tom and Sarah at her bedside. He stopped off to tell Louisa about the meeting with Professor Khan, before heading off down to the Thames, with no particular destination in mind. He found himself drawn back to Tate Modern and to that drawing. As he was standing there, captivated by the image, looking for some hidden meaning that might unlock Richard Friedman's personality, his phone rang.

It was Inspector Paul Cullen of the British Transport Police.

'Sam, I'd like to talk to you about the incident at the weekend. There's been a development. Are you free to meet me now, somewhere in central London?'

Chapter Thirteen

S am, glad you could make it at such short notice.'

Paul Cullen rose from his seat to greet him, his hand outstretched. Sam met his firm but unthreatening grip and nodded a hello. Cullen was wearing a casual open-neck shirt and blue chinos: evidently dressing for off duty or at least to make it appear that way.

'Thought I'd take the liberty and get one in for you,' he said, gesturing at the pint of lager on the table.

'Thanks.' They both sat down, but Sam left the lager alone. He would hear what Cullen had to say first. 'Your colleague isn't with you?'

'DS Beswick?' Cullen said. 'He's ill. Flu, his wife said. So I'm working on my own for the moment. I think I prefer it, really.' He glanced around. The Islington pub was busy with mostly old white Irish men drinking dark ale. 'Hope you don't mind the surroundings. I used to come here a long time ago, back in my training days. It hasn't changed a bit.'

Sam could believe it. It was a genuine London local. There was none of the refurbishment that had occurred in many other of the capital's establishments, which over the past few years had transformed themselves from old men's drinking dens into family eating places. In here, the fittings remained as old and frayed as the clientele.

'Fine by me,' Sam replied, thinking that Cullen's choice of a pub, just like his purchase of the pint, was meant to set a relaxed tone for the discussion. And yet his call, both in the fact that he wanted to meet so quickly and the way he'd mentioned a development, jarred with this supposed relaxed situation.

Cullen smiled. 'It might sound strange, but I find pubs are often the best places to get some privacy.' He looked around. 'No one's bothered about our conversation in here. They're too busy picking this afternoon's winners at Haydock.'

Sam nodded, noting that most of the men were scrutinising the back pages of the newspapers or staring up at the TV over in the far corner, near to the ceiling, which was showing a horse race. A few wandered in and out, clutching cigarette packets. Maybe the location had really been just a pragmatic decision.

Sam watched impatiently as Cullen took a drink. 'So,' he said while the beer was still draining down the officer's throat. 'You said there's been a development?'

Cullen smiled as he placed the glass back on the table. 'All in good time, Sam. First things first. How are you?'

'I'm okay.'

'I see the bruise is fading a little.'

'Slowly,' Sam acknowledged.

'And the memories?'

'Slower.'

Cullen nodded. 'You see a lot of terrible things in my job. Things that you could never dream up in your worst nightmares. Sometimes it can be difficult to get them out of your head, no matter how hard you try. I expect it's the same for you in your line of work.'

93

'I've seen some things that I'd rather not have,' Sam admitted. 'But it's part of the job, and I knew what I was letting myself in for.'

'Me too. But it doesn't make it any easier.' Cullen played with the top of the lager, running a finger along the rim of the glass.

'No, it doesn't,' Sam agreed.

'We've got something else in common,' Cullen added. 'We both lost a sister.'

Sam tensed. 'You've been looking into my history.'

'Of course,' Cullen replied, 'that's what I do. What happened to your sister was a terrible thing. My sister died when I was fourteen. She was five years old. Died from meningitis. One minute she was there, smiling, playing with her toys. The next she was gone.'

So Paul Cullen did understand what it was like. 'I'm sorry to hear that.'

'It was a long time ago,' he said, 'but I still think about her every single day. What she'd look like now, what kind of person she would have grown up to be.'

Cullen seemed to be searching for a reaction, but Sam wasn't going to oblige. He thought those very same things about Cathy. But he wasn't going to discuss this with Paul Cullen.

'I think it was one of the reasons I joined the force,' Cullen added. 'I couldn't help my sister, but I could help other people.'

Again Sam didn't respond to the bait.

'Is that why you became a doctor? Because of what happened to your sister?'

'People always assume that,' Sam replied, 'but I'd already decided to apply to medical school, so no, it's not why I became a doctor.'

Again he shut down the possibility for deeper discussion. He wasn't about to tell Cullen that Cathy had been the one who had finally made up his mind to become a doctor. Not because of her murder, but because of what she had said to him.

'One day,' she'd said, 'you'll be Dr Becker, and you'll save people. That will be your job – saving people. How cool is that?'

Cullen took another sip of his drink, taking the hint. 'Fair enough, I don't want to pry.'

'It's okay,' Sam said, not really believing him – wasn't that what police work was all about, prying? 'How are the children?'

'They're fine,' Cullen replied. 'Being taken care of by their grandparents.'

'There's no father?'

'Left a year ago. No longer in contact.'

Sam shook his head. 'And what about the girl, Alison?'

Cullen went to speak, then checked himself. 'Since we spoke, has anything else come back to you about the accident?'

'No.'

'Nothing else that Alison might have said to you?'

'No.' Sam scanned Cullen's face. 'What's this about?'

Again, a pause. 'We got the preliminary results back from the post-mortem. The body was relatively intact because the train pretty much pushed the car down the tracks rather than crushed it.'

'And that's why the train stayed on the tracks.'

Cullen nodded. 'Mrs Ainsley hadn't been drinking. We didn't find any alcohol in her system. But there were traces of anti-depressants.'

'Which ones?'

Cullen pulled out a small notebook from his trouser pocket. 'Neuroxate.'

'She'd been prescribed those?'

This was potentially highly significant. Neuroxate was one of the stronger anti-depressants on the market. The drug had hit the headlines a few years ago because of an alleged link between its use and increased risk of suicide. Although this fact was denied by its manufacturer, hundreds of bereaved families believed their loved ones were now dead because of the drug. Louisa had once counselled the family of a fourteen-year-old boy who had hanged himself within two weeks of taking those little yellow tablets. She'd described it as the most traumatic case she'd ever dealt with.

'I spoke with the grandparents, Shirley and Eric Ainsley, this morning,' said Cullen. 'They said she'd been depressed for a long time after her husband left, last year. The doctor prescribed them then.'

'Right.'

'But they also said that she hadn't been taking them for a couple of months or so.'

'Meaning something triggered off her taking them again.'

'She met a new man about a month ago. He broke off the relationship the day before the train crash.'

'Hell,' Sam said. 'Have you spoken to him too?'

'No contact details. Shirley and Eric don't know where he lives. The mobile number they had for him isn't working. And the name they've given us hasn't produced any results.'

'But it sounds like that, plus maybe the effect of the drugs, could explain what happened.'

'It makes sense. We still consider suicide to be the most likely explanation.'

The most likely explanation? Surely, it was clearly suicide. 'It couldn't have been an accident.'

Cullen waited for Sam to elaborate.

'Alison said her mother drove onto the track deliberately. If it had been an accident, she wouldn't have locked the doors or had the baby in the boot.'

'I agree,' replied Cullen. 'But we owe it to the family to keep an open mind about this. A verdict of suicide often causes a lot of pain for those that are left behind – guilt especially. I saw it this morning with Shirley and Eric Ainsley. They're already blaming themselves, thinking that they could have done something to save her.'

'I can imagine.'

'So until my team and I have explored every avenue, then we won't close any doors – even if it does look blindingly obvious to you and me.'

'Are you going to be able to trace the ex-boyfriend?'

'Unlikely,' Cullen admitted. 'We have the name Vincent McGuire, but like I said, nothing has come up so far, and who's to say that's his real name? But we'll keep looking and asking around the local area.'

'Of course.'

'Maybe something will come up – sometimes investigations will lead you to the most unpredictable conclusions.'

'If there's any way I can help, then I will.'

'That's great. And I appreciate you being able to meet today at such short notice.'

'No problem.' Cullen was about to say something, and Sam could tell that whatever the officer was holding back was nearing the surface. He decided to pre-empt him. 'The development that's happened, it's about Alison, isn't it?'

This time the pause was more ominous. 'I'm going to ask you a question now, Sam, and think very carefully before you answer.'

Sam felt his pulse quicken. 'Go on.'

'Did you know Jane Ainsley prior to Sunday evening?'

He hadn't expected that. 'What? No, of course not.'

'So on Sunday evening, that was the first time you ever met Jane Ainsley and her family?'

It felt like a question under caution, the conversation transforming from chat to interrogation.

'Yes, of course,' Sam reiterated. 'I'd never seen her before in my life. What's this about?'

Cullen leant forward. 'Last night Shirley Ainsley received a call from Alison. According to Mrs Ainsley, Alison said that her mother's death was your fault.'

———

Richard Friedman knelt over the completed jigsaw, staring at the image that now haunted him. He'd used his computer to scan the painting and had converted it into the wooden puzzle, using a company in the high street. It seemed to add another dimension to the creation – the sense of being broken, fractured, was given even more prominence. He'd planned to frame the thing and hang it on the wall. But now he wasn't so sure. He stared down at the tortured eyes – it was like a warped mirror, reflecting back his torment.

Torment that she had helped to take away.

He stood up, unsteady on his feet, and staggered towards the drawers. He'd taken too many tablets. Pulling out a small jewellery box, he flipped open the lid and took a pinch of the auburn hair that lay inside, bringing it up to his cheek. It tickled his skin, the way it had always done. It still smelt of her.

Carefully, hands shaking, he placed the hair back in the box and returned it to the drawer, which was stuffed with memories. Most of which he had never had the strength to delve into.

She had given him that strength.

Offered him comfort and hope.

But now he had ruined it.

He put a hand to his head and broke down, his mouth wide in a child's silent cry.

Why had he done this? Was it just pure revenge? Whatever, when he got the news, it hadn't made him feel any better. Instead he felt sick and ashamed.

Twisting off balance, he kicked out at the jigsaw, the pieces shooting around the room as his image shattered.

'I'm so sorry.'

He'd scared her. Now he wouldn't be able to see her again, and he would be back to the beginning.

Alone and afraid.

He curled up on the floor, biting on his fist, rocking gently.

'I'm sorry, Margaret, I'm so sorry.'

The car had come from nowhere, travelling at tremendous speed. The driver, a child of eighteen, was drunk. He'd spent all that morning downing extra-strength lager with friends at a barbecue.

'I couldn't help you.'

She was in the middle of the crossing when the car hit her doing sixty. The driver never even braked, and his dear wife of twenty years didn't have a chance. The force of the impact threw her ten feet into the air. At the trial, witnesses likened the noise to that of a small explosion.

She was dead before she hit the ground.

He had seen everything, watching from across the road. She'd stopped to look in a charity shop window, and he'd gone off ahead. If only he hadn't been so impatient. She was smiling at him, and by the time he shouted a warning, it was too late.

All the paramedics could do was take away her broken body.

Twenty years of happiness gone in a split second.

'My beautiful Margaret. I miss you so much.'

He dragged himself up from the floor and moved unsteadily towards the kitchen.

The boy was convicted – death by dangerous driving. Yet there were no signs of remorse, and a few times Richard had caught him smirking in the dock, as if he was proud of what he had done. He would serve a few years in prison. The judge had apologised to the family that the maximum available sentence was not longer. In no time the killer would be free while his wife rotted.

That was not justice.

'It was for the best,' he muttered. 'I didn't do it for myself.'

Reaching the drawer, he gazed down at the knife. He picked up the one Margaret used to use to cut the meat. She was a great cook. They'd invite the neighbours around for dinner, and everyone would be full of genuine praise at her delicious creations.

He grasped the knife so tightly that his knuckles whitened. Richard stared hard at the blade.

This was the only way.

Chapter Fourteen

Eric Ainsley gulped back the last few drops of his beer and peered into the now empty glass. He'd lost count of how many he'd had in the past couple of hours. Looking around him in the near-deserted pub, he briefly thought about going home. He should be with his wife. But Shirley would notice his drunken state in an instant. He could get away with it at night, but not during the daytime.

Still, Shirley needed him.

He looked across to the man who was drinking in the far corner of the bar. He didn't recognise him, and he wondered for a horrific moment if the drinker was actually one of them – that maybe it wasn't really all over and his gamble had backfired. Eric's eyes flashed back down to the glass as he caught the man's eye.

If only Shirley knew the truth. She would never forgive him.

Eric hauled himself out of the wooden bench and made for the door. He would take a long walk, try to sober up and then go home. Then he would put his arms around his wife, hold her and tell her everything.

Emerging into the blinding sunlight, he turned left and headed down towards the canal.

Jane had killed herself, and it was his fault.

He passed through the old industrial area with its boarded-up windows and deserted alleyways. It was once a thriving place, alive with small businesses and honest local people plying their trades. Here he'd worked for thirty years as a carpenter in a successful furniture business, and it was here that he'd met his wife-to-be, who'd come to work there as an office junior, back in 1967. Those were the days. Finishing work and strolling across to the local pub, arm in arm, talking excitedly about the future as the Rolling Stones blasted out from the radio. That was before the jobs went abroad and the business closed its doors, like so many other companies. Now, during the day, the area was an unkempt museum of what used to be, while at night it was the haunt of the area's prostitutes and kerb crawlers, with any vestige of romanticism now extinguished.

The man stepped out from a doorway, just a few feet ahead of him. Eric stopped dead. The guy in his path was well built, pushing six three, with a skinhead and pit-bull facial features.

'Have you got the time, mate?'

The accent was pure South London.

Eric nodded, relieved but still scared, and glanced down at his watch.

'It's half past—'

But before he had a chance to finish, someone charged him from behind, knocking him to the floor. His attackers let fly several kicks to the back and stomach as Eric tried but failed to protect himself.

The pain was crushing.

'Stop,' said a voice that he recognised. 'We don't want to kill him.'

His gamble hadn't worked. The man hadn't been able to deliver what he promised.

Eric grimaced with pain, afraid to open his eyes as he lay on the hard cobbles. He could taste blood and alcohol. From the floor he heard a vehicle approach and stop.

'Pick him up,' the voice said. 'Let's get going.'

Two sets of hands grabbed him under each arm, yanking him upright. Now he did open his eyes. Two men – the one who had blocked his path and the man from the pub – were on either side of him.

They dragged him to the back of the waiting white van. Another man thrust open the back doors.

The man who he already knew was just watching.

Eric looked across at him. 'What are you going to do?'

'Put him in the van.'

And with that Eric was launched into the back of the vehicle, slamming head first against the metal floor.

'Drink some of this.'

Eric took the litre bottle of whisky from the man, who was sitting on the opposite bench that ran along the back of the van. They'd been driving around for ten minutes or so, and without the aid of any windows, he had no idea where he was heading. And little idea why.

'Go on,' pressed the man. 'Drink. I hear you've been getting a real taste for alcohol recently.'

Eric glanced at the other two men in the back of the van, who smiled in amusement. He brought the bottle to his lips and took a couple of gulps, feeling the burn down the back of his throat. He looked across to the man for a reaction.

'Don't be polite. Have some more.'

'I'm okay.'

'Drink some more,' the man insisted, releasing the words slowly.

Reluctantly, Eric slugged back several more gulps. This time it scorched his throat like liquid fire. He'd drunk a quarter of the bottle.

'More than that.'

Eric shook his head.

Within a split second the man was upon him, squeezing his cheekbones so hard that he thought they would crack. He felt the bottle on his lips and the whisky gush down his throat. 'Swallow.'

Eric did as requested. Now there was no burning: only numbness. His assailant pulled back and sat back down, holding the now half-empty bottle. 'That's better.'

The half a litre of whisky had already worked its magic, going off like a nuclear bomb in Eric's head. The inside of the van and its occupants were rising and falling in an alcoholic swell.

'Please, let me go,' Eric heard himself saying.

'Not yet. You still haven't given me what I want, Eric.'

Eric put a hand to his head, trying to steady himself. 'I can't do it. I just can't do it. I've tried, but it's impossible.'

'You will do it, Eric.'

'I will – I promise I will. Just please, leave my family alone, please.'

A cruel smile flickered across the man's lips. 'How is Jane?'

Eric looked up at him, trying not to break down. 'You must know.'

If the man did, his expression didn't give anything away. 'Know what?'

'She's dead. She – she killed herself because of what you did.'

The man's facial expression didn't change. 'I'm sorry that she suffered because of your actions.'

Eric put his head into his hands and started to sob. The man was right. It was all down to him. He had caused all this.

'You give me what I want,' said the man, 'and no one else will get hurt.'

'Just hurt me, not my family,' Eric slurred.

The man scoffed. 'I just want what's owed to me, Eric – that's all.'

'I'll get you what you want, I swear. I swear I will get it, please.'

'Good. Now cover his eyes.'

The two other men moved towards him. One put on the blindfold while the other held him firm. Eric didn't struggle.

'Now we're ready,' the man said as a gush of air rushed into the van through the open doors. Eric hadn't even noticed that they'd stopped moving. 'Get up, Eric.'

Eric tried to get up from the bench but fell back down. His balance had gone AWOL. He tried again, this time really focusing on staying upright. But he straightened up too early, smacking the top of his head into the van's roof.

'Watch it. I think you've had a bit too much to drink, haven't you?'

Eric heard laughs as he was guided out of the van and down onto ground level. He swayed in the darkness, before being led, legs buckling, to a lock-up garage. He heard the door being opened and was pushed inside. The door was closed behind them, and his blindfold removed. Blinding light exploded from a single bare bulb hanging from the ceiling. The inside was spinning. The garage reeked of petrol and was ringed by shelves filled with car accessories. Then Eric's vision cleared slightly, and he saw something on the ground.

A large sack, and it was moving.

'We don't like being messed around with, Eric.'

He couldn't keep his eyes off the sack. Was it really moving, or was he imagining it?

Within seconds his question was answered as the man brought his heel down hard on the object. The sack seemed to spasm and Eric heard a muffled cry.

'People have to learn,' the man said, stamping on the sack with full force. 'That no one messes with me. No one tries to ruin my plans.' He took a few steps back, wiping saliva from his mouth like an animal going in for the kill.

'Now you take over,' he gestured to Eric. 'Kick him.'

Eric felt the bile rise as he contemplated the act. He stood, swaying.

'Do it now!' he shouted. 'Or the next person in that sack will be your wife, and then your grandchildren.'

Eric shook his head, taking a stumbling step back. 'Please, let me go. Please, don't hurt my family.'

'Do this now,' the man said, 'or they will suffer.'

Eric didn't doubt it. He took a step forward, muttering a silent prayer for forgiveness as he kicked out at the unknown person. He felt his shoe against bone. It was the worst feeling, and he found himself crying.

'Harder.'

Eric kicked out again and again. The person in the bag stopped moving and became an inanimate object. It was easier now. He kicked and stamped as the world spun around him.

'It's finished,' the man said as Eric stumbled backwards. 'Congratulations, Eric, you've done a good job.'

Hyperventilating, Eric tried to steady himself against the shelving, but dislodged an oilcan. It fell to the floor and the lid flipped off, spilling out the dark liquid onto the concrete. He watched the sack as the men untied the rope. There was still no movement from whoever was inside.

They removed the sack and Eric caught his breath.

His plan, his one last hope, had failed.

The man whom he'd met two days ago was unmoving, blood staining his teeth. There was a deep red gash along his right eye. His nose had collapsed, flattened by Eric's blows. The man had promised to solve Eric's problems, by warning off his tormentors, for a price of five hundred pounds.

'Now don't try anything like that again, Eric, and everything will be all right.'

Chapter Fifteen

W hy would she say that?'

Cullen shrugged. 'I was hoping that you might be able to answer the same question.'

Sam looked off to the left. 'Why would she say that?' he said out loud, but this time directed at himself. He couldn't see any rationale for Alison's actions – why would she want to implicate him in that way?

'She might just be looking for someone to blame,' Cullen offered, 'and you're the person she's chosen.'

Sam looked back at him. 'Did she say anything else?'

Cullen shook his head. 'Not according to Shirley Ainsley. She just said that and put the phone down.'

'So you still don't know where she is?'

'No.'

'But at least she's safe.'

Cullen nodded. 'Are you certain that you don't remember anything else that might explain what Alison said?'

'No,' Sam replied without hesitation. Why was Cullen not letting go of this? 'You don't believe it was my fault, do you?'

'Like I said, suicide looks the most likely option, but we can't and shouldn't rule anything out at this stage.'

'So you do think I could be involved?'

'Personally, no. I think that Jane Ainsley wanted to die and drove down onto that line. You just happened to be in the right place at the right time. I'd be a fool to think anything different.'

'But you just have to cover your bases.'

'Exactly.'

It was reasonable from Cullen's perspective to consider all the possibilities, and Sam had no divine right to be believed without question. 'So what next?'

'We hope that Alison gets back into contact very soon. She's the one person who really does know what happened.'

He was in the room before Louisa even noticed. She'd had her back to the door, rooting through her filing cabinet for one of her patient's records.

'Miss Owen, I wanted to see you.'

Louisa spun around. Richard Friedman was stood in front of the closed door and moved a pace towards her.

'Stay there,' Louisa heard herself say. Her voice was shaky. 'You shouldn't be here.'

'I had to see you,' he replied, staying on the spot. 'Please, I'm sorry. I need to talk to you. Please, talk with me, Miss Owen, please.'

Louisa ran through her options. She couldn't phone for help without making things worse. And she wasn't prepared to just push past him and fight her way out of the office. So talking was the only way.

She gathered herself as much as she could, trying to calm down inside so her fear wouldn't leak out and risk antagonising the situation. 'Okay, sit down, Richard. But I can't be long. I have to see another client in a few minutes.'

It was a lie, but a worthy one.

He nodded, and almost fell into the seat as Louisa took her place opposite. 'Thank you, thank you, Miss Owen. Thank you so much.'

Louisa met his eyes. They were blood red, and he was looking right through her, as if focusing on some distant point.

Was he drugged up?

She tried to pretend that this was just another consultation, taking a deep, steadying breath. 'How are you, Richard?'

He shook his head, his eyes closing. 'Not good, not good at all. I'm sorry, so sorry.' He brought a shaking hand up to his head.

Louisa didn't really want to ask the question, but she had to. 'What are you sorry for, Richard?'

'For what I've done to you,' he said, his head now buried in his hands.

Maybe he had come to admit it all. If it had been him who had done all those things, she would be relieved. 'Do you want to tell me about it?'

He nodded.

Louisa took a chance, pulling out her new mobile from the desk drawer and holding it below the level of the table. She pressed speed dial 1 and placed the phone on her lap.

'I've done bad things . . . bad, bad things.'

She waited.

'I'm sorry, so sorry.'

'You're sorry for coming to my home?'

He nodded vigorously. 'I'm sorry. So sorry for everything. Please, I just needed to be close to you. I needed to be close.'

'But coming around to my house, you know that's not right, don't you? We agreed that there are boundaries – we have to keep a distance outside of the hospital.'

'I know, I know. I'm just so sorry.'

'I asked you not to do it, Richard, but you keep coming. Like now, just turning up at my office when you know you shouldn't do it.'

'I know. But please, please, Miss Owen, can I still see you here, at the hospital?'

Louisa shook her head as he looked on with pitiful childlike expectancy. 'I'm really sorry, Richard, but it's for the best that you see Karl instead. He's a very nice man, Richard, and a very experienced counsellor.'

'No, please,' he pleaded. 'I need to see you. I can't cope without you.'

Louisa glanced down at the phone. It was still connected.

'Karl will really be able to help you. I've made sure that he knows all the background.'

Richard shook his head. 'No, please, I want to see you.' This time there was force behind the statement.

'It's not possible. I'm sorry.'

'You called the police,' he said, his forehead creasing in confusion. 'They questioned me about stealing your telephone and threatening your friend.'

Louisa had decided not to go down this route, but so be it.

'Did you take my telephone, Richard?'

He started weeping.

Louisa tried a different tact. 'Richard, you said you're sorry for what you've done. What else have you done?'

Richard looked up. 'I did it for the best.'

Louisa was confused. 'Did what?'

He closed his eyes. 'I should have waited for her. I shouldn't have crossed the road on my own. I wasn't there when she needed me. The screams – I can hear the screams; they're getting louder now.'

His mind was blending the past and present again. She wouldn't get any sense out of him now. The priority was to calm him. 'Richard, you still need time to grieve. What you've been through, it takes time to recover, years for people to come to terms with their loss – especially when the event was so traumatic and unjust. What you've been through for all these years, the pain has built up and built up. It would take its toll on anyone.'

Richard nodded. 'I did it for the best.'

This was a new statement, unlike anything he'd said to her in the past. 'I don't understand.'

'It was to make everything better,' he replied cryptically.

'Richard, you need more support to recover from everything you've been through, but I won't be able to help you any more. I'm really sorry. But Karl will be there to help you now. He can help you through all this, and you will come out the other side, I promise.'

'No.'

This wasn't working. Louisa decided it was time to get a little firmer.

'It's best that we don't see each other again,' she said. 'And please, Richard, don't come to my house again. If you do, I'll have to speak to the police again, and I really don't want to have to do that. I don't want to get you into trouble.'

'No, no, no,' he said, his teeth clenched. 'I can't do this any more.'

And then he produced the knife.

Sam stepped inside the flat and headed for the kitchen. Making a cup of tea, he thought about what Paul Cullen had said. Maybe this was just a way that Alison was coping with the tragedy. Who knew what state she was in right now, alone, without any support from family? And she was so young to cope with such an event. Cullen was right. He was an obvious person to blame. After all, he had failed to free her mother from the car. Maybe that's what she had really meant – he was to blame because he had failed to save her mother.

He moved into the lounge with the drink. The house was empty without Anna. Too quiet. She was the one who filled their home with laughter and life. Looking around, he smiled at the slightly scary but exciting thought that in nine months this place would be home to a new arrival.

He glanced at his watch. It would be late afternoon in Bangladesh. He wondered how Anna was getting on. He moved into the office room and booted up the laptop. A couple of minutes later he was online, logging into his email account. Maybe Anna had sent a message.

She had. It wasn't overly long, but it was more than he could have hoped for, given the remoteness of her location and the hectic nature of her task. She had emailed him first thing in the morning. The group were set to travel out to a remote rural area just north of the delta region, which had been especially hard hit by the typhoon. The population had been without clean water for days, and the situation was grave. Sam smiled at the last sentence.

Lots of love from Anna and Baby Becker the first. Can't wait to see you very soon! xxx

He replied, leaving out mention of the meeting with Cullen. He would update her when she got back. Hopefully, by then Alison would have reappeared, the person would have stopped calling him and things would be back to normal.

He returned to his email inbox and began deleting the half a dozen spam messages that had built up over the past two days. Most were offering him the chance to enhance the size of his penis or claiming that he'd won the lottery.

But one message was different.

Cathy B wants you to check out her profile.

Sam hovered over the title with the cursor. Could this really be a reference to his sister? It was from a sender which screamed spam: 06905919909@netmail.com.

He knew it was risky to open such a message. Last year they'd nearly lost their entire hard-drive contents thanks to a computer virus that had been delivered by email. But the title was just too tempting.

He opened the message. It repeated the title of the email, but with an accompanying link to a page on a site called Dream Date.

Again, he knew it wasn't wise to follow the link. But he couldn't resist. He waited impatiently as the computer connected to the destination site. And then it appeared on screen, and Sam caught his breath.

'What the hell?'

It was a profile page for his sister Cathy. On the right-hand side was her photograph. Her bright smile shone back at him. She was just fifteen years old in the photo. Her life lay ahead of her, or so they had all thought. Sam looked across at the text running beside the photo. It listed her likes as camping, walking on the beach and late-night drinking.

'That's sick,' he mouthed. 'Who the hell . . .'

Her dislikes were listed as 'dying young'.

Sam shook his head. He wanted to smash the screen.

There was no more information, apart from a button to click if you wanted to get in touch with her. But when he did, the site asked for registration details.

'Who the hell would do this?'

Before he could think of what to do next, his phone rang.

It was Louisa.

'But coming around to my house, you know that's not right, don't you? We agreed that there are boundaries – we have to keep a distance outside of the hospital.'

Her voice was low. 'Louisa, are you okay?'

There was another voice, a man's, but it wasn't loud enough to hear.

'I asked you not to do it, Richard, but you keep coming. Like now, just turning up at my office when you know you shouldn't do it.'

Sam got to his feet as the horror of the situation dawned. Richard Friedman was at her office. 'Louisa?'

And then the phone connection went dead.

Chapter Sixteen

S am phoned through to the hospital's main switchboard as he threw open his car door and slid into the driver's seat.

The hospital's automated voice recognition system requested a name.

'Operator.'

He started the engine, resisting the temptation to drive off with phone in hand. It would be difficult enough to concentrate on the road, without trying to deal with a phone conversation at the same time.

'Calling Operator,' the system replied.

The phone seemed to ring forever as Sam continued to fight the urge to just sink his foot down on the accelerator.

'Hello, Operator speaking.'

At last.

'Hi, this is Sam Becker. I'm a consultant on the Cardiac Unit. I need you to get security up to the second floor, Clinical Psychology, right away – Louisa Owen's office, 2G27. It's an emergency.' He injected all the authority he could muster into his voice. The operator needed to be in no doubt as to the seriousness of his demand.

'Of course,' the operator replied, her tone acknowledging the urgency. 'What's happened?'

'A patient has forced his way into her office,' Sam replied. 'He's dangerous. Louisa called me, but the phone went dead.'

'Right,' the operator said, 'I'll call security straightaway. I'll also call the police.'

'Great,' Sam said. 'But get security up there right now.'

Sam neared Louisa's office, having parked the car in the drop-off area at the front entrance to the hospital. He wasn't comforted to see a group of security guards talking to a policewoman, right outside Louisa's door. It looked like a crime scene.

Maybe he was too late.

The young police officer broke off her conversation as she saw him approach.

'Can I help you?'

Sam strained to look past the officer towards the door. He couldn't see if Louisa was in there. 'Louisa, is she all right? I'm the one who called security – Sam Becker. I'm a close friend.'

'She's fine,' replied the officer, stepping aside. 'Go on in.'

Sam nodded, passing through the guards and into the office. Thank God, Louisa was okay. She was sitting at her desk, talking with a young male officer.

She looked up and smiled weakly. 'Sam.'

Sam had never been so pleased to see her. She looked exhausted – pale and certainly not her usual self – but at least she was safe. 'Thank God, you're all right.'

'I'll leave you to it for a moment,' the officer said, rising to his feet and exiting.

Sam sat down. 'Are you okay?'

Louisa nodded. 'I am now.'

'Where is he?'

'I don't know,' she replied. 'They think he might still be some-where in the hospital. He left just before security arrived.'

'It was awful, listening to what was happening on the other end of the phone and not being able to do anything. The things going through my mind; I thought he was going to hurt you.'

'At one point, so did I.'

'And when the phone cut out, I thought something terrible had happened.'

'My battery ran out,' she admitted. 'I'm really sorry.'

'Don't be silly,' Sam said, reaching out to her. 'You did well, using the phone like that – very clever. So what happened? Did he force his way in here?'

Louisa shook her head. 'He took me by surprise. I had my back to the door, and by the time I realised he was in the room, ask-ing to talk with me, I couldn't call security, so I thought it was best to just talk to him, try to deal with it the best I could and hope he might just go away. And then I had the idea of calling you.'

'Why did he want to see you?'

'For help, I think. He's really unstable. I've never seen him that bad before.'

'But he didn't touch you.'

'No,' she replied. 'I think he's more likely to hurt himself. He had a knife.'

'A knife? But he didn't threaten you with it?'

'No. He was just holding it.'

'And he just left on his own accord?'

Louisa nodded. 'He virtually ran out of the door – after he said a lot of quite worrying things.'

'Like what?'

'He started reliving his wife's death, telling me that he was responsible. It was like he was standing there, watching it happening. He's been like that before, but never so agitated. He was angry, mostly with himself, but that's when I started to think I might be in trouble. Then he said something else. It was about Cathy.'

'Cathy? What did he say?'

'He starting talking about her – he knew how she'd died, when she'd died, what she looked like. He was speaking as if he'd known her. And then he was mixing up Cathy with his wife, saying he was responsible for Cathy's death.'

Sam shook his head in anger. 'It was him. He's been researching Cathy.'

'What do you mean?'

'He emailed me, Louisa – sent me a link to a dating site which had a profile of Cathy on it.'

'What?'

'Did you ask him about the phone calls?'

'I asked, but he wouldn't answer me.'

'They've got to find him and put a stop to this.'

'I know. They've got all of hospital security out looking for him. People with a description are watching the front entrance. The police are looking too.'

'I just don't understand why he's become so obsessed with Cathy.'

Louisa shrugged. 'The train crash?'

'The crash?'

'He read about you in the news, found out about the connection between me and you, and then did some looking on the Internet. That's probably how you've become caught up in all this.'

'But why do all this? The phone calls, the threats, the website?'

'Maybe, in his head, his wife's death and Cathy's are all messed up together now.'

'And he blames me?'

'He blames himself, certainly for Margaret's death,' Louisa corrected. 'Sam, you've got to understand that he's just not rational any more. He's living in another place. It's hard to empathise. But at the heart of it, he's grieving for a loss that he can't recover from. We can both empathise with that, can't we?'

Sam nodded, holding Louisa's gaze. There were tears in her eyes. 'I still miss her, Sam.'

Sam looked away and fought his emotions. 'We all do.' He turned back to face Louisa. 'He's got to stop doing this.'

Just then the young male officer re-entered the room. 'You're Sam Becker?'

Sam nodded.

'We've located Richard Friedman. He's up on the roof, threatening to jump. But he's asked to speak with you.'

Sam followed the uniformed officer to the lift, travelling up to the top floor. From there, they walked along to a metal emergency exit door and climbed a spiral metal staircase, heading for the roof. At the top, it opened out into a small, concrete floored space. Another police officer was waiting there for them.

'Dr Becker,' he said, proffering a hand. 'Sergeant Robert Anderson.'

Sam shook his hand, glancing towards the door that led out onto the roof of the hospital. This all just seemed unreal. Why did Richard Friedman want to talk to him? Why would this man, whom Sam had never properly met, attach so much meaning to the murder of his sister all those years ago?

'He asked to see you,' the officer continued. 'Any idea why?'

'Not really,' Sam replied.

'Well, he wants to speak with you. Are you okay to do this?'

Sam nodded, even though he wasn't sure at all that this was the right thing to do.

'We don't want to pressure you. I mean, if you're not comfortable doing this, then that is absolutely fine. We certainly don't make a habit of involving civilians in this kind of thing, but he was insistent about talking to you.'

'It's okay,' Sam said, swallowing his doubts. 'I'll do it, if it could help.'

'Okay, as long as you're sure. Well, we've got one officer out there speaking with him. That's Sergeant Will Thomas. There are trained people on the way, but for now we're just trying to do our best.'

'Do you really think he might jump?'

'Who knows – but he's right on the edge of the roof, and he is threatening to do it. We haven't got any reason to suspect he isn't serious.'

'Did he say why he wants to speak to me?'

'I'm afraid not.'

'What do you want me to do? Talk him down? I'm not sure I'll be able to do that.'

'We don't expect you to talk him down. Just listen to what he has to say. Talk to him. Maybe he'll then decide to come down. Or maybe we can keep him talking long enough for the trained officers to arrive. Just do your best, but under no circumstances put yourself in any danger. And if it gets too much, then just turn around and come back inside.'

Sam nodded. Two suicide rescues in one week. He just hoped this one would end better than the first.

'If you're ready, I'll open the door and you can walk out. Take things slowly. Will is expecting you, so just follow his instructions.'

'I'm ready.'

The officer nodded and moved towards the door, pushing it open. Sunlight burst through the growing gap. 'Good luck.'

Sam stepped out into the light, feeling heartsick. Surely, he wasn't the right person. He was a doctor, trained to save people, but not like this.

The second officer was waiting for him on the other side, standing a few yards away on the flat roof. About the same distance on was Richard Friedman, looking out over the drop and the city beyond from the top of the boundary wall. He didn't seem to have noticed Sam's arrival.

'Sam.' Another handshake. 'Sergeant Anderson has briefed you?'

Sam nodded as the wind swirled and buffeted his body. He glanced off to the right, seeing the London skyline spreading out eastwards. They were high up. No one would survive a fall from here. He felt faint.

'Just take it slowly,' advised the officer. 'I'll keep a distance. We don't want to scare him into doing something stupid. And if you want to go back inside, again, just take it slowly, and come back to where I am.'

'Okay,' Sam said, feeling sicker than ever.

The officer patted him on the back. 'Whenever you're ready.'

Sam moved past the officer, walking at a funeral-march pace towards Richard Friedman, who still had his back to him. The wind whipped up again as Sam considered his first words. He feared that calling out might precipitate Richard falling over the edge, but he didn't want to get too close before announcing his presence.

He stopped a few feet away. Seagulls cried out, gliding overhead, looking for their next scavenged meal. Still, Richard didn't turn around.

'Hi, Richard.'

Now he did turn to face Sam, wobbling on the small wall that acted as a ledge along the edge of the roof. He was every bit the man on the brink. His face resembled that of his self-portrait – pulled in many directions, tortured, afraid. Suddenly Sam forgave him everything – all the phone calls, the taunting over Cathy. None of it mattered any more.

'You wanted to speak to me.'

Sam spoke as calmly and softly as he could. The feelings of nausea and his self-doubts had gone, and his professional persona kicked in.

'I'm sorry,' said Richard. 'So very sorry.'

'It's okay,' Sam replied.

Richard shook his head. 'No, it's not okay – really, it's not okay.'

'Everything will be okay.'

'Cathy is dead, and it's my fault.' Richard turned to look down at the ground below.

Sam thought back to what Louisa had said. He was mixing up Cathy with his wife, Margaret. The two had become one in Richard's mind. So Sam played along. Now wasn't the time to challenge these delusions, no matter how much it didn't make sense.

'Don't blame yourself, Richard. There was nothing you could have done.'

Richard closed his eyes, unsteady on his feet. For a split second, Sam thought about making a move, somehow trying to wrestle him to safety. But it was too risky.

'You don't understand,' said Richard. 'I did it. I'm the killer.'

'Richard, please, come down and we can talk about this.'

Richard shook his head.

Despite what the police had said, Sam knew that this was now his responsibility. The officer might have only been a few yards away, but it might as well have been a mile. It was just Richard and he, locked together in this life-changing moment, with the outcome depending as much on Sam as the man on the ledge, threatening to jump.

He wasn't going to let it happen. 'You've been through a lot, Richard. You're still grieving for your wife, but you weren't to blame for what happened to her.'

'I did it. I'm the killer.'

'Come down, Richard. Talk to me. You said you wanted to talk.'

'I have something,' he announced. 'For you, from her.'

Sam watched as Richard delved into his pocket, again swaying on the edge. He brought out something shiny and with trembling hands threw it underarm towards Sam.

Sam caught it, grasping the chain and locket. The shock hit him like a sickening, winding heavyweight blow to the stomach. He shook his head. 'No.'

He opened the locket and there was the confirmation.

A photograph of his parents.

The locket had been Cathy's sixteenth birthday present. Sam had been with his mother and father when they had bought it. It hadn't been seen since her murder. The police surmised that it had either been lost in the struggle or that the murderer had kept it as a trophy. Sam had prayed that it still lay somewhere on those dunes. He went back dozens of times during those first few years, looking for that all-important piece of her, digging through the sand in a vain attempt to recover something of his sister.

He looked up, in total shock, grasping the necklace. Richard was looking back. 'How did you get this?'

'I'm so sorry,' replied Richard, 'so, so sorry.'

And then he pulled out the knife, slicing across his neck in a single sweep. Blood erupted and spewed towards Sam like a large brush flick of paint, splattering his clothes and face.

Before Sam could react, Richard toppled backwards over the edge.

Chapter Seventeen

S am raced towards the ledge, hearing screams from below. As he peered down in horror, the ground seemed to rise up towards him as the true height of the building became apparent. Richard was sprawled out far below on the car park tarmac, surrounded by four uniformed officers, who were standing a few feet away. There was no attempt to touch him.

They could see it was already too late.

Gathering crowds watched from a distance behind the police line. A few spotted Sam, standing where, just a few seconds earlier, Richard had ended his life with that stunning revelation. Maybe they thought he was planning to follow him or even that he had pushed Richard to his death.

Sam looked again at the necklace he was holding, which was catching the sun's rays. He was still in shock as the police officer reached him. 'It's okay, Sam,' said the officer. 'Come with me.'

He placed a shepherding arm around Sam's shoulder and led him across the rooftop. At the same time his radio squawked into life.

'Confirmed one fatality: the jumper. No one else hurt. We've got a lot of shocked witnesses down here.'

The officer pressed on the radio by his lapel. 'He slashed his throat with the knife. It's up here on the roof.'

'Okay, got that.'

'Just take it slowly, Sam.' They continued across to the door, where they were met by Sergeant Anderson. From there they descended the steps, along the corridor and into a meeting room that had been commandeered for the police operation. Several serious-faced officers were gathered in there, watching as the group entered. 'Just take a seat, Sam,' Sergeant Anderson said.

A chair was brought round, and he slumped into it, still grasping the necklace tightly. His world was spinning, but not just for the reason that the police assumed. The horrific suicide of Richard Friedman, right in front of his eyes, was overridden by the significance of what he was holding. It felt as if he were touching Cathy: that the necklace was actually a part of her. And it had been. She had loved it and had never taken it off. But the necklace was more than an emotional link to his little sister – it was a connection to her killer, a clue to what had happened that night.

Had Richard Friedman really murdered Cathy?

Sergeant Anderson pulled up a chair opposite. 'Sam, I'm so sorry it ended like that.'

'He planned to do that all along.' Sam shook his head with the realisation.

Sergeant Anderson waited a beat. 'What did he say to you?'

'That he was sorry.'

'For what?'

'For killing my sister.'

'Killing your sister? I don't understand.'

Sam held up the necklace. 'This is my sister's necklace. The last time I saw this was fifteen years ago, the night she was murdered. He had it.'

'What?'

Just then Louisa walked through the door, led by the female officer. Sam could see that she already knew what had happened. Her face was red and her eyes puffy. 'Sam.'

Sam got up and met her tight, all-encompassing embrace.

'I can't believe he did it,' she sobbed into his shoulder. 'I should have known. He was in such a state – I should have done more to stop this.'

'You couldn't have done anything.' Sam squeezed her harder, looking at Cathy's necklace as he held it behind her back. He wondered for a second whether now was the right time to tell her, but almost instantly he dismissed the thought. They had always gone through this together. It wasn't going to change now. 'He planned this all along,' he said softly. 'He wanted to die in front of me.'

Louisa pulled back, confused.

'I don't understand.'

Sam released his grip and showed her the necklace. 'He gave me this, just before he died.'

It took a second, but then her eyes widened. She looked at Sam and then back at the necklace, focusing on the silver locket, cradling it in her hand. 'It can't be.'

Sam nodded. 'It's Cathy's.'

'Here you go.'

Sam handed Louisa a mug of tea and took the seat opposite. They'd returned to his flat after questioning by the police, exhausted from a frustrating interview. The police were prepared for discussing the acute incident of Richard's suicide, but the link to a murder fifteen years earlier had thrown them. Much of the interview had consisted of an intrigued Robert Anderson being filled in on Cathy's death.

Sam leant back on the sofa, head turned towards the ceiling, and closed his eyes. It was hard to stop the random thoughts, to get some kind of handle on the situation. For a few minutes both he and Louisa sat there in stunned silence. It had been like that since the revelation on the hospital roof – both seemingly unable to vocalise their feelings.

'What does this mean, Sam?'

Sam opened his eyes, looking across at Louisa. 'I really have no idea.'

'This is just so crazy. Absolutely crazy.'

'I know,' Sam agreed. 'It feels so unreal.'

'Totally.' A pause. 'Do you think he really did murder Cathy?'

'I don't know, I really don't.'

'He had the necklace.'

'I know.'

Louisa took a sip from her drink. 'If he did it, then Marcus must be innocent.'

Sam followed the logic; he had run it through his head many times, but there were still so many unanswered questions, so many contradictory facts. He couldn't just reject all that he had believed, even after such a revelation. 'The evidence was there, Louisa, the evidence that Marcus had been lying about being with Cathy. You were in that court room too.'

'I know, I know.' Louisa became more animated. 'But what if Marcus has been telling the truth all along? What if he was just scared of admitting that he'd been with her? And now we might have found the one thing that proves he's innocent. We can't just dismiss it.'

'I'm not. Believe me, if Marcus is innocent, I'd be the first to want to prove it, but it's not that easy.'

Just saying his name was painful. And even contemplating that he was innocent seemed so wrong, like betraying Cathy. The certainty of Marcus's guilt had become part of him – it had become the truth, the explanation that Sam had craved for why his sister had been so cruelly taken from them. But it had never been enough.

Louisa seemed surprised. 'So you think he might be innocent?'

'I don't know what to think, Louisa. But I know I've got to keep an open mind. What do you think?'

'I'd like to believe that Marcus is innocent.'

'But do you think that Richard Friedman could have done it?'

'Maybe.'

Sam sat forward. 'Let's say Richard Friedman did kill Cathy. He took her necklace. Got away with it, and Marcus went to prison. Then, fifteen years later he reappears as one of your patients.'

'It sounds unlikely, I know.'

'Could he have selected you in some way? Deliberately chosen for you to counsel him?'

'Not really,' Louisa replied. 'People can ask to be referred by their doctor to a certain hospital, but not to a particular psychologist.'

'But he could have known that you worked at the hospital, and there aren't that many psychologists there.'

'True.'

'So he could have asked to be referred, thinking it was a way of getting close to you – and me.'

Louisa nodded.

'Maybe he wasn't really unwell. Do you know for sure that his wife really died in a road accident?'

'Definitely,' she replied. 'I've seen the official records. It happened the way he said it happened. And he was ill, Sam. It wasn't an act – you couldn't have acted the way he did. I would have spotted it, I'm sure.'

'Maybe something triggered off a need for him to contact you,' Sam said. 'And things went from there.'

'It sounds like you're starting to believe he did it.'

'I'm just thinking things through. There is the other possibility.'

'Go on.'

'That he got the necklace from someone else.'

'You mean from Marcus?'

'Maybe.'

'But why?'

'I have no idea,' Sam admitted.

'You really think that Marcus has something to do with what Richard has been doing?'

'Oh, I don't know,' Sam said, running a hand through his hair. 'This is just so hard to get to grips with.'

'Why don't you ask him?'

'What?'

'Meet Marcus face-to-face. Look him in the eyes, and then decide whether you think he's telling the truth.'

Sam shook his head. 'No.'

'Sam, consider it. I know it's hard, but after what's happened today, it could really help.'

'I don't think so.'

'I understand, Sam. But don't dismiss it as an idea, please. You might find out more in a ten-minute conversation with Marcus than you could ever find out by just sitting here and discussing it with me.'

Sam looked away.

'Just think about it, Sam.'

Sam put a hand to his face. 'I just don't think I could do it. I don't know how I'd react.'

'I could come with you, support you.'

Sam stood up and moved over to the window, looking out across the park. 'Thanks, but I don't think so.'

Louisa approached him. 'So what now?'

'We wait for the police to contact us,' Sam said, watching the cars go by.

'Do you think they'll reopen the case?'

Sam didn't look at her. 'I don't know. Part of me hopes not. But it's out of our control, isn't it?'

'I guess so. What are you going to tell your parents?'

Now he did turn to face her. 'No idea. But I want to tell them in person. This can't be done over the phone. I know how much this could upset them. I'll go up there tomorrow.'

'I want to come with you,' Louisa said.

'What about work?'

She shrugged. 'I was meant to be on a training day, but it's nothing that can't be missed.'

'Are you sure?' Sam didn't want to pressure her by revealing his happiness at her offer, but it was a great comfort to think that he would have support up there.

'I'm certain. I'd like to speak to my mum and dad too. And I don't think you should be left to do this on your own.'

'You're a good friend,' Sam said. 'You okay for travelling there first thing? I want to get an early start.'

'Absolutely fine by me – just name the time and I'll be ready.'

'Good. I need to get to them before the police do. This has got to come from me.'

Chapter Eighteen

The first call came at ten minutes past midnight, waking Sam from a shallow sleep. He had struggled to settle, lying in bed for over an hour, staring at the ceiling and listening to the traffic outside, wishing beyond anything that Anna were lying next to him. He longed for the comforting warmth of her presence. Instead, his only bedfellow was the haunting image of Richard Friedman slicing across his throat, and those words that changed everything.

'I did it. I'm the killer.'

And then there was the thought that for all these years, he may have been wrong about Marcus.

Could he have been so wrong?

Reaching over to the bedside table, he brought the mobile's illuminated display towards him.

No caller ID.

'Hello?'

Silence.

Sam sat up. 'Who is this?'

Still no answer. But he could hear someone breathing.

'Is that you, Marcus?'

And then the line went dead.

Sam lay back down, thinking, the phone still in his hand, by his side. Who would call at this hour? Just as he was drifting off, the phone rang out again from under the sheets.

He sat up again, this time throwing off the covers and swinging his feet out onto the wooden floor. 'Who is this?'

Again, a moment of silence followed by the cutting of the connection.

Sam stared at the mobile as the display darkened. This time he didn't bother to return to bed, instead getting up and pouring himself a drink of water. Settling down in front of the television, with only a single lamp lighting the room, he channel-hopped, thinking about who the caller might be.

Before his death, Richard Friedman would have been the prime suspect. But now, who? Marcus? Or maybe it was Anna trying to get through on a bad line. But then, she would have called the main phone.

Sam stuck on a sitcom, but he didn't feel like laughing.

Phone still in hand, he got up and moved towards the window, pulling back the curtain. The street outside was quiet, with just a few taxis and a lone bus passing by. Across the street, the park was shrouded in darkness. The trees, silhouetted by the full moon, swayed rhythmically in the breeze. It had been raining again.

He sat on the window ledge, waiting for the caller to return. And three minutes later, the phone rang again.

'Hello?'

Sam did not expect a reply. 'Sam.'

It was a girl's voice.

He stood up and moved back into the lounge, in front of the television, trying to remain calm. He had made contact at last. 'Who is this?'

'Help me, Sam.'

Sam placed a hand behind the back of his head. 'Help you how? Do I know you?'

'Please, Sam, help me.'

And then the realisation dawned.

'Please help us.'

He recognised the voice.

'Alison?'

No answer.

'Is that you, Alison?'

Still no answer. But now he was sure it was Alison. How on earth had she got his number? He strode back over to the window and pulled back the curtains again. Could she be calling from outside?

'Please, Alison, talk to me,' he said, scanning the road outside. There was no one in sight, but if she was in the park, among the trees, she would be next to invisible. 'Your family are worried.'

Still, she didn't respond. He didn't want to push it and risk losing her. Like a fish on a line, she had to be reeled in carefully. This could be his one and only chance. 'You've been through a lot, and you shouldn't have to do this on your own.'

For a horrible moment, he feared that she'd gone. But then he heard a low sob.

He tried to make his voice appear as calm as possible. 'Alison, where are you? I can come and pick you up. Or I can call someone else – anyone you like – to come and get you.'

'It's too late,' she stated.

'I don't understand.'

'It's too late.'

The ominous nature of that statement chilled Sam. 'Too late for what?'

A louder sob now.

'Alison, please talk to me.'

'I can't take it any more,' she spluttered. 'It's all my fault, and I can't take it any more.'

Sam continued to look out of the window, hoping that he might see a movement in the tree line that would reveal her presence. 'Let's talk,' he offered, 'face-to-face. Let me know where you are, and I can be there right away. You don't need to come back with me – just meet me to talk. We can sort things out.'

'It's too late,' she repeated, stifling another sob. 'I'm already here now. I'm going to do this. I'm going to jump.'

Dear God, not again! Please! 'Where are you, Alison? Please, tell me.'

'Oakley Bridge.'

'Oakley Bridge,' Sam mouthed, rushing back towards the bedroom. The bridge was about five minutes at pace from the flat. He knew it well and sometimes ran that way in training. 'Please, Alison,' he pleaded, 'just stay right there until I get to you, okay? Please, just stay right there. Don't do anything.'

Silence.

He grabbed his jogging bottoms from the bedside chair and threw on a T-shirt and tracksuit top, cradling the phone awkwardly between his ear and shoulder as he put on his socks. 'Please, Alison, promise me you won't do anything until I get there.'

Another sob.

Now dressed, he grabbed his keys and headed for the door. 'Alison, stay where you are, I'll be there in just a few minutes. Promise me you'll do that.'

But she had already put the phone down.

Sam closed the door behind him and set off up the path, glancing back to see the light on in the flat upstairs. He needn't have worried about disturbing the neighbours.

Days were long for city traders.

He set off at pace, pulling out the mobile from his pocket and punching in the number. The rain, a light drizzle, was cool against his face.

'Police, please. There's a girl threatening to jump off Oakley Bridge in Islington, North London, just off Central Street . . . No, I'm just on my way. I think she's serious. Please, get someone there quickly. You might need an ambulance too.'

He believed that he would get there first, but then again, there might be a patrol car nearby.

He picked up the pace, lengthening his stride, occasionally glancing down at his phone, in case she called back. But the phone, which he held like a relay baton, slicing through the night air on the rain-washed deserted streets of North London, remained silent.

Just a minute or so from the bridge, he cut straight across a junction. Too late, he saw the car speeding around the bend, towards him.

Sam froze in the headlights as the black BMW screeched to a stop no more than a couple of yards from him. The horn blared angrily as Sam held up an apologetic hand. He couldn't see past the tinted windscreen and the blinding halogens, but the horn blared again.

'Sorry,' he said.

Then the front passenger door opened, and a towering Jamaican man got out and headed towards him, gesticulating. Sam took a step back in the otherwise deserted road.

'What d'ya think you're doin'? Tired of livin', eh?'

'I'm sorry,' Sam repeated, 'but I've got to go.'

He sprinted off past the man.

'Yeah, you just run, man, and keep runnin'.'

Shaking off the near miss, Sam raced along the road that ran parallel to the stone bridge, which was just off the main road. It wasn't open to traffic, instead being used for walkers and cyclists to get to and from the adjacent park.

As he turned the corner, the rain came down harder, sweeping across in a sudden, swirling gust that made him wipe his eyes. A sharp turn to the left, and the bridge was ahead of him, lit only by an ageing, dull, yellow-hued street lamp. It was completely deserted.

Sam shook his head. 'Oh, no.'

He slowed as he reached the bridge, scanning three hundred and sixty degrees for any signs of Alison. But there was nothing. He peered over the side down to the blackened water below, praying that it wasn't already too late. But he saw nothing amid the gloom. Crossing over to the other side, he repeated the exercise, but still he could see nothing but the reflective ripples of the water.

'Where the hell are you?'

Maybe she'd changed her mind. And now she was somewhere safe. Maybe that short phone conversation had been enough to convince her that she had something to live for. She could be on her way back to be reunited with her grandparents.

Or it could have all been a hoax. She could have just been playing with him, making him suffer for what she believed he had done to her mother. After what she had told Shirley, blaming him for her mother's death, it was a possibility.

But she'd seemed so genuine on the phone.

She had been afraid and distressed, just like by the railway track. There was no faking that.

Again the thought returned: How did she get his mobile number?

He crossed the bridge once again and peered over. And then he saw something, up against the bank on the left-hand side, resting against the reed bed.

'My God, please, no.'

It was too dark down there to see exactly what it was, but the size and shape could have been that of a young girl.

'Please, no.'

He raced around to the side of the bridge, vaulting over the safety gate that led onto the bank. He slid down the small bank, and then he knew.

It was a body, face down in the water.

'Oh my God!'

He waded into the cold, murky water, up to his knees, and grabbed the body, pulling it towards him. He dragged it onto the bank and turned it over.

It was Alison. Unmoving, eyes closed. Her skin was ghostly white, her lips purple.

Although expected, it was a hammer blow to his system. Why had she done this? Why?

There was no pulse. He began resuscitation, pressing his mouth onto her cold lips, blowing in life-giving, warming air, before pumping on her chest. *Fight, Alison, fight, for God's sake!* But with each passing second, hope faded. After two minutes of determined, frantic effort, that hope was extinguished.

She was gone.

He cradled her head in his hands. Her wet hair spilled through his fingers as her body slumped against his. That's when he noticed the wound on the back of her head. An impact from the bridge, or maybe as she had hit the river bottom – blood covered his hands, blackened against the night. Sam rocked her back and forth. 'I could have helped you. I could have helped. I'm sorry I couldn't save your mum.'

He was crying now, sobbing again for the second time that week. It was like fifteen years of well-constructed dam had just burst.

What must she have been going through to do this?

He looked up at the bridge, sensing something. Someone was standing there, watching. Light from the street lamp illuminated the observer's face – it was a teenage girl. Their eyes met, holding a gaze as Sam continued to cradle Alison. The girl was crying too.

And then she turned and ran.

Chapter Nineteen

Jody watched from the bridge as the man pulled the body from the water and brought it onto the bank. She stood there, keeping an eye out to her left, as he tried to save the girl. For a moment she thought everything was going to be all right, but then he stopped and just held her.

And then he looked up, and their eyes met as the tears started to fall. She thought about staying and explaining everything. But then a noise and a flash of headlights ended that delusion. The car had turned into the side road and was approaching the bridge. She couldn't tell whether it was the people she was running from, but there was no room for taking chances.

She had to escape.

Fear rippling through her, she ran into the park and sheltered behind some thick bushes, safe in the darkness, listening to the noises coming from the bridge. It sounded like the police. She waited, but not for long, then took her chance, moving through the park and out onto the road on the opposite side. She hurried through the deserted back streets, not sure where she was heading, all the time looking out for signs of them.

She decided to try Locky's place. It would be as good a place as any to lie low. And it was only a few minutes away.

Locky didn't exactly look pleased to see her. He'd been asleep when she knocked and was obviously drunk and stoned, but he had let her in without question. She hadn't needed to explain anything, which was good, because all she wanted to do was sleep and try to forget about what she had witnessed. She had seen many terrible things over the past three years, and she would have to deal with this the same way: just try to block it out, place it in that mental box inside her head, and lock it securely.

Tomorrow she would decide what to do next. Now she should rest.

But sleep was impossible. She lay weeping against the flat, mildew-smelling pillow, pulling the covers tightly up to her neck. Although she was still strong, each trauma had left its mark, and maybe this one had dealt the fatal blow to her will. She needed to escape this world.

If only she could find a way.

'I love you, Mum.'

The words surprised her. She hadn't said or even thought that in a very long time.

As she finally started to drift off, thoughts of her mother soothing her mind, there were three loud bangs from the direction of the front door. She shot out of bed, still fully clothed, and crept towards the door of the spare bedroom, peering through the gap, her body on edge. Locky staggered by and descended the stairs towards the door, muttering a dictionary of swear words as he rubbed at his face.

She held her breath, pushing gently at the door and straining to listen.

'Is she here?'

They'd found her.

'Who?' Locky asked in his strongest Irish accent.

'You know who. Is she here?'

'You mean Angelina Jolie? Sorry, mate, she's out.'

And then she heard Locky cry out in pain.

'Is she here?' The voice still calm, but more insistent this time.

'No.'

'I don't believe you.'

She didn't have much time. Turning to the window, she pushed it open and climbed through, out onto the sloping roof. Fortunately, she'd used this exit before. Within twenty seconds she was at ground level, running as fast as she could.

Too far away to hear Locky's screams.

———⌣———

Shirley Ainsley knew as soon as she opened the door that the news was bad. No visit at six in the morning could herald good news, especially when that visit was from the police. The uniformed officer, the same woman who had met with them shortly after the train accident, stood there, smiling tightly.

'Sorry if I woke you, Mrs Ainsley. Is it okay if I come in?'

The truth was she hadn't been asleep. She'd been up, waiting for her husband, who hadn't come home last night. She nodded and led the officer through into the living room, not daring to ask anything. If the news was bad, she wanted to delay it as much as possible. Until then, she could continue hoping.

'Would you like a drink?'

Her voice was shaking, and the officer noticed and shook her head. 'Would you like to sit down for a moment, Shirley?'

Shirley nodded, her emotions suddenly overcoming her. She put a hand to her mouth to stifle the sob and sat down onto the sofa next to the officer, her eyes clouding.

'We've had some bad news about Alison,' the officer began.

'No,' Shirley said, trying to shake away the thought. 'Not Alison – she's okay, isn't she? She's okay? Please say it's okay.'

The officer reached forward and took her hand, gazing deep into her eyes. 'I'm really sorry, but Alison was found a couple of hours ago. They found her body in a river.'

'No. She's not dead – she's not. She can't be!'

The officer squeezed her hand. 'I'm so sorry, Mrs Ainsley.'

Shirley broke free of the officer's grip and clamped her hands across her face, trying to block out reality. Then she picked up the cup next to her and hurled it against the wall, crying out as it smashed on the other side of the lounge.

She buried her head in her hands and felt the officer put her arm around her shaking body.

'I'm really sorry, Shirley, really sorry.'

For a moment they just sat there in silence. Then Shirley raised herself up. 'Where is she?'

'At the hospital. Would you like to see her?'

'Yes.'

Eric wasn't answering his phone, so she would have to do this on her own. Her neighbour was looking after the children. In the police car, en route to the hospital, she didn't speak to the officer, didn't ask for any further details. None of it mattered. The officer respected her desire for silence and concentrated on driving.

They reached the hospital, and Shirley was led through the A&E unit, down several corridors, until they reached their destination. Outside the doors, the officer turned to face her.

'Now, are you sure you want to do this, Shirley? If you've changed your mind, I can take you back home, and we can do this later with your husband.'

Shirley shook her head and pretended to be stronger than she was. 'I want to do this now.'

The officer nodded. 'Okay, we'll go in. I'll be there with you, so just let me know if it gets too much.'

'Okay.'

They passed through the double doors, to be met by a doctor who introduced himself as the pathologist. Shirley didn't take in what he was saying. She had tunnel vision for the curtained-off bay just off to the right. That was where Alison lay.

They moved forward as three, the doctor pulling back the curtain to reveal a trolley with a white sheet covering her granddaughter.

Suddenly, Shirley felt strong. This was her first granddaughter. The always smiling, kind girl with the infectious laugh who had delighted everyone she met.

She needed to do this.

She nodded at the doctor.

He nodded back and gently pulled back the sheet to reveal the body.

Shirley took a sharp intake of breath and grabbed the guard rail for support. She thought she had been prepared for anything, but she had been wrong.

Sam ran hard, trying to block out the night's events. He passed through Regent's Park, up around Primrose Hill, and then across

Camden, which was busy with commuters. He longed to run further, heading for nowhere in particular in the early-morning brightness, but the stresses of the previous few days had taken its toll on his body.

He felt drained, both physically and emotionally.

He decided to head home and then call Louisa. They would still travel up north to his parents, but it might have to be later. No doubt the police would want to talk to him about Alison before then.

He'd tried to come to terms with her death in the hours since pulling her from the water. But it was all such a waste. Such a young girl. He'd failed to save her mother, and now he felt he'd failed her too. It was just so hard to comprehend.

He couldn't get the image of her out of his head – her cold and lifeless body on that bank, blood still seeping from her head.

And then Richard Friedman's suicide and the link to Cathy.

It all felt too much.

He nodded a hello to the upstairs neighbour as he passed him on the path up to his flat. Suited up and off into the City, briefcase in hand.

Entering the flat, he had a shower, bathing under the warm water, not wanting to get out. He thought of Anna and the baby – how much he would give to have her waiting for him when he got out. But there were things to do.

He'd just dressed, still before nine, when the doorbell rang. Paul Cullen was waiting for him, accompanied by a female officer Sam hadn't met before. The young, blonde officer introduced herself as Police Constable Alice Stapleton, a liaison officer who had been supporting the Ainsley family.

Paul Cullen inched forward impatiently. He looked drained. Maybe he'd also not been sleeping. 'Can we come in, Sam?'

'Sure,' he replied, 'come on through.'

He led them into the living room and took a seat opposite them.

'How are you feeling, Sam?' Inspector Cullen asked. 'It's been yet another traumatic event.'

'I've felt better,' Sam replied. 'How are Alison's family? They must be distraught.'

There was a slight hesitation, and Sam caught PC Stapleton glance nervously at Cullen.

'We spoke with Shirley and Eric Ainsley,' confirmed Cullen. 'PC Stapleton took Mrs Ainsley to see the body at the hospital.'

'It must have been difficult,' Sam noted.

Another glance from the female officer. This time Cullen spotted it and nodded her to speak. 'It was a very traumatic experience for Mrs Ainsley. But not for the reason we had envisaged.'

Sam looked across to Paul Cullen. 'I don't understand.'

Cullen dipped a hand into his jacket and pulled out a photograph. He handed it to Sam. It was a smiling image of a young girl in her school uniform, posing for the camera.

Sam looked up at Cullen for an explanation.

'This is a recent photograph of Alison Ainsley,' he explained. 'This wasn't the girl you pulled from the river.'

'What?'

'The girl you pulled from the river – are you sure it was the same girl who led you to the train tracks? Or could it have been this girl, here in the photo? There is a striking resemblance between the two.'

Sam looked again at the photograph and shook his head in disbelief. There was a resemblance, but he'd never met this girl.

He looked back at Inspector Cullen. 'The girl I pulled out of the river last night was the same girl who led me to the car, definitely. And that girl told me she was Alison, and that it was her mum in there. This girl,' he said, lifting up the photo, 'I've never seen before in my life. I don't understand what the hell's going on here.'

'That makes two of us.'

PART TWO

Chapter Twenty

Are you sure you want to do this?'

Sam nodded as Louisa fastened her seat belt, her overnight bag having been placed in the boot alongside Sam's belongings. The plan was to stay for the night at his parents, to make sure they were okay. He couldn't just turn up at their door, drop the bombshell about Richard Friedman, and leave after a few hours. Louisa would stay at her family home, while Sam would have his old room.

Louisa waited until they had passed through the city's outskirts and onto the motorway before speaking again. 'How are you, Sam? After what happened at the river?'

'I've been better,' Sam replied, negotiating around a slow-moving lorry into the middle lane. He accelerated to seventy, as if trying to outrun the painful memories of his desperate efforts to breathe life back into the drowned girl.

'It's just so weird,' Louisa said. 'I mean, the girl – she pretended to be Alison Ainsley. Why? Who was she?'

'I was up most of the night thinking about it,' Sam admitted, moving back into the inside lane and slowing slightly. 'I can't think of any explanation. I've also been wondering how she got my mobile number. But it's all questions and no answers.'

'Are you sure you're in the right frame of mind to be doing this today? Dealing with your mum and dad, telling them about Richard Friedman?'

'I've got no choice,' Sam replied. 'I don't want them to find out from some policeman they don't know, knocking on the door without warning – it could be too much for them, too much of a shock. It needs to be me who tells them. I owe it to them to be there, to look after them, to break the news gently.'

Louisa nodded her understanding.

The journey up to the North West was torturous. An accident just north of Stafford resulted in a ten-mile tailback, meaning the three-hour trip became a five-hour crawl. Sam and Louisa hardly spoke in that time, letting Radio Four fill the void. By the time they reached Sam's home village, ten miles west of Manchester, it was four o'clock. Sam hoped the police hadn't already broken the news to his parents; he was desperate to get there before them. But before then, there was something else he had to do, and ten minutes probably wouldn't make a difference.

He sensed Louisa stiffen as he turned left before the village boundary and headed down a small country lane.

'You're going to the church?'

Sam nodded, keeping his eyes on the road.

Louisa didn't say any more. She didn't need to. Sam knew how long it had been since she'd visited this place. Not since the days after Cathy's funeral. It was too painful, she had once admitted. Sam felt guilty for bringing her back to the spot, but he needed her with him, and despite the element of selfishness, he truly felt it could do her good. They reached the church and came to a crunching stop on the gravel path just next to the churchyard. The ancient Norman stone building had played host to some of the happiest moments of his family's life – thirty-seven years ago his parents had married there, two years later Sam had been baptised, and three years after that it was Cathy's turn. And then the dark moment – Sam had walked the same gravel-lain route, holding Cathy's coffin, struggling under the weight, fighting back tears as he pressed his ear against the wood. His mother had been against the idea, worried that it would be too much, but Sam had insisted on joining his father and two uncles as pall-bearers – he had wanted to be as close to Cathy as possible.

Sam looked across at Louisa, who was staring straight ahead as if her mind was somewhere else. 'You okay?'

Louisa nodded, even though she didn't look okay at all. The happy, carefree Louisa seemed a world away, and for a moment Sam thought about turning the ignition and driving straight off. 'You can stay in the car if you like.'

Louisa shook her head.

They climbed out of the car and passed through the rusting iron gate, Louisa following in Sam's wake. The churchyard was a picture of tranquillity, sun bathing the area in a mild late-afternoon glow. A blackbird was singing from one of the overhanging trees that swayed in the gentle breeze. Sam scanned the area – no one else was around.

They turned left and headed for the far corner. Sam stopped in front of Cathy's grave. The plot was adorned with fresh flowers, left by the family just a few days earlier at the remembrance service. But he noticed a new bouquet, a spray of yellow roses, with a note from his mother. He crouched down and ran a finger and thumb across one of the delicate petals.

'My mum has visited here virtually every day since Cathy was buried. I only found that out last week.' He looked up at Louisa. 'She's been coming every day for all these years, and I never even knew.'

He looked back at the grave, thinking back again to the day of the funeral. The pain on his parents' faces, the sobbing of his grandmother, who had always been so close to Cathy. 'I don't really have any idea what my parents went through. I ran away and let them deal with it. They had to cope with Cathy's death on their own.'

Louisa moved towards him and placed a hand on his shoulder. 'We all had to deal with it the best way we could.'

Sam shook his head. 'But I ran away, Lou. I went to London, got on with my life, tried to forget about what had happened.'

'You went to university to train to be a doctor,' Louisa said. 'What good would it have done anyone if you'd just thrown your future career away?'

Sam stood up and faced her. 'I didn't have to throw my career away. I could have stayed around here, supported my parents more. After Cathy was gone, I looked at local courses. I contacted the admissions at Manchester, and they said that they'd offer me a place. But I decided I needed to get away, so I went to London.'

'Did your parents know?'

Sam shook his head. 'I didn't mention it. How could I? Basically, tell them that I'd had the chance to train in medicine and stay close to home, but rejected it because I wanted to be anywhere but here?'

'I'm sure it wasn't like that, Sam.'

'Wasn't it? I ran away, Louisa. I saved myself by running away and trying to forget.'

'You're being too harsh on yourself.'

Sam turned back to the grave. 'I hardly ever came home in the holidays – because I couldn't face being back here and having to walk past Cathy's bedroom. Everything here reminded me of my sister, and it was easier to just get away and surround myself with new places and new friends.'

'You did what you had to do.'

'I didn't help my friends and family when they needed it the most.'

'You helped me,' Louisa countered. 'Without you, I wouldn't have been able to get through what happened. You might not realise it, Sam, but you saved me back then. Really saved me. I don't know what I would have done without you there to support me. I really was losing my way, and you pulled me out of it. With all those letters and phone calls, you supported me more than anyone.'

Sam shook off the comment. 'You helped me more than I helped you.'

'We helped each other. We were closer to Cathy than anyone, and we helped each other. You might have regrets, Sam – we all can think of things we should have done, but it's easy to say that now, all these years later. You were only eighteen. You were just a boy, Sam, having to cope with a very traumatic event.'

Sam nodded. 'But I'm not eighteen any more. And I'm not going to run away this time.'

Louisa smiled, placing a hand on his arm. 'Good. I wouldn't expect you to.'

'I mean it, Lou. Whatever it all means, Richard Friedman having Cathy's locket, saying that he murdered Cathy – whatever it leads to, I'm not going to run away this time. This time I'm going to protect my mum and dad. I'll be there for them.'

'How do you think they'll handle the news?'

'Badly probably – just when it looked like they were moving on, it could bring them back to square one.'

'They might surprise you,' Louisa replied.

Sam dismissed the notion. 'They still look really fragile, Lou. Dad especially – I could see it in his eyes last week at the remembrance service. He's trying to move on, but something like this could drag him right back.'

'Last week, back here, was harder than you've admitted, wasn't it?'

Sam nodded. 'It was one of the most difficult things I've ever done. I missed you being there, you know.'

Louisa surprised Sam by looking away guiltily. 'I'm really sorry, Sam.'

'You don't have to apologise.'

'No, I do,' she explained. 'The wedding I said I was going to that day – it didn't exist. I made it up. It was an excuse not to go.'

Sam waited.

'You're not the only one who can't face being reminded of Cathy,' she added. 'I wanted to come, but the thought of celebrating her thirtieth, when she's – she's just – dead, I couldn't do it, Sam. I just couldn't. I'm so sorry.' She started to cry.

Sam's thoughts turned to the note in her locker. She'd been beating herself up over this for days. But he could understand why she had done it, totally. He knew all about running away from the pain.

'It's okay,' he said. 'Honestly.'

'I was dreading coming with you here,' she revealed, 'but I just had to do it. After last week, I couldn't let you come up on your own.'

Sam smiled. 'I'm really glad you came.'

They hugged briefly and then both turned to face Cathy's grave once again. It felt as if a weight had been lifted, albeit temporarily.

'Mum says that she feels closest to Cathy when she's here,' Sam said. 'She believes that there's some kind of link here, to Cathy in heaven.'

'Do you think that?'

Sam shrugged. 'I'd like to believe. But I don't have any evidence.'

'But you're a Christian. You believe in heaven?'

'Lapsed Christian,' he corrected. 'Maybe. Just after Cathy's death, I came to this church every day, sitting there, listening out for something. Some sign that she was out there. But I didn't hear anything.'

'I did the same,' Louisa admitted. 'Not in church – in my bed-room. I talked to her for hours, like we used to do on the phone after school, telling her about my day. I think my parents thought I was going crazy. My dad walked in on me one night and made me go and see Dr Philips at the surgery to discuss it.'

Sam smiled. 'So we're both as mad as each other.'

'Seems like it.'

'I wish I could hear her voice now.'

'Is that why you came here? To see if you could hear Cathy?'

Sam lifted up his arms. 'What can I say? I'm desperate. But it would be good if she could speak to us. She knows who really killed her.'

'True.'

'Maybe if I closed my eyes I'd hear something. A whisper. A name.'

'Try it,' Louisa said.

Sam closed his eyes, concentrating on his breathing. The bird song faded, and suddenly everything seemed to be shut out. He could hear Cathy's voice, full of fun and laughter, teasing her big brother on the day she had beaten him at his then-favourite racing computer game.

'What can I say? Some people are just naturals, Sammy.'

And then a sadder time: Sam consoling her on the day that their pet rabbit died, squeezing her tightly as she sobbed into his shoulder.

'I'll miss him so much.'

He opened his eyes to find Louisa watching him intently.

'Anything?'

He shook his head. 'Bit of a long shot, though, wasn't it?'

Louisa smiled. 'Keep listening out, Sam, just in case.'

He took her by the hand. 'C'mon, let's get going.'

They walked slowly and silently, hand in hand, through the churchyard, back towards the car. As Sam started the engine, he took one last look across the cemetery towards Cathy's grave. He might not have had a divine revelation, but maybe something had happened in those few minutes at the graveside.

He turned to Louisa. 'I think I might have made a terrible mistake.'

Chapter Twenty-One

What if Marcus really didn't do it,' he said, looking out of the car window towards the churchyard. 'For all these years, I've been so sure, but what if he was innocent all along?'

He couldn't really believe he was saying this. For so long he'd been so sure of Marcus's guilt. Or had he? Had there always been that doubt, bubbling just under the surface? The doubt that had pressed him to reply to Marcus's letters, the doubt that had coaxed him into arranging the prison visit. For the first time in fifteen years, he had vocalised that doubt, and it felt strange, but liberating.

'I know,' Louisa replied. 'To think that Marcus might have spent all that time in prison for something he didn't do – it would make what happened even worse.'

'He was locked up for fifteen years. I didn't go to see him once, didn't speak to him, even when he wrote to me pleading his innocence. And now, maybe he was telling the truth.'

'You had no reason to believe he didn't kill Cathy.'

'I had his word,' Sam replied. 'And he was my best friend. I could have just trusted him.' He thumped his hands against the steering wheel. 'God, I don't know what to believe any more.'

'Don't beat yourself up over it, Sam.' Louisa touched his shoulder. 'We all thought the same thing, every one of us. You weren't the only one who didn't go to visit him or didn't believe what he said. And remember, for a long time even he couldn't say for sure whether he'd done anything wrong. So it wasn't straightforward.'

Sam turned to face her. 'And now, do you believe he's innocent?'

Louisa paused. 'Do you?'

'I asked you first.'

'Yes,' she replied, without missing a beat. 'I don't think he killed Cathy. I really don't, Sam.'

Sam was taken aback by the certainty of her answer. 'You really think he's innocent?'

Louisa looked uncomfortable voicing her feelings. 'I had doubts for a long time, wondering how he could have done it, wanting to believe he was innocent despite all the evidence. Now, after what happened with Richard Friedman and the locket, I'm as sure as I can be that he didn't do it.'

Sam held her gaze.

'So what about you?' she pressed. 'Do you still think your best friend killed Cathy?'

'To be honest, I don't know,' he admitted, 'but for the first time, I really want to believe Marcus.'

'Then go and see him. Listen to what he has to say.'

Sam's parents had moved into Clarence Avenue, just half a mile from the parish church, the week before they got married and had lived there ever since. Built in the early 1970s, the attractive tree-lined street had kept most of its original inhabitants, who had moved through the life course together – having kids and watching them leave home. Twenty years ago the street had been alive with the sights and sounds of children, especially in those heady summer months. Footballs spun and bounced off parked cars, into gardens, and occasionally off windows. Multicoloured chalk adorned the pavement with the artistic flair of the best urban graffiti. And paddling pools, filled with laughter, sprang up as the sun blazed.

Now the children had gone, returning only to visit from their varied bases around the country. The street had mellowed, lost some of its life, but one day it would regenerate with the arrival of a new generation of homeowners, and the process would start again.

Sam half-expected there to be a police car parked outside his parents' house, with officers already inside breaking the news, but the street was empty of vehicles.

He pulled into the driveway, coming to a stop behind his father's Civic, and glanced across at Louisa. 'I'm not looking forward to this.'

She gave him an encouraging smile and squeezed his arm. 'It'll be fine.'

He still had a spare key, but it was a long time since he'd used it – it didn't feel right any more just to walk in as if he still lived there. So he knocked and waited, nerves plucking at his insides.

His mother opened the door. Irene Becker was a petite lady, around five foot five. She'd just turned sixty but could easily have passed for ten or fifteen years younger, with her almost wrinkle-free skin and subtly coloured blonde hair. Cathy had shared many of their mother's facial features – her bright blue eyes, the shape of her nose and mouth – even the way her hair curled around her ears. Sometimes looking at his mother offered a painful reminder of what they'd lost, and Sam had wondered whether his mum sometimes felt the same when she looked in the mirror.

She'd been crying – maybe not in the last hour or so, but definitely recently. Her eyes always took a long time to recover. Sam had grown used to that over the years. The smile was genuine, but it seemed born out of relief, like someone who had just been rescued. 'Sam . . .' She noticed Louisa as she stepped into view. '. . . Louisa, what are you doing here? Come in, come in.'

Sam and Louisa followed her through the hall and into the lounge. 'Take a seat,' she said. 'I'll go and make you a cup of tea.'

'Mum,' Sam said as she was about to leave the room in suspicious haste. Irene Becker froze at the doorway, her back to them. Suddenly her shoulders sagged, and she let out a loud sob, bringing her hands to her face.

Sam moved over and placed an arm around her back. 'They've been, haven't they? The police – they've told you what happened.'

She nodded. 'About an hour ago.'

This was just what he had feared might happen. He held her tightly, smelling the familiar scent of her favourite perfume. It reminded him of his childhood more than any memory or photo ever could. 'I'm so sorry. I should have called to warn you.'

He looked over his mother's shoulder at Louisa, who was watching, solemn-faced. He nodded to her, and immediately she knew what to do. 'I'll go and make that cuppa,' she said, leaving the room.

Sam led his mother to the sofa and sat down next to her. She wasn't crying now, but she looked on the brink. It broke Sam's heart to see her like this again. The situation was just so cruel. Last week at the remembrance weekend, she had looked so well. Would she ever be allowed to move on? 'I wanted to tell you myself, in person,' he explained. 'That's why we're here. I didn't want to tell you over the phone.'

'It's okay,' she said, trapping a stray tear with her finger.

'Where's Dad?'

'At the allotment – he said he needed to get some fresh air.'

'You shouldn't be on your own,' Sam replied, angry that his dad had abandoned her to wallow in the news alone. He should be there for her.

'I'm worried about your father,' she said, as if reading his thoughts. 'He's really upset, Sam. Will you go and see him, now? I'll be okay here with Louisa.'

Sam nodded.

The allotments were five minutes' walk away, on the other side of the village. Sam went on foot, leaving his mum in the care of Louisa. He wanted to talk to her about what had happened and what it all might mean, but he also wanted to do something to make her feel better. And seeing his father was it – for all these years, his mum had worried about other people more than herself, and she wasn't stopping now.

It had been years since he'd walked through the village, and it brought back happy memories. The village – its streets, hidden lanes, fields and footpaths – had been their childhood playground. As he reached the outskirts, he looked out across the sunbathed fields, breathing in the countryside air, remembering the good times with Marcus and their close circle of friends.

His father was busy at work in the otherwise deserted allotment and didn't see him approach. Sam watched as he dug into the soil, pushing down hard on the spade with his right boot. Releasing his grip, his father took off his cap and wiped sweat from his forehead. He had taken over the allotment ten years ago from Sam's grandfather, and from what Sam heard he'd spent most of his time down there since retiring. His mother called it his 'oasis', but Sam thought 'refuge' was a more apt description. His father came here to escape from his demons, and to avoid facing up to his emotions. Sam knew all about that.

'Hi, Dad.'

Graham Becker turned around, seemingly unsurprised and unmoved, and straightened up. Still an impressive bear of a man, his full head of hair now greyed, Sam's father had aged less well than his mother. Cathy's murder had put years on him – he'd changed physically since that day, his face trapped in the terrible moment when the call had come through from the campsite.

There was no smile of relief from him. 'Sam. I wondered if you'd turn up.'

'Mum told me the police have been.' Sam shaded his eyes from the dipping late-afternoon sun. 'I wanted to get up here sooner, and tell you in person. I didn't want you to find out from someone else. Not from the police.'

His father shrugged. 'Doesn't matter – what's happened has happened.'

He had never been one to reveal his emotions – he worked hard at not letting the mask slip. And Sam knew it was a mask. His father had never cried in front of anyone about Cathy, but a week after her murder, Sam had crept upstairs and listened to him sobbing uncontrollably in the locked bathroom. Five minutes later he was downstairs, barking out orders and exuding an air of solidity, the mask back.

Sam's feet toyed at some soil. 'I am sorry it happened like that, though. Mum's really upset, isn't she?'

'I'm sorry for your mother, Sam. That she has to have all of this dredged up again.'

'Louisa is with her,' Sam said.

His father nodded. 'Louisa is a nice girl.'

'How is Mum?'

'You saw her yourself.'

'She's been crying.'

Again, just a nod.

Sam wanted to ask his father why he'd abandoned her, why he wasn't with her now, comforting her. But it wouldn't help the situation. 'What did the police say?'

His father looked frustrated at being asked to revisit it. 'They told us that someone else admitted to killing Cathy and that he had her locket.'

'And they told you what happened to him?'

'Yes. It must have been hard for you, Sam, watching someone do that in front of your eyes.'

'It was.'

His father moved back to his plot, picking stones out from the soil. 'You've had a terrible time this past week, haven't you? With the crash too – they were all talking about it at the club.'

'It's been difficult.' Sam didn't elaborate. It wasn't the right time to talk about the latest twist. Not now. There were other priorities.

His father recommenced his digging.

Sam moved closer. 'We should talk about what's going on.'

His father stopped, seemingly annoyed by the interruption, and faced him. 'Why?'

'Because we need to talk about what this means for us all.'

'It doesn't mean anything,' his father replied sharply.

Sam was taken aback by his reaction and his hostile tone. 'But Dad, if Richard Friedman did kill Cathy—'

'Then he's now where he belongs.'

His father rarely got angry, but he was now. His eyes were wide, seething with fifteen years' worth of pent-up fury.

'But what about Marcus?'

'Marcus is out of prison,' replied his father, suddenly checking himself, trying to regain control. 'He's a free man.'

'But if he was innocent all along . . .'

'Then we all made a terrible mistake, including the police. But what good would it do to rake over it all now? We'll never know what happened to Cathy, and it certainly won't bring her back to life. It's best left. That's what I told the police.'

'You told the police you want them not to investigate?'

'Yes. Not that my opinion matters. I'm sure they'll do what they feel they have to do.'

'But don't you think that if Marcus is innocent, he deserves them to look into it?'

His father laughed. 'And you think that will be enough for Marcus and his family?'

'I don't understand.'

'No, you don't understand.'

They were squaring up to each other, their faces just a few inches apart. This wasn't what Sam had planned at all.

'Then tell me, talk to me.'

His father turned away. 'Tom Johnson came round to our house the day after the trial ended. I never told you about it. He said he was sure that Marcus didn't kill Cathy. There wasn't even a shred of doubt in his mind – you could see it. He said that one day we'd find out the truth. I told him that he was blind and as good as threw him out. Three months later they moved out of the village, and I haven't seen him since. I was good friends with the man, Sam, for years and years. Your mother used to babysit Marcus.'

'They deserve the case to be looked at too.'

'No.'

Sam shook his head. 'Dad, I can't believe you're saying this. Don't you want to find the truth? Isn't that what Cathy would want? To find out who's responsible?'

And then his father's face darkened. 'You really want to know who's responsible, Sam? You really want to know?'

'Yes.'

'Well, take a long, hard look, Son,' he said, pointing to his own face, 'because I'm standing here, right in front of you.'

Sam shook his head.

'Yes, Sam,' his father continued, the carefully constructed mask beginning to crack, 'Cathy was my responsibility, *my* responsibility.' He was crying now. 'It was my job to look after her, make sure she was okay in life. I was her dad. And I failed, Sam, I failed. She was so fragile, so beautiful, and I let that happen to her. So blame me.'

Sam wanted to embrace him but didn't feel able to. It just wasn't what they did. 'No, Dad, it wasn't your fault. You couldn't have done anything. For years I blamed myself – I still do really. I promised to look after her over that weekend – I promised you. That was the only reason you let her go away with us. So it's my responsibility too. But we didn't kill her. Don't you think she'd want us to find out the truth?'

'Cathy's dead, Sam. She doesn't want anything. She's dead. Let her rest in peace. This family has had enough suffering.'

———

Sam retraced his steps back to the house, leaving his father at the allotment. This time he did let himself in. Louisa met him in the hallway.

'How's Mum?'

'Okay,' Louisa replied. 'I think she's just been really thrown by everything and doesn't know what to think. She's asleep upstairs. What about your dad?'

'Not great,' Sam revealed. 'He's in defensive mode. He's afraid any police investigation will harm the family.'

'I can understand that.'

'So can I – but it's about more than this family, isn't it? There's another family to think of.'

'I know. So what are you going to do?'

Sam looked up towards the top of the stairs, thinking of his mum. 'Definitely stay here tonight, if that's okay with you. I'd like some more time with them, although I think Dad's mind is set. Then tomorrow, assuming he still wants to meet, I'm going to go and speak with Marcus.'

Chapter Twenty-Two

Sam woke early, the morning sun blasting through the curtains just the way he had always liked it. It was strange waking up as a thirty-four-year-old in the same bed, and the same room, as he had spent his childhood – like going back in time. The room hadn't changed much since his teenage years. The wooden desk was still in the corner, on which he had written his application for university. The same wardrobes ran across the back of the wall, except that now they were full of overflow clothes from his parents' room, instead of his own jumpers, jeans and shirts. Cathy's room was different. Some grieving parents can't bear to alter the room of a dead child, and it becomes a shrine, frozen at the moment before the pain came. But just two weeks after her murder, his dad had gutted the place, enlisting Sam's help to repaper the walls, re-carpet and move out Cathy's belongings. Cathy's room became an office.

Sam had understood why he'd done it, but he couldn't quite forgive him.

For a while he just sat there, enjoying the sun's glow, thinking about everyone – his mum, his dad, Cathy, and Anna. He'd received a text message from Anna just before midnight. She was still good, but looking forward to coming home. And he was really looking forward to seeing her. *Then,* he thought, *everything will seem all right again.*

But he knew that before then there were important and difficult things to do.

The time was just approaching half past seven. He rolled out of bed, dressed quickly and went downstairs. The kitchen was empty. When Cathy and he were young, his dad used to be the first downstairs, always. His dad's job was preparing the breakfast – Weetabix for all, plus toast with strawberry jam – before he travelled off to work in Manchester. That was then, though. That was when things were so different, before the spectre of Cathy's murder changed everything.

He'd just filled the kettle when he heard someone move behind him.

'Morning, Sam.'

Sam turned to see his mum enter the kitchen. He could see straightaway that she was worrying about something. He recognised the same facial expression from his own – it was a dead giveaway. 'You okay?'

His mother nodded unconvincingly. She was also dressed. She moved towards the oak table and pulled out a chair, lifting it up from the floor so as not to make a noise on the wooden floor. 'Don't want to wake your father,' she explained, taking a seat.

Sam continued preparing the tea as his mother watched. He would wait for her to tell him what was troubling her.

'You know I'm very proud of you, Sam.'

He turned around. 'Thanks.'

'I mean it, Sam. Sometimes I can't believe that our son is a heart surgeon in London. Cathy would be so proud of her big brother.'

Sam abandoned the preparations and took a seat opposite. She was going to tell him something. The breakfast could wait. 'How are you feeling?'

She managed a weak smile and shrugged. 'I'm okay. I was so shocked yesterday when the police came, but I'm okay this morning. Talking to Louisa helped a lot.'

'That's good,' Sam replied. 'And what about you and Dad – have you talked about it?'

'You know your father doesn't like to talk about Cathy. I tried to talk to him after the police left, but he wouldn't say a word. He just went off to the allotment. But I could tell how upset he was. He tries to hide it from me, but he can't.'

'He's worried that going back over all this will hurt you.'

She seemed surprised. 'Is that what he said?'

Sam nodded.

She smiled sadly. 'Did he tell you what he told the police? That he didn't want them to investigate any further?'

Sam nodded again.

'Sam, when Cathy died, it was devastating for all of us. For everyone, a part of us died that night along with Cathy. But for your father, it totally changed him. He isn't the same person he was before. I know you saw the change too. Cathy was always a daddy's girl, and he just couldn't deal with the thought that she was gone and that she'd been hurt. He buried his feelings so deep because he couldn't cope with them, but they're always there. He's scared, Sam, for himself, of how he's going to cope with all this again.'

Sam stared down at the grains in the wood on the kitchen table. 'I'm so sorry, Mum; I wasn't there when it mattered. I went away to London and left you two on your own. You shouldn't be proud of me.'

His mother put her arm around his neck. 'Sam, we're both proud of you, and you shouldn't feel guilty about going to London when you did. Knowing you were getting on with your life helped us both to get over what happened. Honestly.'

'I'm still sorry I wasn't around more,' Sam said, meeting her gaze.

'Well, don't be.'

'We went to Cathy's grave yesterday, on the way here. I was hoping she might give me a message about what was really going on.'

His mother didn't seem surprised. Sam knew that she often 'spoke' to Cathy there. 'And did she?'

'I'm not sure,' Sam said. 'Maybe.'

She waited for further explanation.

He decided this was the moment. For years he had wanted to broach the subject, and now was the time. Now it was his mum's turn to recognise the worried expression. Sam took a deep breath and spoke. 'What would you say if I said I was going to see Marcus?'

Her reply was instant. 'I would say, make sure your father doesn't find out.'

Sam didn't expect that. He'd always assumed that his mum had agreed with his father, who, since day one, had made his hostile views on making contact with Marcus crystal clear. 'But what about you – what do you think?'

She waited a few seconds. Again that worried look. 'Sam, I've got something to tell you.'

'What?'

She leant forward. 'You must promise not to tell your father about this.'

'I won't. What's the matter?'

There was another nervous pause. 'I've . . . I've been meeting with Janet Johnson ever since Cathy died.'

Janet Johnson, Marcus's mother. Even though the circumstances appeared to have changed dramatically in the last couple of days, even though Sam had dared to think that Marcus might have been innocent all along, the revelation still brought a strong sense of betrayal.

'I don't understand. Why?'

'I can understand why you might be upset, and by God, I would never tell your father, but you've got to understand, Sam: Janet and I were friends ever since you and Marcus were babies. I thought after what happened I could just cut ties, but then I thought, why should I? What happened wasn't Janet's fault. She was suffering just as much as we were. We'd lost a daughter, but in many ways, they'd lost a son. So we started to meet up, and it helped a lot. It helped us both.'

'But you never told Dad.'

'No.'

'And did you talk about Marcus?'

'Not at first, but later, yes. She was so certain that he didn't kill Cathy.'

'And what did you say to that?'

She shrugged. 'I started to think the same.'

Sam couldn't quite believe what he was hearing. But it was a familiar sentiment, echoing Louisa's recent words. How could he not have known? How had this stayed so hidden for all these years? 'You believed that Marcus was innocent?'

'I went to visit him.'

Sam's eyes widened at the shock of her revelation. 'You went to visit Marcus in prison?'

His mother nodded, looking extremely uncomfortable. 'With Janet.'

He struggled to take it in. His mother had dared to do what he hadn't – to go face-to-face with Marcus, in search of the truth. 'When?'

'Eighteen months into his sentence. I only went once. I had to see for myself what he had to say, to ask him myself if he killed Cathy.'

'And?'

'He said that he couldn't remember what happened because he'd been so drunk. But he didn't believe he could ever have hurt her.'

'So, no different from what he said in court.'

'Not in *what* he said. But it was different, Sam. Sitting just a few feet away from him, I could see that he meant it – he really meant it. You could see it in his eyes. He told me he loved Cathy.'

Sam tried to take in the information. For years he had cemented the painful belief that his best friend had raped and murdered his sister. But now he found out that his own mother didn't even believe it. Now yesterday made sense, the unexpected calmness when she'd opened the door. It hadn't been the shock. 'So when you heard about Richard Friedman yesterday, you weren't surprised at all. You always thought Marcus was innocent.'

'I could never be sure, but no, I wasn't surprised when the police told me someone else had confessed.'

'But you never shared this with Dad?'

'Your father wouldn't have wanted to hear it. It would have just made things worse. It helped that he had someone to blame, and there were no other suspects until now.'

Sam put a hand to his neck and let out a steadying breath.

'I can understand that you're shocked,' his mother said. 'I just hope you can understand why I had to do it. I would never do anything to hurt you or your father, but I just thought this was the right thing to do. I don't enjoy the lies, but I can't tell him. It could tear us apart.'

'I do understand,' Sam replied. 'It's just a lot to get your head around.'

'I know it is, Sam.'

'So what now? Where do we go from here?'

'I want you to go and speak to Marcus. Do what I did: look him in the eyes, and ask him the question. And help the police however you can. For Janet's sake – for all our sakes – we need to find out the truth about what happened to Cathy.'

Sam filled Louisa in on all the details during the journey back to London. She didn't seem surprised about the news that his mother had visited Marcus in prison, and Sam suspected that it might have come up in their conversation the previous night. Maybe Louisa had even persuaded her to tell Sam. But Louisa was well versed in client confidentiality, and she didn't reveal anything about their discussion. She just sat there and listened. By the time they reached the capital, it was early afternoon, and the traffic slowed to a crawl as they moved through the dreary outskirts, past tired office blocks and fast food outlets, heading for the hospital. The rain was falling again, drenching the dirty streets, washing them clean. They passed Waterloo Station and the gigantic IMAX cinema, turning left past the London Eye, through a series of traffic lights and down into the hospital's underground car park.

They parted at the hospital entrance. Louisa had a team meeting to attend, and for Sam it was a chance to catch up with the progress of Sophie. With all that had gone on, and being away from the hospital, it would have been easy to forget about her, but he wasn't going to allow that to happen. First he headed for the cardio-thoracic unit to pick up his mail.

Doug intercepted him as he approached the post trays.

'Sam,' he said brightly, his wide smile a welcome sight. He looked well, toned underneath his royal-blue shirt and fresh-faced despite being at the back end of a long shift. His marathon-training regime was obviously going better than Sam's. 'Great to see you back.'

'Just a flying visit,' Sam explained. 'Have you heard how Sophie is?'

'Sorry, no.' Doug's Scottish accent seemed to be getting stronger. 'It's been so busy today, absolutely manic, I haven't had time to come up for air.'

'I'm going to go up there now,' Sam said, 'to see how she's doing.'

Doug nodded his approval and then clicked his fingers as he remembered something. 'I nearly forgot. You had a visitor about an hour ago. I didn't think you'd be in today; otherwise, I'd have told her to wait around. She seemed pretty keen to speak with you.'

'A visitor? Who?'

'A woman. She came up to the nursing desk, asking to speak with you – said it was very important. I just happened to be at the desk.' He fished around in his trouser pocket and handed Sam a piece of paper. 'She left this number.'

There was no name.

'Who was she?'

Doug shrugged. 'An older woman, probably in her early seventies, maybe late sixties. Reddish hair, quite short. London accent. Feisty. Ring any bells?'

Sam tried to think of who it might be but couldn't. 'She didn't leave a name?'

'No. Just said for you to call her as soon as you get the message. She seemed very keen to speak to you.'

Chapter Twenty-Three

Sam retreated to a quiet corner of the department and dialled the number. It went straight through to a generic answer service, giving no clues as to the phone's owner. He left a short message, explaining that he was now back at work and would try to call again later. He then checked his mail and found the letter that he had been waiting for. It was a brief but important message. He'd been invited for an interview in a week's time for the consultant post. But the rare feeling of good news was tempered by the thought of whether getting the job was important any more. How could he focus on that with everything that had happened? Still, life went on. He slipped the letter into his trouser pocket and turned towards his office. Miles was waiting for him by the door.

'I assume that you got the letter too,' he said, gesturing towards Sam's trouser pocket.

Sam nodded. He must have been watching him at the post station.

'I just wanted to say good luck.'

Miles turned to walk away, not waiting for an answer, but Sam called him back. 'Miles.'

He turned around, hands in his pockets and raised his head expectantly.

Sam gestured towards his office. 'Can you talk for a minute?'

Miles nodded and followed him inside.

'Take a seat,' Sam said.

Miles did as requested and sat facing Sam. He still didn't look at his best, his eyes betraying a genuine tiredness. His tired face was combative, as if ready for hostility, and Sam wondered whose fault this all was – he'd certainly played his part in maintaining the bad atmosphere between them over the past couple of years. It was easy to get caught up in things, rising to new levels of animosity, so much so that it became the norm. But now Sam decided to do what Anna had advised him to do a long time ago – really try to make peace. She knew Sam had never liked the situation. And anyway, there were too many problems in the world without this.

'I didn't thank you properly,' Sam said, 'for picking up the slack while I've been off.'

'No problem,' Miles said, wary but obviously taken by surprise at Sam's comment.

'I'm especially grateful for what you did with Sophie Jackson. You saved her life.'

'For now,' Miles replied flatly.

Sam nodded. 'How is she doing?'

'Better than I thought she would,' Miles admitted. 'You were right about her, Sam; she is a little fighter.'

'Do you think she'll pull through?'

'Maybe. Depends on whether a suitable heart becomes available. But if one does, I think she could make it.'

'So do I,' Sam concurred. 'And I really do mean what I said, so thanks for everything you did the other day. You're a good surgeon. Whoever gets the consultant job will have deserved it, be it you or me.'

Miles's forehead creased with suspicion and confusion. 'Why are you doing this, Sam?'

'What do you mean?'

'Being so nice.'

Sam shrugged. 'I just want things to change around here, between us both. We might never be the best of friends, Miles, but it doesn't mean we have to be enemies. At the end of the day, we're both here to do our best for our patients – patients like Sophie.'

Miles just sat there for a second, as if weighing up a decision of national importance. 'Fair enough,' he said, 'that's fair enough.'

He held out a hand across the table, which Sam shook. Miles's grip was strong, and Sam responded, fighting to suppress a smile – it would be very difficult, if not impossible, to banish the air of competitiveness between them. But this was a good start.

When Miles left, Sam powered up his computer and waded through the stack of emails that had built up over the past couple of days. There was very little of interest. Carla Conway had sent him a message, concerned about how he was coping following Richard Friedman's suicide. She offered any support she could, in the way of private counselling, and also emphasised that the board had committed to inject more money into hospital security. There would be more security staff, and from next week all CCTV cameras would be fully operational. Access to the roof would be secured.

Sam wondered, maybe cynically, whether Carla was trying to protect staff and patients, or the hospital's reputation. Suicides on hospital property certainly weren't a welcome news story.

He closed the email and logged onto the Internet, quickly checking his private email account. There was a message from Anna. Relief work that day had gone well, and they were on target to finish connecting a health centre back to the mains water supply before she returned in three days' time. She was looking forward to coming home and seeing him. Sam typed out a brief but warm reply. He didn't mention any of the recent events, including the visit to his parents, as it would just raise her suspicions that something was going on. There would be plenty of time for explanations when she returned. He pressed 'Send' and scanned down his inbox. The message from Richard Friedman was still there, along with the link to the dating website. Sam highlighted the message and selected 'Delete'.

There was a knock at the door.

He rose from his chair. 'Come in.'

A woman entered, moving confidently into the room as the door closed behind her. 'Dr Becker?'

Sam nodded. She looked to be in her late sixties, and he immediately assumed that this was the woman whom Doug had described. 'Can I help?'

'Not unless you can tell me where my granddaughter is.'

'Sorry?'

She straightened up and proffered her hand, grim-faced, clearing her throat. 'Shirley Ainsley.'

She didn't need to offer any further explanation.

Sam shook her hand, thinking quickly about how to approach this. He hadn't expected to have to speak to the family face-to-face, and he wondered how wise it was to do so when the police investigation was ongoing. He doubted whether Inspector Cullen would appreciate it at all. But it was too late really to stop it now, so he would just have to be cautious. 'Please, take a seat.'

He pulled his chair from around the back of the desk so that there was no obstacle between them. 'First of all, I want to say how sorry I am about your daughter. I'm so sorry that I couldn't save her.'

'Thank you,' she said solemnly, her lips pursed and her hands cupped on her lap. She looked down to her left, frowning at some thought. 'They won't let me have her back yet. We can't bury her, can't say goodbye properly.'

'I'm sorry.'

She looked up. 'They're keeping her, doing some more tests – I don't know what. I just want to bury her in peace.'

'I know how difficult it must be,' Sam offered.

Her face was now set hard. 'Tell me about what happened. I need to know from you what happened to my family.'

Sam steeled himself to recount the horrific events once again. He didn't want to have to do this. Each time he had spoken about the incident, it was as if he'd been transported back to the scene, time-travelling to the point where it all began and playing it through like a horror film. But Shirley Ainsley deserved to have her wish granted, so he swallowed hard and prepared once again to relive the pain. 'I was driving home; it was late on Sunday evening, and from nowhere a girl ran out in front of my car—'

'Alison,' she interrupted.

'She said her name was Alison,' Sam replied.

Shirley Ainsley pulled out a photograph from her pocket and handed it to him. 'That's a recent photograph of Alison. Was it her who ran out in front of you?'

Sam studied the photograph more intently than he needed to, feeling that he owed Shirley his close attention. It was clear that this wasn't the girl. It was the same girl Paul Cullen had asked him about before. 'No, this wasn't her,' he said, handing the photograph back to her. 'I'm sorry.'

'It had to be her,' she responded, looking down at the photo. 'It doesn't make any sense if it wasn't.'

'I'm really sorry, Mrs Ainsley, but it wasn't your granddaughter.'

She seemed to struggle to take in the statement, closing her eyes and grimacing slightly, as if her mind was physically fighting the truth. 'You said it was the girl who died in the river, the girl I was taken to see.'

Sam nodded.

'Who is she?'

'I don't know. I thought she was your granddaughter.'

She put a steadying hand to her head. 'I don't understand why someone else would pretend to be Alison. I don't understand what that girl would have been doing there, with my daughter and her family on the train line.'

'Neither do I, Shirley. I've tried to make sense of what happened, but I just can't explain it.'

She looked at him. The steel had returned. 'Are you telling me the truth?'

'Of course,' Sam said, rattled by the accusation. 'You think I might be lying?'

'I don't know what to believe. But I do know what Alison told me on the phone. She said it was your fault. Why would she say that?'

'I don't know,' Sam admitted. 'I've never met your granddaughter. And as I said, I really don't understand why someone else was there pretending to be her, but you've got to believe me, Shirley, I'm telling you everything I know. I did what I could. I wish I could have saved your daughter's life, and I truly hope Alison comes home safe and well.'

'She would want to come home,' she stated, stony-faced. 'She was very close to her mother, very close to me and my husband and the children. If it was up to her, she would be here with us.'

Sam leant forward on his chair. 'You think someone has her?'

'I've been thinking about it all night. I didn't sleep at all. I *couldn't* sleep – all these thoughts going around in my head. I don't know what's happening. I don't know where Alison is, but it's something to do with him. I think he's the cause of all this.'

'Who? Who do you think did this?'

'The man she dated, Vincent McGuire. I told the police, but they haven't been able to find him. To be honest, I don't think they believe me, but I just know he's something to do with all of this.'

'You think he was the reason your daughter wanted to die?'

'I don't believe she killed herself,' she stated. 'My daughter would not have tried to kill her own children. She just wouldn't.'

Sam paused, knowing what he was about to say might be painful. 'I'm sure under normal circumstances you'd be right, but she wasn't thinking straight, Shirley. She'd driven down there herself. She was in the driver's seat.'

Shirley was unmoved. 'The car was already on the tracks when you got there, wasn't it?'

'Yes.'

'Then how do you know she was the one who drove the car on there? Maybe it was the girl from the river, the one pretending to be Alison. Maybe she did it.'

'I don't think so.'

'But you don't know, do you?'

'No, but the police—'

'The police think they have all the answers,' she scoffed. 'But they haven't found my granddaughter.'

'I wish I could help you. But we've just got to let the police deal with this.'

'You seem like a good man,' she said, seemingly ignoring his plea as she stood up. 'I usually read people well. And having met you now, spoken to you face-to-face, I'm as sure as I can be that you're telling the truth.'

Sam stood too. 'I am. You've got to believe that.'

Shirley held out a hand. 'I want to thank you for saving the lives of my grandchildren and trying to save my daughter.'

'Thanks,' he said, shaking hands.

'But,' she continued, maintaining the grip, 'I will stop at nothing until Alison is back where she belongs, safe with her family. And if I find that you are responsible for what has happened or are keeping something from me, then I swear, your life won't be worth living.'

Sam watched in contemplative silence as Shirley Ainsley left the office.

Chapter Twenty-Four

Sam called Paul Cullen the second Shirley Ainsley left his office. There had been no significant developments in the case. Or at least none that Cullen was willing to disclose. The girl who had claimed to be Alison Ainsley had yet to be identified despite police checks using the missing persons' database and an alert to homeless charities and shelters around London. No one had reported anyone missing who matched her description. A post-mortem had confirmed that she had died from drowning, but there was also the damage to the back of her head, thought to have been caused by a blow from the bridge as she jumped. Her age was estimated at fourteen or fifteen. There were no distinguishing marks, and she hadn't been carrying any ID. Cullen assured Sam that they weren't about to give up and would put in serious man-hours to identify her. It seemed he was as determined to explain what had happened as Shirley Ainsley was, although he was cool when Sam relayed her suspicions, merely repeating the mantra of not ruling anything out.

Sam pushed away thoughts of the train crash and headed up to ICU to check on Sophie. She had definitely improved since the last time he had seen her. Although still sedated, the colour had returned to her cheeks, and she just looked as if she were in a peaceful sleep. If a heart were to become available, she would have a chance. But it would need to come soon. And if it did, he would be there, ready to do whatever it took. He sat there for a while, amid the electronic beeps and artificial breaths coming from the half a dozen patients who were currently being cared for on the unit. Of those, about half would not survive long term – those were the cold, hard statistics. But he would be damned if Sophie became one of them. A passing nurse gifted him a smile, which he returned.

'Are Sophie's parents around?' he asked.

'Her mum was in earlier.' The nurse scanned the notes of the adjacent patient – an old woman with severe burns who had set herself on fire by falling asleep in bed with a lit cigarette in hand. She was wrapped in what was in essence hi-tech cling film, to give the skin a chance to heal as much as possible. The poor woman was still heavily sedated and knew nothing yet of her experience. 'I've not seen Mr Jackson for a few days now,' added the nurse.

Sam was surprised. Tom, the epitome of the dedicated dad, hadn't missed a day before now. 'Really? Any idea why?'

The nurse shook her head, replacing the patient notes in the holder on the end of the bed. 'Didn't like to ask his wife, you know, in case it was personal. I thought maybe he's away on business. He hardly left her side in the first few days Sophie came up here.'

Sam pondered that. Being away with work was an unlikely explanation given that Tom Jackson worked at a local employment advice centre. Maybe he was sick. Sam made a mental note to give him a call.

Louisa sat through the team meeting without really hearing a thing. Her mind was somewhere else, thrown back in time by recent events. She was in the car travelling to Anglesey, four friends packed tightly into Marcus's rusting white Ford Fiesta, alongside the rucksacks, tents, food and drink. Full of high spirits, laughing and joking about everything and anything. Exams were over, and a great summer lay ahead. Cathy was squashed next to her in the back, her blue eyes shimmering with excitement. In the front were Marcus and Sam. It was the last time they had all been together, happy.

The meeting finished, and Louisa made a hasty exit, desperate to get out of the hospital. She felt uneasy now, walking down the corridor, half-expecting to see Richard Friedman standing outside her office, wearing that chilling halfway-to-insane smile. But of course there was no one there; Richard Friedman wouldn't be able to hurt her any more.

She closed the office door and glanced up at the clock. It was just before five, and she could legitimately leave for the day. But first she went about clearing her desk of the recently opened post, binning the junk mail and filing the rest into the various drawers of her desk. It was when she opened the bottom drawer that she saw the envelope marked with her name.

She just looked at it for a few seconds, fear rising from her gut. Who had placed it there? Fighting back the anxiety, she grabbed the envelope and tore it open with trembling hands. As she read the single typed sentence, she brought a hand over her mouth, trapping in the horrific realisation that Richard Friedman knew much more than she had understood.

She gripped the letter, staring at the words in disbelief and shock, wanting to destroy it there and then. But she resisted, instead stuffing it into the bottom of the drawer, underneath a half-foothigh pile of musty papers.

He must have put the letter there before he died. Somehow he'd got into the office and left this for her, a mocking message from beyond the grave.

She held her head in her hands, trying to control her breathing. He was gone now, and everything would be all right.

Everything would be fine.

Unless he had told someone else what he knew.

She pulled out her mobile and pressed speed dial 1.

⌣

Sam stood just before the ticket barriers at one of the entrances to Waterloo Underground Station, deciding whether to go through with what he had planned. He felt Marcus's letter in his jacket pocket as the rain-soaked, night-time commuters hurried past. To his left, a family with two small children, a boy and a girl of about six, scrutinised the tube map on the wall, the dad tracing a finger towards their destination. On his right a dishevelled man in his early twenties navigated the oncoming torrent of people, picking up discarded tickets from the floor, looking for one that might get him onto a train. The girl who called herself Alison, had she done this too, to survive on the streets? Sam looked beyond the barriers.

Northbound would take him back home.

South would take him somewhere altogether different.

He decided that it was now or never and took the tube south, then jumped onto a bus that his rapid research on the Internet back in his office had told him went within a few minutes of the address given in Marcus's letter. During the bus ride, peering out at the passing, darkening South London streets, his nervousness began to grow. It had been fifteen years without contact, at least on his part. How would Marcus react to seeing him? How would *he* react himself? What would they say?

And then the more serious question: Was Marcus really innocent?

The bus travelled deeper into what was relatively unknown territory for Sam. Like a lot of North London residents, he didn't visit south of the river often. The bus was now in one of the city's most deprived areas. A never-ending series of decaying flats lined the road, their contents spilling out onto balconies in a way that revealed the overcrowding within: washing, bicycles, prams, furniture.

He exited the bus and walked the remaining few minutes through the scented, bustling streets. He felt uncomfortably out of place here. The residents on the streets were a rainbow mix of ethnicities, most notably Somali, but also Caribbean, South Asian and Chinese. There were very few white faces, and certainly no one in a suit. Not that anyone gave him a second glance. The sense of alienation was obviously all in his mind.

He reached the flats where Marcus lived. He hadn't been expecting to see a palace, but the state of the building that Marcus now called home was still a shock. Its drab, grey, battered concrete exterior exuded destitution. Several of the windows were boarded up. He checked Marcus's letter to make sure he hadn't got the wrong address. He hadn't.

Now he was here, so close, the anxiety rose. He entered the ground-floor landing, which was too dark to be comfortable, lit by a single yellow strip light. A cocktail of alcohol, urine and cleaning solution pervaded the air. He decided against the lifts, instead heading for the stairs. Flat 136 was on the third floor. He didn't meet anyone as he climbed the concrete steps. But as he went to push at the door to the third floor, it was kicked open at high speed.

He fought back the urge to say something as he narrowly avoided being struck in the face by the swinging door. He watched as the man who had burst through, a heavily built skinhead wearing a tightly fitting white T-shirt, stomped down the stairs without any acknowledgement or apology.

Shaking his head, Sam passed through the still vibrating door and emerged onto the third floor. As at ground level, the lighting was terrible. But at least the smell was better. He followed the numbers until he reached 136. The wooden green door was badly damaged in several places, revealing the inner part of its structure. It looked as if someone had taken an axe to it.

He stood there for a moment, staring at the number, with his hand raised. Maybe he should have called rather than just turning up out of the blue. He had decided to arrive unannounced because he thought the less warning Marcus was given, the more honest his reactions might be to his questioning. But now he wondered whether the element of surprise would just make things harder. There was also the possibility that Marcus wouldn't even be in.

But it was too late now.

He knocked three slow knocks, stepped back and took a steadying deep breath.

He heard movement from behind the door.

Followed by the sound of gunfire and smashing glass.

Chapter Twenty-Five

S am wanted to run. But he had no idea where the shot had come from, so any movement might have brought him face-to-face with the gunman. Instead, he flattened himself against the wall by Marcus's door, staying as still as his body could manage. He stood there, trying to slow his breathing, pushing away the fear without success, looking one way, then another down the corridor. No people had been brought out of their flats by the commotion. The place appeared deserted. But he knew that it wasn't. Someone was in Marcus's flat. He had heard somebody.

Deciding to make a move, he fought the urge to flee and instead knocked again on the door, this time lightly. Again he heard movement. So he knocked again.

This time the door moved open slightly.

Desperate to get out of the corridor and reach some kind of shelter, he instinctively pushed at the door and moved through the opening.

'Marcus?' He closed the door quietly behind him.

The room was in darkness. The curtains were drawn on the far side, but he could see what looked like glass on the floor at the base of the window. The shot had come from, or been aimed from, here. He thought about turning around now, but it was too late to retreat. He moved tentatively inside, holding his breath. There was a light coming from behind a door on the left, and he could hear water running. He moved over to the door and knocked, his heart thumping against his ribcage as if it were trying to break free.

'Marcus?'

He reached for the doorknob and then paused, fearing the horror that might lurk on the other side. He could hear his own breathing and feel the blood pumping in his head.

'Marcus, are you in there?'

He pushed the door open and saw the bath. The cold water tap had been running for some time, as the water lapped close to the rim, threatening to spill over. Instinctively, he went to turn it off, but as he reached for the tap, someone moved up from behind the door and kicked the back of his knees, buckling his legs and sending him crashing into the bath. Grabbing the back of his hair, whoever it was plunged him into the ice-cold water, holding him firm as he struggled for life.

Jody knocked hard and fast at the door and waited impatiently for Locky to appear, all the time looking around in case she had been followed. It had been like that in the days since she had first run from Locky's place – always on the move, from hostel to hostel, convinced that they were on her tail, just a few steps behind.

So why come back here?

Why not get as far away as possible and start again?

She considered the questions, her thoughts then turning to whether Locky was all right – she had left him at the mercy of those men. But just as her concerns grew, he answered the door with his customary Irish stoner swagger.

'Jody.'

Unlike all those other times, he didn't immediately stand to one side and let her in. Instead, he blocked the doorway. He sported two black eyes, and his nose looked as if it had been broken.

'Locky, are you okay?'

He nodded unconvincingly, glancing nervously up and down the road. 'Look, Jody, you've got to leave.'

'What?'

'You've got to go,' he insisted. 'Please, just go.'

'I've got nowhere to go to,' she replied. 'Please, let me in, just for a couple of nights, and I'll find someone else.'

Locky shook his head.

'Look,' Jody continued, 'I know I shouldn't be asking you to do this again, after what happened, but I'm desperate. I'm really sorry about what they did to you. I'm so sorry.'

'They know you come here,' he stated, 'and they'll be back. You wouldn't be safe.'

'I'll take the chance.'

'But what about me?' he said, raising his voice uncharacteristically. 'What about when they come around here the next time and finish what they started?'

'I am really sorry for what they did to you,' she repeated, realising that the argument was being lost. She'd never seen Locky so determined or, for that matter, so scared.

'I don't give a damn about what they do to me. But I've got to think about Cheryl. They said they'd give her a homemade abortion. And I believe them, Jody – you know what they're capable of. You know what *he's* capable of.'

'They wouldn't do that.'

Locky shook his head, exasperated. 'Jody, they would do that, and you know it. Please, just go, will you? Just go. Go to Mel.'

He went to shut the door.

Jody reached out a hand to block it, her fingers narrowly escaping being trapped in the gap between door and frame. 'She's dead.'

He opened the door again, his face twisted in disbelief. 'What?'

'Mel's dead.'

He rocked back on his heels. Locky had known Mel for as long as he'd known Jody – four years. They'd met at the homeless hostel in King's Cross, all three of them newly on the street, scared, lonely and confused. When the bad people came, drawing them into their world of violence and vice, they gained strength from one another, ensured each other's survival, offering friendship. Locky referred to Mel and Jody as his 'little sisters', and Jody truly regretted breaking the news to him like this. It broke her heart, but she was desperate.

'How? When?'

'The night I came to yours. I don't know how – she was in the river. I think he killed her, Locky.'

His face twisted with disgust. 'But why? Why would he do that?'

'I don't know.'

'Jody, you've got to get away from here, away from London if you can. Get yourself into a hostel in another city: Leeds, Manchester, Bristol – anywhere.' He delved into his jeans pocket and stuffed some crumpled notes into her palm. 'Save yourself from that sick, evil piece of scum.'

'But I need to find out what happened to Mel. I need your help.'

'Don't, Jody. Just leave it.'

'So you won't help?'

'I am helping,' he replied. 'For the first time in my miserable, messed-up life, I'm giving some bloody good advice. Now take it.'

Jody watched helplessly as Locky closed the door in her face.

She knew then exactly why she had come back here, risking both her life and his. Now that Mel was gone, Locky was the only person she had, the only person who could make her feel safe. Without him, all that was left was the fear.

———

Sam held his breath, trying desperately to break free from the hold. The water was fighting to enter his mouth, pushing against his lips like a river threatening to burst its banks. He reached up over his head with his right hand, trying to grab at his assailant. But he was out of reach. Sam was pushed harder and deeper, and that's when his lips surrendered against the onslaught, sending cold water gushing down his throat and up his nose. Struggling even harder, he remembered a technique Doug had taught him: that sometimes it's more effective to use the opponent's strength than to fight against it.

Instead of fighting to raise himself up, Sam relaxed and plunged deeper into the water, at the same time twisting his back and throwing the attacker off balance. He then threw out a speculative backward kick, hitting the person full on in the abdomen. Now free, he burst out from the surface, staggering back against the wall, gasping for breath. He looked across the room to see his attacker lying on the floor, dazed.

It was Marcus.

Marcus Johnson – older, yet instantly recognisable as the person he had shared so many childhood experiences with. Instinctively, Sam moved to his aid. Old habits die hard, and anyway, Marcus seemed no threat now as he lay motionless against the base of the sink. Sam crouched down and checked his pulse. Marcus opened his eyes, his face creasing in confusion.

'Sam?'

Sam watched him warily as he came to. 'Are you okay?'

Marcus nodded, trying to suppress a grimace of pain. 'Nice kick. Can you help me up?'

Sam grabbed his arm and pulled him upright. Marcus stretched his stomach, then reached out and handed Sam a towel from the rail. 'Sorry. I didn't know it was you.'

'Who did you think it was?' Sam said, trying to catch his breath, holding the towel. In truth, he didn't want to take his attention away from Marcus, in case he launched another attack.

'The same people who just shot out my window,' he replied. 'You heard the gunshot?'

Sam nodded.

Marcus grimaced again. 'I thought they'd come back to check out their damage.'

Sam looked down at his clothes. His shirt was drenched, and drips from his saturated hair fell onto the bathroom floor. 'You know who these people are?'

'Local youths.'

Sam was amazed by Marcus's apparent nonchalance. 'And have they done this sort of thing before?'

Marcus nodded, again feeling his stomach. 'Mostly low-level harassment – schoolyard stuff mainly – name-calling, throwing a couple of stones – they're only about fifteen or sixteen.'

'But why?'

'Somehow they found out that I'd been in prison, and why. And as a convicted rapist and murderer, I'm a legitimate target.'

Sam tried to distance himself from that reality. 'Have you told the police?'

Marcus snorted. 'They gave them a warning, but as you can see, it hasn't exactly put them off.'

'But they tried to shoot you.'

'It was a ball-bearing gun,' Marcus said. 'They were aiming for the window, not me.'

'But still, you could have been hurt.'

Marcus shrugged off the suggestion. 'Better dry that hair; otherwise, you'll catch your death of cold. Isn't that what your mum used to say?'

Sam nodded, managing a thin smile. 'She still does.'

They looked at each other, and the smiles vanished, both knowing what this was all about. The nervous banter was over. 'The police,' said Sam, 'have they been to see you?'

Marcus nodded. 'They told me about the guy who killed himself, Richard Friedman.'

'So you'll know why I'm here.'

'You want to decide for yourself whether I killed Cathy. You want to look me in the eye and ask me the question. Well, go on, ask me.'

Sam swallowed hard, not expecting to have to deal with this so soon.

'Go on, ask me,' Marcus pressed.

'Did you kill her?'

Marcus met his stare and stepped a pace closer. Sam realised now how much bigger Marcus was than he used to be. He was not only physically larger but also taller, now a good few inches above Sam. And his face, once quite thin and angular, had filled out. You could see the muscles in his cheeks as he bristled with emotion. 'What do you think, Sam? Do you think I killed her?'

'Don't play games, Marcus.'

'I'm not. Look at me.' He gestured to his eyes. 'Do you think I killed Cathy? Do you think I went out that night on the beach, raped her and then left her for dead?'

Sam clenched his teeth, feeling his fists tighten by his side.

'Do you?' Marcus pressed.

'No,' Sam said, surprising himself with the strength of his conviction. 'I don't think you did it.'

If Marcus felt any satisfaction, he didn't show it. 'That's good, Sam. Because I've learnt over these years that it doesn't matter what I say or what I think. It's all about what other people believe.'

Chapter Twenty-Six

Sam watched from the sofa as Marcus inspected the window. The ball bearing had shattered the lower pane, leaving jagged shards of glass scattered over the carpet and jutting out from the wooden frame, but fortunately it had missed the main part of the window.

'Will you tell the police?' Sam asked.

Marcus nodded, picking up a particularly nasty-looking shard of glass with the tips of his fingers and depositing it in a black bin bag. 'I'll give them a call.'

As Marcus continued the clean-up, Sam took the opportunity to survey the flat. It was a small, dingy space, with one room serving as the lounge, kitchen and bedroom. The putrid orange carpet was threadbare, the brown wallpaper was 1970s kitsch and there were sure signs of damp in all four corners. So this was life after prison. It all felt thoroughly depressing.

'I know what you're thinking,' Marcus said, catching Sam looking. 'It's a dump.'

'It's okay,' Sam lied.

'The best I could afford.' Marcus put down the bag and grabbed a coat. 'C'mon, I can't be bothered with this now. Let's get out of here.'

'What about the police? You're not going to call them first?'

'It can wait. Believe me, they won't be in a rush to get here anyway.'

Sam followed Marcus out of the flat and down the stairwell, emerging into the courtyard at the base of the tower block. He didn't ask where they were heading, instead just staying at Marcus's shoulder, not speaking. Walking side by side with the one-time friend whom he hadn't seen for fifteen years, he reflected on the strangeness of the situation. He couldn't quite believe he was here, now, back with Marcus. It felt unreal and uncomfortable.

'You still play snooker?' asked Marcus.

Sam shook his head. 'Not since we used to play together.'

'I know a place,' Marcus explained. 'Time you started again.'

They approached a row of shops. A group of teenagers huddled around a bench outside an off-licence, chatting and laughing. Sam ignored the stare from one of the male youths as they passed. Marcus made for an unmarked red door on the far left-hand side of the block, and Sam followed him inside and up the flight of bare wooden stairs that led up directly from the door. They turned right at the top, into a large open-plan room that must have spanned the entire upper level of the block. The room was full of snooker tables, half of which were occupied with players of varying ages, all male. There was a bar on the far side and a small reception desk directly to their left.

The whole area was awash with tobacco smoke, as if to emphasise its separation from normal society. This obviously wasn't a place where the authorities came.

Marcus spoke with the man at reception, handing him cash, and then beckoned Sam to follow him to one of the free tables. Setting up the table and handing Sam a cue, Marcus broke off. For a couple of games, the only words exchanged between the two were compliments about one another's game play. Although rusty, by the middle of game three Sam was back into the swing, leaving the score at two to one, in Marcus's favour, with an impressive shot across the length of the table.

It was during the fourth game, an hour in, that the conversation began.

'It means a lot to me that you're here, Sam,' Marcus said as he lined up a shot. He slotted the blue ball deep into the middle pocket and then turned to face Sam. 'I've waited a long time to hear you say that you believe me.'

Sam didn't really know what to say.

'Did you get my last letter?' Marcus asked, turning back to the table to make another shot.

'Yes.'

'I don't mean the one I sent the other day. I mean the one from prison, three years ago.' Marcus took another shot – this time narrowly missing the pocket.

'I got it,' Sam said.

Marcus straightened up and nodded. 'I guess deep down I knew you wouldn't reply, but part of me hoped you would. Part of me thought that you'd believe me.'

'I didn't know what to believe,' Sam stated. 'You said you couldn't remember what happened. Don't you think that I wanted to believe that you hadn't done it?'

'I believe you wanted someone to blame,' Marcus replied. 'You wanted someone to be punished for what happened to Cathy. And I don't blame you. I feel just the same.'

Sam looked away. 'The evidence was there. And the jury found you guilty – not me or Louisa or anyone else.'

'You're right, Sam. But they didn't know me like you do.'

They finished the fourth game in near-silence, letting the comments from their exchange mature before migrating over to the bar and moving to a table with their beers.

'I was going to visit you,' Sam revealed, taking a sip from his pint, 'but at the last minute I changed my mind.'

Marcus looked confused. 'Why?'

Sam shrugged. 'Because I was afraid where it might lead. I didn't want to risk inviting you back into my life without being one hundred per cent certain that you didn't kill Cathy.'

'And are you one hundred per cent certain now?'

'I think so.'

'You think so?'

Sam faced Marcus head on. 'I'm trying to shake off the doubts. But it's difficult after so many years.'

'Sure,' Marcus replied, stony-faced. He shook his head at some unknown thought. 'You don't know how much of a nightmare it is, not being able to remember. Being sure that you couldn't do something so terrible, but just having that doubt. Do you know, my legal team suggested that I plead guilty so I'd get a lesser sentence?'

Sam wondered how Marcus thought he would know such a thing. 'I didn't know that, no.'

'Well, they did. They said the evidence was so stacked against me that it was highly unlikely I would be found innocent, and that my best chance was to plead guilty and express remorse. But I knew I couldn't have done that to Cathy. I would never have hurt her – never. And I didn't care if it meant more time in jail. It didn't matter as long as someone out there believed me.'

'I wanted to believe you from the beginning,' Sam said.

Marcus declined to reply directly to Sam's statement or indeed to reveal any internal reaction to it. 'I always had the support of my family. Really, I don't know what I'd have done without their belief in me. My mum and dad, they never wavered – or at least they never let it show. They were my lifeline, totally. Without them I'd probably have been brought out of there in a box. You don't know how powerful it is, to be believed, how it keeps you going. In there, it's like oxygen.'

Sam felt some discomfort at Marcus's unspoken accusation – some had believed in him, but others hadn't. But despite the feelings of guilt, it was still remarkably difficult to consider Marcus as anything but the man who had killed and raped his sister. His brain had been hardwired to make that association, make that neural link, and it would take time to disconnect the two. 'I haven't asked how you are.'

'I'm okay,' Marcus said. 'Better now I'm out of prison.'

'What was it like?'

'Prison?' He shook his head as if dismissing some unwelcome memory, then took a gulp of beer. 'You remember what it was like in our first year of high school? Being scared of all the older kids, the bullies? We just tried to blend in, disappear, so they wouldn't bother us.'

Sam nodded. 'I remember.' They'd both had some problems in the early years with a few of the lads in the top year. Marcus had taken the brunt of the bullying, targeted by a vile boy who had taken a particular dislike to him. Sam had been drawn into being tormented too through association with his friend.

'Well, prison's like that. It's a brutal playground with all the same bullies, but in there there's no hiding place, no way out, no going home to Mum and Dad for even just a few hours of peace. And when you're in there for rape and murder – well, it's open season, and even the prison guards can't, or won't, help you. You think at first someone will come, someone to save you, and tell you they've realised there's been a big mistake. But you soon realise that isn't going to happen.'

Sam couldn't really even begin to empathise with Marcus's experience. He'd never even set foot in a prison, and all he had were the images offered by Hollywood movies and British crime dramas. 'You got singled out?'

Marcus nodded. 'Oh yes. Especially at first – I got lots of attention.'

'Physically?'

'A few times,' Marcus revealed. 'Two weeks in, three guys cornered me in the toilets and gave me a beating. They kicked me until I lost consciousness. Had to be rushed to the medical centre, woke up not knowing where the hell I was and had the scars for a few weeks. But it taught me a lesson. I got smarter and didn't leave myself open like that again.' He took another gulp of beer.

Sam shook his head, trying to imagine how he might have dealt with such an experience. Would he have had the strength to survive? 'I'm sorry.'

'For what?'

'For not believing you. For not visiting you in prison. For not replying to your letters.'

'It's okay.' Marcus waved away Sam's apology. 'Honestly. It's in the past, and I just want to move on and forget about it all. Life's for living, and all that.'

His response rang hollow when Sam looked at his one-time best friend. It was as if Marcus said these things enough times, he would start to believe them himself. Sam realised that this whole conversation, this historic reunion, was necessarily polite. The emotions were just too raw at the moment, too strong, needing to be restrained for the time being. Just as Sam hid his unease and stubborn suspicion, Marcus's bitterness surely had to be there. Bitterness at losing fifteen years of his life through a miscarriage of justice, bitterness at the best friend who had abandoned him to his unjust fate.

'And what about now – what will you do?' Sam said.

Marcus shrugged, playing with the rim of his glass. 'Try and get some money together, work my way out of that hole of a flat. I've got a job in a warehouse, loading food containers for supermarkets. It's not great; it's nightshift work, cold, but it pays pretty well.

Although the prices of property in London are astronomical, so I won't be living in a palace anytime soon.'

'I was surprised you moved down to London.'

'I just ended up here,' Marcus said. 'I didn't plan to, but after I got out, I went home, and it just didn't work out. People were talking, and I was getting looked at in the street. Then kids started shouting things outside the house. It was affecting my family. So I got out. I like the anonymity here.'

'But you're getting your windows shot out.'

'True,' Marcus conceded. 'I've tried to run away from the past, but I haven't quite managed it yet.'

'But if the police announce that you're innocent and people then get to know—'

'Then it will help,' Marcus said. 'But mud sticks. There will always be that element of doubt in some people's minds.'

Sam didn't know whether that was directed at him, but it certainly felt like it. 'What did the police say to you?'

'Not much. They just told me that someone had claimed that he'd murdered Cathy and that he had her locket. But they still treated me as if I was the guilty one. They even suggested that I might have given him the locket. Can you believe that?'

Sam kept quiet and Marcus continued, now revealing at least some of the bitterness and anger that he harboured.

'I think as far as they're concerned, I'm out of prison, a free man, so what's the problem? I lost my trust in the law a long time ago. This guy Richard Friedman might be guilty, but to be blunt, I don't think the police give a damn.' He let out a bitter chuckle.

'Did they tell you anything about him?'

'No.'

Marcus had a right to know the full story. 'He was one of Louisa's patients – she's a psychologist at the same hospital as me.'

'Right.'

'And he'd been ringing me up, taunting me about Cathy.'

Marcus looked perplexed. 'So he tracked you down and targeted you both?'

'Looks like it.'

'What else do you know about him?'

'Not much really, apart from that his wife was killed by a hit-and-run driver. According to Louisa, he became depressed after that.'

'But you don't know anything that might link him to Cathy? Whether he used to live in that part of the country or even work on the campsite?'

'No.'

'Aren't you interested in finding out more?'

''Course I am,' Sam replied.

'So why don't you?'

'I don't understand.'

'He was a patient at your hospital.'

'Yes.'

'So his details must be on the computer system – where he lives.'

'I'm sure the police can handle the investigation,' Sam replied. 'I don't want to interfere. It's best to leave this to the professionals.'

Marcus pulled a face.

'You don't think so?'

'It's up to you,' Marcus replied. 'You always were a stickler for doing the right thing. I just wish I shared your confidence in the ability of Her Majesty's Police.'

Chapter Twenty-Seven

L et me know if you hear anything,' Marcus said as they stood outside the snooker club for what felt like an uncomfortable goodbye – like the culmination of a first date, with both parties unsure whether this was the start of something more or simply the end.

'I will,' Sam replied. 'You too – if anything happens, call me.'

Marcus nodded, then glanced over his shoulder. 'Better head off home.'

'Me too.'

'It's been good to see you, Sam.'

Recognising Marcus's discomfort at how this was ending, Sam decided to make the first positive move. 'We should do it again. Soon.'

Marcus nodded, then smiled, visibly relaxing. 'Definitely. I'd really like that, mate.'

Sam stood at the bus stop, running over the reunion with Marcus. It was too early to take it all in, to fully assess what had happened and how he felt. The truth was, he didn't know how he felt. But one thing was certain – despite his best intentions, he hadn't been able to completely rid himself of the feelings he'd cultivated for Marcus over all those years. Maybe that explained the vague sense of self-loathing he now felt. For the first time since Cathy's murder, he was facing up to the hatred he'd carried but buried for so long.

As he waited at the stop, he remembered the comment the ICU nurse had made about Tom Jackson. He pulled out his mobile and dialled Tom's number. It rang through to voicemail, but he didn't bother leaving a message. Instead, he called their home number.

Sarah answered. 'Hello?'

'Sarah. It's Sam Becker . . .'

'Oh my God, has something happened to Sophie?'

'No, no,' Sam reassured her, trying to stem her panic, 'everything's fine, as far as I know.'

'Oh, thank God, I thought for a second that . . . I thought that . . . oh God, I really thought . . .' She broke down on the other end of the line.

'I'm sorry I scared you,' Sam said. This was why you weren't supposed to call the family of patients outside your professional capacity. But he had crossed that line with the Jackson family many years ago – it was too late to play the dispassionate medical professional now, even if he wanted to. 'I just called to see if Tom was all right.'

The sobbing continued.

Sam moved a few paces away from the bus stop as two elderly Afro-Caribbean ladies approached and sat down in the shelter. He didn't really want anyone overhearing this, even if they didn't know whom he was talking to. 'Sarah, what's happened?'

'Tom's left.'

Sam was shocked. 'What?'

'Two days ago. I came home from work, and he'd gone.'

Sam couldn't believe it. Tom had always been so devoted to Sarah and Sophie. It seemed inconceivable that he would abandon them. 'He just disappeared?'

Sarah had recovered some of her poise now. This was, of course, a young woman who had dealt with trauma very effectively for years. 'He left a note saying that we'd be better off without him and that everything was his fault.'

'And you've not heard from him since?'

'Nothing,' she confirmed, sniffling. 'He didn't say where he was going, and he's not answering his mobile. I've been worried sick.'

'I just tried to call him,' Sam revealed.

'He's not been to see Sophie,' she continued. 'He wouldn't do that, Sam. You know how much he loves her. He wouldn't do that unless he wasn't himself. I'm worried about what he might do.'

'Have you told the police?'

'No. Do you think I should? He's a grown man, and he decided to leave on his own accord, so I didn't think they'd care.'

'Tell them everything,' Sam advised. 'Tell them about Sophie, that it's totally out of character for him to leave like this and that he's anxious and depressed. Call them right now. If they want to speak with me, give them my number. I'll do anything to help.'

***

Sam returned home just before ten. He would never get used to the quietness of the place without Anna. He'd just made himself a drink when someone knocked on the door. But when he reached the front door, no one was there. Two minutes later, just as he had switched on the radio, a knock sounded out again, this time more insistent. This time he reached the door more quickly, but again there was no one there. He scanned the path and front garden, and looked out towards the street and the parkland beyond. There was no sign of anyone.

'Very amusing.' He spoke out into the darkness, his voice not sounding as confident as he'd intended.

It was probably kids knocking on doors and then running away. They'd played the game themselves when they were young, nine or ten years old – running around the village, goading one another to linger longer at the door while still evading the homeowner. At the time it felt like harmless fun, but as an adult he now understood the more sinister effects on the victims.

By the time the knock sounded for a third time, he had decided not to give them what they wanted. He ignored the door and settled back on the sofa.

Then the phone rang.

Feeling more on edge than he had realised, he moved over to the phone. 'Hello?'

The line was dead.

He'd only just replaced the handset when the phone again called out. He snatched at the receiver. 'Hello?'

Again dead.

'What the hell is this?'

Sam thought of Richard Friedman and the unknown girl who had called herself Alison. It was as if their ghosts had returned. He moved into the centre of the lounge, his heart rate increasing as he waited for the inevitable next call or knock.

And then the phone rang for a third time.

This time he let it ring for a few seconds before picking it up.

'Hello?'

There was a blast of interference down the line, but battling through it was a familiar voice. 'Sam?'

Sam experienced a rush of joy. 'Anna? Is that you?'

'Sorry, the line's terrible,' she shouted.

Then suddenly the interference disappeared.

'Anna?'

'Phew, that's better,' she said. 'I've been trying to get through for minutes now, but the phone lines around here aren't the best. They're still repairing a lot of the network from the flooding, so you have to take your chance while you can.'

Her voice was instantly soothing. 'It's great to hear from you,' Sam said, pressing the receiver closer to his cheek. He wanted to reach down the phone and embrace her, feel the comforting warmth of her skin.

'You too,' Anna replied. 'Email's okay, but . . .'

Sam smiled. 'I know what you mean. It's so good to hear your voice.'

'Ditto.'

'So how's it all going?'

'Great,' Anna said, her voice upbeat and now even clearer down the line. 'We've pretty much finished setting up the new water supplies to the local area. We've connected up the health centres and schools, and most of the villages have now got access to fresh water for the first time in weeks. The situation was really terrible, Sam; cholera had really got a grip, but the number of cases has dropped back a lot in the past few days.'

'That's great.' Sam knew from his time in India just how horrific cholera could be, striking at areas of weakness and picking off the most vulnerable with a ruthlessness that was genuinely frightening – both for the local population and those trying to care for them. 'So, are you on schedule to come home on time?'

'Ahead of schedule,' Anna replied. 'I'm already booked on a flight for tomorrow morning.'

This was fantastic news, and Sam didn't hide his joy. 'Tomorrow? That's great. I can't wait to see you, A.'

'Me either.' There was a pause, then – 'I'm worried about you, Sam.'

The statement took Sam totally by surprise. 'Worried? I'm okay,' he said, trying not to sound defensive.

'I know what's been happening since I've been away – with that guy Richard Friedman.'

There was shock, closely followed by anger that someone had told Anna the news that he'd wanted to protect her from. 'How? Louisa told you? She had no right—'

'It wasn't Louisa,' Anna interrupted. 'It was your mum. She emailed me – she thought I knew.'

Sam put a hand to his head. He hadn't wanted Anna to find out like this. But it was his fault. He should have told her himself. 'She told you everything?'

'Yes. I can't believe it, Sam. After all these years, for someone to just appear out of nowhere and say they killed Cathy. Well, it's unbelievable. Shocking. You must be going out of your mind. I called as soon as I could get to a phone.'

'I'm okay,' Sam said. 'I'm slowly getting my head around it.'

'Do you really think this guy murdered Cathy?'

'Did my mum tell you about the locket?'

'Yes.'

Sam paced up and down, twisting the phone lead tighter. 'Well, I just don't know how he could have got the thing if he hadn't really done it. I mean, he could have found it on the dunes or been given it by someone, but he said he did it.'

'So what about Marcus – are you going to meet with him? If this guy did kill your sister, then Marcus is—'

'Innocent, I know. I just went to see him, tonight.'

'Really? How was it?'

'Strange,' Sam replied. 'After so many years of being sure that he killed Cathy, it was just so weird to sit there talking to him. Did my mum mention that she visited him in prison?'

'No.'

'She said she thought he was innocent pretty much all along, but she didn't want to say anything because of how Dad and I felt.'

'And how do you feel now?'

'Confused. Guilty. Angry. I don't know.'

'It's totally understandable, Sam. You've been through a hell of a lot. I'm sorry I haven't been there for you. Don't be mad with your mum for telling me, will you?'

'I'm not,' Sam replied. 'I just didn't want you to find out like that while you're away.'

'You should have told me, Sam.'

'I didn't want to worry you.'

'People care about you. You should let them.'

'I know, I know – it's just I thought that what's the point of you worrying about me when you can't do anything about it?'

'I can do things like this.'

Sam knew she was right. 'I'm sorry. I should have told you. And it is good to talk about it with you. It feels good.'

'Glad to hear it,' she said. 'But seriously, Sam – are you really okay?'

Sam untwisted the telephone cord. 'I've been better, but honestly, I'm okay. I'll be better when you're back though.'

'I can't wait. Expect a big kiss in under twenty-four hours.'

'I'm counting on it.'

───────────

Thankfully, the knocks stopped, and with thoughts of Anna's imminent return, Sam began to relax. He powered up the laptop and logged into his email account to read the message that Anna had said she'd sent earlier in the day. Her email was there. But there was also another message that caught his eye, sent just ten minutes ago. The title of the email message read: 'The Good Samaritan'.

And the sender was catherinebecker@netmail.com.

It was sickening, like an unexpected, winding blow to the stomach.

He opened the message without a second thought. The only text it contained was a link, just like the previous message that had led to the page about Cathy on the dating website. But this time he recognised the website to which the link would take him: YouTube.

He clicked on the link and waited nervously as the page loaded.

The page appeared, revealing a box headed 'The Good Samaritan'. Below the box were video control buttons. Sam clicked on Play'.

It wasn't a video – just a black screen. There was sound, but it was too low to make out. Sam turned up the volume to maximum.

'It's going to be okay . . . You'll be safer staying here.'

It was his voice.

'Jessica's in the back.'

And the girl who had claimed to be Alison.

Sam leant into the screen, his world turning around him. Audio from the train crash. But how? *What the hell?*

'Please, God, no . . . Look away! Look away, please.'

'Please, help Jessica! She's in the back! Jessica's in the back!'

And then the recording ended.

Chapter Twenty-Eight

S hirley Ainsley heard the door and intercepted her husband before he could reach the stairs. He stood there in the corridor, a pale imitation of the man she loved, just staring at her, swaying slightly, eyes glazed and reeking of beer.

'Did you have a good night?' she asked, keeping her tone light, trying to hide her revulsion at what he had become.

He looked at her with a mixture of defiance and embarrassment. It made her feel sad, as this was so unlike him. Eric was her rock, the man who had comforted her after the devastation of the miscarriage, and thirty years later supported her through the frightening battle with cancer. He went to move past her, but this time she wasn't going to ignore it and let him slope off to bed.

She put a hand on his chest. 'We have to talk, Eric.'

He shook his head. 'Not now.'

'Yes, now,' she demanded. 'Otherwise I'm walking out of that door, and I might not come back.'

She surprised herself with that comment, but it seemed to shock Eric into instant submission. 'Okay,' he said. 'Let's talk.'

They moved into the lounge and took seats opposite one another. Shirley watched her husband holding his head in his hands, and wondered whether this was going to be the break-through conversation that she so longed for. Until now she had resisted questioning him when he was drunk, worried that the conversation could spiral out of control. But having got nowhere during his increasingly brief sober hours, she was now desperate enough to take the risk.

'Do you feel sick?' she asked. 'I can fetch a bowl.'

He raised his head. 'I'm okay.'

Shirley nodded. He looked anything but. 'I'm really worried about you, Eric. Really worried about what's happening.'

He didn't say anything.

'Ever since the accident, you've not been yourself. I've been expecting you to come back to me, to see something of the man I've been married to for forty years. But you seem to be getting worse.'

'I buried my daughter two days ago,' he shot back, not looking at her.

'I know,' she replied. 'She was my daughter too. That's why we need to support each other.'

The intensity of Eric's glare shocked her. His jaw was working overtime, clenching. 'I've always done my best to try and support my family.'

Maybe this was a bad idea. The mixture of alcohol and raw emotion might, as she had feared, lead to something she didn't want. But it was too late.

'I know you have,' she replied. 'You're a wonderful husband, father and grandfather. You always have been.'

'No,' he said. 'No, I'm not, I'm . . .' He broke down. Shirley had never seen him cry. Not even at the funeral. She moved over to him and placed an arm around his broad shoulders – the same shoulders that many times had carried an excited, giggling Jane. Eric made a move to shrug her off, but then relented and moved in closer to her instead. She just held him for a few minutes.

'I've been thinking more about what happened to Jane,' she said. 'The other day, at the funeral, I was running over in my mind what could have happened. I was trying to imagine Jane putting the kids in the car and driving off, knowing what she was going to do. And then I knew – Jane couldn't have done that to the children, no matter what state she might have been in. She didn't kill herself.'

Eric didn't answer.

'I went to see him yesterday. Sam Becker. The man who saved the children – the doctor. I wanted to hear from him what happened.'

'You shouldn't have done that,' Eric replied.

'But I needed to do something, Eric. Alison is still missing, and I just feel helpless, waiting for something to happen.'

'What did he say?'

Shirley hesitated. 'He said he didn't have anything to do with it. He thought Jane wanted to die.'

Eric shook his head. 'Why are you doing this?'

The tone of the question stung. 'Doing what?'

'Acting like you're some kind of private detective. You should let the police get on with their job, and not be interfering.'

'But I have to do something.'

Eric shook his head again as he got to his feet.

'The girl wasn't Alison.' Shirley stood up and pulled Eric back as he tried to leave the room. 'He said it definitely wasn't her. Why would someone else pretend to be Alison?'

'I don't know,' he said, shrugging her off and heading for the door.

'Maybe it was her boyfriend, Vincent. Maybe he killed her.'

'Don't be stupid,' Eric said, clutching the door for balance.

'Well, where is he? He must have heard the news. Why hasn't he come around here? Why wasn't he at the funeral?'

'Because he doesn't give a damn,' Eric shot back. 'He broke up with her, if you remember. The guy just doesn't care.'

215

'You've seen him?'

'No, no, of course not. But Shirley, it's obvious – can't you see? He used her. I'm going upstairs.'

'And what about you?' she shouted. 'Do you care? Because it doesn't look like it from where I'm standing.'

She regretted the accusation immediately.

Eric ignored the comment and left the room.

'I'm sorry, Eric. I didn't mean that.'

She pursued him into the landing and watched helplessly as he trudged up the stairs and entered the bathroom. For a minute or so, she stayed at the bottom, her eyes focused on the bathroom door, waiting for him to come out. But when he didn't, she crept up the stairs and put her head close to the door.

Her husband was sobbing like a child.

Jody lay on her bed and looked up at the ceiling. The shelter room, with its bare, clinical white walls and lack of furniture, was far from homey, but it was the best place she had slept in for many years. Run by a Catholic charity, it offered board and lodgings for homeless young people, with the proviso that no drugs or alcohol were allowed on the premises. That wasn't a problem for Jody. She'd never used drugs and only drank alcohol for its numbing qualities, which hadn't been needed in the past year: not since she'd made the deal with him – if she brought him girls, she would never have to suffer at the hands of those men. It was a deal that still haunted her.

But there was one rule she now had to break.

The night-time curfew.

She looked across at the clock that hung on the wall, just above the gold crucifix. It was coming up to eleven, and within minutes the front door would be locked.

She pulled herself up from the bed and ran through the plan one last time. Then, grabbing her jacket, she left the room and walked down to the next door on the right. A young girl answered. Clara, a thirteen-year-old runaway from Scotland, nodded at her, without either exchanging a word. She knew what she had to do. Clara was a good kid. And Jody hoped and prayed that she would never fall into the company she herself had.

Jody waited around the corner from the reception desk as Clara gave an impressive performance. She feigned illness, threatening to vomit, and the woman at reception, a stern but kindly nun, left her station to accompany her to the toilet.

Jody waited until they were out of sight before edging around the corner, past the reception desk and out the door into the cool London air. She turned back to look at the building. She had been so lucky after leaving Locky's to find this place, this refuge from the grimness of what her life had become. For the first time in years, it seemed like somebody cared and that maybe there was a way out of all this. What she had just done had jeopardised that. But she was willing to risk it all for Mel, who had been her friend, a lovely girl who had reminded her of her little sister. She would do whatever it took to make that man suffer for what he had done.

Jody travelled across London by night bus. She sat with her head resting against the window, ignoring the occasional glances of the sole fellow passenger on the bus's bottom deck, a drunken man to her right. As she watched the lights of London flash by, the fear rose, and the stop-and-go movement of the bus began to make her feel sick. She was going against Locky's advice, travelling back into the lair, risking everything.

She reached the house after almost an hour, fighting the nauseating combination of travel sickness and nerves as she watched from across the road. The comfort of the refuge seemed a lifetime away. The building and its entrance looked so innocuous, but looks were definitely deceiving. She stepped back behind a parked van as the front door to the building opened and a man emerged. She recognised him as one of the regulars – one of the more pleasant ones, relatively speaking, but still not someone she wanted to see.

She waited behind the van until he was out of sight, before crossing the road, keeping a wide berth between her and the front entrance. With no one else in sight, she hurried along the side of the building and up to a metal door: the emergency fire exit. Crouching down, she performed the act she had done many times before, running her fingers along the underside of the frame until she found the catch. One flick and the door popped outwards. Within a second she was inside, with the door closed behind her.

She took a few seconds to gather her composure as she stood at the base of the stairs, running through things one more time in her mind. It was crucial that it all went to plan. Then, as quietly as she could, she ascended the metal staircase, reaching the next door. She was pretty confident there would be no one in the linen room at this time of night, but still, she ensured that she opened the door with almost painful slowness. The room was in darkness, so it took time to make her way through the piles of sheets and boxes, being careful not to make any noise that might draw attention to her. She emerged into the corridor on the upper level of the building. Again, thankfully, there was no one around, although she could hear familiar sounds coming from the adjacent room. She longed to burst in there and spoil the party, but now wasn't the time.

Instead, she moved downstairs, avoiding the entrance where security would be on guard, and reached her destination. She knew that he was never in at this time of night – he would be in the casino by now – but still, as she put the stolen key to the lock, a sudden sense of fear gripped her. Fighting this off, she opened the door and closed it behind her, only then flicking on the desk lamp.

Now she had to move fast.

She moved quickly, searching the room for something – anything – that might explain what had happened to her friend – folders, papers on his desk and the contents of the desk drawers. But there was nothing here. Then she moved on to the computer. But as she went to turn on the device, she realised it was already in standby mode. She moved the mouse, and an image of a woman appeared on the screen.

It changed everything.

So shocked was she by the image, Jody didn't realise he was standing behind her. He had been hiding in the room.

Two powerful arms held her down at the shoulders, pushing her into the chair with considerable force.

'Welcome back, Jody. What's it like to see Mummy after all these years?'

Chapter Twenty-Nine

S am sat there, stunned, just staring at the computer screen. He pressed the 'Play' button and, eyes closed, listened to the recording for a second time.

'Please, God, no . . . look away! Look away, please.'

Someone had recorded the train crash. And there had been microphones in more than one location.

He put a hand to his head as he tried to absorb the revelation and what it meant.

The whole thing had been set up. Was that possible?

And if so, by whom?

He went back to his email account and examined the message that had led him to the video: catherinebecker@netmail.com.

Richard Friedman was dead. Yet there was someone still out there, goading him about Cathy. And now, the evidence that the events of the past week could somehow be all connected. He thought back to the terror on the railway track. The terrified young girl, those poor children strapped in the car and the baby in the boot, Jane Ainsley's vacant stare and her death. And the girl's suicide in the river.

Was all that for him?

And did this now link to Richard Friedman?

It was late at night, but not too late to take action. He pulled out his mobile and called Paul Cullen.

'Sam, good to see you.'

Just twenty-five minutes after the phone call, Sam led Paul Cullen through to the living room. 'I didn't expect you to get here so quickly,' he replied.

'I'm only staying just down the road,' Paul revealed, 'in a hotel just near Euston Station – while I sort out some personal problems.'

'Sorry to hear that,' Sam said as they entered the lounge. 'I didn't realise.'

Paul Cullen shrugged. 'It's a long story. But I'm hoping for a happy ending.'

Sam didn't want to probe any further. 'Well, thanks for coming so late at night, even if you are nearby.'

'No problem. I was glad to get out of that hotel room – expensive, but grubby as hell. So, what's this about? You said it's something very important.'

'Take a seat.' Sam gestured to the chair in front of the laptop.

Paul Cullen did as requested, with a flash of something resembling anticipation. Sam sat on the chair next to him and worked the mouse, clicking through to his email account.

'I got this email about fifteen minutes before I called you,' he said, opening up the message. 'The sender has used the name of my sister.'

'Catherine Becker,' Cullen thought out loud.

'The link takes you to this,' said Sam as the web page loaded. He clicked on 'Play' and sat back as it started up, switching his focus between the monitor and Paul Cullen, gauging the other man's reaction.

'What am I watching here?' Cullen asked, not taking his attention away from the screen.

'Just listen,' Sam replied. He went to turn up the volume, but it was already on maximum.

'Please, help Jessica! She's in the back! Jessica's in the back!'

Paul Cullen turned to Sam as the screen went black and the video ended. 'I don't understand, Sam – what is this?'

Sam was disappointed by his reaction. 'Don't you recognise my voice?'

'It's difficult to hear,' Cullen replied. 'I can just about make out some words, bits of sentences.'

'It's an audio recording of the train crash.'

Cullen looked more confused than shocked. 'What?'

Sam gestured towards the screen. 'Someone had microphones there and recorded everything.'

'I don't understand.'

Sam should have realised this would take time to sink in. 'I know it sounds crazy, but someone set this up, recorded it and posted it on the Internet for me to find.'

Cullen's face was a picture of scepticism, but it looked as if his mind was whirring. Sam had certainly got his attention. 'Play it again.'

The recording began to play through again. This time Sam added his commentary, explained who was saying what, filling in the words when it was difficult to hear.

When the audio ended, Cullen sat there in contemplation, kneading his chin.

'Someone recorded the whole thing,' Sam repeated. 'And just under an hour ago, they sent me the link on that email, using my sister's name.'

Cullen turned to face him. 'You really believe that this is a recording from that night?'

'Definitely,' Sam replied. 'You're not convinced?'

'It's pretty poor quality.'

'But you can pick out the voices. And I know what was said.'

'It could be a hoax,' suggested Cullen. 'Someone playing games with you. They could have re-enacted the events.'

Sam didn't buy that explanation, although he understood it was a logical and necessary one for Cullen to voice. 'But how would they know what happened?'

'From what they've heard in the media.'

Sam shook his head. 'As far as I remember, it's word for word what was said – no one else apart from me and the girl knew that. And that voice is definitely mine.'

Cullen gave that a few moments of thought. He was coming around to the idea, Sam could tell. 'Say this is a recording of the train crash. What do you think this means?'

'Like I said, it was a set-up.' Sam knew it sounded unbelievable, but it was what he believed.

'Who was set up? Jane Ainsley?'

'Me.'

Paul Cullen looked intrigued. 'You think this was set up for you?'

'Yes. But maybe it was just chance that I was driving down that particular road when the girl ran out in front of my car. It could have been a set-up for anybody, but I became part of it.'

'You said "maybe",' Cullen replied, picking up on Sam's choice of words.

'Or maybe it was always meant for me.'

Cullen's forehead creased. 'You really think that – that all this could have been set up for you? Why?'

'I don't know,' Sam admitted. 'But what I do know is that some-one recorded everything that happened. Someone else was involved in this. Maybe they were there watching; I don't know.'

'You're talking about murder here.'

'Shirley Ainsley doesn't believe that her daughter committed suicide.'

Cullen couldn't hide his surprise. 'You've spoken to Shirley Ainsley?'

'She came to see me.'

Cullen shook his head with barely concealed anger. 'What did she say?'

Sam felt uncomfortable under his glare. 'That she didn't think her daughter was capable of doing something like that, especially taking her children with her.'

'Nobody wants to think their child would be capable of something like that.'

Sam decided to add one last bit of information. 'She thought it might have something to do with her ex-boyfriend.'

'Did she?' Cullen replied flatly. 'Sam, what are you trying to do here?'

'I don't know what you mean.'

'You shouldn't be talking to Shirley Ainsley about the case, or to anyone else for that matter.'

Sam knew he was right, but he hadn't gone looking for Shirley. 'She came to see me.'

'Then you should have refused to talk to her. Shirley Ainsley is a very upset and confused lady. She's grieving and looking for answers. Surely you can empathise with that.'

Sam nodded. Maybe he should have done that, but it would have been difficult and cruel under the circumstances just to have shown her the door, not to mention that it would have fuelled Shirley's suspicions about him.

'Shirley Ainsley was adamant until a few days ago that you were somehow responsible for her daughter's death.'

'I know,' Sam said, 'but she doesn't think so now.'

'Not at the moment,' Cullen corrected, pressing home his point, 'but things can change, Sam, and you don't want to put yourself in a vulnerable and dangerous situation. If she contacts you again, call me.'

Sam conceded with another nod.

Cullen seemed satisfied with that gesture. He turned his attention back to the screen. 'Sam, I'm not convinced by this.'

Sam wanted to protest loudly, maybe replay the recording again and again until he was convinced. But it wouldn't be wise. Cullen would make up his mind in his own time. 'Why not?'

'Because I'm still not sure what I'm listening to here. I know you say you're certain, but I'm not. Not enough to be sure anyway. And the idea that all this was set up for you just seems so far-fetched.'

Sam tried one last time. 'But what about the girl who pretended to be Alison Ainsley? Surely that indicates that something isn't right about what happened?'

Cullen was impassive. 'Sam, we still only have your word that the girl at the scene wasn't Alison Ainsley.'

'But she wasn't.'

'So you say. And I've got no reason to disbelieve you. But still, it's just your word.'

Frustration was now getting the better of Sam. 'So you think I might be lying?'

Cullen held up his hands. 'Or remembering incorrectly. After all, you went through an extremely traumatic event. The mind can play tricks after something like that.'

Sam checked himself. 'But the girl in the river – it was the same girl.'

'And we're still trying to identify that young lady. Tell me, Sam, do you think that this has something to do with the murder of your sister?'

Sam was thrown by this unexpected line of questioning. 'I – I don't know.'

'I read about what happened. It must have taken a lot of getting over.'

'I've never got over it,' Sam admitted, meeting Cullen's gaze.

'I also know about what happened during this past week – I know about Richard Friedman, what he said and did.'

Sam felt on the defensive. 'What's that got to do with the train crash?'

'I don't think it's got anything to do with it. But do you?'

Sam considered his answer. 'I don't know.'

Cullen nodded to himself, as if his suspicions had been confirmed. 'Sam, thanks for drawing my attention to the recording. And I assure you we will take this seriously. But please, for your own sake, your own sanity, stay out of this investigation, and let me do my job.'

Carla Conway looked over at the stack of papers piled high in her in-tray and blew out her cheeks. It was late, too late, and her husband was once again manning the fort, ensuring that the children were fed and put to bed with a story. *Alice in Wonderland* was their current favourite. This wasn't the way she ever wanted it to be, and she had sworn to herself upon taking up the job that her family would no longer come second best. Of course, the job had always demanded long hours, and she'd known that from the outset, but in the past few weeks things had become intolerable. She picked up the next bundle of papers and slid it across the desk. Skimming through the paperwork, she signed where needed and moved on to the next item.

Then the phone rang.

Her first reaction was to let it ring and cut onto divert. But Chrissie, her PA, was long gone by now – some five hours ago, in fact. She grabbed for the phone, wondering who was calling at this late hour. Possibly it was security. Sometimes they called just to check that everything was okay. After all, she was the only person left up here on the top floor. Everyone else had more sense and less responsibility.

'Hello, Carla Conway speaking.'

Less than a minute later, she put the phone down, shocked by what she had just been told and hoping to God that it wasn't true. She called through to the security room and requested that a senior member of the team be sent up to her immediately. Then she dialled Adil Khan's number.

'Adil. It's Carla. Sorry to disturb you so late, but we've got a potentially extremely serious situation here. It's regarding Sam Becker.'

Chapter Thirty

S am strode into the cardiac centre and immediately longed to be back at work. He missed it all so much. This was where he belonged – the general bustle of the team as they moved purposefully between stations, the adrenalin as the operation approached, the camaraderie of a team that was really making a difference. He nodded hellos to a couple of the nursing staff, who looked pleasantly surprised to see him as he made his way past the nursing desk and down the corridor towards Professor Khan's office. The Professor had called him first thing, requesting that he come in as soon as he could. He hadn't expanded on why, but that was Adil Khan's way – if he had something to say, he would do it face-to-face, not over the telephone and certainly not by email.

The door was closed, so he knocked and waited.

'Sam,' Professor Khan said, too solemnly for Sam's liking, as the Professor opened the door and the two men locked eyes.

His face matched his tone. Whatever this was about, it didn't look good. Sam followed him inside; Professor Khan shut the door gently and gestured to him to take a seat. For a few seconds they eyed each other across the ornate desk. With anyone else, Sam would have already asked what the matter was, but not with this man.

There was something in his dark brown eyes, in his expression, that Sam had never seen before.

Disappointment. Pity, maybe. It made his stomach lurch.

Professor Khan clasped his hands together and cleared his throat. 'Sam, I'm not sure how to approach this.'

Sam waited, dreading what was about to be said. Maybe they'd decided to withdraw the new consultant post – after all, these were tough economic times, and the hospital may have decided to make do with what they already had. If that were true, then he would handle it. But maybe it was much worse than that. It could be what all doctors feared, a serious complaint from a member of the public or a clinical error from an unsuccessful operation that had been picked up on post-mortem.

Professor Khan exhaled. 'When we last met, I asked how you were dealing with everything that has happened to you recently. You said you were okay.'

'I am,' Sam replied. 'It's difficult, but I'm dealing with it.'

'Dealing with it,' Professor Khan repeated slowly, as if processing something of great significance.

'The time off has helped,' Sam added. 'You were right. I feel I'll be better prepared for the interview.'

Professor Khan pinched the bridge of his nose, lost in thought. 'Sam, is there anything you would like to tell me?'

'Tell you?'

He faced Sam with those searching brown eyes. 'Yes. Anything you would like to tell me?'

'I don't understand.'

'Stress can lead us to desperate actions, Sam. I've seen it happen before, to strong people who have buckled under intense strain.'

Desperate actions? Now this did sound serious. 'What is it you think I might have done?'

Professor Khan shook his head. 'I shouldn't be doing this, Sam, I really shouldn't, but I wanted to tell you first, give you chance to say something to me, explain things, before the board meet. It might help.'

The drip-feed approach was killing him, and the Professor must have known it. 'Tell me what? What's happening with the board?'

'If I said that they have found some items in your possession, in your locker, would you now be ready to talk to me?'

This was so crazy. Items in his locker? Someone had been searching his personal possessions? 'What items?'

Professor Khan went to speak, then checked himself. 'Sam, have you ever used controlled drugs to – help you – help you through difficult times?'

The question, no matter how delicately it was asked, still came like a shock to the system. 'No,' Sam said, struggling to believe this conversation was really happening, 'of course not. I've never taken drugs – never. Is that what they've found? Drugs in my locker?'

'I'm sorry, Sam, I can't say any more than that.'

He needed to know more. 'What drugs were they?'

'I can't say any more than that,' repeated Professor Khan.

Sam's mind worked quickly through the possible explanations for this. There was only one. But who would have done such a thing? 'Whatever they are, they're not mine,' he said. 'Someone must have put them there. Someone must have set me up.'

Professor Khan put up a finger. 'Do not name names. Not here, or now.'

'I wouldn't,' Sam said, struggling to hold back his emotions. His whole professional life was on the line. This could end everything. 'But if drugs have been found in my locker, then someone has put them there. I swear it's got nothing to do with me.'

Adil Khan remained silent, just watching Sam, scrutinising him.

Sam took the opportunity to continue his defence. 'I would never do anything to jeopardise my career; I love this job too much. You believe that, don't you?'

'It doesn't really matter what I believe.'

'It matters to me.'

Professor Khan considered the question. 'I had to ask you, Sam, given the uncomfortable reality of the circumstances with which we find ourselves. But now that I've heard what you have to say, you have my full support. I trust my team, and I especially trust you. I know you wouldn't let me down.'

Sam felt a genuine rush of gratitude. If the Professor, his own mentor, doubted him, then there would surely have been no hope. 'Thank you. It means a lot to me.'

Professor Khan's expression remained solemn.

Sam knew there was more. 'What happens next?'

'The board have called a meeting. It takes place this afternoon. They are planning to tell you this morning. You are expected to attend.'

'What time?'

'Three o'clock.'

Sam bit his lip. He wouldn't be able to pick Anna up from the airport. He would have to make alternative arrangements. 'Will you be there?'

'I will. And I will support you. But I do not have control here. Some influence, that's all, but I know my limitations.' He spread his hands. 'In the theatre, Sam, I am all powerful, but up there, in the board room, things are very different.'

Sam needed all the allies he could get. And he knew how well respected the Professor was among the hospital's hierarchy. 'I'd still really value your support.'

Khan nodded. 'Use these precious few hours to think extremely carefully, Sam. The implications of what you say will be great. For you, and for others who work here.'

'Did the drugs come from hospital supplies?' Sam asked, guessing what Professor Khan was alluding to. If they were, then it meant he had been set up by a colleague. Only they would have access to the secure drugs cabinets located on each ward.

Professor Khan remained poker-faced. 'I can say no more, Sam. Just use these hours wisely.'

Sam retreated to his office, trying to come to terms with what was happening and also consider who might be responsible. As far as he knew, there was only one colleague who disliked him, and that was Miles Churchill. But to plant drugs and destroy his career? Would he really be capable of that? And for what – so he could get the consultant post? There were other jobs in other hospitals. It seemed too much. But if not Miles, then who? Desperate to talk this through with Louisa, he journeyed down to her office, but she was in clinic.

He got the call just twenty minutes later. It was from Carla Conway herself. She requested that he attend an emergency meeting of the hospital board at three o'clock but didn't offer an explanation of its purpose. Instead, she informed him that one of the hospital trust solicitors was waiting to speak with him. Sam didn't reveal what he knew – Professor Khan had put his own job on the line by telling him the details, and he wasn't going to betray that act of bravery. So he acted suitably confused and promised to wait in his office until the solicitor arrived.

Five minutes after the phone call, there was a knock on his door.

'Come in.'

The solicitor, a man in his mid- to late thirties, with trendy messy hair, entered and smiled tightly. Sam had seen the guy before; he'd been involved in supporting and vindicating a senior nurse who had been accused – wrongly – of verbally abusing a patient. Word had it that this guy was good, and on the side of staff.

The solicitor proffered a hand while cradling a file against his chest. 'Ed Stansfield,' he said. Sam stood up, and the two men shook hands.

'Sam Becker. Take a seat. So, what's this all about?' began Sam, aware that he wasn't supposed to know any details.

Ed Stansfield opened up the file he had been carrying and cleared his throat. 'I'll get straight to the point. Last night, the hospital commenced a search of staff lockers, and they found a quantity of tablets from the hospital stock in your locker.'

He searched Sam for a reaction. When he got nothing, he continued, glancing down at the file. 'The tablets were Alprazolam, a controlled drug, used for the treatment of—'

'Anxiety and insomnia,' Sam finished.

'Yes, of course, you'll know all this . . .'

The tablets were strong stuff. And yes, one of the drugs of choice for doctors who, unable to cope, sought a lifeline in a desperate attempt to save their career. Professor Khan's earlier line of questioning made total sense. 'How much was there?'

'Half a box – thirty tablets,' Stansfield replied.

Although it wasn't a large amount, no more than a few days' supply, it was still enough to raise serious questions, especially given their source. 'And they definitely came from the hospital?'

'Definitely. The stock number matches those in the hospital pharmacy.'

'They're not mine,' Sam said. 'Someone must have put them there.'

Ed Stansfield blinked a few times, never taking his eyes off Sam. 'You're claiming that someone has set you up?'

'Yes,' Sam replied, facing him down. 'Why did the hospital start searching people's lockers?'

'They received a call tipping them off.'

This was all now so transparent. 'From who?'

'The caller didn't give a name.'

'Was it a man or a woman?'

'A man.'

'And did the caller specifically mention my name?'

'Yes. The person named you.'

Sam shook his head, consumed by confusion and anger. This person aimed to ruin him and might yet succeed. 'Then someone has definitely set me up. Someone's trying to wreck my career.'

Ed Stansfield let that claim sink in. 'Have you got enemies, Sam? Someone who would go to these lengths? Someone who works at this hospital, maybe?'

Again, Sam thought of Miles. 'There's only one person I don't get along with, but I'm sure he wouldn't do this.'

'Don't rule out anything, Sam. If what you say is true, then you have to consider everybody. Think the unthinkable. Who is it?'

Sam put a hand to his head, wondering whether to say the name. He felt terrible making the accusation. 'Miles Churchill. He's a surgeon too, a colleague. We're going for the same job next week. We don't get on.'

'But you said you don't think he would have done this?'

'No, I don't think he would. I don't think he'd go to such lengths, I really don't.'

'Then if not him, who?'

Sam closed his eyes. Maybe there was someone else – someone who would certainly do something like this, although Sam didn't know how this person would have got access to the drugs. 'Did you hear about the rail crash last week which I was involved in?'

Stansfield nodded. 'I saw it on the news.'

'The whole thing was a set-up. They made it look like a suicide, but it wasn't. They wanted to get at me.' No matter how many times Sam said this, to himself or others, it didn't sound any less crazy.

Ed Stansfield remained silent as Sam explained the YouTube posting of the train crash and the mystery of the girl who had led him to the scene.

'So you think this person might have also set you up with this?' His voice was neutral, with no clue as to whether he took this idea seriously.

Sam shrugged. 'Maybe. I don't know what to think. But I can't rule it out.'

'But this person would need to have access to the pharmacy stock of controlled drugs.'

'I know.'

'Or would need to know someone who does have access.'

Sam had already thought of that. 'Maybe.'

Now Stansfield did look interested. 'And what do the police say about all this? About the train crash being a set-up?'

'They're not convinced.'

Ed Stansfield drummed his fingers on the desk, looking off into mid-air for inspiration. 'Sorry,' he said, realising what he was doing. 'Old habit.' He pulled at his lip. 'We've got to play this very carefully. I want you to defend yourself in there – hold your ground and don't let the board bully you into saying something you might regret. But I don't think at this stage it would be at all helpful to tell them what you've just told me. Don't talk about the rail crash, or this person who you think might be responsible. Keep to the bare facts – the drugs aren't yours, and you don't know how they got into your locker.'

'And do you think they'll believe me?'

'Maybe. Your record is exemplary. You have a fantastic character reference from Professor Adil Khan. And there's been no report of erratic behaviour that might indicate the abuse of controlled drugs.'

Sam sensed Ed was holding a negative back. 'But?'

'But,' he said, 'the drugs *were* found in your locker.'

Chapter Thirty-One

Immediately after Ed Stansfield left, Sam called a local taxi company and arranged for them to pick up Anna from the airport. He then left a message on Anna's mobile, explaining that he had to attend an urgent meeting at the hospital – he didn't expand on that – and that a taxi would be waiting for her in the arrivals hall. Anna was currently thirty thousand feet in the air, but Sam hoped that she'd switch on her phone soon after landing, so she wouldn't have a chance to wonder where he was.

For the following few hours, Sam did as Professor Khan had advised. He spent the time hidden away in his office, drinking cups of tea and thinking through how he was going to handle the situation. Emotions battled for supremacy within him: fear, anger, confusion. It was hard to know what to do, and he longed for Anna to be there. She was always so good at helping him to see through the fog. But eventually he came to the conclusion that Ed Stansfield was right – it wouldn't be sensible to talk about conspiracies or links with his sister's murder, Richard Friedman and the train crash. It would just risk him looking paranoid or delusional. And for the board that might be enough to confirm their suspicions that he was indeed using the very drugs that had been found in his locker.

But still, there was a link between these events. Sam was sure. The board meeting just wasn't the right time to voice it.

When he had exhausted his thought processes, he emerged from his hideaway, seeing just one nurse as he passed quickly through the department. He headed for the lift and down towards Louisa's office. It was now twelve thirty, and she would have just finished her morning's consultations.

She was indeed in her office. As Sam approached, he could see her through the window of the door, talking on her mobile. He peered through the glass and tapped a hello. Louisa looked startled to see him. She held up a hand for him to wait and then turned her back to him, finishing the call in just a few seconds. She faced Sam and beckoned him in.

'Sorry,' she said, 'my cousin, Helen. She's going through another one of her man crises.'

'She okay?' Sam said, closing the door behind him, his mind not really on the well-being of Louisa's cousin.

'Oh, you know Helen.' Louisa gave a dismissive wave of her hand. 'She gets like this from time to time, worrying about whether this man or that man is Mr Right. Anyway, how are you? No more calls or emails?'

Sam sat down, feeling guilty about injecting another dose of negativity into Louisa's life. He looked across to her, wondering how to word it. In that moment Louisa knew that something had happened, and her face tensed.

'What is it, Sam? What's happened?'

'Professor Khan called me this morning,' he began. 'The hospital did a search of my locker last night and found half a packet of Alprazolam tablets. The board now think I'm a drug abuser and have called an emergency meeting in three hours' time.'

'My God,' Louisa said. 'But that's rubbish, Sam – it's rubbish. How did they know to . . . what made them look in your locker?'

'Someone called and tipped them off.'

Her anger was palpable. 'Who?'

Sam shrugged. 'They don't know. Or if they do, they're not saying.'

'But this is just crazy. Someone's set you up.'

The strength of her certainty surprised Sam. He had expected support, of course, but her instinct was total rejection of the allegations – there was no doubt in her eyes. 'Thanks.'

'For what?'

'For believing me.'

Louisa looked offended at Sam's insinuation: that he may have doubted that she would believe him. 'Of course I believe you. I'm your friend.'

'It doesn't mean I have any right to expect such rock-solid support from you.'

'Of course you do,' Louisa hit back. 'You have every right.'

Sam smiled his gratitude. 'It means a lot.'

Louisa had already moved on with her thoughts. 'So who the hell's done this?'

'The drugs came from hospital stocks.'

'No!' Louisa exclaimed. 'It's someone at the hospital?'

'To get the drugs, you need staff access to the controlled drugs cabinets on the ward. So it must be someone who could get that access.'

'You think it could be Miles?'

'I don't think so,' Sam said. 'I don't think he'd do it.'

'Probably not. He's not that bad or desperate – at least I don't think he is. But if it isn't Miles, then who?'

Sam waited a beat. 'The same person who sent me the link to the train crash recording.'

Louisa didn't look that surprised. 'You think this is all connected?'

'I know it sounds outlandish, but it does make sense in some ways. Someone is targeting me, Louisa. This could be just another example.'

'But the access to the drugs. It means that the person works here.'

'Or maybe,' Sam said, repeating Ed Stansfield's earlier thought, 'it's someone who has contacts in the hospital.'

Louisa shook her head. 'This is all so crazy, Sam.'

'I know.' Sam decided not to discuss his suspicions of Marcus at this point. He wasn't sure why exactly – maybe because it just felt like too much. He would talk to Louisa about it at some stage, but not right now.

'So what are you going to do? You have to attend the board meeting?'

Sam nodded. 'Three o'clock sharp.'

'And who's going to be there?'

'I don't know. Carla, for certain. And whoever in the senior management team can make it, I guess. Professor Khan too.'

'And does he support you?'

'Yes,' Sam said. 'But there's only so much he can do.'

Louisa let out a sigh of frustration. 'Do you think they're going to suspend you?'

'I don't know.'

'But what about the job interview?'

'I really don't know.'

'This is awful, Sam, just awful. Whoever's doing this, we can't just let them get away with it.'

'I know,' Sam said. 'They won't.'

He wasn't sure whether he really believed that, but he had to think positively. He had to think this would all end happily.

Just then his mobile buzzed in his pocket. He excused himself and pulled out the device.

It was a message from Louisa's stolen phone.

Cathy died in my arms, Sam. Where were you?

Sam made his way up to the boardroom, still seething about the taunting text message. Somehow he had to put the actions of this sick individual to the back of his mind, at least for the next hour – but how? The doors to the lift opened, and Ed Stansfield, as promised, was waiting for him on the other side.

'Hi,' he said, unsmiling, still clutching his file. 'Are you ready for this?'

Sam nodded.

'Remember,' Stansfield said, dropping the volume, 'try not to be drawn by the board into saying anything you might regret. If you feel uncomfortable answering any of their questions, just glance over at me, and I'll take it.'

'Sure.'

Stansfield patted his back. 'Let's go then.'

They walked along the corridor, silence descending, and came to the boardroom. Ed Stansfield knocked, and they were called in. The room layout had been changed to an interview style. The long board table and its occupants faced them along the back window, with two empty chairs in between. Unlike a few days ago, the table was fully occupied. Sam did a quick scan of the people present. Carla Conway was seated in the middle. To either side were six of the permanent board members, with Professor Khan at the far end. And immediately on Carla's right, a middle-aged man whom Sam didn't recognise but assumed was the hospital solicitor. Sam looked back at Professor Khan, who nodded an almost imperceptible greeting, sending a hidden message of support.

'Sam,' Carla began, 'if you wouldn't mind taking a seat.'

This time there were no smiles.

Sam sat down, and Ed Stansfield took the seat next to him.

'Thank you for coming at such short notice,' Carla began, stony-faced. 'The board appreciates your co-operation in this serious matter.'

Sam nodded.

'I know that Mr Stansfield explained the situation to you earlier today,' she continued.

'He did,' Sam replied.

Carla Conway picked up a piece of paper from the desk and peered at it from over her glasses. 'Yesterday evening we received a call from an anonymous individual who claimed that you had been taking controlled drugs from hospital supplies for your own personal use. We launched an immediate investigation and found a quantity of controlled drugs – Alprazolam – in your locker. The batch code confirmed that they were from hospital supplies.'

She looked up at Sam and held her gaze, awaiting a response.

'The drugs aren't mine,' Sam stated, trying to erase any emotion from his statement. He needed to stay professional, calm and controlled. 'Someone must have put them there.'

Carla didn't flinch, as if she'd already known what he was going to say. 'So you're denying that you took the drugs from hospital supplies, for your own personal use?'

'Yes.'

She glanced down. 'Then how did the drugs get there?'

Again Sam fought to maintain a professional tone. 'Like I said, someone put them there – the same person who called you.'

She looked puzzled at that suggestion. 'You're saying that another member of the hospital staff has deliberately set you up?'

'Someone at the hospital must have accessed the controlled drugs stocks.'

'Who?' she said, looking far from convinced.

'I don't know,' Sam admitted. 'But I'm just telling you that it wasn't me. I don't take drugs, and I don't steal from this hospital.'

Carla took off her glasses, leaning towards him across the table. 'Why would someone do this, Sam? Why would someone who works here do this to you?'

'I don't know.'

She sat back. 'I want to believe you, Sam. I really do. But try and see this from our point of view. The drugs were found in your locker.'

'Someone put them there.'

'So they had a key? The locker wasn't forced open.'

Ed Stansfield hadn't mentioned that. Sam resisted the temptation to look over at him for confirmation. 'They must have had a master key.'

'So they had a key to your locker, and they also had access to the controlled drugs stock?'

'They must have.'

'So you think maybe this person works in security, if they have access to master keys?'

'Maybe,' Sam said. 'I don't know, but all I do know is that someone put those drugs there and then called to tell you about it.' He addressed each of them in turn across the table. 'I don't know who, I don't know why, but that's all I can come up with.' He was struggling to keep his anger and frustration in check now. 'Do you really think I'd throw away my career for this? I love what I do, and you know that, Carla.'

'Sam is as baffled by this as anyone,' Ed Stansfield interjected, aware of the need to dampen down the escalating emotional tension. 'But he is willing to do anything it takes to find out who did this, and offers his full support in the investigation.'

Carla nodded. 'Sam. You've been through a series of traumatic events during the past two weeks. And I must admit, I take some responsibility for increasing the stress which you undoubtedly have been under. I should not have encouraged you to liaise with the media when it was obvious you were not keen.'

Sam waited.

'And it would be understandable that under those extreme circumstances you might turn to other forms of support—'

'No,' Sam interrupted.

'You have a record that is second to none, Sam. You have a fantastic character reference from Professor Khan, who I must add, is unwavering in his support for you and has been extremely vocal on that score.'

Sam glanced over at Professor Khan, but he was just looking down in a way that rang alarm bells of what was to come.

'But even so,' Carla continued, 'we have a duty to take this matter extremely seriously.'

'You're going to suspend me,' Sam said.

'We need a few minutes to deliberate,' she replied, 'and then we'll call you back in to explain our decision. But before I ask you to leave the room for a moment, is there anything else that you wish to say?'

Sam exchanged a look with Ed Stansfield. 'No.'

Chapter Thirty-Two

'You did the right thing,' Ed Stansfield said as they moved a few paces down the corridor, out of earshot from the boardroom. 'You kept it simple, to the point.'

'Carla didn't look convinced,' Sam said, musing on what had just happened. He should have expected it to turn out the way it did. They had to go through a process, reserve judgement until the evidence was clear. But the lack of support still hurt, especially from Carla. Even Professor Khan had been noticeably quiet, although hopefully behind closed doors he would argue Sam's case. Sam looked at his watch. Anna's flight would be landing any moment. Why couldn't he be there to welcome her home, hold her tight?

'I'm afraid it looks likely that you will be suspended from duty,' Ed Stansfield said. 'But if the investigation is swift, you could be back at work within a matter of weeks.'

'Assuming they decide I'm innocent,' Sam replied, still thinking of Anna. He reached into his pocket and pulled out his mobile. It had been on silent during the meeting, but the screen display registered a message. It hit him like a jab to the ribs, knocking him back a pace.

'My God.'

Ed Stansfield moved towards him. 'What's the matter?

'I've got to go,' Sam replied, already moving towards the lifts, his head reeling from what he had just read.

Ed Stansfield followed, spooked by his client's behaviour. 'Sam, don't leave! If you're not here when the board calls you back, it could make things much worse.'

Sam reached the lifts and hit the button. He knew this one action was potentially career ending, but he had no other choice. 'Tell them I've got a family emergency.'

'What sort of emergency? Is everything okay, Sam? If I can tell them something specific, it would help.'

'Sorry.' Sam stepped into the lift and pressed the ground-floor button several times. 'Please, just tell them I had no choice.'

The doors closed on an open-mouthed Ed Stansfield.

Anna Becker leant close to the window and looked down on the patchwork-quilt countryside as they approached Heathrow. The plane banked anti-clockwise in a wide circle, waiting its turn to land. It couldn't come soon enough. The flight had been pleasant, as a long-haul flight could be, but it had seemed to take forever, so desperate was Anna to get home. This time the homing instinct had been worse than ever, and although she was in some ways disappointed at cutting the visit short, the need to be with Sam was too strong.

Two minutes later the plane straightened up and touched down with only a gentle kiss of the runway. Anna smiled. It was great to be back. She placed a hand on her stomach as she thought of Sam.

He would be waiting for her in the arrivals hall.

Anna waited for the rest of the passengers to disembark before grabbing her bag and making her way out of the plane and down to the luggage collection area. She waited at the empty conveyor belt along with the rest of the flight, many of whom were obviously people who had visited or were coming to visit relatives. With the baggage yet to arrive, she took the opportunity to check her phone.

But it wasn't in her pocket or her bag.

She searched again, but the phone definitely wasn't there. Thinking it must have fallen out during the flight or maybe on the way from the plane, she retraced her steps back towards the aircraft. The crew had left, but one of the cleaners accompanied her down to her seat. There was no sign of the phone.

Defeated and annoyed, Anna returned to the luggage collection area. By now the cases had arrived, and she soon spotted her black case with its distinctive red and white trim. Mulling over where the phone could be, she realised the last time she had seen it was just before taking off. It had been on the plane. So maybe one of the crew had already found it.

She would contact the company the next day. One day without the phone would probably be as much of a blessing as an inconvenience. And anyway, Sam was waiting right outside, so she had no need of it right this moment.

But when she emerged into the arrivals hall, Sam wasn't there. She scanned the crowds but couldn't see him anywhere. She stopped, turning three hundred and sixty degrees. And then she saw the man with the sign: Anna Becker.

'Hi, I'm Anna, Anna Becker,' she explained to the man, who was wearing a chauffeur's suit. He was young, late twenties probably, with closely cropped hair and stubble.

He smiled. 'Taxi back to Clerkenwell?'

'Yeah,' Anna answered, thrown and disappointed by this unexpected welcome – she had been so looking forward to seeing Sam. 'My husband arranged this?'

He nodded, glancing at his clipboard. 'Sam Becker.'

Anna nodded. Sam must have been called into work.

The man reached out for her case. 'Let me take this for you.'

Anna fought the urge to refuse. She didn't really want to relinquish it for some reason.

'We're right outside the door,' he said as they walked through the hall and out through the main doors. 'Over there.'

He pointed towards a white BMW just a few yards away.

While the man loaded her case into the boot, Anna climbed in the back, still thinking of her lost phone.

Sam tried Anna's mobile as the lift descended, panic rising as the call went straight to the answer service. Her flight should have landed by now, and she would have switched the phone on, surely. He waited impatiently as the lift made its way down to the second floor. He ran through the opening doors and along to Louisa's office. She wasn't there, so he headed for the consultation rooms. This wasn't time for protocol, so he knocked on the first door and opened it before hearing a response.

Louisa was sitting there, alone and crying. The sight threw Sam for a second as he just stood there, not knowing how to react.

She dabbed her eyes, embarrassed. 'Sam. How did it go? I didn't think it would be over so—'

'I think something terrible might have happened to Anna,' Sam interrupted. He handed his phone to her. 'I got this message, sent from your stolen phone.'

I have your wife. She smells sweet. Like your sister. Call the police, she dies too.

Louisa brought a hand to her mouth. 'Oh my God.' She looked up at Sam. 'Could they be making this up?'

Sam shook his head, fighting back the panic. 'I can't get through to her, Louisa. Her flight was supposed to have landed twenty minutes ago.'

'Maybe it's delayed,' Louisa said, standing up. 'Can you check?'

Sam was already moving out of the door. 'The Internet.'

They hurried over to Louisa's office and logged on to the Heathrow airport website. As Sam tried Anna's phone again, Louisa pulled up the list of arrivals.

'It's there,' Sam said, pointing at a flight. 'It landed on time.'

He put a hand to his head, trying to think.

'This person might still be bluffing,' Louisa said. 'Just saying he has Anna to scare you.'

'The taxi,' Sam said. He found the company's number in his contacts list and dialled, hoping to God that they were going to be the ones to banish his growing fears.

'Hi, my name's Sam Becker, and I booked a taxi to collect my wife, Anna Becker, from Heathrow Airport. I was just checking that she was picked up okay.'

'One moment,' the operator replied. 'Anna Becker, you said?'

'Yes.'

There was a brief, painful silence. 'And you booked the taxi, did you say?'

'Yes,' Sam said. *Please let it be good news.* 'This morning.'

'We did have your booking, but it was cancelled shortly afterwards.'

Sam's world spun. 'What? Who by?'

Louisa looked on.

'According to our paperwork, you cancelled it.'

'No,' Sam stated, the shock hitting him that this wasn't just a bluff – someone had Anna. 'I didn't.'

'Well, that's what is down here, I'm afraid.'

Sam exchanged a worried glance with Louisa. 'So you're saying that you didn't send a taxi to collect my wife?'

'No, I'm afraid not.'

Sam cut the call. His hands, and the phone receiver, were soaked in sweat. He couldn't believe this was happening. 'Louisa, someone cancelled Anna's taxi.'

'Sam, call the police.'

'I can't,' he replied, 'you saw what the message said, no police.' He moved to the door.

Louisa pulled Sam back as he went to exit. 'Where are you going?'

'To the airport.'

'But if something has already happened—'

'Then I'm too late. But I have to try.'

It took just over an hour to reach the airport. Sam spent the journey fighting horrific images of Anna being held captive by whatever psychopath might have her. On the way to the car, he had tried their home number, just in case Anna had found another way back, but the call had rung through. Another call to her mobile was unsuccessful.

But still he clung on desperately to the hope that this was all one cruel, sick joke.

He parked up in the drop-off zone and ran through to the arrivals hall to be met by the crowds meeting and greeting incomers from all over the world. After a few minutes of frantic searching, he decided to try the information desk for the airline.

'Is there any way to check whether my wife landed on the flight from Bangladesh?'

'We can,' the woman behind the desk answered, 'but it will take some time. If you're looking for her, we can arrange to put out an announcement.'

'That would be great, thanks.'

Two minutes later the announcement echoed out across the arrivals hall. Sam prayed that Anna would appear, smiling in that way that always got to him. She would explain that there had been a problem on landing, that she'd been delayed through customs. And then they would hold one another and the nightmare would end. But three minutes after that, Anna hadn't arrived at the information desk as requested.

It was then the call came.

'That will be the last public announcement you make about your wife,' the caller said, in a voice deepened and disguised by some kind of distortion device.

Sam gripped the phone tight, turning away from the information desk, his heart pumping hard. 'Who are you? Where's my wife?'

'No questions and no police. Or your wife dies.'

Again that terrifying threat. 'Please, just let her go.'

And then, a split second before the line went dead, Sam heard something that confirmed with heartbreaking certainty that this was all so very real.

Anna's cry for help.

PART THREE

PART THREE

Chapter Thirty-Three

S am brought the phone down from his ear. His arm was
shaking and his head reeling as the terrifying echo of Anna's
scream reverberated through his head.

'No, please no. Please, God, this can't be happening.'

Paralysed by fear, he scanned the arrivals hall, searching desperately for his wife. But there was no sign of her.

What the hell was he going to do?

He bit down hard on his lip to stop himself from losing it totally.

This couldn't be happening.

He punched in the speed dial for Louisa's office number, hardly able to hit the right key, his hand was shaking so much. He didn't know what he was going to do if Louisa did answer, or how she could help, but he just needed someone who understood, and there was no one who understood more than her.

He raised the phone to his ear, his eyes continuing the sweep across the hall in the vain hope that Anna would appear, smiling and safe. But among the crowds, the families, the businessmen, the airport staff, there was no sign of her. 'Please, Louisa, please be there.'

The call rang through. She would probably be in consultations, possibly for the next hour or so. But maybe she would have her mobile on.

He dialled that number. 'Pick up, Louisa, please pick up the phone.'

After a dozen or so rings, it cut through to the answer machine. 'Louisa, it's Sam. Call me as soon as you get this message, please – just call me.'

Sam cut off the call, took one last look around the arrivals hall and, gripping the phone like a relay baton, sprinted out of the terminal building, hurrying towards the car. As he raced across the road, he spotted two heavily armed police officers just off to his left. His first instinct was to run straight over and tell them everything. They would know what to do.

He slowed to a stop. They could put out an alert across the airport and access security cameras to track Anna and whoever had taken her.

But the man on the phone had been clear. No police. Or Anna would die.

It could be a bluff. Was he willing to risk it?

Sam watched the two officers. One turned and their eyes met briefly. In that instant he decided.

Sam fought the urge to approach them and instead continued towards the nearby car. Reaching the vehicle, he threw open the door and jumped inside. But as he raced to turn on the ignition, he caught a glimpse of himself in the rear-view mirror and reality hit.

Someone had Anna and was threatening to kill her. He didn't know who, or why. What the hell was he going to do?

'Christ.' Sam put a hand to his head and sat back in the seat, slowing his breath, trying to think through his options. He pulled out his mobile again and dialled Paul Cullen's number. Cullen picked up on the second ring.

'Sam, what can I do for you?'

Sam went to speak, fighting with the conflicting voices in his head. One begged him to tell Paul Cullen everything. He felt he could trust him. But the cautionary voice won out – what if the person who had Anna was watching or listening to him right now? He struggled to maintain an even tone of voice. 'Hi. I was just wondering if there's been any news on the case.'

'Afraid not,' Cullen replied. 'But I've got some guys looking at that audio clip, Sam, seeing if they can clean it up.'

'Good,' Sam said, thinking about Anna. 'That's good.'

'You okay, Sam?'

Sam snapped back to the situation. 'Yeah, fine. I'm fine.'

'Are you sure?'

'Yeah, I'm okay,' Sam lied, fighting back tears of frustration and fear.

'I promise you, Sam,' Cullen said, 'I'll do everything in my power to get to the bottom of this. And as soon as I do, you'll be one of the first to know.'

'Thanks.'

Sam drove back to the flat with the phone on the front passenger seat, all the time simultaneously hoping for and dreading another call from the person who had Anna. But the mobile remained silent. The drive seemed to take forever, and he didn't know what he was going to do when he reached home. He parked up and entered the house, rushing into the living room, clinging to the desperate hope that Anna would be sitting on the sofa waiting for him.

She wasn't there.

He moved into the hallway and checked the answer machine. There was one message. It was from Professor Khan, wanting to know how he was. He didn't mention anything about Sam having walked off before the panel had given their verdict. And he didn't reveal the outcome of the disciplinary hearing. He just sounded concerned. So much so that for a second Sam considered calling the Professor and telling him everything. Professor Khan was a great mind, a clear thinker who could offer valuable advice.

Then the doorbell rang.

Sam's body stiffened as the echo of the bell faded. He moved over to the window to try and see who was there. But whoever was there must have been stood right up to the door and he couldn't see around the porch wall. He grabbed the nearest object at hand, a decorative crystal candlestick that had been bought for their wedding, and edged out into the corridor. He moved towards the door, and just as he reached for the handle, the person on the other side pressed the doorbell again. He gripped the candlestick and spoke through the door. 'Who is it?'

'It's Doug.'

Immediately Sam relaxed and opened the door. Doug, dressed in grey jogging bottoms and T-shirt, smiled warmly. He was carrying a small Jiffy-bag package down by his side. 'Thought I'd come and see how you are.'

'It's good to see you, Doug.'

Doug followed Sam into the lounge, and they sat down.

'I heard about what happened,' Doug said. 'Are you okay?'

For a moment Sam thought he meant with Anna, but then realised he was talking about the panel. 'I haven't even thought about it.'

'I'm afraid it's got around most of the hospital, Chinese-Whispers style. I heard from one of the nurses in paediatrics. By the time the story got to me, you'd told Carla where to stick the job and had resigned on the spot. Obviously, I knew that was a load of rubbish, so I got the real story from your solicitor.'

The whole hospital was talking about him, his career and reputation in ruins. But Sam didn't care about that any more. 'So you haven't spoken to Louisa?'

'No,' Doug replied. 'I tried to, but she wasn't around; I looked for her everywhere. So as soon as I could, I thought I'd come and see how you are – ran all the way from the hospital. You look terrible, mate.'

'I feel terrible,' Sam replied.

'What happened? Ed Stansfield said there was some kind of family emergency.'

Sam put a hand to his head, wondering how to play this. He didn't know if he was capable of vocalising the situation. It was as if just by telling someone would somehow make it more real – less likely that it was all a terrible mistake.

'What is it?' Doug said, his face darkening. 'Has something happened to Anna?'

Sam nodded.

'My God, Sam, what's happened?'

'Someone's taken her,' Sam said, hardly able to speak the words.

Doug looked incredulous, as if it was some kind of sick joke. 'Taken her? What . . . I don't understand.'

Sam forced out more information, the words catching in his throat like sharp barbs. 'Someone picked Anna up at the airport, and they've taken her. They're holding her somewhere and threatening to kill her.'

'My God, Sam. You're not joking, are you?'

'I wish it was a joke,' Sam replied, tears welling up and spilling down his cheeks. 'But it's not. It's not a joke, it's totally serious.' He regained his composure, but his head began pounding with the strain of holding it all together. 'Someone's taken Anna.'

'But who? Why?'

'I don't know. Someone wants me to suffer; they're playing games with me, Doug.'

Doug looked just as incredulous. 'What?'

'They murdered Cathy, set up the train crash, planted the drugs in my locker and now they've got Anna.'

'You're saying that this is all connected with your sister's murder?'

Sam nodded, getting to his feet and moving towards the computer.

'This just seems unbelievable, Sam,' Doug said as Sam booted up the computer.

Sam waited for the computer to load. 'The train crash was set up. It wasn't a suicide at all. And I think it was all meant for me.' He clicked on the audio file. 'Listen to this.'

Doug moved towards the computer and listened intently.

'What can you hear?' Sam asked.

'Your voice,' Doug replied without hesitation.

'And?'

'A girl's voice.'

'The girl who ran out in front of my car. The girl who said she was Alison Ainsley, but wasn't.'

Doug looked puzzled. 'How did you get this?'

'I was emailed the link.'

Doug turned to Sam. 'Sam, this is crazy, just crazy.'

'But it's happening.'

Doug was still trying to come to terms with the situation. 'You said they also murdered Cathy?'

'That's what the person implied.'

'But what about Richard Friedman? He had Cathy's necklace. He *admitted* murdering her.'

'I don't know. But it's all connected. All of it. And they've now got Anna.'

'But who?' Doug scrutinized Sam for a sign. 'You think this is Marcus Johnson?'

Doug had read his mind. There was, after all, only one likely suspect. But there was no evidence. 'Maybe.'

'What have you told the police?'

'Nothing. I haven't called them.'

'What? Why?'

'Because this person said he'd kill Anna if I did.'

'My God. Then what are you going to do? I mean, what does this person want?'

'I don't know, Doug, I just don't know. I'll just have to wait until he contacts me again.'

Suddenly Doug's face registered something. He moved back towards the sofa.

'What is it?'

Doug returned with the Jiffy-bag package. 'This was in your pigeon hole. I assumed it might be to do with the investigation, but . . .'

Sam cradled the package. 'This wasn't there before I went up to the board.' He ripped open the tape, pulling out a note. Sam tipped up the bag, and a ring fell out into his palm. It was Anna's engagement ring. Tied around it was a lock of strawberry-blonde hair. It could have been anyone's. But Sam knew it was Cathy's. And then, reaching into the bag, sickened to the core, he found something else.

A photograph of Cathy, smiling on the small dance floor, drink in hand, caught up in the moment.

And on the back, a handwritten note.

Young and sweet. Never seventeen.

Sam had never felt such rage.

Chapter Thirty-Four

What is it, Sam?'

Sam slipped the photograph into his back pocket and started towards the door. 'He's got her – he's got Anna.'

Doug followed him. 'Who has?'

Sam grabbed his coat as he reached the hallway. The anger was burning so intensely. All along it had been him. He'd looked him in the eye, pleading his innocence, asking for his trust. And he'd really started to believe, had wanted to believe. 'Marcus.'

Doug moved between Sam and the door, worried. 'What are you doing, Sam?'

'Going to get my wife back.'

Doug put out a hand as Sam approached. 'You can't just go around there, Sam. Call the police.'

Sam shook his head. 'No, I can't.'

'You can, Sam. Do it now, call the police. You really think it's the best thing for you to go charging around there like some super-hero? You don't know what the hell could happen. He's probably waiting for you – this could be his plan, to get you around there.'

Sam thought about that. Doug had a point. Why else would Marcus make it so obvious? And then it became clear – if Sam wanted to see Anna again, he would have to give Marcus what he wanted, he would have to play the game.

'I have to go,' Sam stated. He went to move past Doug, who held firm his position.

'This is crazy, Sam.'

'I know,' Sam admitted. 'It's all crazy. But I've got no choice. Now let me go.'

'Then I'm coming too,' Doug announced. 'I'm not letting you go there on your own – no way.'

Sam nodded. 'Thanks.'

<hr/>

'You know this is crazy,' Doug repeated as they drove across the capital in darkness towards South London. 'Absolutely crazy.'

Sam nodded as he stopped at a red light. It took all his self-control not to plant his foot down hard on the accelerator and burn rubber, such was his desire to reach their destination.

'I don't think Claire believed me. I'm a terrible liar,' Doug continued, having just explained to his wife that there was a last-minute meeting at the hospital, so he wouldn't be home for dinner. 'Not that it's important right now.'

Sam nodded, not really listening to his friend. He was too busy thinking through what he was going to do once he reached Marcus's flat. The more he considered it, the more he thought about what could go wrong. Marcus was the one in control here. Was he just handing Marcus everything on a plate? Maybe now was the time to tell the police.

'So are you going to tell me what was in the bag?' Doug asked.

Sam pushed away thoughts of the police. He couldn't risk it. He didn't want to risk it. 'The ring is Anna's engagement ring, with Cathy's hair wrapped around it.'

'Christ. And the photograph?'

Sam reached behind him and pulled out the photograph from his back pocket, handing it to Doug. 'A photograph of Cathy – it was taken the night before she was murdered.'

'Really?' Doug looked at the note on the back. 'You sure?'

'I know who took the photograph. I was standing by him when he took it.'

Doug looked stunned. 'Marcus Johnson?'

Sam nodded. 'He took it with his Polaroid camera. The night before Cathy was killed – we were in the clubhouse on the campsite. It had a bar and dance floor. They started playing ABBA and Cathy jumped up and started dancing like there was no tomorrow.'

'She seems so carefree, so happy,' Doug said, looking again at the photo.

Sam nodded.

Doug re-read the message. 'What a sicko.'

'Yes, sick.'

Twenty minutes later they slowed to a stop.

'We'll stop here,' Sam said. 'Marcus's flat is just around the corner. I don't want to go any nearer in case he sees us.'

Doug nodded. A new tension had descended during the final few minutes of the journey as the reality of the situation hit hard.

Sam turned to Doug, who looked genuinely fearful. 'I want you to wait here.'

'No, I'm going with you.'

'I need you to wait here,' Sam said, 'in case anything goes wrong. If I'm not back in ten minutes, I want you to call the police. Tell them everything.'

'But—'

'And if Marcus is watching, I don't want to spook him by his seeing you there too. He wants to see just me.'

'But you don't know what he'll do to you. If he's killed before—'

'He could have done it before now,' Sam said, 'when I was in his flat. I don't think that's what he wants.'

'You can't be sure, though.'

'I know. But I'm just going to have to take the chance.'

'Sam,' Doug said, 'we've known each other for a long time, and I really trust your judgement – I do. But this just seems mad, really mad. Are you sure about this? Are you sure we shouldn't just call the police now?'

'I'm sure,' Sam lied. In fact, he wasn't sure at all, but he had made his decision.

'Okay,' Doug conceded, but not looking happy about it. 'I'll wait here. But if I don't hear anything from you in exactly ten minutes, I call the police.'

'I expect it.'

Sam climbed out of the car, leaning in for one last word to Doug, who looked sick with worry. 'I have my mobile with your number on speed dial. If I get into trouble, I'll call. So be ready.'

Doug nodded. 'Please, Sam, be careful.'

Sam strode across the concrete area towards the tower block, running through various scenarios, trying to push any negative thoughts from his mind. He glanced up at the tower as he approached the entrance, trying to pick out Marcus's flat. He scanned across the third floor, trying to remember how many flats along it was – but he couldn't remember exactly. And none of the windows gave anything away – there was no shadowy figure watching him from above, or at least no one he could see.

He reached the entrance and made for the staircase, making light work of the concrete steps. He didn't feel nervous or afraid.

Instead, anger remained the dominant emotion, driving him on. Anger that this man, his onetime friend, had once again sought to hurt those closest to him.

He emerged onto the third floor and made straight for Marcus's door. This time he knew exactly where he was going. He knocked three times as the anger rose within him, priming him for what was to come. He heard movement from within the flat, and then the door opened.

Sam launched himself at Marcus, taking him by total surprise and knocking him off balance as they both fell into the flat. He kicked the door shut as he held Marcus firmly by the collar and dragged him over to the sofa.

Marcus was in total shock, his face contorted. 'Sam, what the hell are you doing?'

Sam held him down on the sofa, using all of his weight to subdue him. 'Where's my wife?'

'What? Your wife, I don't know what—'

'Tell me where she is,' Sam demanded, tightening his grip.

Marcus's face reddened as the blood welled up. 'Sam, I don't know what you're—'

'Tell me, damn it,' Sam shouted. 'What have you done with her?'

'I don't know what you're . . . talking about,' Marcus strained to say through the constriction that Sam was applying.

Sam reached back and pulled out the photograph, thrusting it in Marcus's face. 'You remember this?'

Marcus looked at the photograph, his eyes searching its every detail. 'I . . . don't . . . understand.'

'You took this, remember?'

'How . . . did . . . you . . . get . . . it?'

Sam pressed down harder, as if he could physically force the truth from within him. 'Stop playing these sick games, Marcus.'

'You're . . . really . . . hurting . . . me, Sam.'

Suddenly, Marcus found room for manoeuvre, thrusting his right fist deep into Sam's solar plexus. The pain was intense, and Sam folded, releasing his grip. Within seconds Marcus was on top of him, pressing his knees into Sam's arms. Sam waited for the next blow, but it didn't come. Instead Marcus just held him there, breathing heavily.

Sam tried to move.

'Don't fight me, Sam,' Marcus gasped. 'I don't want to hurt you.'

'If you've hurt Anna—'

Marcus shook his head in anger and frustration. 'For Chrissake, I haven't got your wife. Where did you get the photo?'

'Don't pretend you don't know.'

'I don't know, Sam,' said Marcus, his voice raised. 'Where did you get it from?'

'It's your photo. You sent it.'

'What? I haven't seen that photograph for over fifteen years. I gave it to Cathy that night on the dunes. It was the last thing I ever gave her . . .' Marcus trailed off but his grip remained firm. He seemed to snap back from his thoughts. 'You really think I did this?'

Sam said nothing.

'You still don't believe me, Sam, do you?' Marcus said, tightening his grip. 'After all these years, you still can't bring yourself to believe me. You can't believe me that I didn't kill Cathy.'

Sam still remained silent.

'Your first reaction was to assume it was me. You were sure that it was me. You came around here without any doubts.'

'I just want to find my wife,' Sam said, torn about whether or not to believe him. Was this just another part of his game, or was he really telling the truth? 'If you have her, Marcus, then please let her go.'

'Sam, please, just believe me. I had nothing to do with Cathy's death, and I don't know what has happened to your wife.'

'I don't know what to believe.'

Marcus softened. 'When did she go missing?'

'About three o'clock today.'

'It wasn't anything to do with me. I swear it, Sam. Please, believe me.'

'I want to.'

'He couldn't have done it,' a familiar voice said from behind. Sam, amazed, turned to see Louisa emerging from the bathroom. 'He's been with me all afternoon.'

Chapter Thirty-Five

'You've been with him?' Sam said, sitting up as Marcus climbed off him.

Louisa nodded as she edged towards him. 'I came over here just after you left for the airport.' She glanced at Marcus, who simply nodded. 'Marcus couldn't have had anything to do with it, Sam. I really believe that.'

Sam looked down to his left, his chest feeling as if it were being crushed with the strain. This changed everything. Suddenly, there was no one to suspect, no one to blame and no way to find Anna.

'Sam, I want to explain,' Louisa continued, taking a seat next to him.

'I just want my wife back,' Sam replied as his stomach turned in knots.

'I know, I know.' There was an uncomfortable pause. 'What happened?'

Sam looked up at her. 'You didn't get my call? I left a message.'

'I left my mobile at work by mistake,' she explained. 'In my desk drawer.'

'But you didn't call to find out what had happened,' Sam stated.

Louisa reddened. 'I was over here with Marcus before I realised I didn't have my phone with me, and I didn't know your mobile number.'

'It doesn't matter,' Sam dismissed.

'I called your home phone, but there wasn't an answer. I'm so sorry, Sam.'

Sam refrained from saying what he really thought: that he felt genuinely betrayed by one of the few people he truly trusted. Instead, he held his tongue, knowing that to say such a thing would hurt Louisa deeply. 'Anna wasn't at the airport when I got there. Someone's got her, Louisa – the person who killed Cathy. I got a call warning me not to go to the police, and I heard Anna scream. Then this was left in my pigeon hole.'

He brought out Anna's engagement ring, still with the blonde hair wrapped around it.

Louisa took it from him. She looked at Sam with a mixture of disgust and amazement. 'Cathy's hair?'

Sam nodded. 'And Anna's ring.'

Louisa looked across at Marcus, gesturing towards the photograph he was still holding. 'And the photo.'

Marcus handed it to her. She studied it, front and back. 'My God, Sam, I remember this. I remember it so well. We were on the dance floor . . . the night before she died.'

'I have to find who did this,' Sam said, watching as Louisa scrutinised the photograph once more. 'Before they hurt Anna.'

'Do you still think I'm behind all this, Sam?' Marcus asked. 'Do you think I have your wife? Do you think I killed Cathy?'

Sam looked at him but didn't answer. Instead, he turned to Louisa – a thought had just occurred to him. 'If you think Marcus hasn't got anything to do with it, why did you come straight over here?'

'Because he is part of this, Sam, but not like you think. Whoever's doing this, whoever has Anna and whoever killed Cathy, is targeting all of us. We're in this together, and we need to work together.'

'You really believe that?'

'Totally,' she replied. 'Marcus didn't kill Cathy – he didn't do any of this, I just know he didn't. I've never been as sure of anything in my whole life, Sam.'

'How can you be so sure?'

'Trust,' Marcus said.

Suddenly Sam realised. 'You've seen him before today, haven't you?'

Louisa nodded. 'We've been meeting for the past few weeks.'

Sam shook his head and smiled ruefully. 'All this time, and you didn't tell me. All the things we discussed, and you just kept quiet.'

'I wanted to tell you, Sam – believe me I did. I nearly told you, but I just couldn't find the words.'

'Couldn't find the words?' It was such a cliché.

'No, I couldn't. I was going to tell you, but then when all the strange things started happening, the phone calls and the notes and you starting talking about Marcus maybe being involved, it just got harder.'

Another suspicion rose. 'Have you two been in touch since the very beginning, since the trial?'

'No, Sam, I swear. Just these last few weeks – I hadn't seen or spoken to Marcus since the trial, just like you. But a few weeks ago I got a call from Marcus's parents—'

'They were worried about me and thought I could do with a friend,' Marcus interjected. 'I didn't ask them to do it, but I was glad they did. Louisa's been a big help for me. I'd probably have gone crazy without her support.'

'They said Marcus had just moved down to London,' Louisa continued, 'and that they were worried about him being here on his own after what had happened since he got out of prison and went back home. He'd been attacked, Sam. The people there, they wouldn't let him get on with his life.'

Sam looked across at Marcus, who sat impassively, his arms folded across his chest.

'He was forced to move out of the area. That's why he came to London.'

'Why did his parents call you?'

'You know our parents were always good friends. They knew I was working down here and thought I could help.'

It didn't add up. 'But why would you agree to see him? You thought he killed Cathy, just like I did. Why would you meet with the person who you thought killed your best friend?'

Louisa hesitated just long enough. 'I . . .'

Suddenly for Sam it all became clear. 'You didn't think he'd killed Cathy, did you?' Just like his mother, she had kept this from him for all this time.

Louisa looked away, her eyes glistening with tears. 'I didn't know what to believe, Sam. At one time, yes, I thought Marcus had done it, long ago, but then – I don't know – I wasn't so sure any more. I just wanted to do the right thing. And I wanted to find out the truth.'

Sam ran a hand along his face. 'It was only ever me, wasn't it? I was the only one not to see it. All these years, the real murderer has been out there, free. And now he's got Anna.'

'Someone's playing with us all, Sam,' Marcus said. 'And I want to find out who it is just as much as you do. This person is trying to hurt us. We've got to start working together and trusting each other.'

Sam looked across. 'Is it really that easy after everything that's happened?'

'We haven't got a choice,' Marcus replied. 'Look, I'm only going to say this one more time, but here goes.' He looked straight at

Sam. 'I didn't kill Cathy. I did lie to you, Sam, but only about our relationship. And yes, I do feel bitter about what happened – really bitter. I went through fifteen years of hell in prison. But I'm still here, and if I thought it would bring Cathy back, I'd do it all again. We were young, but I loved her, just like you and Louisa did. Please, believe me.'

Sam considered Marcus's words. 'I believe you.' He was pretty sure that he meant what he said, but it still sounded strange to say it.

'So where do we go from here?' Louisa asked. 'Have you contacted the police?'

Sam shook his head.

'Why not?'

'I told you, the person said he'd hurt Anna if I involved him.'

Louisa didn't look convinced. 'So what are you going to do?'

'I'm not saying that I won't involve the police. But right at this moment, I just don't think I can risk it. I have to do something, though.'

'Then what?'

Sam turned to her. 'Louisa, I need a massive favour from you – Richard Friedman's address.'

Louisa looked puzzled.

'You said he lived with his sister,' Sam explained. 'I need to talk with her, try to understand more about how he fits into this – how he got Cathy's locket. Maybe there will be something in the house that might explain things.'

'But won't the police be doing that kind of thing?'

'Maybe, maybe not, but I've got to do something, Louisa. I can't just wait for something to happen. And it seems that whoever has got Anna wants me to play the game. Engaging with this person might be the best chance I have of getting Anna back safe.'

'If the hospital finds out I've shared patient details, I could lose my job.'

271

'I know,' Sam replied. 'That's why you're not going to give me his details.'

'I don't understand.'

'I'm going to take them. Have you got your office keys with you?'

'Yes, but if someone sees you doing this, looking through confidential records, you'll never work as a surgeon again. Your career will be over.'

Sam shrugged. 'If that's what it takes.'

'I'll do it,' Marcus said. 'Give me the keys, tell me where to find his file, and I'll go in there and get his address. I've got nothing to lose.'

Sam shook his head. 'I can't ask you to do that.'

'Please, let me,' Marcus replied. 'I want to do it.'

'You're both crazy,' Louisa said. 'I'll get you his address.'

Shirley Ainsley paused by the doorway of the spare room. The three children were sleeping downstairs. She felt sick to her stomach, fearing imminent confirmation that her husband had fallen back into the nightmare of alcohol abuse from which he had emerged ten years ago. Back then it had been another traumatic event – the death of his younger brother from a heart attack at the age of just forty-five. The grief had led to depression – and drinking. It was to be another two years before he came back to her. Shirley blamed herself for letting things get out of control at the beginning. But this time would be different. This time she was determined to tackle the problem head-on, no matter how painful it might be.

Eric had left the house ten minutes ago, having spent just half an hour in her company since coming home from work. Barely enough time to eat his evening meal. He had hardly spoken in their time together, save for muttering that he was off to see some work colleagues.

Shirley hadn't believed him.

He had made his way straight upstairs upon his arrival home, taking his work bag up with him. He had come back down, saying that he had desperately needed the toilet, and indeed she had heard the flush. But his breath smelt of alcohol. And from the creaking of the floorboards above, Shirley was pretty sure that Eric had also been doing something in the spare room. Hiding drink, she suspected.

She looked around the room. Nothing seemed to be out of place. She moved around, pulling out each drawer in the cabinet and running her hands through the piles of ageing underwear and socks – items that should have been thrown away long ago.

She found nothing – no hidden bottles of whisky or vodka.

Then she turned to the bed. It was the last place. She crouched down at its base, and reached for the valance, slowly pulling it back. Peering underneath she used the small torch she had brought from the kitchen to sweep across the darkness. The space was empty. But then, just as she was bringing the torch out, something caught her eye – a cut in the fabric across the roof of the bed's base. She slipped her hand inside and it met an object, balanced on the wooden slats that ran along the underneath of the bed.

She pulled out a brown, battered leather bag. She'd never seen it before. It felt too light to contain bottles of alcohol. She looked at it for a few seconds, fearing where all this was leading. How would she approach Eric, and how would he react to knowing she had gone snooping like this?

But she would deal with that later.

She pulled back the zipper and gasped.

This was much more serious than she had ever imagined.

Chapter Thirty-Six

Sam finally gave up on sleep at 4 a.m. For hours he'd struggled to find rest in a shallow slumber. His body just wouldn't relax. He reached the realisation that he just didn't want to sleep. Sleep was about rest and relaxation, but that was the last thing he wanted to do while Anna was still missing.

He paced around the flat for a few minutes, checking his mobile and home phone for any messages, texts or missed calls. There was nothing. He made himself a strong coffee and then booted up the computer. He checked his email, just as he had done on returning from Marcus's some five hours ago. But there was nothing new there either. Now he craved what only yesterday he'd dreaded – contact from this sick individual.

He listened again intently to the audio of the train crash, eyes closed, hoping that something would rise from the recording that would help to explain all this. But all the recording served to do was to transport him back to that horrific event. It set his skin on edge, listening again to the girl's desperate cries over the noise of the oncoming train.

He thought back to what Louisa had said about telling the police. Was he wrong in not telling them? It hadn't been an easy decision, and it certainly didn't feel comfortable. Would the person who had Anna find out if he did tell the police? It all depended on how closely he was being watched.

He slid across a pad of paper and wrote out his sister's name in the centre of the blank page. Around that he wrote several other names: Jane Ainsley, Shirley Ainsley, Alison Ainsley, girl at scene of train crash (drowned), Richard Friedman, Marcus Johnson, Louisa, Sam, Anna. And then two more names: Vincent McGuire, boyfriend of Jane Ainsley, and the girl watching from the bridge. Between those names he wrote the words: 'Cathy's murder, train crash, drowned girl, drugs in locker, Anna's kidnap, Richard Friedman's suicide'.

He stared at the page until his head throbbed. He underlined Richard Friedman's name three times. He still seemed the key to this. He'd had Cathy's necklace. He said he'd killed her, whether that was now true or not. Sam flicked on the stereo and selected Coldplay's 'Fix You' from the hard drive: one of Anna's favourite songs. He sat back, closed his eyes and could almost feel his wife's warming breath on his neck. It made him feel like crying, but he needed to be strong.

He woke with his head flat against the computer desk, the piece of paper stuck to his cheek. He grimaced from the pain in his neck as he pulled himself upright. Sunshine bathed the room in an early morning hue of yellow. He looked at the clock. Just after eight. He might not have wanted to sleep, but he had needed it.

He dressed quickly before travelling over to the hospital. As promised, Louisa was waiting for him in the far corner of the cafeteria. But unexpectedly, Marcus was with her. Sam nodded a hello to him as he sat down, uncomfortable with his presence. Although he no longer believed Marcus was behind all this, it didn't necessarily mean he wanted him so close this soon.

Marcus seemed to pick up on his unease. 'Hope you don't mind me being here. I can leave if you like.'

'It's okay,' Sam said.

'Any more news?' Louisa asked.

'Nothing,' Sam replied. 'Total silence.'

Louisa smiled sadly. She then reached into her bag and slid a piece of paper across the table. 'I hope this helps. I really do.'

Sam pulled it up. Richard Friedman's address. He lived in the London borough of Hackney, in the northeast of the city. 'Thanks,' he said, recognising Louisa's discomfort with all this. 'It means a lot.'

Louisa nodded. 'Just don't do anything silly, Sam.'

'I won't.'

She glanced at her watch. 'I've got to go. My first appointment is in five minutes. Let me know what happens.'

Marcus remained seated as Louisa walked away. 'She really cares for you.'

'I know,' Sam replied.

'She really didn't enjoy keeping it a secret, you know, that we were seeing each other.'

Sam just stared down at Richard Friedman's address.

Marcus continued. 'She didn't want to hurt you. She wanted to help me, but she felt as though she was betraying you.'

Sam nodded. 'I know she did it for the right reasons. She always does do things for the right reasons.'

'I've missed you both,' Marcus revealed. His face flushed with embarrassment that the words had sprung out. 'We were all such good friends.'

'I know,' Sam agreed. 'I never stopped missing our friendship.'

Marcus looked surprised. 'Even though you thought I'd killed Cathy?'

'I'm not saying I wanted to be your friend, but I did miss our friendship.'

'And now?'

'At the moment I can't think any further than getting Anna back.'

'Of course.'

'I'd better go,' Sam announced, looking once more at the address. A short tube trip and he would be there.

'Let me come with you,' Marcus said.

'No,' Sam replied, without hesitation.

'Please, Sam.'

Sam shook his head and got up from the chair, determined to do this alone. 'I want to do this on my own, Marcus. It's nothing personal.'

'Please, Sam, say yes,' Marcus pleaded. 'That's why I came here this morning. I want to help. You need someone to help you with this.'

'I'm sorry. I'll let you know what happens.'

Sam turned and walked away, feeling a pang of guilt that he'd shut out Marcus so cruelly. But as much as he did believe that Marcus was innocent, it was still easier not to be around him. Marcus brought back too many bad, hurtful memories. Maybe one day that would change, and things could go back to being the way they were – two friends together, there for each other, nothing in between them.

But today was not that day.

Marcus caught up with Sam just as he'd exited the main doors.

'Sam, wait a minute.'

Sam stopped and turned around to see Marcus jogging up to him.

'Sam, why are you doing this?'

'Doing what?' Sam said, aware that there were colleagues – nurses mainly – within earshot. He guided Marcus away from the groups who were mingling at the entrance of the hospital.

'Shutting me out, pushing me away.'

'I just think it's best if I go alone. Why can't you just accept my decision?'

'Because I need to do this as much as you do.'

'Need to do what?'

'I need to redeem myself, Sam. I need to put things right.'

'I don't understand.'

'I didn't kill Cathy, but it doesn't mean that I don't blame myself for what happened. I left her, Sam, on her own, on those sand dunes.'

'You said you were drunk, that you didn't remember anything.'

'I was drunk, and I don't remember anything, Sam, but I still left her alone. If I hadn't drunk so much, I'd never have just walked off, and Cathy would probably be alive today.'

'You don't know that.'

'I do, Sam, I do. And I know you understand. You feel the same. I can see it in your eyes whenever Cathy's name is mentioned. I can see the guilt. You blame yourself, just like I blame myself.'

'Cathy was my responsibility on that trip,' Sam said, feeling the pain of his regret just as much as the day she died. 'She was my little sister. I'm the one who persuaded my dad to let her go – I promised to look after her. So yes, I do blame myself.'

'Then we're both in this for the same reason, Sam. We want to make amends. We want to find out who's behind all this. We want to do this for Cathy.'

Sam paused, thinking. All these years later, and Marcus still knew how to push the right buttons.

'Please, Sam, I really need to do this. For Cathy and for myself. Please let me come with you.'

Sam examined Marcus's face. It was like looking in a mirror. 'Okay, let's go.'

Sam and Marcus stood in front of the house, a Georgian terraced property. Its painted white bricks contrasted markedly with the natural dark brown of the rest of the row. Sam had expected something run-down, reflective of a man in mental torment, but the windows top and bottom were adorned with flowers, and it all looked thoroughly presentable. He glanced at Marcus to indicate that now was the time. They hadn't spoken much during the journey to Hackney, both content to mull over the situation in their own heads. But they had talked briefly of a strategy for approaching Richard Friedman's sister, Victoria. Both had agreed that it wouldn't be easy.

Sam stepped forward and knocked three times. It was more than possible that she wouldn't be at home. But just a few seconds later someone approached the door.

'Can I help you?'

The woman, unsmiling, peering at them over half-moon glasses, resembled an old-style school headmistress, with silver-grey hair tied back in a tight bun that seemed to pull her face taut. She wore a uniform-like outfit of dark blue blouse and skirt.

'Hi. My name's Sam Becker.'

There was no discernible emotional reaction, her face remaining serious, business-like even. 'Victoria Friedman. You'd better come in,' she said, in impeccable Queen's English.

Sam and Marcus followed Victoria through the house. The place was immaculate, furnished with antiques, including an impressive grandfather clock in the hallway. The burgundy carpet was thick and luxurious.

They reached the living room.

'Please, do take a seat. Would you like a cup of tea?'

Both Sam and Marcus declined as they sat down on the high-backed sofa. It looked like the kind of furniture that usually resided in a stately home with security ropes around it.

'So,' said Victoria as she sat on the chair opposite, 'how can I help you?'

Sam spoke first. He and Marcus had agreed that, as far as possible, he would do the talking. 'I wanted to talk to you about your brother.'

'Well, I gathered as much as that,' she shot back.

'Specifically about what he said to me about my sister.'

'That he murdered her?'

Sam nodded.

'My brother couldn't have killed your sister,' she replied. 'He could never have killed anyone. He was the gentlest man I've ever met.'

'But he said he'd killed my sister, and he had her necklace.'

Victoria didn't register any surprise. The police had already been through this with her, probably at great length. In fact, Sam was possibly repeating the questions that the police had asked her, so it was little wonder if her responses were assured. 'He wasn't himself. He didn't know what he was saying.'

'But the necklace?' Sam pressed.

'I don't know how he got it.'

'And that doesn't make you suspicious?'

'It makes me wonder how he got hold of it, but it doesn't make me think he killed your sister.'

Sam thought about his next question, wondering if there was a better way of getting more useful information from her. She was being defensive, abrasive even, but that might just have been her manner. After all, she hadn't had to let them in – she would have been well within her rights to say no at the door. But instead she had chosen to engage. 'How do you think he might have got the necklace?' he asked.

She shrugged. 'He liked to collect things, antiques, like me. Maybe he bought it from a shop.'

'Or maybe someone gave it to him?' Sam suggested.

'Probably not.'

'What makes you say that?'

'Because Richard didn't really have any friends, not since Margaret died.'

'He didn't have any friends?'

'He spent most of his time in the house or at the hospital. He used to have friends before Margaret's death, but not after. He retreated into his own world and pushed people away.'

'You said that Richard was gentle,' Sam said. 'But you heard about what he did? How he stole my friend's phone and threatened us both? He talked about my sister's murder too.'

Victoria Friedman sucked on her top lip, as if thinking of an appropriate response. For the first time she looked rattled. It excited Sam that he might have found a way through. Is this how Paul Cullen felt when interviewing him?

And then Victoria was back in control. 'Richard was a gentle man, but you've got to understand that after Margaret's death he was not the same person as he was before. He was in his own world. I'm sure he didn't know what he was doing. I'm sorry for what he did to you and your friend, but I think it was just a cry for help.'

'Did he live here ever since the accident?'

She nodded. 'I asked him to come and live here because I was worried what he might do. He'd started to talk about harming himself. I thought I could save him from the demons, but I couldn't. Deep down I knew it was going to end like it did. I think he was waiting for justice before ending it.'

Sam leant forward, intrigued by the remark. 'Justice? What do you mean?'

She blinked several times. 'Do you know how Richard's wife was killed?'

Sam nodded. 'By a hit-and-run drunk driver.'

'On a zebra crossing,' Victoria added. 'And do you know how many years her killer received?'

Sam shook his head.

'Seven years,' she said, blinking through her anger. 'He could have been out in four. That's next year. He could have been walking around, free to do whatever he wanted, free to enjoy life to the full. Free to kill again and destroy another family's life. He wasn't sorry for what he'd done. He didn't show the slightest bit of remorse.'

For the first time Marcus spoke. 'You said he could have been out next year?'

'Yes,' she replied, straightening up, her facial muscles tightening. 'He could have been out. But not now; he's dead.'

Chapter Thirty-Seven

S am sat forward, with Marcus doing likewise. 'Dead? How?'

Victoria shrugged. 'I don't know. I know it might sound heartless to you, but I don't care how he died. I'm just glad that he did die.'

Sam just looked at her. Out of the corner of his eye, he saw Marcus glance at him.

She continued in an even tone, as if she were talking about some everyday occurrence rather than a man's death. 'I'm not a vengeful woman, but it really was the best thing that could have happened for everyone. That individual was a danger to us all, and I was happy when I heard the news. I can't pretend otherwise.'

Sam thought about what she had said. There was a time when he had felt the same way about the man now sitting to his left. He had wished him dead. Not out of revenge, but for justice. 'You said you thought Richard had been waiting for justice. Did this happen recently?'

'Late last week,' she replied. 'Richard got a call from the police to let him know what had happened.'

'The man committed suicide?'

'Like I said, I don't know how he died, and I don't care. I didn't ask Richard for the details, and he didn't offer me any.'

Sam continued. 'But you think this is what led to Richard's death? You think he killed himself because he felt that justice had been done – that this guy wouldn't walk free?'

'Yes, I believe he did.'

'Did Richard say that to you?'

'No,' she replied. 'After he told me the news, he didn't say anything more about it. I tried to talk to him.'

'So you're just surmising that he killed himself because of it.'

'I suppose I am. But I know in my heart of hearts. After the news I saw him change, withdraw even further. He was readying himself for death. And I couldn't do anything about it.'

'And you're happy with that?'

'If that's what Richard wanted, then I suppose I have to be.'

Sam didn't really know what else to say.

'I can see you're horrified by what I'm saying here,' she said. 'But this is how I feel. My brother had everything before that day; afterwards, he had nothing. He died at the same second that Margaret did. His life was over. And if I'm honest with myself, I always knew that really. You lost your sister. Surely you must understand what it's like.'

'It's difficult, yes,' Sam acknowledged.

'And did it change you for good?'

Sam hesitated, not wanting to talk about this. 'Yes, it did. But I didn't die the night my sister was murdered.'

'Then you're fortunate. But it's obviously still affecting you greatly. I can see it in your eyes when you talk about her. The wounds are still fresh for you.'

'No,' Sam said.

'I think you're lying,' she stated. 'But it's none of my business.'

Sam was taken aback by the accusation. Was he really that obvious? Could everyone see it? The way it still hurt, every single day? He let that accusation fade away before turning the conversation back to Victoria. 'So you're sure that Richard couldn't have murdered my sister?'

'Positive,' she replied. 'I'll tell you just what I told the police. At the time of your sister's murder, my brother wasn't even in this country. He was working in India with Margaret, teaching English to children. They were there for about five years in all. Did you know Richard was a teacher and a fine artist?'

'I knew he was artistic,' Sam replied.

'But did you know how good?'

'I saw one of his drawings in Tate Modern.'

She smiled, evidently pleased that Sam was aware of her brother's work. 'And what did you think of it?'

'To be honest, it was a bit disturbing,' Sam admitted.

'It's not one of my favourites,' she revealed. 'He used to be a highly skilled portrait and landscape artist – sold many of his paintings at exhibitions for several hundred pounds apiece. This is one of his.' She gestured to the wall behind her, upon which was hung an impressive beachfront vista in watercolour. 'But since Margaret's death, his drawings tended to reflect his inner torment. It became his way of communicating with me and the world, I suppose. He wouldn't really talk to me about his feelings, so I would try and understand what he was going through by examining his artwork.'

'Can we see some more?' Sam asked.

She looked surprised by the request. 'Of course. It's all upstairs in his art room.'

Marcus exchanged a knowing glance with Sam as they followed her upstairs. It had been a clever way of gaining access to more of the house. But also Sam couldn't help thinking that if art had been Richard's prime method of communication, then maybe, just maybe, there would be something somewhere in his art that might help explain more.

'I'm thinking of organising an exhibition of Richard's art,' Victoria said as they reached the top of the stairs. 'I just don't think that this should all go to waste. It deserves to be enjoyed by the public, and I hope that as many people as possible can enjoy Richard's talents.'

Sam and Marcus looked around the room. Unlike the rest of the house, this room in no way could be described as pristine. It was a working art studio. There was no furniture. The floor was covered with white sheets dotted with paint, and there were pieces of art everywhere. Some of it hung on the walls, but most was stacked up along all the edges of the room, three or four canvases deep. There were three stands there, each with half-completed artworks on them.

Sam looked around in wonderment as Marcus, from a respectful distance, examined a sketch of what looked like a moonscape.

Victoria smiled that same smile as before. 'Richard had his own art studio at his previous home, so when he moved in, I cleared some space for him. He spent most of his time up here. As you can see, he was extremely productive.'

Sam nodded, still surveying the room and its contents. Suddenly, one of the artworks caught his eye, and he moved towards it. It was in the far corner, propped up against the wall.

He recognised something in it. 'My God.' The hairs on the back of his neck bristled.

'That's one of the last complete artworks he did,' Victoria said as Sam crouched down before the canvas.

The sketch was of a young man's face, eyes bulging and tongue flopping down from his mouth. A noose hugged his neck, below which the words 'I did it. I'm the killer' were etched.

'I did it. I'm the killer.'

The exact words Richard Friedman had spoken up on the roof, just before slitting his throat.

Sam reached out and held the frame, his breathing shallow. In the background was the silhouette of a figure, arms out almost at right angles, which seemed to be looming over the foreground somehow.

He'd seen that figure before.

Sam turned to look at Victoria.

'Is this the person who killed Richard's wife?'

She nodded. 'Wayne Cartwright. I can hardly bear to say the words.'

'Did Richard draw this after he found out the news of his death?'

'Yes.'

'What does it mean? Who's the figure in the background?'

'I don't know.'

Sam turned back to the artwork. He looked again at the man's anguished face and the linked rope around his neck. Then suddenly he realised. He turned the canvas upside down, stifling a gasp, wanting to cry out. The noose around the man's neck – it wasn't a rope.

It was Cathy's necklace.

Detective Inspector Paul Cullen sat down on the edge of the bed, looked around the sparsely furnished hotel room and exhaled loudly, running his hands through his thinning hair. This wasn't how he wanted to be spending his fortieth birthday. He hoped that things could be patched up between him and his wife, but wondered whether that would ever happen. There had been no birthday phone call, not even a text. Hell, even DS Beswick had managed a text message of congratulations, and he was still in his sickbed.

He pulled out his mobile and checked the caller display, just in case he had missed a call from her – or more likely from the analysis lab. They'd had the audio from Sam Becker's computer for over twenty-four hours. Surely by now they must have had time to sharpen the sound and produce a definitive transcript. It couldn't be that difficult.

Cullen turned his attention back to Sam Becker. Little of this case made sense, but one thing that he'd been convinced of from the beginning was that Sam was trustworthy. He believed what he said. Even when it seemed that there was something really wrong about the situation, he'd fought against doubting Sam. Was he just being blinded by the guy's profession? If Sam had been a builder, not a doctor, would Cullen have been so sure that he was telling the truth?

There was a rasping knock on the door that ripped Cullen from his musings. 'Hello? Room clean.'

Cullen took his cue, grabbed his jacket and headed out. There wasn't anywhere to go, but it wasn't healthy to hang around on your own in hotel rooms on such a day. Better to get outside and at least pretend that you were with other people. He'd only got as far as a few blocks away, walking towards central London, when the call came that he'd been waiting for.

'Detective Inspector Cullen?'

'Speaking.'

'We've completed the analysis on the audio file. Are you able to come over now? We've got some surprising findings.'

Cullen smiled – nothing about this case surprised him any more. 'I'll be there right away.'

He took a taxi and was at the laboratory in less than fifteen minutes. The building, a grim 1960s affair that resembled an oversized public lavatory block, was situated down a back street just off Kensington High Street in West London. It was as if the planners had always intended to hide this deeply ugly building from public view. The windows were stained black with sun-baked London filth. They didn't look like they'd seen a cleaner in a long time.

But as Cullen had told himself just that morning as he'd looked in the mirror, it was what went on in the inside that counted. You might look terrible, over the hill, but if it was all working inside, then you were all right. Hell, it might even lull others into a sense of false security.

This building was certainly a case in point. The vile exterior hid the beauty of the work taking place inside – work that solved crimes, brought murderers and rapists to justice, and placed public safety at its heart. The unit carried out analysis for the British Transport Police, investigating all crimes on Britain's transportation network. This included not only forensic investigation but also, increasingly, analysis of digital data such as that gained from CCTV. They were well placed to investigate Sam Becker's audio file.

Cullen approached reception, gave his name and waited impatiently for his host to arrive. A minute or so later, a short balding man appeared, introducing himself as Charles Holloway. He didn't speak as they headed for the stairs, descending into the basement, through two sets of double doors, and into a small, windowless meeting room.

Holloway gestured to one of the uncomfortable-looking plastic seats. 'Please, do sit down.'

Cullen did as requested. The seat was as uncomfortable as it looked.

'We spoke on the phone yesterday,' Holloway said. 'We ran the audio through our system, cleaned it up, removed the background noise, to leave you just with the spoken words.'

He handed Cullen a typed transcript. It looked like a film script. But instead of actors' names, the cast was headed 'Male 1' and 'Female 1'.

Cullen read the pages. He remembered how Sam had described the incident.

This seemed to reflect what he had said exactly.

But if this was really a recording of the incident, then it could mean only one of two things – either what Sam had said was true, and someone had set this up, recorded it and sent it to him, or Sam himself had made the recording and this was all part of some elaborate game he was playing with the police.

Cullen looked up. 'Is it genuine?'

Holloway looked surprised by the question. 'Genuine?'

'Yes, is it a recording of the actual train crash? Or could it have been recorded afterwards, to make it sound like it was from then?'

Holloway nodded his understanding. 'It was certainly recorded outside. Our team have examined the other noises on the file, and as far as we can deduce, the noise of the train is genuine and is from the same time as the speech – it wasn't overlaid afterwards. The other noises on the audio – car doors being opened, the sound of shoes on stones, smashing glass – they all appear to be from the same time period.'

It seemed his gut instincts about Sam Becker had been right. 'Then it is genuine.'

Holloway nodded.

'You said there were some surprising findings.'

'There are. Something we really didn't expect.'

Chapter Thirty-Eight

Shirley Ainsley sat at the kitchen table and thought again about what she had found underneath the bed in the spare room. Hours after finding the bag stuffed full of banknotes, she still couldn't come to terms with it all. Why would Eric have so much money? She hadn't counted, but there must have been thousands of pounds in the bag. And why hide it from her? She'd fought the urge to walk to his workplace and challenge him there. It would not go well, and it was much better leaving this until he got home. But the wait was painful and just left her feeling so alone, wallowing in her dark thoughts.

Eric was in trouble.

Or maybe he was planning to leave her. Was the money his ticket out of the marriage?

She rose from the seat and put the kettle on, moving slowly, as if her body wasn't quite connected to her brain. If Eric was planning to leave, she didn't know how she would cope. One thing was certain though – she wouldn't give up on their marriage without a fight. And if he were in some kind of other trouble, she'd be there for him.

She'd just poured the tea when there was a knock at the door.

She crossed the lounge and approached the door, seeing a silhouette through the glass. The second she pulled the door inward, someone stepped through the gap, pushing her against the wall. She went to scream, but a large, rough-skinned hand clamped itself over her mouth as she was held firmly against the wall. She now saw her assailant as another two men entered the house from behind him and closed the door.

'Try and stay calm, Shirley.'

It was Vincent. The man Jane had dated.

He burned into her with those ice-blue eyes. 'Stay calm and we won't hurt you. We won't be here long.'

Still with his hand tightly across her mouth, he turned to the two other men, who were dressed in black. Both were comfortably over six foot and had close-cropped hair. One had a tattoo of an animal on his neck. None had concealed their face. 'Start upstairs and work your way down. Be quick.'

The men nodded and made for the stairs. Thank God, the children were staying at their aunt's house – Shirley's instinct that it was best for them to be away from the house for a few days had proved correct.

Vincent smiled as he watched the two men moving swiftly upstairs. Then he turned his attention back to Shirley. 'In the lounge.' He half-dragged her down the corridor and through into the living room. 'Sit,' he said, throwing her onto the sofa.

Despite being free of his grip, Shirley did just as she was told. She was scared of what these men might do. 'We have people right outside the house,' he explained, 'so there's no point trying to get away.'

Shirley looked at the man. He'd been to the house twice, as far as she knew. She'd never been totally sure of him, but Jane had really liked him, had trusted him – she'd always been a trusting girl. Suddenly, Shirley wanted to fight back, to make him suffer for what he had done to her daughter.

He swung over a chair, straddling it the reverse way around, with his legs either side of its back. His hands rested on the top, and he smiled, his eyes narrowing. 'I liked your daughter. What happened was unfortunate.'

She was so angry, but just as afraid. 'Why did you—'

'Do what? Kill her?' He smiled. 'Ask your husband.'

Shirley shook her head. 'No . . .'

'Oh yes. Ask Eric why Jane died. See what he says.' He glanced at his watch. 'He should be along in a few minutes.'

Shirley pushed the insinuation to one side. 'Where's Alison?'

He went to speak but stopped as the men burst into the room, brandishing the bag. 'It was under one of the beds.'

Shirley's stomach lurched. What the hell was Eric involved in?

Vincent smiled as he peered inside the open bag. 'Very good,' he said, standing up.

'What have you done with Alison?' Shirley yelled, getting to her feet as the men headed for the door.

Vincent turned around and walked slowly back towards her. She shrank away as he grasped her head in both hands and whispered in her ear.

'No,' she said, shaking her head and fighting back tears. 'You're lying, you're lying. Eric wouldn't do that – he would never agree to that.'

Vincent smiled. 'Like I said, ask him yourself.' He went to leave but stopped at the door. 'Do you know the really sad thing, Shirley? This isn't about you, or Eric or your daughter. You're just part of a bigger plan – one that's been playing out for a long, long time.'

He turned and left as Shirley slumped onto the sofa, clutching a cushion to her to try and muffle the pain.

Sam and Marcus approached the café, which they'd passed on the way from the tube to Victoria Friedman's house. Sam had noticed a customer on a computer by the window, so he hoped that it meant the place had Internet access. As they entered, someone else, an older man, was on the computer, and he was indeed on the Internet. Sam approached the bar and the server, a young girl, probably a student, looked up from cleaning glasses and flashed a smile.

'Have you got any other computers with Internet access?' Sam asked.

The girl shook her head. 'But we've got Wi-Fi.'

Sam looked around at the man on the machine. 'Do you think he'll be long?'

She shrugged. 'It's pay by the minute, and cheap, so he could be awhile.'

Sam decided to do something he'd never done before – abuse his position. 'Look, I'm a heart surgeon, over at St Thomas's, and I really need access to the Internet. It's kind of a medical emergency.'

Excitement flashed across the girl's face. 'You're a surgeon? I'm a medical student. At St George's. This job helps with the bills.'

Sam couldn't believe his luck. He tried to hide his joy. 'Then you'll know that this is important.'

'Sure, yes,' she said, suddenly flustered. She looked over at the man on the computer and then back over to her left, biting her lip. 'There's a computer in the back office. You can use that one.'

'Fantastic.'

They followed her around the back of the bar and into a cramped office that was littered with papers. In the corner was the computer. It was already switched on, and the girl loaded up the Internet. 'There you go,' she said, standing back, 'it's all yours.'

Sam recognised her expression from that of the many junior doctors who had worked underneath him – a longing for validation that what they had done was worthwhile. 'Thanks, that's fantastic. I'm sure you'll make a great doctor.'

She beamed back at him. 'Happy to help. I'd better get back to the bar.'

Sam slid into the seat next to the computer, and Marcus pulled up a chair next to him.

'Nice job,' Marcus noted as Sam pulled up the search engine. Sam typed in the name 'Wayne Cartwright' and hit 'Search'.

Nothing of note came up. Just lots of articles with 'Wayne' or 'Cartwright' in the title – the search hadn't been specific enough.

He tried again. This time he put Wayne Cartwright in quotes and added in 'HMP Bristol' and the word 'death'.

And there it was – the second result down, an article from the *Bristol Evening Post*, the local newspaper, dated the previous week.

Prisoner death mystery.

They scanned the short piece, describing how Wayne Cartwright had been found dead early the previous morning. The prison authorities and police had refused to comment, but an unnamed source claimed he was found hanging in his cell.

Sam shook his head as he read on.

The source said that suicide had been ruled out and that they were working on the assumption that he had been murdered.

'Wow,' Marcus said.

Sam re-read the revelation. 'Do you think that's likely – that other prisoners did this?'

Marcus nodded. 'Prison's a very dangerous place. Believe me, I've met plenty of people who were capable of much worse than that.'

Sam didn't linger on that thought. Instead, he thought of Richard Friedman's drawing. 'He must have known. Richard Friedman must have known that he was found hanging.'

'Looks like that,' Marcus agreed.

'But how? How did he know?'

Marcus shrugged. 'Maybe the police told him. They might not have wanted to tell the press, but they might have told him more details.'

'Maybe. But Victoria Friedman said she didn't know how he died.'

'Maybe he didn't tell her.'

'I don't think so.'

'I did it. I'm the killer.'

Marcus studied Sam. 'What are you thinking?'

An idea had formed: a possible explanation. 'What if Richard knew what was going to happen?'

'You think he could have set up his murder?'

'It's possible, isn't it?'

Marcus thought for a second, then nodded. 'It's possible. There are always people who are willing to sort out grudges or exact justice for those on the outside – for the right price. But he would need to have access to someone in the jail that was prepared to do it. It's not easy to do that kind of thing without the right contacts on the outside.'

He might have been wrong, but this was starting to make sense. 'A go-between?'

'Yeah – someone who knows people in the prison that can do the job. Someone who can set it all up, make sure everything runs to plan.'

'Did you ever see this happen?'

Marcus waited one beat too long.

'You did, didn't you?'

Marcus nodded, somewhat reluctantly. 'I saw it happen once or twice. But I don't want to talk about it. I'm trying to forget all that.'

Sam respected Marcus's wishes. 'But you think that this could be a possibility?'

'I think it's much more likely that this guy made enemies while he was inside,' Marcus replied. 'And that whoever these people were took their opportunity to punish him. What makes you think Richard Friedman has anything to do with it?'

'The words on the drawing. And what he said to me up on the roof. "I did it. I'm the killer." Maybe he wasn't talking about Cathy. He could have been talking about Wayne Cartwright. Maybe he felt responsible for his death.'

Marcus didn't look convinced. 'From what his sister said, and from what Louisa said, he doesn't sound like the kind of person who would do that.'

'I agree. But he wasn't thinking straight. His sister said how he was dreading the possibility that Cartwright would be released. Maybe he panicked, wanted to get rid of the pain, and this seemed like the best way.'

'But he'd still have to have the right contacts to be able to do that kind of thing.'

'Just say he did.'

'Okay,' Marcus said. 'Say that Richard Friedman did arrange for someone to murder Wayne Cartwright. What has all this got to do with Cathy and the person who has Anna?'

'I have no idea,' Sam admitted. 'But Richard Friedman holds the key to this, I just know it. We've got to find out more, and quickly.'

'How?'

Sam thought back to the artwork. 'From Richard Friedman himself.'

Chapter Thirty-Nine

Eric Ainsley returned home barely five minutes after Vincent and his men had left. Shirley was still on the sofa, tears wet against her cheek and head buried against the cushion, as she heard him enter the room.

His face fell. 'Shirley, are you okay?'

She didn't look up.

He knelt down beside her, trying to get a glimpse of her face. 'What's the matter? Tell me.' He was panicking. 'Is it Alison?'

She turned to look at his tortured face. 'They've taken the money.'

His face flashed horror.

'They've taken the money,' she repeated in what was now more an accusation.

'No,' he said, shaking his head. He jumped up and raced upstairs. Shirley could hear him in the spare bedroom, frantically banging doors and drawers.

She rose up and looked at the bag that he had left on the floor. It wasn't his normal work bag. Instinctively she unzipped it and was met by the sight of yet more banknotes – thousands more. 'Dear God.' She felt dirty, contaminated.

'I'm so sorry, Shirley, so, so sorry.' Eric swayed at the door, totally shell-shocked. He was crying. 'I don't know what to do, I don't.'

She looked up, her blood boiling for her dead daughter and missing grandchild. 'Tell me everything. Now.'

Eric slumped against the wall, sobbing into his hands.

'Tell me everything, Eric, now.' Her voice was deliberately hard. 'Before it's too late.'

He nodded, struggling to compose himself as he sat down next to her. 'It's all my fault.' He looked at her through drowning eyes. 'Everything is my fault.'

She maintained the hard tone. 'Tell me.'

Shame forced him to look away. 'I borrowed some money,' he said, his forehead creasing. 'A lot of money.'

'How much? Why?'

'Fifteen thousand pounds – I lost my job twelve months ago.'

The shock was immense. *'What?'*

'I should have told you, I know – I should have, but I didn't want to worry you, and I thought that I would find something else. But I couldn't. No one wants to employ someone of my age. So I borrowed some money from a man I met in the pub. He said it would be interest-free – he said it was a favour.'

Shirley felt sick. 'Vincent McGuire?'

Eric nodded, his eyes closing. 'Six months ago he said he wanted the money back, with interest. And if I didn't pay, bad things would happen. Then one day I came home, and he was there with Jane, smiling at me, and I didn't know what to do. I tried to get together the money, from friends. Bob lent me some; so did Arthur and Tony. But it wasn't enough.'

She shook her head, disgusted by what she was hearing. 'He murdered our daughter because you needed money.'

Eric started sobbing again, nodding into his hands. 'It's all my fault.'

Shirley let him cry for a moment. He deserved to drown in his tears. 'How long have you known?'

'I thought he might have done it,' he mumbled, 'but I didn't know for sure. I wanted to believe it was just an accident. But then he said he had Alison.'

Shirley fought to control her anger. She didn't recognise the man in front of her. 'My God, Eric, you should have told me.'

'I thought if I could get the money together then he would give her back – I nearly had enough.'

'You're a fool. We need to tell the police, right now.'

'No! We can't. He'll kill Alison.'

'The police will help us.'

He shook his head. 'He'll know we've done it, and he'll kill her. They're watching us, Shirley, all the time. You don't understand who we're dealing with. He has people everywhere. And he doesn't care who he hurts – he enjoys hurting people. He's enjoying watching us suffer.'

'Then what? What do we do?'

'I don't know, now they've taken the money. I just don't know.'

'Do you think they might let her go, now they've got what they want?'

'I don't know.'

Shirley thought back to what Vincent had said to her just before he left. 'He said this was just part of something bigger. That it wasn't really about us. Do you know what he means?'

Eric shook his head. 'No, I swear, I don't. Please believe me, Shirley.'

Then Eric's mobile rang.

He brought it to his ear and listened without replying, before handing the phone to Shirley. He looked confused. 'They want to speak to you.'

Sam and Marcus retraced their steps back to Victoria Friedman's house, deciding that it was worth quizzing her again now, armed with their additional information. With it they might be able to unlock some more answers – something that could take them further forward. And although there might be nothing more to be gained, it was worth a shot. Unfortunately, this time when they knocked on her door, there was no answer.

'She was quick to leave,' Marcus noted.

Sam nodded, placing a hand on the door, turning around to scan the street. 'Too quick.'

'You think she knew about what happened and just didn't tell us?'

Sam shrugged. 'Who knows? Maybe.'

'So what now?'

'We go and take a look at Richard Friedman's artwork.'

Marcus's face creased. 'But I thought . . .'

'Not here,' Sam revealed. 'Follow me.'

They headed for the tube, travelling towards Embankment, and Sam explained about the artwork at Tate Modern.

'It's the same figure as the one in the drawing of Wayne Cartwright, the silhouette of the man with arms outstretched, lurking in the background.'

'You're thinking that it could be the man who has Anna, the man who killed Cathy?'

'Maybe.'

'Do you know when he drew it?'

'Recently – Louisa said all the artworks were produced in the past few weeks, especially for the exhibition.'

'So there might be clues in it?'

'Hopefully – I just need something to go on. I can't stand feeling so powerless.'

'You're not tempted to call the police?'

'I'm fighting my instincts not to call them,' Sam revealed. 'But I'm scared that this guy isn't bluffing. What if I get them involved, and he carries out his threat?'

'I know,' Marcus replied. 'I think you're doing the right thing, for the moment anyway.'

They spent the majority of the journey in silence, and Sam's thoughts turned again to Anna. It hurt so much to think that someone had her, maybe the same person who had murdered Cathy, and that the police didn't even know about it. There were no search teams, no rooms full of officers chasing up leads and considering possibilities: just him, Marcus, Louisa and Doug. As the tube pulled into Embankment, he uttered a silent prayer that she was safe. It seemed futile, but there was little else to do.

On the way to Tate Modern, Louisa called to check how things were going. Sam updated her on the revelations about Wayne Cartwright and their suspicions that Richard might have been involved somehow in his death. She was just as puzzled as to a connection with Anna's disappearance as they were.

Reaching the gallery, Marcus followed Sam through the main hall and up the stairs towards the exhibition space. Both stood in front of the large canvas and took in the powerful feeling of chaos and despair that it exuded.

Sam pointed. 'See the figure in the top right-hand corner?'

Marcus nodded.

Sam examined it carefully. 'It's exactly the same figure. Exactly the same pose.' He glanced at Marcus, whose eyes seemed to be taking in every detail of the piece. 'It's disturbing, isn't it?'

'Yes.'

Sam turned back to the work, looking for anything that might shed some light on things. But he saw nothing that seemed relevant. There was no message, no sign of Cathy's necklace, just the tortured image of Richard Friedman staring out from a mass of gravestones and twisted faces.

'I can't see anything new,' Sam said. He turned again to Marcus and was shocked to see the expression on his face, drained of colour. His eyes were fixed on the drawing. 'Are you okay?'

'Yeah,' Marcus answered unconvincingly. He looked away. 'I've just remembered I've got to be somewhere really important, Sam. I'm sorry; I'll be back as soon as I can, I promise.'

Sam watched Marcus walk away at pace and noticed that even before he had left the hall he'd pulled out his mobile phone.

He followed, pulling him back at the shoulder as Marcus reached the stairs. 'Marcus.'

Marcus turned around.

Sam held on to his friend. 'You saw something in the drawing, didn't you? What was it?'

'Nothing,' Marcus replied.

'You're lying.' Sam hit back. 'You saw something, I know you did. Tell me what you saw.'

People were watching.

Marcus tried to shrug him off. 'Let me go, Sam.'

Sam tightened his hold. He would be damned if Marcus was going to keep something from him that could help them find Anna. 'Tell me.'

They had now attracted the attention of a security guard, who was watching them from across the hall. He moved slowly towards them.

Marcus glanced across at the guard, then back at Sam. 'You've got to trust me, Sam, please. I want to help, but you've got to let me go.'

Sam considered his response as the guard neared. He released his grip.

'I'll phone you later, I promise,' Marcus added. He turned and made for the stairs.

Sam waited until Marcus had disappeared from view before following.

Chapter Forty

Sam spotted Marcus about fifty yards ahead, walking along the side of the Thames and heading towards the direction of the hospital. He was walking purposefully. Sam hung back and hoped that he wouldn't turn around. Fortunately, being just after half five, there was a lot of cover, with commuters on their way home or going for a post-work drink, mixing with late-afternoon tourists enjoying the autumn sun.

When Marcus reached Westminster Bridge, he crossed it and entered the hospital grounds.

Why was he going back there?

He didn't head for the main entrance, instead moving towards the rear of the building – to the gardens. Sam thought for a second about following further. The grounds were invariably quiet, and it would be much harder for him to hide. But then he remembered an alternative route, around the back, via a small gate that emerged just behind a thick clump of bushes that would give him cover. He hurried across the road and arced towards the back entrance, losing sight of Marcus for about half a minute.

He entered through the gate and crouched low behind the bushes, watching as Marcus took a place on the very same bench where Sam had been so upset days earlier. It did feel wrong, spying like this, but he was doing this for Anna.

Marcus's body was folded, his head in his hands.

What the hell was going on?

For a good two minutes, Marcus held that position. And then, from the left, came Louisa. She approached from behind, touching Marcus on the shoulder and then sitting down next to him. It was too far away for Sam to hear any words, but from their facial expressions the conversation looked intense. Marcus stood up, with Louisa clinging to his arm. There was a hug, and then a kiss. Not a friendly kiss goodbye.

A lovers' kiss, full on the lips, held for seconds.

What the hell?

And with that, Marcus walked away. Sam decided not to follow. Realistically, the chances of him being able to pursue Marcus across the city were slim. Instead, stunned by what he had just seen, he watched Louisa dab at her eyes and then turn back towards the main entrance. Only when she was gone did he emerge into the main gardens, already rehearsing how he was going to play this.

It was time he found out the truth.

Sam made his way up to Louisa's office, still trying to decide how to tackle this. He felt angry, betrayed, although in reality there was no real reason for him to be – Louisa had every right to date whomever she liked. But still, she'd kept it a secret, even at Marcus's flat, when she'd had the chance to tell Sam everything, to bring it all out into the open. He knocked on her door, and she looked up from her desk, startled. Her eyes were swollen with recent tears, but she tried to gather her composure. 'Sam.'

Sam closed the door without a word and stood with his back against the cool glass.

Louisa looked tense. 'What's the matter? Have you heard something?'

'I saw you.'

Louisa looked confused. 'What?'

Sam held his tongue. He needed to approach this in the right way, keep things calm; after all, he hoped Louisa would be part of the solution, not the problem. 'What's going on, Louisa?'

'I don't understand.'

'Tell me about you and Marcus.'

Louisa let out a nervous, defensive laugh, but Sam could see the shock ripple across her face. 'What?'

Her instinctive denial angered Sam. 'I saw you together. I saw you kiss. Now tell me what's going on.'

Louisa looked away, her face reddening. 'I'm so sorry, Sam.'

Sam moved towards her. 'Sorry for what?'

'For lying to you – for not telling you what was going on. I should have told you. You weren't meant to find out like this.'

'Tell me now, Louisa. Tell me everything.'

'I don't know if I can.'

Sam brought his fist down hard on the desk, making Louisa jump. 'Damn it, Louisa, Anna is in danger, held by God knows who, and you still don't know if you can tell me? For God's sake, this isn't a game, you know.'

Louisa winced. 'Please, Sam, don't shout. I'll tell you everything I know – I promise. Just sit down.'

He sat, already feeling remorse for losing his temper. 'I'm sorry. I just want Anna back.'

'I know.'

'Then tell me what you know. What were you and Marcus talking about in the gardens? Was it something to do with Anna?'

307

'No,' Louisa replied.

'Then what? Was it about the drawing?'

'Drawing?'

'Richard Friedman's drawing in Tate Modern. We were looking at it for clues when Marcus left. I think he saw something in it.'

Louisa dabbed her eyes. 'He didn't mention anything.'

'Then what?'

'He called and asked to see me straightaway, somewhere private – said it was really important. So we arranged to meet around the back of the hospital. He said he was in trouble, but he was going to sort it out. I tried to get him to tell me what was wrong, but he wouldn't. He said he just wanted to see me, in case things . . . didn't . . . work . . . out.'

'Did he say where he was going?'

She shook her head. 'No. He wouldn't tell me.'

Despite her keeping so much from him, Sam believed her this time. 'And you've got no idea at all what trouble he might be in?'

She closed her eyes.

So there was something else. His hopes rose. 'Louisa? Anything might be helpful.'

She nodded. 'A few days ago I was with Marcus, in his flat, when two men came.'

'Go on.'

'I heard Marcus talking with them at the door, and then they just walked in and started taking things. They took the TV and some money.'

'From you?'

Louisa nodded. 'Fortunately, I only had fifty pounds on me.'

'And what did Marcus do?'

'Nothing,' she replied. 'He just stood there, watching them. I don't think he had a choice. They just did what they wanted.'

'Who were they?'

'Marcus wouldn't say at first – said I was much better off not knowing. But later that night he told me. They know him from prison.'

'The men were in the same prison?'

'Not those two, but the gang, the same gang were in his prison. Marcus said they ruled the place, even had contacts with the prison guards. They bullied people in there.'

Sam remembered what Marcus had said to him about his time in jail, the punishments he had taken and the playground hostility that pervaded. Maybe he'd been underplaying just how much he had suffered. 'And now they're harassing him on the outside?'

'It started a few weeks after he was released. He got a call from one of the gang who offered him work – collecting money from people.'

'A loan shark?'

'I assume so. Marcus said no, and from that point on they've never left him alone.'

Sam thought back to the skinhead he had passed on the stairs when approaching Marcus's flat. And then there was the shot-out window. Marcus had said it was local youths, but now Sam wasn't convinced.

'But why are they so interested in Marcus? Did he associate with them in the prison?'

Louisa shifted in her seat. 'Marcus swore to me he wasn't involved with them at all. He said he kept out of their way, was friendly to them when he had to be, but nothing more. He doesn't know why they're pursuing him. It's been a nightmare for him.'

'But he didn't tell the police?'

'He said it would just make things worse. He thought if he ignored them, they'd get bored and leave him alone.'

Sam thought for a second, trying to piece things together. Could this all be connected to Anna and to Cathy? 'The trouble he says he's in – is it related to the gang?'

'He wouldn't say, but I think it must be. I'm really worried about him, Sam. These aren't the kind of people you mess with.'

'We need to find out how all of this is connected with what's been happening.'

'Do you really think it is?'

'It must be, Louisa. Marcus saw something in that drawing, and it made him run. Whatever trouble he says he's in is connected to the picture, it's connected to Richard Friedman and it's connected to the person who has Anna. It has to be.'

'What are you going to do?'

'I need to speak to Marcus.'

Louisa took her cue and picked up the phone. 'I'll call him now.' But the call rang through to his answer service. 'Now what?'

Sam didn't know whether she would agree to what he was about to suggest, but it was worth a try. 'Have you got a key to his flat?'

Louisa nodded.

'Maybe there will be something there . . .'

'I can't, Sam. I can't just break in like that.'

Her reaction was understandable, but Sam pressed home his request. After all, she owed him. 'Please, Louisa, do this for me.'

'I don't know, Sam – it just feels wrong.'

'I understand, but Anna is in danger, and it sounds like Marcus is too. We might find something that we could take to the police, something that might help save them both. Please, Louisa. I wouldn't ask if I thought there was any other way.'

'Okay,' she said finally. 'Okay, I'll do it.'

Chapter Forty-One

Louisa knocked on the door for the second time, but once again there was no indication that Marcus was in the flat. She cupped her hand against the wood.

'Marcus, are you there? Marcus?'

She turned to Sam, her face asking the question.

'It's okay,' Sam said. 'We're doing it for the right reasons.'

She didn't reply. Instead, she pulled out the key from her pocket and unlocked the door. Sam followed her, closing the door quietly behind them. Louisa flicked on the light and stood uneasily in the centre of the living space. 'What are we looking for, Sam?'

Sam scanned the room and then headed for a set of drawers. 'I don't know,' he replied, already hunting through Marcus's underwear. 'Anything that can help us find Anna.'

Louisa stood at his shoulder as Sam moved on to the next drawer. 'I feel sick being here, Sam, really sick. I'm betraying his trust. We shouldn't be doing this. It's not right.'

Sam moved on to the third and final drawer, not really hearing her, such was his single-minded determination to find something, anything that could help. But the drawer was just stuffed full of socks. He turned and looked for the next place to search. There was a small wardrobe across the room, jammed between the fridge and the entrance to the bathroom. Inside was a complete mess. Bails of clothes collapsed on top of each other in multicoloured piles. Sam reached in and scooped up armfuls of jumpers and shirts, placing them on the floor. He searched the back of the unit, in case anything had been hidden behind the mess. But there was nothing.

'At the hospital, Marcus asked me if I still believed in him,' Louisa said. 'I said I did, and I meant it, Sam. I believe in him. In his face, you could see how much it means to him, just to have someone say that they believe. That's all he ever wanted from you – just to be believed.'

Sam turned, wounded. 'You know it was never as easy as that. Don't you think I wanted to believe he was innocent? I lost my sister and my best friend in one night. They both might as well have been dead. Do you really think I wanted that? I would have done anything to bring Cathy back. And I prayed that it wasn't Marcus who did it. I wanted the police to find someone else to blame. I wanted them to find some other person who did it, so I could have my best friend back. But they didn't, Louisa. No clues, no fingerprints, no fibres or bodily fluids from anyone else. If there had been something for me to believe in, I'd have grasped it in a shot.'

Louisa flinched, as if she'd been slapped across the face. 'I should have told you,' she said tearfully. 'I should have said something at the time.'

Sam moved towards her. 'Told me what?'

She flinched again as he touched her arm.

'Louisa, told me what?'

She put a hand to her head. 'I wanted to say something, but I didn't, and then it was too late. I was scared, so I kept quiet.'

'Louisa, you're not making sense.'

Louisa looked up. 'I've done a terrible thing, Sam.'

'What is it?'

She looked as if she was going to be sick or faint. Sam guided her towards the sofa with a steadying hand. 'Sit down, Louisa.'

They both sat down. 'I knew that there was something going on between them.' She was taking ragged breaths, struggling to get the words out. 'I knew about it, but I didn't say anything.'

'Knew about what?'

'About Marcus and Cathy – the night before she was killed, we were out at the clubhouse, at the disco. Cathy and I were at the bar, and that weird guy came talking to her.'

'I remember.'

Sam had watched the encounter from the other side of the dingy clubhouse, praying that the lad would leave his little sister alone. Marcus and Sam had run into him and his friend earlier that day, while playing pool in the bar. Cocky and threatening, he was not the kind of person Sam wanted anywhere near his sister, and he had never been so relieved as when the guy, who seemed both drunk and stoned, walked away and left without his prize.

'He was horrible, leaning right in to Cathy and suggesting that we go back to his tent. Said that Cathy had eyes like stars in the midnight sky – how lame is that for a chat-up line? We didn't know how to get rid of him, but then when he went to the toilet, Marcus followed him in.'

Sam had been standing next to Marcus. He remembered the point at which he'd gone to the toilets, as Marcus had given him his camera for safe keeping. He'd joked about not using up the film while he was gone, taking pictures of the girls in the place. But not for a second had Sam suspected his bathroom stop had been for a reason other than the obvious. 'He definitely followed him? It wasn't just a coincidence?'

Louisa shook her head. 'He told me about it a few weeks ago. He said he'd watched the guy with us, then decided to warn him off – tell him that Cathy and he were seeing each other and to back away.'

'And what happened?'

'Marcus said the lad just smiled at him and walked right past.'

'But he did leave you alone after that?'

Louisa nodded. 'We didn't see him again. He never came back to us.'

So Marcus had been the knight in shining armour. 'But you said you knew about Cathy and Marcus back then. It wasn't just from watching Marcus follow that guy into the toilets.'

'I'd had my suspicions for a few weeks,' Louisa explained. 'One day Cathy said something about Marcus which gave me the first clue. I can't remember what it was exactly, but it just made me think that something might be going on.'

Sam thought back. He'd never had any suspicions that Cathy and Marcus were an item. Neither of them had said a word. 'Cathy didn't confide in you?'

'She couldn't. Because she knew how much I liked him.'

Sam swallowed his surprise. 'You liked Marcus back then?'

'Always.' Louisa smiled sadly. 'Cathy wouldn't have known how to tell me.'

Now it made sense. 'So you just kept quiet.'

Louisa nodded. 'Part of me wanted to say something, to challenge her, but another part of me just wanted to pretend it was all in my imagination. If things came out in the open, then I'd have to face up to the facts – Marcus liked Cathy, not me.'

'But you knew, really.'

'I knew. From that point on I watched for signs and saw the stolen glances between them. Times when Cathy would be out of contact coincided with times when I knew you weren't with Marcus. And then that night, I knew for certain. I saw the way Marcus watched while that guy was talking to her. And then later, when

Cathy was on the dance floor, dancing to ABBA, I saw the smiles between them. That's when I decided to get things out in the open.'

'You said something?'

She nodded. 'I was drunk and angry, and it just came out when we were getting ready for bed in the tent later that night. We kept quiet because neither of us wanted you to hear. Cathy said she was sorry, but I just didn't want to hear it. I said our friendship was over. The next day we didn't speak. Cathy tried to make peace, but I wouldn't. The last thing I said to her was "Go to hell". I was awake when she left the tent to go and meet with Marcus, but I was too angry and hurt to say anything.'

The revelations were stunning, and Sam couldn't quite believe what he was hearing. There had been so many secrets. 'And you didn't tell the police anything about this?'

It was difficult not to make it sound like an accusation.

'No.'

'But why?'

'I don't know why. Marcus said he wasn't with her that night, so I just didn't mention it. And then the police found all that evidence, and I started to think that Marcus had really killed her. I just pushed it all out of my mind and tried to get on with things. I've asked myself a thousand times why I didn't say something at the court case, but the police had all their evidence, and maybe I thought it would confuse things, get me into trouble. And then, when I did start to question whether Marcus was innocent, it was too late.'

Sam put a hand to his head. If only he'd known all this at the time. He would have believed his friend; he would have fought for him. And the details about Marcus and Cathy's relationship might have been enough to clear him. Maybe then, the real killer wouldn't still be out there. 'Marcus doesn't know any of this?'

'No, no.' Louisa looked panicked at the thought. 'I can't tell him, Sam. He'd never forgive me.'

'But you're hoping to build a future with him, built on lies.'

'I know. I'm trying to make amends, Sam, I really am.'

'Then help me find out what's going on, Louisa. This isn't about not believing Marcus – or betraying him; this is about helping him – and Anna. Help me to help them.'

Louisa nodded, sniffing back more tears. 'I will.'

They continued searching the flat. Despite what he had told Louisa, Sam did feel a sense of betrayal as he hunted through Marcus's private possessions – his underwear, clothes, mail, financial papers, bedding, toiletries. It was impossible not to think about the gross invasion that he'd instigated. He'd also lied to Louisa. This was about not believing Marcus. Not in relation to Cathy's murder maybe, but certainly about Anna's disappearance. And if the search yielded anything that could help get her back safely, it would all be worth it.

Five minutes into the search, he found the first item of significance.

The box of tablets were right at the back of a drawer stuffed full of papers. He brought them up to the light.

Alprazolam.

Louisa moved towards him.

'Did Marcus tell you he was taking these?'

'No.'

'The same drugs that were planted in my locker.'

'I know. You're not saying—'

'A coincidence,' Sam said. 'Those tablets were from the hospital pharmacy stock. These have been prescribed to him.'

Louisa held the box, studying it. 'I know he's been really down since he came out of prison. He told me he's had anxiety attacks and hasn't been sleeping. Especially since moving down here – he didn't say he'd been to his GP about it.'

Sam placed the tablets back in the drawer and pushed it shut, guilty that Marcus's confidentiality had been breached.

They continued searching but were running out of places to look. Sam turned to the bed, one of those cheap all-springs-and-not-much-mattress affairs. Crouching down, he looked underneath. But there was nothing. Then he lifted the mattress and saw the mobile phone.

'Louisa.'

Louisa emerged from the bathroom, shaking her head in disbelief as she saw the device.

She took the phone. 'No, it can't be.'

But Sam already knew. He'd seen the name etched on the phone's back.

It was Louisa's stolen mobile.

Chapter Forty-Two

At first Susan Blackmore hadn't taken much notice of the girl sitting on the railings and looking in her direction. It had happened so many times before in such similar circumstances, especially during that first year. She would be out shopping, and then someone, a young girl matching her daughter's build, or with the same hair colour, would catch her attention. On more than one occasion, she had been so convinced it had been her that she'd approached the individual, even touching the girl on the shoulder as she walked down the high street with friends.

It had never been her daughter.

Now she managed to suppress her instincts. No longer did her heart leap at the sight of a girl matching her daughter's description. In some ways Susan had moved on. At least that's what her friends thought – and even celebrated in some macabre sense. But in truth she hadn't moved on at all.

And that's why she looked back.

The girl was gone.

Susan felt a stab of pain. She'd allowed herself to hope, and it hurt.

She turned back around, and there she was, standing just a few feet away. It felt like a dream – one which she was desperate not to wake from. It had been three years, but she still looked essentially the same: the almost-black hair she had inherited from her father, still shoulder length, the bright blue eyes from her grandparents and the face that seemed to always offer a challenge.

Her attitude had come from her mother.

'Jody? It's really you?' She stepped forward, wanting to touch her and confirm that this was actually happening.

Jody nodded, holding her gaze but taking a step back. 'We need to go somewhere quiet. Over here.'

Susan followed her daughter around the back of the buildings and towards a car park, her head reeling from what was happening. She felt dizzy, sick.

They stopped at the back of a van, hidden from view. Susan wanted to reach out and hold Jody, but she resisted, instead taking in her face. Close up, time and experience had left its mark.

'Jody, I can't believe it's you, I can't believe you're standing here. You're okay. I thought you might be dead. We looked so hard – the police looked – for years we searched the streets, put up posters, but we couldn't find you.'

Jody looked at her feet. 'I'm sorry, Mum.'

'You should have called. I know you weren't happy with school, with your dad and me, the way things were, but you should have called. Just one phone call to let us know you were okay.'

Jody seemed unmoved. 'We haven't got time to discuss this now.'

Susan flinched. 'Not got time?'

'You and Dad need to get away.'

'Get away?'

'For a few weeks. Go on holiday, go visit Aunt Edith in Scotland, go anywhere.'

'I don't understand.'

319

'You don't need to understand. Please, just do it.'

'But we can't just go away. Your father has got work. He can't just decide to go on holiday without any notice.'

'Mum, please, this isn't about going on holiday. This is about saving your life, Mum.'

'What?'

'You've got to get away, or I don't know what they'll do to you.'

'"They"? Who are "they"? You're in trouble, Jo. We can help you.'

Jody laughed at the suggestion. 'You can help by doing what I say. Take Dad and go to Scotland. Do it today. Don't tell anyone where you're going. Stay there until I call you.'

'But . . .'

'No "buts", Mum. Just do it.'

Louisa stared at the phone as she turned it over in her hand, as if willing it to disappear. Her jaw clenched, and she was lost in thought. Sam waited next to her on the sofa, staying silent. They needed to talk about this, of course, but he felt it was appropriate if Louisa took the lead. She would speak when she was ready.

'I've been crazy to trust him,' she stated finally, still glaring at the phone. 'Blinded by love. It was Marcus all along. He killed Cathy, and he's got Anna.' She turned to Sam. 'That's what you think, isn't it?'

'No,' Sam said, studying her surprised reaction.

'You don't think Marcus is behind all this?'

'Do you?'

Louisa looked down at the phone, her brow creased in concentration. 'No,' she said, her relief obvious. 'I don't think he's behind all this, I really don't. And I don't think he killed Cathy.' She held up the phone. 'But what about this?'

'I don't know,' Sam admitted.

Silence again descended for a few seconds.

'Why are you so sure?' Louisa asked.

'About Marcus?'

'Yes. A few days ago you still thought he murdered Cathy, and you suspected he was the one doing all this. I mean, I can explain the way I feel as being blind loyalty, or love. But it's not the same for you. You were so sure. What's changed?'

Sam pondered that. 'I just know. I looked in his eyes when he said he had nothing to do with it, and I believed him. For the first time since that night, I had the courage to listen to what he was saying. And now, no, I don't think he killed my sister. What you told me about Cathy and Marcus being together just reinforces that.'

'But what about the phone? What does it mean?'

'Marcus is connected in some way. I saw his face at the art gallery. Something shocked him, and I'm sure it's about Anna. I'm not saying that he knows where Anna is or who has got her. But he knows something. He knows something. That's why we've got to find him.'

Louisa pulled out her other phone. 'I'll try and call him again.' Once again, there was no reply.

'Can you think of anywhere where he might be? Some place he might have mentioned during the past few weeks? Or a name – anything? The people who have been hassling him, the gang, did he ever say where they're based?'

Louisa shook her head.

Sam sat back, frustrated with the lack of leads. Then he had a thought. 'Victoria Friedman. Marcus said that he thought she'd known more than she was letting on. Maybe he went back to challenge her about whatever he'd seen in the drawing.'

'Maybe,' Louisa said.

'Come on,' Sam said, moving up from the sofa. 'It's the best option we've got at the moment.'

They left the flat and headed downstairs. But Sam's mobile rang just as they exited the building.

'Sam, how quickly can you get to the hospital?' It was Professor Khan. His voice had an uncharacteristic edge to it.

It wasn't like him to be anything other than calm. Something out of the ordinary was happening. Sam thought quickly. 'Twenty minutes.'

'Good. I need you here right away. Your little patient Sophie has got the heart she's been waiting so long for. It's due to arrive here by helicopter within the hour, and I need you to be there by then.'

A donor heart had been found. This was amazing news: news a lot of people had been longing for all these years. But how could he help? 'I don't understand. I'm suspended.'

'Not any more,' replied Professor Khan. 'Things have changed. You're now assisting me in this extremely important operation.'

⌣

Just over twenty minutes after the conversation with Professor Khan, Sam entered the cardiac centre. The place was on red alert. This was the most high-profile surgery of the year so far – all the staff had followed Sophie's progress since her very first visit to the hospital those years ago – and now was the time. The adrenalin was flowing.

The young nurse Maria Hennessey was by the nursing station, sorting out paperwork. She looked up, saw Sam and beamed. 'Welcome back.'

'Thanks,' Sam replied. 'Has the organ arrived yet?'

'No, but it's just a few minutes away. They've flown it in from France.'

Sam nodded, thinking through how the day might go. It was a high-risk operation, and there were certainly no guarantees it would work. 'Are Sophie's parents here?'

'We've called them. They're on their way.'

'And how's Sophie?'

Maria handed Sam a blue folder. 'All in here. But she's doing well. Professor Khan seems confident.'

Sam leafed through the folder. Her observations looked good. It would give Sophie every chance. And he was being entrusted with the shared responsibility of giving her the best chance at a new life. For now he would have to try and compartmentalise the torment of Anna's whereabouts.

Looking up from the notes, he glanced around and then asked the question he'd been desperate to ask since that initial phone call requesting his assistance. 'Where's Miles?'

'I don't know,' said Maria. 'He was around early on, but he just disappeared.' She lowered her voice. 'There's a rumour that he's been suspended.'

Sam couldn't believe it. 'What?'

'Sam, better get ready.' It was Professor Khan, standing behind them, his face serious.

Sam nodded, resisting the temptation to ask him for more details about Miles's whereabouts.

Now was not the time.

For the moment, despite everything else that was going on, Sophie was all that mattered.

Chapter Forty-Three

'Are you sure this is a good idea?'

Sam paused at his office door and turned to face Louisa. It was nearly time. The heart had arrived by air ambulance direct from Toulouse. The surgical team were primed. Sophie had undergone her pre-theatre checks.

'Two hours ago,' said Louisa, 'the hospital weren't even letting you in the building. And suddenly, with no explanation, they're asking you to assist in a life-or-death operation?'

'I have to do this.' But Sam turned over Louisa's words in his mind. It was true: in the pre-operation briefing Professor Khan hadn't even mentioned the suspension, despite the fact he and Sam were alone, nor did he explain Miles's absence. Instead, he had stuck to script, outlining Sophie's case and how he was going to play it. But such focus wasn't out of character. Professor Khan always had tunnel vision in the time leading up to surgery, which was certainly no bad thing.

'It isn't exactly the best of circumstances for you to be operating,' emphasised Louisa. 'You're under so much pressure. And you're tired, Sam, I can see it.'

Sam pinched the bridge of his nose. She was right. He had felt exhausted, and the operation – certain to take several hours and last well into the night – would be punishing, even for someone who'd had adequate rest. But since Professor Khan's phone call, a river of adrenalin had gushed through his body. And now he was like an athlete ready for the hard race. There was no turning back. Not because he couldn't, but because he didn't want to.

'Tell Professor Khan about what's happening,' urged Louisa. 'Tell him that Anna is missing.'

Sam shook his head.

'If he knew what was going on, he wouldn't let you anywhere near that theatre, Sam, and you know it.'

Sam avoided her gaze.

'Tell me I'm wrong,' she pressed.

Now he met her challenge, eye to eye. 'You're right. If I told Professor Khan what was happening, he'd tell me to go home. Then he'd have to draft in someone else for the operation. That would take time: time we haven't got.'

'They could get someone else, though.'

'Not quickly enough. Sophie needs me.' Sam surprised himself with what he'd just said.

Louisa looked almost amused. 'Sophie needs you – or you need Sophie?'

'What?'

'You need this, Sam. You need to save this little girl.'

Sam knew exactly what she was alluding to. 'I want to save all of my patients.'

'But Sophie is different. It's more than just a doctor wanting to save a patient; it's personal.'

'You sound like Miles Churchill.'

'Can you deny that this case is different?'

Sam laughed off the suggestion, but Louisa was undeterred.

'It has been from the start, Sam. From that very first moment when I heard you talk about Sophie, when I saw how you were with her and her parents, I could see what was happening. For you Sophie represents the chance to save an innocent girl in a way that you couldn't save Cathy. Tell me I'm wrong.'

The comment hurt. She was right, and he couldn't deny it. Sophie did represent something more than he'd admitted, even to himself. He turned away.

'I shouldn't have said that.' Louisa's voice softened. 'Just be sure that you're okay to do this. If something does go wrong, I don't want you to come out thinking that it was your fault. I want you to go in there knowing that you're going to perform at the top of your game. If you go in thinking about Anna or Marcus or me, then you're asking for big trouble. And I know you – if something goes wrong, you'll never forgive yourself. Just like with Cathy.'

Sam placed a hand on the wall, exhaling one long breath. 'You're right. I do need to do this for myself.' He turned around. 'And maybe Sophie is all about me wanting to make up for not being able to save Cathy. Maybe you're right, maybe that's what my whole career has been about – saving as many people as I can because I couldn't save my own sister from the person who raped and murdered her.'

'I'm sorry, Sam.'

'But even with all that, I want to do this because I feel like I'm the best person to be in there with her. Maybe that's arrogance – I don't know – but I really feel she's got a better chance if I'm in that theatre. And if I thought for one second that I wasn't up to the task, then I wouldn't go in there, Louisa. I really wouldn't. You've got to trust me.'

Louisa contemplated that.

'I wouldn't do anything that I thought would put Sophie at risk,' he added. 'You know I wouldn't.'

Eventually Louisa nodded.

Sam smiled his appreciation. 'Thanks for trusting me.'

Louisa looked thoughtful. 'You couldn't have done anything to save her. None of us could. It took me a long time to realise it. Maybe I only just have.'

Sam didn't need to ask for clarification. He simply nodded. 'I know. I think I'm only just realising that too.'

Louisa placed a hand on his arm. 'I'll be there when you come out, for as long as it takes.'

'You don't have to,' Sam replied. 'It could be a very long night.'

'That's fine. I offered to wait with Sarah in the family room. She doesn't want to be on her own tonight.'

'Tom's not with her?'

'No, he's still missing. She hasn't seen him for days.'

Sam shook his head. 'He should be here with his family. Where the hell is he?'

———

Sarah Jackson managed to raise a smile as Sam stepped into the family room. But her face told a different story, revealing the stress and strain of the situation. She looked like a woman on the edge: as if a gentle puff of wind could send her plummeting into the abyss. Sam would have to tread very carefully.

'I'm so glad it will be you in there,' she said. 'Is everything going okay?'

Sam nodded. 'All the preparations have gone fine.'

'So this is really it?'

'Yes.'

Sarah ran a hand through her hair, and then sat back, her head against the wall, looking up as if wishing for divine intervention. 'I wish Tom was here.'

'I know,' Sam agreed. 'Have you heard anything from him?'

'Not a word. He's still not answering his mobile. He hasn't turned up for work since he disappeared. I've called friends, family, his work colleagues. I've been to places where I think he might go – places we visited together – parks, museums, the cinema. I even went to the zoo.' Her laugh was humourless. 'Can you believe it? I actually paid and walked around, looking for my husband in London Zoo.'

'I'm sure he's okay.'

'Oh, I'm sure he is. But what about me and Sophie?' She turned to face Sam, as if searching desperately for an answer. 'Doesn't he care about us at all?' Her face registered regret as soon as she asked the question.

'I'm certain he does,' Sam said comfortingly. 'I know it's hard to understand what he's done, but I'm sure it's because he's upset. It's not because he doesn't care about you or Sophie. He loves you both more than anything.'

'I should have seen it coming. The other day, when Sophie deteriorated and I just left him here on his own to deal with things, something changed in him. I should never have left him like that. I don't know why I did it. I think I just had to get away. I felt like I was suffocating with everything that was going on.' She shook her head. 'I just wish I'd realised things were that bad.'

'You couldn't have done anything.'

'I've left a message on his phone,' she said. 'I've told him you're doing the operation tonight. Maybe he'll be here.'

'I hope so.'

Sam waited a few beats. 'The nurses have explained the operation and how long it's likely to take?'

She nodded.

'And you know about the bed next door?'

'I won't be sleeping.'

Sam nodded. 'Louisa will be with you. If you want anything, just ask – drinks, food, something to read . . .'

'Will there be updates? Updates on how it's going?'

'I can't promise anything,' Sam replied. 'Possibly – but usually we don't tend to comment until after it's over.'

Sarah nodded.

'But as soon as it's over, I'll come to see you.'

She smiled. 'Thanks, Sam.' For a second she just looked at him, and Sam could see the question in her teary eyes. 'What are the chances?'

This was of course what any relative really wanted to know, but ironically it was the one question he could never really answer. 'As good as they can be,' he replied. 'Much better than they were a week ago. Sophie is a fighter. And she's in the best hands. Professor Khan is a world-class surgeon.'

'So she's probably going to be all right?' asked Sarah hopefully.

'We can never say that.'

The brutal honesty seemed to land an almost physical blow on her fragile frame. 'Please don't let her die.'

Sam watched Sarah Jackson crumple before him, and it took all of his inner strength not to fold with her.

⁓

The call came through ten minutes later from the surgical team.

'They're ready. Professor Khan requests your presence in theatre.'

'Thanks.' Sam replaced the handset and moved towards the door. But as he swung it open, he found Ed Stansfield on the other side, his fist raised to knock.

'Hello, Sam,' said Ed, startled. 'I wonder if I can have a quick word?'

'It'll have to wait. I've got to get straight to theatre.'

'I know. That's partly why I'm here. Just one second? It's really important.'

Sam sucked on his top lip, not really wanting to spare a moment. 'Okay, one second.'

Ed Stansfield didn't waste any time. 'I wasn't sure whether to tell you now or after the operation, but I've decided you should know the full facts before you go in there.'

'Go on.'

'The hospital has withdrawn its allegations against you. You'll be notified officially tomorrow. The board are going to offer a full and unreserved apology, and the incident will not be kept on your record. Carla wants to see you personally to express her regret at what happened.'

The news was fantastic, but puzzling. 'Why are they so sure now? I mean, they obviously weren't convinced by what you or I had to say.'

'Someone has confessed to setting you up.'

'What? Who?'

'Miles Churchill.'

'Miles? What – they caught him with drugs?'

'No,' replied Ed. 'He came forward and confessed. He said he'd planted the drugs in your locker and then called security.'

Sam thought it over. Even though Miles had always been a name in the frame, the news still came as a great shock – to think one of his colleagues could do that. 'Did he say why?'

'Not yet, no – but it's fair to assume that he saw it as a way of getting the consultant post. With you discredited, he was the clear favourite.'

Sam shook his head in disbelief. Miles had never been the most ethical of characters, and he was as desperate for the job as Sam was – but to plunge to those subterranean depths was terrible.

'I thought it might put your mind at rest before the operation.' Ed watched Sam carefully as he took the news in.

'It has, thanks . . .' Sam trailed off, still lost in his thoughts. In truth, it had done the exact opposite.

Chapter Forty-Four

S am watched Sarah Jackson as she slept in what looked like the most awkward position imaginable. Her legs were tucked underneath her body, which was wedged across two plastic chairs. Her head lolled back like a broken puppet, and her mouth was set open. Sam looked across at Louisa, who was just waking up, holding her neck and grimacing. She threw him a glance that was somewhere between bewilderment and hope.

Sam reached for Sarah, touching her lightly on the shoulder. This conversation would transform her life forever. He wondered whether she was dreaming of Sophie – dreaming of that knock-down smile as she held her daughter in her arms.

'Sarah.'

She woke slowly at first. But then realisation dawned, and her eyes snapped open. She almost scrambled upright in what could only be described as blind panic. 'Sophie – is she okay? Is she—'

Sam smiled. 'It went really well.'

The news didn't seem to register at first. It was as if she was waiting for some cruel punchline. When none came, her face exploded with joy and she leapt up, embracing Sam and squeezing him tightly, burying her head in his shoulder. 'Thank you, thank you, thank you.'

Sam smiled across at Louisa. 'It's my pleasure.'

'My little Sophie, she's going to be okay. She's going to be okay . . .' Suddenly Sarah began sobbing, and she pulled back. 'She's really going to be okay? She's going to be fine?'

Sam nodded. 'Though it's early days,' he said, not wishing for one moment to puncture her joy but also mindful of the reality of the situation. The first few hours after an operation, especially one of such magnitude, were fraught with dangers. Internal bleeding, rejection of the heart by Sophie's body, a reaction to the drugs used to suppress her immune system's response, a post-operative infection – the list went on.

'But you think she'll be all right?' Sarah's tears had stopped, but there was a new cautiousness in her voice.

'I'm as sure as I can be that Sophie will be okay,' Sam comforted her. 'The operation went better than I could have hoped.'

Indeed, during the eight-hour procedure, everything had worked like a dream. The team had performed brilliantly. Professor Khan had directed with confidence and skill, giving Sam a leading role while also being a rock for everyone in the theatre. Sophie had remained strong throughout. There hadn't been one moment when Sam feared it wouldn't work out.

It was amazing, really.

Sarah's smile returned. 'I can't thank you enough.'

'Like I said, it's my pleasure. Would you like to see Sophie?'

Her face lit up with joy. 'I can see her now?'

'Yes.' Sam smiled. 'She's not awake yet, but you're welcome to go in and see her.'

Sam and Louisa stood back as Sarah Jackson approached her daughter, who was sleeping in a private room in the ICU. Sarah looked back at them for confirmation that it was okay to get closer, and Sam nodded. He watched as Sarah cupped Sophie's head with her palm and gently brushed away stray strands of blonde hair from her forehead.

'She looks so well,' she said, turning to them.

Sam nodded. It might have only been a matter of minutes since the operation, but already the difference in Sophie was noticeable. Her skin was glowing, her body radiating the new chance of life that the donor heart had gifted.

Sarah turned back to admire her daughter. 'I'm so happy you're okay. You'll never know how happy.'

Louisa stole a glance at Sam and squeezed his arm. 'Well done,' she whispered. 'Miracle man.'

Sam gave a tight smile. Although this was a happy occasion, outside of this there was nothing to smile about. Despite his best efforts, he had been unable to stop himself from thinking about Anna during the operation. He leant in close to Louisa's ear. 'Have you heard from Marcus?'

Louisa shook her head. 'I've called a few times, but he's not picking up.'

'We need to find him, Louisa.'

'I know.'

Just then the doors to the room opened, and Nurse Hennessey entered. 'I've got a visitor for Sophie,' she said, her eyes bright and excited. 'Would you like me to bring him in?'

'Definitely,' Sam replied, realising instantly who the visitor was.

'Tom?' mouthed Louisa as Nurse Hennessey left.

Sam nodded.

Sarah seemed oblivious to what was happening, so engrossed was she in her daughter. Even as Tom entered the room, almost cowering behind Sam and Louisa, she didn't notice his presence. Tom Jackson looked like a man who had been living on the streets. His hair was all over the place, his face bearded. His blue eyes seemed shrunk against his skin, which was tanned with an accumulation of London dirt.

Suddenly Sarah sensed something and snapped out of her worship. Her eyes widened with amazement, and she broke into a wide smile. 'Tom!'

'I'm so sorry for leaving you,' he said, his body poised for surrender against the expected oncoming onslaught of emotion. 'I'm really sorry.'

But there was no anger, no recriminations. Instead, it was Sarah who surrendered to him, throwing herself into his arms. They hugged tightly for several seconds. Sam thought of Anna and how, just days earlier, they had embraced in the same way, two people joined as one. What he wouldn't do to have that again.

'It's okay, Tom, really.' Sarah cupped his face and looked deeply into his eyes. 'Everything's going to be fine now, everything's going to be okay.'

Tom, still holding his wife, looked over at Sam. 'Thank you, Sam. Thank you so much.'

Sam acknowledged the appreciation. 'Go and speak with your daughter.'

As Sarah and Tom moved towards Sophie, Sam gestured to Louisa that it was time for them to leave. They moved out of the room, standing just outside the door.

'Did you have something to do with this?' Louisa asked, nodding through the window to where Sarah and Tom were now cooing over their daughter.

'I called him straight after coming out of theatre and left a message,' Sam said. 'Told him to get the hell down here and be with his wife and daughter.'

'Good work. They look really happy.' She turned back to Sam. 'How are you feeling? I mean, physically? You must be exhausted.'

'Not too bad. I can feel the tiredness creeping up on me, but I'll be okay after a few strong coffees.'

Louisa frowned. 'You're not going back home to sleep?'

'I've got to keep looking for Anna. I thought I might go over to see Victoria Friedman.'

'But you've been awake all night.'

'I know,' Sam conceded. 'And if I really flag later in the day, then I'll have no choice, but for the moment I don't want to waste any time.'

'I wish I could come with you.'

'It's okay. You've got a job to do. Just let me know as soon as Marcus gets in touch.'

'I will,' she promised. 'Sam, I really am sorry, you know, about not telling you about Marcus.'

'It's okay. Let's just focus on getting Anna back.'

'Agreed.'

They said their goodbyes. It was now just after 8 a.m. Sam decided he would head back home, change and shower, then travel over to speak again with Victoria Friedman. It was still the only avenue of investigation he had. But before he could leave, he got a message from Professor Khan, requesting his presence in his office.

The Professor was sitting at his desk, and he beckoned Sam over. 'Sam, take a seat.'

Sam did as requested, even though sitting down only served to remind him how tired he was really feeling.

'I wanted to congratulate you before you left,' said Professor Khan. 'You did a fantastic job in there. Showed everyone exactly why your reputation is so high.'

'Thanks. But I was just assisting.'

'Nonsense. I was just watching. You were the lead, Sam. If I hadn't been in the theatre, I don't think anyone would have noticed.'

Sam didn't believe that for one moment, but you didn't challenge Professor Khan, especially to flatter him.

'I know you care for the child,' continued Professor Khan. 'You were happy with the way things went?' He raised a single bushy, inquisitive eyebrow and leant back in his chair, his fingers resting against the desk.

'Very happy,' Sam replied. 'I don't think it could have gone better.'

'Excellent. I couldn't agree more. And the parents – how are they?'

'They're good.'

'Excellent, that's excellent.' He seemed distracted, looking down at his palms as he trailed a finger along the lines. Then he chuckled, somewhat embarrassed, realising what he was doing. 'My grandmother used to read our palms when we were children,' he explained, smiling. 'I used to think it was all nonsense, but I didn't dare tell her so. When I was eight years old, she told me I was going to be a famous doctor in England. Can you believe that?'

Sam smiled.

The Professor looked back down at his palms. 'Ever since then I've wondered whether my grandmother really saw the future, or whether what she said merely influenced me to want to become that person she saw – a self-fulfilling prophecy that an impoverished boy from rural Pakistan would become a doctor and come to London.'

'Does it matter?'

'No, I suppose it doesn't. Whatever way, her prediction came true.' He smiled. 'And now when I look at my palms, I too can see into the future.'

'How do you mean?'

He held up his palms. 'I look at these palms, Sam, and I see an ageing man.' He smiled with regret. 'I see that my future does not lie here for much longer.'

'You're not that old.'

'You'd be surprised. I'm not saying it will be this year, or even next or the year after. But soon. And when I leave, I want to be sure that the place is in the best of hands. Your hands, Sam.'

The proclamation took Sam by surprise. 'Mine?'

'Of course. Nothing would make me happier.'

Hearing those words from a surgeon as great as Professor Adil Khan was more than Sam could have ever dreamt of. 'I don't know what to say.'

'You don't need to say anything. Just make sure that you perform well at the interview.'

'I'll do my best.'

'On the basis of today's exploits, that will most definitely be good enough.'

Sam paused, wondering whether to raise the issue of Miles's suspension. He decided there would never be a great time, so it might as well be now. 'I heard about Miles.'

'Yes, Miles.' Professor Khan pursed his lips. 'Miles was misguided. He's a skilled surgeon, but it's not enough. He knew that in the end, and that's why he did what he did. Sam, I hope you still want to be here after what has happened. I know you may well feel aggrieved with the suspension, but the hospital had to follow due process.'

'I understand. And I don't want to move. I love it here.'

'Good. I was worried we might lose you.'

'As long as you want me, I'm here.'

'Very good news, very good news indeed.' He smiled at Sam with evident satisfaction. 'So,' he continued, 'how is your good lady wife?'

Sam paused. 'She's good,' he lied, biting down hard on his emotion, 'very good.'

For a second he almost told Professor Khan everything. But the wall quickly came back up – he couldn't risk telling any more people about what was happening. He needed to remain as in control of the situation as possible, even though it was increasingly clear that he didn't know what the hell to do.

'She's away at the moment,' he added, 'but I can't wait to get her back.'

Chapter Forty-Five

S am got back to his empty house, checked the answer machine, then headed straight for the bathroom and jumped in the shower. He turned the temperature right down to cold and gasped as a jet of icy water blasted onto his body, shocking his system into life. It was a necessary wake-up call. On the tube home he had struggled to stay awake against the now relentless advance of tiredness. It threatened to overwhelm him, but he planned to fight it all the way.

The cold did seem to re-energise him, and by the time he got out, he felt ready for the confrontation with Victoria Friedman and for whatever else the day might bring. He dressed in fresh clothes and checked his emails. Again, there was nothing from the person who had taken Anna. After all that contact, now it was as if the lines had been cut for good.

He stared at the computer screen.

What the hell did this person want?

He tried Marcus's mobile and then his home phone. Nothing. Moving into the kitchen, he paused by the breakfast bar; he could almost see Anna there in her pyjamas, cheerfully snapping off an edge of toast. Closing his eyes, he heard her voice.

'*We're having a baby.*'

His eyes were still closed when the doorbell rang, and at first he wondered whether he'd imagined it. But by the time he emerged into the hallway, it rang again.

He opened the door to Paul Cullen, looking tired, but smiling, his hands in his coat pockets. 'Sam, can I come in?'

Sam stood aside and beckoned him inside. Cullen knew where he was going and headed straight for the living room. 'May I?' He gestured at the sofa.

'Of course.' Sam took the seat opposite and looked at Cullen's serious face. 'Has something happened?'

'A few things. We got the results back from the audio message.'

'Right . . .'

'And the guys in the analysis labs have confirmed that, as far as they can detect, it is genuine.'

'So they agree it's a recording of the incident?'

'Not exactly,' replied Cullen. 'They can't be sure when the recording was made. But they concluded that the sounds on the file did match both your statement of what you said happened and that of the train driver, and also that they align with the investigations that took place at the scene.'

'So it's not just someone playing a sick joke.'

'Like I said, they're as convinced as they can be that this is an accurate audio recording of the event.'

'And what do you think?'

Cullen laughed. 'What do I think?' He ran his tongue along the underside of his top lip as he contemplated the question. 'When you first played me this, I thought it was a joke – a sick joke, yes, but a joke nonetheless. Now I'm certain that it's for real.'

The happiness that Sam felt on hearing that Cullen believed him was tempered by the thought that he couldn't tell him about what had happened to Anna. Not without fear of reprisals. 'So what does it mean?'

'Well,' began Cullen, looking around the room as if searching for the right answer among Sam's possessions, 'it means that what you claimed was true, in the sense that the whole incident was pre-planned by someone. Somebody took the trouble to plant recording equipment at the scene – positioned in more than one location – to gather that information, and then email it to you. Unless, of course, you were the one who set up the incident and did the recording.'

His statement hung in the air like a challenge.

Sam sensed that Cullen didn't believe that but had to ask. 'And do you think I did that?'

'No, no, I don't,' replied Cullen with a certainty that both surprised and heartened Sam. 'I've never really believed you did this. I've asked myself countless times whether I was being blinded by who you are, the fact that you're a surgeon, an everyday hero. I've wondered whether if you were someone else – someone in another occupation, someone less worthy – I might have been more suspicious. But I don't think it's that at all. I just have a very strong feeling that you're telling the truth, and I trust that feeling.'

Sam nodded his gratitude before firing off his own challenge. 'Do you believe this is linked to my sister's murder?'

Now Cullen didn't look so sure. 'Maybe,' he said finally.

That he was even entertaining the possibility came as a shock, evidently to both of them. Cullen looked around the room again. 'Any chance of a tea?'

'Of course – sorry. Come through.'

Sam prepared two cups while Cullen leant on the breakfast bar. 'This case has been the most baffling of my career,' he admitted as Sam boiled the kettle. 'Transport police matters aren't usually so mysterious – plenty of grisly stuff, you know, deaths on the line, assaults, rape, the occasional murder. But nothing like this.'

Sam popped a tea bag in each cup and poured on the boiling water. 'But you do think that this might be all connected to what happened to Cathy?'

'At first I thought it was crazy, but I'm coming round to the theory, yes.'

Sam handed him the tea. 'What's changed?'

Cullen shrugged. 'You believe there's a connection.'

'But me believing it didn't convince you initially. Why now?'

'You were right about the rail crash. Believing that someone had set up that incident was, for me, the most unlikely part of your theory. If we now believe that, the next step is to consider who had the motive to do such a thing. It isn't a massive jump to conclude that it could be the person who murdered your sister.' He took a tentative sip from his tea. 'Have you spoken to Marcus Johnson since his release?'

'You think it could be Marcus?'

Cullen looked faintly amused. 'Don't you?'

'I don't think so, no.'

Cullen looked surprised. 'But you said you think the person who murdered your sister did this.'

'I don't think he killed Cathy.'

Cullen's eyes narrowed. 'Why are you so sure?'

'Because I've met with him, and I don't believe any more that he did it.'

'You asked him?'

'Yes. I asked him and I believe what he says.'

'But why now? You didn't believe him before.'

'I never listened,' Sam said. 'I didn't want to listen to what he had to say. I wanted to believe it was over, finished, and I tried to move on. But I think I was wrong.'

'You think you were wrong?'

'I'm as sure as I can be that he didn't do it.'

'Maybe you should keep your options open. Can you think of anyone else who might have a motive?'

Miles Churchill was the only name that came to mind. 'This week my colleague Miles Churchill tried to frame me,' Sam said. 'He planted drugs in my locker.'

Cullen was interested. 'Do you know why he did it?'

Sam shrugged. 'We're going for the same job, so I guess he wanted me out of the way – he wanted to smear me.'

Cullen let out a long breath, considering the statement. 'Do you think he could have done this?'

Sam considered the possibility. But surely it was ludicrous to believe that Miles Churchill had the resources to carry out such a complex plot. 'He stole a pack of drugs from the hospital supplies and planted them in my locker. I don't think he'd be capable of setting up something like this.'

'Maybe,' Cullen said, 'but it doesn't mean he didn't do it. I'd still like to speak with him.'

Sam nodded. 'I can give you his address.'

'Thanks. I'll also want to talk to Marcus Johnson.'

'He's away at the moment.'

'Away?' Cullen asked. 'Away where?'

'I don't know.'

Cullen looked exasperated, then angry. 'Look, Sam, I really need your help here. Three people linked to this case are dead, and a young girl is missing. And if your theory holds, it's all connected to you.'

He reached out and picked up the photo of Sam and Anna that stood on the breakfast bar. It had been taken by the wedding photographers two weeks before the ceremony, as part of a special pre-wedding shoot. Anna had looked especially stunning that night.

'If this is all some kind of plot directed at you, Sam, then you and your family are at risk.' He held up the photo to illustrate the point. 'You and your wife could be in great danger. So if there's anything else you know that could help, then please tell me.'

Sam swallowed hard. Should he just tell Cullen, here and now? He wanted so much to do it, but the threat of her captor still held too much power to risk it. 'I really don't know where Marcus is,' he said, sidestepping his own thoughts. 'He's not answering his phone, and there's no one at his flat.'

Cullen snorted in disbelief. 'And you still don't think he's got anything to do with this?'

'I don't know,' Sam admitted. 'I really don't know.'

'When was the last time you spoke with him?'

'Late yesterday afternoon.'

'And you've got no idea why he disappeared?'

Sam shook his head.

'I definitely want to speak with Marcus Johnson,' mused Cullen, 'as well as your work colleague. The second Marcus contacts you, you contact me, okay?'

'Okay.'

'Good.' Cullen went quiet, and Sam could tell by his eyes that there was something else: something that he was wondering whether to tell Sam.

'Have you found out the identity of the girl?' Sam tried.

Cullen shook his head. 'We found something else on the audio tape,' he began, 'something quite strange – it was buried underneath the main track, some kind of hidden file. I don't pretend to know the first thing about this sort of technology, but the guys in the lab are sure that it was deliberately laid down so that someone with a bit of technical knowledge would find it.'

Sam frowned. 'What was it?'

Cullen went to speak, then checked himself, as if wondering whether to take this last chance at keeping the information secret. 'Does the term "black wolves" mean anything to you?'

'Black wolves,' Sam repeated. 'No. Why?'

Cullen's disappointment was evident. 'The words "black wolves" were repeated several times throughout the hidden portion of the audio file.'

Clearly this was a key clue, and Sam was frustrated that he couldn't make any sense of it. Surely he'd remember something like that – but it held no meaning whatsoever. 'Was it a man's voice?'

'A male voice, yes, but it was distorted.'

'Black wolves,' said Sam again, as if repeating the words might unlock something deep down in the recesses of his memory – something that he should know.

'I think someone was sending you a message, Sam. Are you certain it doesn't relate to you in any way?'

'I don't think so. I can't think of anything.'

Cullen looked deflated. 'Just keep thinking, Sam. Keep thinking.'

⌣

Sam watched from the window as Paul Cullen walked away. Part of him desperately wanted to chase Cullen up the road and tell him everything. For the next few minutes, the thought grew stronger, until he was just staring at the phone, Cullen's number on the screen, his finger ready for pressing the 'Call' button.

Of all the life or death decisions he had taken in the operating theatre, this was the toughest decision of his life. The call could signal help, and the beginning of the end, which would see Anna back safe and well in his arms. But if he believed her captor, it could also spell disaster. He stared at Cullen's number some more.

And then he pressed the green 'Call' button.

He stood, readying himself. But the call went straight through to the answer service. And then, just as he brought the phone down from his ear, deciding not to leave a message, he heard a noise from the kitchen. It sounded like the back door closing.

He moved tentatively around the corner and through the archway. The room was empty. But then he sensed a presence, and before he could react, someone kicked his knees from behind, sending him crashing onto the tiled floor. A powerful, rough hand clamped over his mouth. Sam twisted, trying to see the person holding him, but caught only a brief glimpse of a balaclava before the person shoved him closer to the ground. 'Don't fight, Sam,' the man said with eerie calm.

Sam continued struggling, but now he saw the boots of a second person looming above him.

'We told you, no police.' The second man, also wearing a balaclava, knelt down and spoke inches from his face. 'No police, Sam. Lift him up.'

Sam was hauled upright and received a shockingly powerful punch to his lower abdomen that seemed to jolt all the major organs. The pain radiated into every part of his body. A second equally devastating blow sent him reeling back onto the floor. Gasping for air, he clutched at his stomach, rocking for comfort. 'My wife, where's . . . my . . . wife . . . ?'

A mobile was placed against his ear.

'Sam, please, they said they'll kill me.' Anna's desperate words sent even more of a shock through Sam's system.

'Anna!' Sam cried. But the phone had already been snatched away.

A final kick, and he blacked out.

PART FOUR

Chapter Forty-Six

S am woke with his cheek flat against the cold kitchen tiles. For a second or two, he just lay there, listening to his own breathing, half-expecting the men to be waiting above him, ready to administer the next act of violence. But there was no discernible noise coming from the house, and a quick, nervous glance around the kitchen from his floor-level vantage point revealed that there was no one else in the room. He rose up on his hands and struggled to his feet, grasping out at the nearby chair for support. As he moved, his stomach throbbed, and a wave of pain rippled across his back.

'Anna.'

Grimacing from the pain, he shuffled out to the phone and dialled Louisa's number.

There was no answer.

'Louisa,' he said, grimacing again as another wave broke across his body. 'They're watching the house; they knew Cullen had been here. We can't tell the police. They came here, but I'm okay. Call me on my mobile as soon as you get this.'

He considered his next move. He struggled upstairs, each step seeming twice the normal height. He entered the bedroom and looked out from the window. They were out there somewhere, watching the house, making sure he did as he was told. A few people passed by along the pavement, and in the park beyond, a couple of people were playing fetch with their dogs. One was a youngish-looking woman, dressed in jogging attire; the other, an older man. Sam watched them both, but there seemed nothing suspicious about either of them. He scanned the scene further, trying to spot anywhere that might offer a vantage point for those who were watching him. There was a clump of oak trees off to the left. It was some distance away, but if you had a decent pair of binoculars, it would afford a good view of the property, with adequate cover.

Sam sat on the edge of the bed, his mind in turmoil. There seemed no way out, no way forward. Whoever these people were, they were organised and violent. But the most shocking thing hadn't been the violence itself; it was the cold ruthlessness with which they had come into his house and dispensed the punishment. They had taunted him about Anna, without offering any clue as to their intentions.

But their visit had given him some vital knowledge. Most importantly, that Anna was still alive. Although he'd refused to acknowledge openly that she might not be, the dark thought had lurked under the surface, pricking him every so often. He also now knew for sure that this was not just the work of one lone person. A group of people were behind this. He thought of the words that had been discovered on the audio file.

Black wolves.

And then he ran through what Louisa had told him about those who had been targeting Marcus – it was the same organised, violent approach. Under those balaclavas it could have been the guy who had passed him on the stairs to Marcus's flat or the two men Louisa had said had entered the flat and taken away the television.

Surely all this was connected.

Marcus was the key.

Sam called Marcus's number, but still there was no reply. This time he left a message. 'Marcus, it's Sam. If you get this, please, call me back straightaway.'

He thought for a few seconds. His options were limited. He could wait in the house for the next phone call, the next knock at the door, the next attack. But that was what these people wanted. Or he could defy them and continue what he had been doing. He thought some more, then rose from the bed. There was no way he could just play the waiting game. He moved a little more quickly now, defying the pain, which had eased slightly. Downstairs he threw back two paracetamol and turned on the television, drawing the curtains just enough to allow the light to be seen from outside. Then he grabbed his keys and left the house by the back door. At the bottom of the garden, he peered over the fence into the garden of the house beyond. Alongside the garden was a path that opened onto the road running parallel to his. It was a useful alternative exit. The men had intended to use their revelation that they were watching him as a way of subduing his activities, but in a way it had had the opposite effect. Now he knew to be more careful.

He scaled the fence, hauling himself over, hoping it wouldn't collapse under his weight. His body aching, he jogged down the path, through the latched gate, and turned left towards the tube station.

———

The moment that Alison Ainsley had been dreading had arrived. Two days ago they had told her that she would begin to participate in the full life of the house. And after God knows how long there, trying to block out the animal-like moans and groans from behind the grubby walls, she knew exactly what that meant. She already felt dirty and without hope, but soon there would be no return. They would take the last thing from her, and she would never get it back.

The door opened slowly, and a girl whom she hadn't seen before entered. She looked a few years older than Alison, though it was difficult to judge the ages of the various girls who'd brought her food and water during her ordeal. Most bore the signs of drug abuse – the skeletal facial features, the skin taut over the bone, as if their bodies were being stretched and would one day just tear apart. A few wore make-up so garish it was almost clown-like. This girl, however, looked healthier and stronger than the others; her face was fuller and free of excessive make-up. 'Hello, Alison.'

Alison edged up the bed and backed up against the wall. She thought about running, and her eyes darted around as if looking for a portal to freedom that would magically open up in the wall. But the door was covered, and she knew that even if she got out, he would be waiting for her. Just like last time.

The girl moved closer. 'It's time, Alison.'

Alison shook her head and began to cry. 'Please, leave me alone, please.'

The girl shook her head. 'You know I can't do that.'

'Leave me alone,' Alison repeated. She rose from the bed, but the girl moved forward quickly, holding her down by the shoulders. Her grip was firm without being threatening.

'Please,' she said, looking deep into Alison's eyes, 'please, just do everything I say, and you'll be all right.'

What did that mean? Alison hardly dared think that it was another attempt to free her, but the girl's face seemed to convey something that offered that promise.

'What are you going to do?'

'Just follow me.'

Alison held back.

'You'll be all right,' the girl repeated. 'Come with me.'

'Are you here to save me?' Alison was almost scared to speak the words for fear that the answer would destroy her hope totally.

'Follow me.'

Alison prayed that she would be walking to freedom rather than a greater horror. The truth was, whatever her destination, she had no choice but to do as she was told.

She followed the girl out onto the landing, and for a moment thought they were heading for the same store cupboard from which the first failed escape had been launched. But instead, the girl took her downstairs.

Alison's hopes rose as she scrutinised the girl's behaviour. She was hurrying, and her nervous glances were the mark of someone who didn't want to be discovered.

By the time they reached the lower floor corridor, Alison had convinced herself that this was the beginning of the end. Soon she would be free. The nightmare would be over, and she would be home with her family. She was so sure of this that when the girl beckoned her through the door, she rushed through with excitement, almost elation.

She hadn't expected a man to be waiting for her on the other side.

Chapter Forty-Seven

As she answered the door, Victoria Friedman tried to maintain her composure, but something in her expression told Sam that Marcus had been right – she knew more than she had claimed.

'Ms Friedman,' said Sam, 'can I come in for a few minutes?' He resisted the temptation to put his foot in the gap between the door and the frame. Instead, he stood his ground, hoping she would let him in.

Her face creased, and then she nodded. 'Okay, a few minutes.'

Sam followed her inside and into the living room.

'What can I do for you now?' she said, blinking. Her tone was meant to convey annoyance, but Sam detected something different: nervousness, maybe even defensiveness.

'I need your help,' he said.

She looked surprised. 'My help?'

Sam nodded. 'I think you can help me.'

'How?'

'By telling me who killed Wayne Cartwright.'

Now she looked stung, and again, those now telltale blinks. She snorted incredulously. 'He killed himself.'

'No. Someone made it look like a suicide.'

She shrugged. 'So what? Some prisoners killed him, or he killed himself. Like I told you before, I'm afraid I don't really care.'

Sam just stared at her for a few seconds. 'How did you find out?'

'Excuse me?'

'How did you find out what Richard had done? Arranging Wayne Cartwright's murder. Did Richard tell you himself?'

A micro-expression of guilt, an almost subliminal message, flashed across her face. 'I really don't know what you're talking about.'

Sam sensed that he had her on the ropes. If he pressed some more, she would give way. 'Who killed Wayne Cartwright, Ms Friedman? How did Richard come to meet these people?'

She tried to remain defiant, but the mask was slipping. 'You should be careful, throwing wild accusations around.'

'Do the words "black wolves" mean anything to you?'

Again a micro-expression. 'I think you'd better leave.'

Sam stayed seated. 'You've heard those words before, haven't you? They're linked to the people who killed Wayne Cartwright, aren't they? The people Richard asked to kill him.'

'He didn't ask them to kill him – they offered,' she shot back.

Sam tried to remain composed, hardly daring to believe the breakthrough he'd just made. 'Who are they?'

Victoria Friedman looked wounded and refused to meet his gaze.

'Who are they?' Sam repeated.

'Why are you so concerned?' She sounded as if she was almost pleading for an end to the questioning. 'What does it matter to you? It's all finished with now.'

It was time. She needed to realise the gravity of the situation. 'The people who killed Wayne Cartwright: they've taken my wife.'

She looked genuinely shocked. 'Your *wife*?'

'It's all connected. My sister's murder, your brother, Wayne Cartwright, my wife.'

'But I don't understand.'

'Neither do I, but I'm beginning to. Someone – some people – killed Wayne Cartwright for your brother. And then they wanted something in return. He stole my friend's mobile phone and called me, taunting me about my sister's murder, because they told him to do it.'

She shook her head. 'Richard wouldn't do that kind of thing; it wasn't in his character.'

'Richard had no choice. These people would have forced him to do whatever they wanted.'

'You don't know this.'

'Your brother is dead because of these people.'

She tried to dismiss it. 'He's dead because of what Wayne Cartwright did – killing Margaret.'

'No. He's dead because of these people. They drove him to it. They offered to kill Wayne Cartwright, then made him do things he didn't want to do, and the guilt was too much for him.'

She put a hand to her head, as if an explosion of pain had just detonated inside her skull.

'Please,' Sam pressed, 'they have my wife. I need your help.'

She lowered her hand. 'How do I know that you're not one of them? That this isn't a test?'

'I don't understand.'

'They said they might do it. They might send someone around to the house to ask questions, to check that I would keep quiet.'

Now the extent of the gang's web of fear was apparent. Sam pulled out his wallet and showed her his driving licence. 'Sam Becker,' he said, gesturing towards the card. 'I am who I say I am.'

She nodded, satisfied. 'I want Richard to be remembered for who he was: a good man. A troubled man, but still a good man. He never would have gone down this road if it hadn't been for me.'

Sam blinked. 'You? You arranged for them to kill Wayne Cartwright?'

'I don't have to tell you anything, and I certainly won't tell the police anything. I just don't want Richard's memory to be besmirched. He's finally at peace now, and that's how I want it to stay.'

Sam leant towards her. 'I just want to find my wife.'

She nodded, as if considering her response. 'Richard spoke to a man on the telephone several times. His name was Vincent.'

Another breakthrough.

It had to be the same Vincent who had dated Jane Ainsley. Who was this guy?

'You don't know his surname?'

'No. I don't know anything else about him, apart from his first name, and I'm not naive enough to believe that his name really is Vincent.'

'What about "black wolves". Does it mean anything to you?'

'Just a moment.' She rose from the chair, and Sam heard her trudging up the stairs. He waited, dry-mouthed. When she returned, she handed him a canvas. The pencil drawing seemed to burst out of the frame. The wolf's jaws appeared to be heading for the viewer's throat; saliva was spitting from its open mouth. And in the background, once again, was the mysterious figure with its arms open wide.

As with Richard's other artwork, Sam was transfixed. 'But you don't know what "black wolves" refers to?'

'No. Just that Richard drew this shortly before he died.'

'And who is this?' Sam gestured at the figure.

Victoria Friedman shrugged. 'Richard would never tell me. But it always made me think of the devil.'

Sam could see why. 'One last thing – has my friend Marcus been to see you again?'

'No.'

She could have been lying, but Sam saw no reason for her to. Wherever Marcus had rushed off to, it hadn't been here.

Sam exited onto the street and watched as Victoria Friedman closed the door. Now he had confirmation, as much as she was willing to give, that Wayne Cartwright had been murdered to order. And that name, Vincent – undoubtedly it was the same Vincent whom Shirley Ainsley had spoken of. Her suspicions, which a few days ago had sounded outlandish, even paranoid, now made sense. Sam opened his wallet and pulled out the address that Shirley Ainsley had handed him shortly after storming into his office and quizzing him about his role in her daughter's apparent suicide. As she was another caught in the web, the next logical step seemed to be a visit to her.

On the way to the bus stop, in between checking to see if anyone suspicious was following him, he tried Marcus and Louisa. But again there was no answer from either. He did get through to ICU for an update on Sophie. She was still doing well. The bus had just appeared when his phone rang. It was Paul Cullen.

'Sam. I've got some news about the case.'

Sam stepped onto the bus. 'Go on.' He took a seat near the back.

'We've determined the identity of the girl who claimed to be Alison Ainsley.'

Sam held his breath. Another piece of the puzzle was coming together. 'Right. Who was she?'

'Her name is Stacey Bond,' replied Cullen. 'Sixteen years old, from Newcastle-upon-Tyne. She ran away from home three years ago after a family argument and hadn't been seen since.'

'Are you sure it's her?'

'The family came down and gave a positive ID.'

The bus stopped, and a large man thumped down next to Sam, pressing against him. Sam switched ears. 'Did they come forward?'

'No,' Cullen replied, 'we found them. We had a call yesterday. The person gave us the name Stacey Bond, and we worked back from there to find the family.'

'Who gave you the name?'

'No idea. They rang the Crimestoppers line and reported it anonymously. The caller was female, but that's all we know.'

Another mysterious aspect to events. 'So what now?'

'At the moment it doesn't give us much,' Cullen admitted. 'This girl dropped off the radar for three years: no contact whatsoever with the family. But we obviously know she was in London, at least for a time, so we're sending people out to the hostels and other places to ask again. Maybe the name will lead to something.'

Sam doubted it. The photograph had yielded nothing, so he didn't have any reason to believe that a name would make any difference. But there was no point in being defeatist. 'Hopefully it will.' Cullen might not have been in the loop regarding Anna's kidnap, but he was still an important ally, and the big break might yet come from his side. 'Any news on what "black wolves" means?'

'No,' Cullen said. 'How about you? Any new thoughts?'

Sam glanced around the bus, suddenly realising again that there could be someone watching and listening from a nearby seat. It was time to end this call. 'No new thoughts,' he lied, 'but I'll keep thinking.'

Chapter Forty-Eight

S am stepped off the bus in unfamiliar surroundings. The Ainsleys' home was only a mile and a half from his own, but as was the nature of the capital, with its many inter-twined villages and communities, he had never been around this way before. The area was noticeably poorer than Clerkenwell. There were no chic cafés, no shops or pleasant social green spaces. Here, pubs, scruffy fast food outlets and betting shops predominated, and the people looked jaded, heads down as they passed Sam on the street. Once he was through the high street, it took only a couple of minutes to reach the Ainsleys' house, a redbrick mid-terrace, sandwiched together with five other properties between two ugly tower blocks.

Shirley Ainsley answered after the first knock. She looked worn and troubled, quite different from the feisty character who had challenged him in his office. She looked surprised when she saw Sam, and shepherded him in quickly, as if embarrassed at her visitor. In the living room sat a man who, Sam presumed, was Shirley's husband. He glanced warily up at Sam, looking tense, even frightened.

'Eric, this is Sam Becker,' Shirley said.

Sam shook Eric's hand. 'Pleased to meet you.'

'You too, Doctor.' Eric seemed relieved at the identity of their guest, but he avoided eye contact.

While Shirley went to make a cup of tea, Sam looked around the room and noticed a photo of Jane. She was beaming at the camera, her expression far removed from the vacant one she'd had as she'd faced down the oncoming train. Sam pondered that in silence; Eric too sat silently. The stillness was only broken when Shirley returned. 'Here you are,' she said, handing Sam a cup. 'Careful – it's very hot.'

Sam cradled the drink and looked across at Shirley, now sitting next to her husband. She readied herself, flattening down her skirt and forcing a smile. 'What can we do for you?'

Sam decided to come straight out with it. 'My wife has been kidnapped.'

With such a statement, he realised that he had in some way detached himself from its horrific meaning, in the same way that he sometimes coped with breaking bad news in the hospital. The truth was almost too painful to bear: that someone, some people, had Anna and could be doing anything to her.

But the reality of what his statement meant was not lost on Shirley Ainsley, who reacted with dismay. 'Oh my God – kidnapped?'

Sam nodded, glancing at Eric, who was sitting there, not revealing any emotion. 'It's all connected, Shirley. Everything that has happened to your family and everything that's happened to mine – it's all connected.'

'I don't understand.'

'I think the same people are behind all of this,' Sam explained. 'The people who killed your daughter also killed my sister, and now they have my wife and your granddaughter.'

'But why?'

'I don't know. But I'm sure that it's all connected. That's why we've got to help each other.' He paused and caught Eric glancing at Shirley. 'What is it?'

Shirley and Eric hesitated, but Sam pressed. 'If you know anything, tell me, please.'

Shirley nodded, placing a hand on Eric's knee. 'It's going to be all right,' she said to her husband. 'We can trust him.'

'You tell him,' muttered Eric, looking at his feet.

'Eric lost his job some time ago,' said Shirley quietly. 'He didn't tell me; he was ashamed, and he couldn't find other work. So he borrowed money from a man who approached him in the pub. He thought it would just tide him over until he found a job, but the interest rate was so high, he got deeper and deeper into debt. Then they started threatening him, wanting the money back.'

Eric continued staring down.

'The man was Vincent McGuire,' continued Shirley. 'Dating our daughter – it was just another way of threatening Eric, threatening our family. He came to the house yesterday and told me he had set up Jane's death and that he has Alison. That's when Eric told me everything.'

Sam closed his eyes for a moment. So it was the truth. The train crash was a set-up.

'What you said,' Shirley added, 'about everything being connected? Vincent said that this wasn't about us – it was part of a bigger plan. Is it all about you?'

Sam swallowed. As much as he didn't want to believe it, it now seemed obvious. 'I think so, yes.'

'So he's using us to get at you? Jane murdered, Alison taken. Why? Why would he do that?'

'I don't know,' Sam admitted. 'I really don't.'

Shirley digested that for a moment. 'Yesterday we got a call,' she said, 'from someone who said she knew where Alison was.'

Sam sat forward. 'And?'

'And she said we should wait to hear from her.'

'She didn't say who she was?'

'It was a girl, but she didn't give a name.'

Sam thought about what Paul Cullen had said about the anonymous tip-off having come from a female. Maybe he had one more ally than he realised.

'So, you're just waiting?'

Shirley shrugged, upset. 'What else can we do? She warned us not to tell the police; otherwise, Alison might come to harm. She said Vincent has got friends in the force. So this person is our only hope.'

Another tantalising step forward, but it wasn't the leap that Sam needed. 'What do you know about Vincent McGuire?'

'Nothing. Only his name.'

'But you know he has money,' Sam said, directing his statement at Eric.

'Oh, he has money,' Eric said. 'He got the fifteen thousand pounds to me the same day he offered it.'

'From where?' Sam thought about what Louisa had said about the gang intimidating Marcus and about their offer of a job. 'He's got people working for him, violent people. Is he a loan shark?'

'Maybe,' said Eric. 'But I hadn't seen him before that time in the pub. I don't know what he does, really.'

It was a long shot, but worth asking. 'Do you have a contact number?'

'No,' Eric said. 'He always contacted me either in person or via an unknown number. And the number he gave Jane is now not working.'

Sam pressed on in the hope that Eric might unlock another part of all this. 'Do the words "black wolves" mean anything to you?'

Eric shook his head, but Shirley looked thoughtful.

'What is it?' Sam asked.

'One of his men, when he came to the house, he had a tattoo of something on his neck, an animal. I thought it was a dog, but it could have been a wolf, couldn't it?'

Sam nodded, tempering his hope that they were making real progress here: if it didn't result in the safe return of his wife, it meant nothing. 'Is there anything else you can think of?'

When both came back with a negative, he tried again. 'What's he like, Vincent McGuire?'

'Ruthless,' Eric shot back, resentment flowing. 'Inhuman. He enjoys making people suffer. He's enjoyed every second of making me and my family go through hell.'

Sam considered Eric's description of Vincent. Was he Cathy's murderer? Could it really be him?

'He can be charming though,' Shirley interrupted. 'Jane was smitten with him, really smitten. I remember her coming home one night and telling me about this new man she had met. Sounded like a real smooth character – said her eyes looked like the two brightest stars in the midnight sky.' She snorted bitterly. 'I guess we were all fooled by his words. I blame myself, Sam, because I was her mother, I should have seen through that man. Jane was lonely, naive, a young mother with four children whose husband had upped and left. She needed someone to look out for her, to see things for how they really were.'

'It wasn't your fault,' Sam said, although he had stopped listening properly halfway through her speech. What had she just said? 'None of this is our fault.'

Stars in the midnight sky.

'Are you okay, Sam?'

'What did he say to Jane? About stars in the midnight sky?'

'That her eyes looked like the two brightest stars in the midnight sky. Why?'

Sam's heart was pounding, his body in overdrive at the thoughts going through his head. 'What does he look like?'

'Tall, thin, dark hair, pointed nose, very blue eyes,' Shirley replied.

Sam thought back fifteen years to the night at the campsite bar. The guy who had been pestering Cathy and Louisa, the one who Marcus had warned off. My God, could it be?

'I think I know who it is,' he said out loud.

He pressed his fingers into each side of his temple and trawled his memory for an impression of that person. It was a long time ago, but he did remember the guy being tall and thin, with those piercing blue eyes. But it was those words that were so powerful: the two brightest stars in the midnight sky. Almost exactly what Louisa had said just the other day, the chat-up line he had used on Cathy. It had to be.

'Who?' Shirley said. 'Who is he?'

But before Sam could answer, there was a loud knock at the door.

He poured himself another glass of whisky and walked towards the chair, flopping down into it. Some of the golden liquid leapt out from the glass and dribbled down his hand. He licked it from his skin, on one level repulsed by the taste, but on another eager for more. He took a generous gulp from the glass and looked around the penthouse apartment, surveying everything that he could be about to lose: the television, the stereo system, the carpets, curtains – everything. He looked out towards the balcony and thought, not for the first time, about ending it out there. But this time felt different. The thought was no longer consigned to some future scenario. It was a here-and-now consideration.

What the hell.

Who would miss him? Certainly not Sam Becker, surgeon extraordinaire.

He got up and wandered over to the glass doors. For the first time in a long while, he felt as if he was in control. Sliding back the doors, he stepped onto the balcony and was blasted by a cooling gust from the Thames below. Up ahead he could see Canary Wharf. That was where the big money was made. How he could do with some of that now. Placing both hands on the brushed metal railing, he peered down towards the ground, some eleven storeys below. The ground seemed to rise towards him – the alcohol, he figured.

He balanced the drink precariously on the railing and brought one leg over the metal bar, steadying himself so that he didn't fall, in the ultimate irony. One leg each side of the rail, he tensed and screwed his eyes shut, wishing away the situation yet also feeling more invigorated than he ever had in his whole life.

Then, from within the apartment, his phone began to ring. He dared to hope. Maybe they had kept their promise after all.

Chapter Forty-Nine

Someone knocked for a second time. Shirley and Eric stayed rooted on the sofa, their faces frozen with fear. Sam looked at them for direction.

'It could be them,' Shirley said, her voice fearful. 'Vincent's people.'

Sam looked towards the direction of the door. A thought came to him – they could have been following him all along. He could have been the one who had brought them here. Despite his own fear, he decided to take control. 'I'll get it.'

'Thank you,' Eric said eventually. 'Thank you.'

Sam nodded and rose from the chair, his body tense.

'Please be careful,' Shirley said. 'And if it is them and they want to come in, please, let them.'

'I don't think I'll have a choice,' Sam said, becoming aware again of the bruising across his ribs as the tablets wore off. 'Don't worry,' he added, 'it will be all right.' He was trying to convince himself more than anyone else. As he approached the front door, nerves playing havoc with his system, the knock came again. 'Who is it?' Sam called.

No reply.

He reached for the door, with no idea how he was going to handle this should those men be on the other side. Taking a deep breath, he opened the door.

The man on the other side frowned suspiciously, looking Sam up and down. There was only this guy, a lank man in his mid-twenties, with dirty blonde hair that fell to his shoulders. He looked like a particularly scruffy surfer. 'This is where Shirley and Eric Ainsley live, right?'

'Who are you?' Sam said, evading the question.

'Antony McLaughlin,' he replied, his accent somewhere close to Dublin. 'Now, mate, are you going to tell me whether I've got the right house or not?'

'Depends what you're here for,' Sam said.

The guy laughed, opening his arms. 'I'm here to . . .' The smile vanished, as if something had just come to him. He took a faltering, panicked step back. 'You're not one of them?'

'One of who?'

'Who are you, mate? Tell me who the hell you are, or I'm outta here.' He glanced down the street, as if he was thinking of running.

Sam took a chance. 'My name's Sam Becker.'

The guy laughed, reacting as if he should have known that fact all along. 'Sam Becker, the doctor.'

Sam held his ground, but his suspicions had lifted. 'Who the hell are you?'

'I've told you already: Antony McLaughlin – Locky for short. Now can I come in, or what?'

Shirley and Eric flinched as Sam walked back in, with Locky following close behind.

'It's okay,' Sam said, 'he's not one of them. At least I don't think he is.'

'Too right I'm not,' said Locky, shifting from one foot to the other as if he were on hot coals. 'I'm one of the good guys, here to get you back your granddaughter.'

Shirley stood up, her face full of hope and anticipation. 'You know where she is?'

Locky nodded. 'She's safe. Now are you coming with me to get her, or what?'

Shirley looked at Sam for guidance.

'How do we know you're telling the truth?' Sam asked.

Locky shrugged. 'You don't, but you must be a smart man, Doctor. Go with your instincts.'

Sam looked back at Shirley. Of course, there was a risk that this was a trap of some sort, but Sam didn't think so. And he wasn't about to waste the big break that might lead him to Anna. 'I'll go with him.'

'If you're going, I'm going too,' she replied. 'She's my granddaughter.'

'Me too,' Eric added, his face determined. 'I'm coming as well.'

'Great,' Locky said, clapping his hands. 'Everyone out to the car it is, then.'

They followed him out of the front door and into a battered blue car that was parked a few yards away.

'Don't forget your seat belts,' he advised, starting the engine. 'I'm a bit of an erratic driver.'

'Where are we going?' Sam asked from the front passenger seat.

'Can't tell – sorry,' he replied, pulling away from the kerb and hitting the accelerator. 'Under orders to keep information to a minimum.'

'Under orders by who?'

'Can't tell, or she'd bust my balls.'

'She?'

'The girl who called me yesterday?' asked Shirley.

Locky seemed infuriated by his slip. 'Yes.'

'The same girl who phoned the police about Stacey Bond?' Sam said. 'Who is she? The girl I saw at the river?'

'No more questions, please.' Locky changed lane suddenly to overtake a slow-moving car. 'Otherwise I might crash this bloody thing.'

'Just one last question,' Sam persisted. 'My wife, Anna Becker, do you know where she is?'

'Look, Doc, I'm really sorry, but I don't.'

Was this guy telling the truth or not? Sam's instincts told him Locky was genuine, both regarding where Alison was and not knowing Anna's whereabouts. So there were positives and negatives. How much he would give to have Anna waiting for him at their destination. He sat back and remained silent for the rest of the fifteen-minute journey. Occasionally he glanced back to check on Shirley and Eric. Both looked in a permanent state of edginess. The car raced around the London streets, across junctions, over bridges, the cultural landscape changing as they went.

Finally Locky spoke.

'We're here,' he said as the car turned a sharp left and slowed to a stop next to a block of low-rise maisonette flats. 'Now, when you get out,' he said, wrenching up the handbrake and turning off the ignition, 'don't be hanging around. Get out of the car as quick as you can, and get through that door over there.' He gestured over to the entrance.

They all nodded.

'Great,' said Locky, 'now follow me.'

The three of them followed him across to the entrance and up a set of concrete steps. They stopped outside the first flat, and Locky led them inside. 'She's in here,' he said, stepping through the door. 'Don't worry – she's okay.'

Sam followed him in first and saw a young girl sitting cross-legged on the sofa, remote control in hand, watching TV just like any normal teenager. She looked up at Sam and frowned. But on seeing her grandmother appear behind Sam, she burst into life, joy spreading across her face like a flame. 'Gran!'

Shirley ran forward with her arms outstretched. 'Oh my God, Alison, my Alison, you're safe! My God, you're really safe!'

They embraced in a tight hug. Then Shirley stepped back and looked at Alison as if unable to believe that she wasn't imagining it. She stroked back some stray hair from Alison's forehead. Alison looked remarkably well, and it gave Sam hope about Anna's condition. 'Oh, my Alison,' said Shirley, 'we're so glad to have you back.'

They hugged again. Eric moved forward and put an arm around the two of them. 'I'm so happy to see you, Alison, so happy.' He was crying. They all were. Sam stood back slightly, side by side with Locky, feeling like a voyeur to an intensely private moment.

'Is everyone okay?' Alison asked over Shirley's shoulder. 'Mum and the rest? They're all okay, aren't they?'

Sam found himself looking straight at her pleading eyes. 'I'm so sorry, Alison,' he found himself saying. 'I couldn't save your mum.'

Sam and Locky retreated to the next room while Alison was comforted by Shirley and Eric. They needed their private space, although Sam knew from bitter personal experience that the real grieving would come in time. Some minutes later, they were called back into the living room, and Sam took a seat. Alison was sitting in between her grandparents, her tears now drying.

'Thank you,' she said, 'for saving my sisters and brother.'

Her gratitude at such a time of grief took Sam by surprise. 'You don't need to thank me. I just wish I could have saved your mum.'

'I know,' she said, displaying remarkable maturity beyond her teenage years.

371

Sam looked across at Locky, who was standing a few feet from them, gnawing at a fingernail. 'What now?'

He shrugged. 'Wait until we hear what to do next.'

'Hear from who? The girl?'

Locky refused to answer.

'What's this all about?' Sam asked.

'I've told you,' he said, 'I can't tell you anything. I'm really sorry, Doc, but I can't say a word.'

Sam turned to Alison. He was unsure about whether to question this girl, who had not only been through a horrendous experience but had also just found out that her mother was dead. However Anna's life was at stake. 'Alison, my wife has been taken by the same people who took you. Do you know where she might be?'

She shook her head. 'They kept me in a room in a big house. There were lots of other women, and men that came to, you know . . . to . . . er . . . have sex with them.'

'My God,' Shirley said, horrified, 'please say they didn't—'

'It's okay, Gran, they didn't touch me,' Alison reassured her, 'but I thought they would.' She addressed Sam again. 'I don't know where the house was, and I don't know anything about your wife. I'm really sorry.'

'It's okay,' Sam replied, trying not to think about what they might be doing to Anna. 'Do you know who it was that took you?'

She nodded. 'Vincent. Mum's boyfriend.'

Mentioning the name 'Mum' upset her again, and she sank into Shirley's arms. Sam wished he could take the pain away. He turned to Locky. 'You know who this guy is, don't you?'

Locky started biting at his fingers again.

'Who is he?' Sam pressed. 'And where's the house? You must know.'

'I can't say – I really can't. Don't you think I'd like to tell ya?'

Sam's anger flared at knowing that this man was keeping something so important from them. 'Why can't you?'

'Because it's not safe!' he spat. 'It's not safe. That's why we've got to stay here until it is. And the less you know at the moment, the safer you'll be.'

'And what about my wife?'

'I've told you, I don't know anything about your wife, I swear.'

Sam's mobile rang, and everyone in the room looked on.

'Hello?'

It was Miles.

Sam listened to the single sentence, not quite believing what he was hearing. He snapped the phone shut and made for the door, blood pumping hard. Locky followed. 'Hey, where are ya off to?'

'To get my wife back,' he replied.

Chapter Fifty

Sam knew where Miles lived. Everyone working in the cardiothoracic unit did, as he'd invited the whole department over for a flat-warming party when he'd first purchased it eighteen months ago. Most thought that it was a way of demonstrating to everyone how successful he was. It was an upper-floor apartment that looked out across the Thames, bought at the height of the London property boom. It wasn't in the premier league of capital residences, but it was still very exclusive, and Sam had wondered at the time how he'd been able to afford the astronomical asking price.

He knocked three hard knocks and waited impatiently.

Please let him be in. Please let him be telling the truth.

Eventually Miles answered. He looked terrible: bloodshot eyes and corpse-like, ashen skin, as if he hadn't slept in days. He shifted from one foot to another. As he went to speak, Sam smelt the alcohol on his breath. He was well past drunk. 'Sam, do come in,' he slurred.

'You said you know what's happened to my wife,' Sam said, letting the door swing shut and squaring up to Miles. Part of him still thought that this was some sort of sick joke. But no one except him and his close friends knew that Anna was missing.

'Would you like a drink, Sam?' grinned Miles. 'I have plenty of drinks. How about a whisky?'

Sam got another blast of alcohol. 'You're drunk,' he stated.

Miles shrugged. 'And what if I am? Can you blame me? I've lost everything, Sam. My career has been flushed down the toilet.'

'You brought it on yourself, Miles,' Sam replied, impatient to get back to the reason he was here. 'What do you know about Anna?'

Miles wagged a finger. 'Ah, no, no, no. I didn't' – he put up two fingers as quotation marks – 'bring it on myself.' He jabbed Sam in his chest. 'It's all because of you, Sam.'

'How?'

Miles smiled. 'Because they used me to get to you.'

'What?'

'They reeled me in and then used me, Sam. They used me as a pawn to do their dirty work. They told me to plant the drugs in your locker. I didn't want to do it – they made me do it. Do you see? It's all because of you, Sam.'

'Who are "they"?'

'I don't know,' Miles replied. 'But they don't like you. I guess we have one thing in common there, Sammy boy.'

Sam ignored the jibe. It wasn't the time for petty games. 'How did you meet them?'

'They found me. Got talking to a guy at the Victoria Casino. Said he could help me out. I was in a spot of bother. Lost a lot of cash, you see. Bet you didn't know I liked a gamble, did you, Sam?'

Sam didn't want to hear about Miles's addictions. 'Who was he? Was his name Vincent?'

'Haven't got a clue. But he had money. Lots of money. Said it was going to be a loan, low interest, but he came asking for it back pretty quickly. Pity I'd already lost it on the roulette. You see, Sam, I'm one of life's risk-takers. You don't get ahead in this life without taking a risk.'

'So they forced you to plant the drugs in my locker?'

'Indeed they did, Detective. They're extremely persuasive.'

The story was startlingly familiar – they'd used the same strategy with Richard Friedman and Eric Ainsley: the offer of help made only to gain total control.

'My wife, Miles,' Sam said, returning to his only priority, 'you said you know something about her.'

'They took her,' he said. 'They're holding her.'

'I know that. Where is she?'

'I don't know, exactly.'

Sam struggled to keep his calm – he wanted to grab Miles by the throat and shake the truth out of him. 'What's that supposed to mean? Do you know where she is or not?'

'I know where she might be.'

'Then for God's sake, tell me, Miles, please,' Sam implored. 'This isn't a game, you know.'

'Oh, I know it's not a game, Sam,' Miles shot back, his expression darkening. 'I've lost everything, remember? And I might lose the apartment too.'

Sam backed down, not wanting to rattle Miles for fear that he'd just shut down or start rambling about himself again. He tried softening his approach. 'Miles, I'm sorry about what's happened to you – I really am – but this is my wife's life we're talking about. You called me over here. Now please, tell me what you know.'

The tactic worked. Miles nodded. 'I have a telephone number. The number they call me from.' He handed Sam a piece of paper with the number scrawled on it.

Sam looked up. The London number looked familiar. The combination of numbers was similar to another number he knew. 'Is this everything?'

Miles nodded. 'I don't know where they are, I don't know any names, but I have that number.'

Sam looked at the number again, trawling his mind for the reason why it seemed so familiar. 'Why give it to me now?'

'I want to help,' Miles said. 'And I'm scared of what they might do to me. Please, help me, Sam.'

He cut a pitiful figure. Sam should have known. This wasn't an act of altruism; it was self-serving. But it didn't matter. 'Did they ever say why they were doing this?'

'No, never.'

Sam left the apartment block and pulled out his phone. He began to type in the numbers on the piece of paper. He didn't know whether this was the right thing to do, but he did it anyway. The last number keyed in, the phone began to dial through. It was then that the text appeared on the screen.

Sam cut the call off immediately.

The phone had recognised the number, already stored in its memory. It had been the landline number of their friends who, until a few months ago, had lived in the flat upstairs. The people who had Anna were calling Miles from there.

Chapter Fifty-One

S am sheltered behind a tree in the park and watched the upstairs window for signs of life. The flat above his had its living room facing the front. He had approached the house from the opposite side of the park, hoping that it would afford him cover. There was nothing to say that there already weren't people watching him in the trees off to the left, but he just had to hope that wasn't the case.

Was he doing the right thing?

A few minutes more, and still no movement. He thought about his new upstairs neighbour, the man who had introduced himself as David Braithwaite. The supposed City banker. Tall, thin, blue eyes, pointed nose. Vincent. The guy had moved in about five months ago. It had certainly been a long-term plan. Sam thought back to the handful of times he had seen the neighbour and the two times they had spoken. The first was the day after he moved in, when Anna and he went around to welcome him to the neighbourhood. He'd been friendly enough but hadn't given much away, and they'd spent just five uncomfortable minutes there.

The second time was the night of Stacey Bond's death.

Vincent couldn't have been with Stacey; he hadn't been the one to inflict the blow and send her crashing into the water. But he had probably directed the operations. And he'd watched Sam rush out of the house on his futile mission to save the poor girl.

Sam decided to go for it. He crossed the street and as quickly and quietly as possible entered his home. Once inside, he headed straight for the kitchen drawer, stuffed full of accumulated junk. They'd been meaning to clean it out for years but somehow had never got around to it. He found what he was looking for right at the back of the drawer. Fiona and Martin had given them the spare key some years ago, when they'd gone on what would be the first of several trips to America.

He pulled out his phone and called the number upstairs. The call connected and then just kept ringing. It didn't mean there was no one there, though.

Now Sam called Louisa. Again there was no answer, so he left another message.

'Louisa, it's Sam. I'll explain things later, but I know who has Anna. He's been staying here, in the upstairs flat. Call me as soon as you get this.'

His next call was to Paul Cullen. It was time to involve him.

There was no answer there either, so again he left a short message, not wanting to waste time.

'Paul, please call me as soon as you get this message. It's Sam Becker. My wife has been kidnapped. But I know who has her. Come over to the flat as soon as you can.'

Saying the sentence sounded unreal. Was he really close to seeing her again? Was she just a few feet away from him?

He ended the call and stared at his phone. Should he call 999 too? His finger hovered above the number. Locky, Miles, the gang themselves, had all warned him that Vincent McGuire had contacts within the police. It might have been a bluff, but Sam wasn't prepared to take the risk. He trusted Paul Cullen, but no one else.

He held up the key and twisted it in the light, pondering whether what he had in mind was a good idea. But the thought of Anna being so close was enough to dispel any doubts. He couldn't wait for Cullen.

He left the house and moved to the side of the building, to where the front door to the upstairs flat was located. The guy might have had the locks changed, but then again maybe he hadn't.

The key worked, and within seconds he was inside. He moved quietly up the stairs that directly faced him, expecting that Vincent or one of his men would be waiting. But as he emerged onto the landing, the place was in silence. He went from room to room. It looked like any average bachelor flat, with the usual mix of functional items and boys' toys. But then, in the back room, was the evidence.

It took him aback. Anna's suitcase.

Sam knelt down and unzipped the case. All her belongings were still there. He could smell her perfume on the clothes. As he knelt over the case, his phone rang. If anyone was in the flat, the shrill tones would alert the person to his presence.

'Hell.' He wrenched the phone out of his pocket. It was Louisa.

'Louisa, I can't talk right now,' he whispered, cupping a hand around his mouth.

'Sorry, Sam, I only just picked up your messages. Are you okay?'

'I'm fine.'

'I can't believe it,' Louisa continued. 'It's the guy from the campsite bar – he's done all of this?'

'Yes.'

'There's something else. Something about the name "black wolves" . . .'

'Go on.'

Louisa hesitated. 'It's – well, it's to do with Marcus, it's something I saw. He's—'

Sam never got to hear the end of the sentence.

Chapter Fifty-Two

S am woke in darkness. He could tell immediately from the rolling and turning that he was in a moving vehicle. Now he was aware that there was some kind of material wrapped tightly around his head, squashing his cheeks, hindering his breathing. Trying to raise a hand, he realised they were tied in front of him. He tried to get some kind of bearing. He was sitting on something hard. Through the material he could smell oil and grease. He was in the back of a tradesman's van, maybe.

They had taken him.

Through the terror he felt an unexpected sense of hope. Maybe this would lead to Anna, to some kind of resolution.

But now the decision not to call 999 seemed unwise. Louisa might alert the police, or Paul Cullen might have picked up his message. But what could they do? They would have no idea where he was.

He considered whether to let his captives know that he was awake. Whoever had attacked him in the flat must have used a knockout substance, as he had that vague sense of nausea that his post-operative patients often complained about. They'd held the cloth firm against his mouth and nose, and the last thing Sam had remembered was slumping to the ground, his vision fading in the all-enveloping fog.

He remained silent and still, listening to see if he would hear something, anything that might better explain the situation. But he heard nothing. He had just decided that he was alone when a hand came down hard on his right shoulder.

Whoever it was didn't speak. The unseen hand grabbed Sam's sleeve and pulled him along the wooden bench. Then he heard what sounded like the back doors being unlocked, and some light penetrated through his hood.

'Out.'

The hands grabbed at him again, hauling him outside, with Sam blindly feeling the way down onto the ground. The nausea grew. He followed the person like a dog on a lead, half-tripping over a shallow step as they entered a building.

Sam was led along a series of twists and turns. Then, without warning, he was pushed down hard onto a chair. He heard a door slam shut, and then someone began untying his hands. Finally the person removed his hood.

'Hello, Sam.'

Marcus Johnson took a seat opposite.

Chapter Fifty-Three

Sam just sat there, looking at Marcus, stunned. He couldn't quite get his head around the situation.

'Aren't you going to say anything, Sam?' Marcus asked. The question was almost business-like, as if this were some kind of bizarre job interview.

When Sam didn't reply, Marcus tried again. 'Don't you want some kind of explanation?'

The nausea returned. 'What's going on, Marcus?'

'I did all this,' Marcus said.

'No,' Sam replied. 'You didn't.'

Marcus blinked several times but held his gaze. 'I killed Cathy. We were out on the dunes, we were drunk and we got into an argument—'

'No.'

Marcus continued flatly. 'She started shouting and pushing me, I pushed her back, she slapped me. And then I took a swing at her. I didn't even know I had the bottle in my hand.'

'I don't believe it,' Sam replied. It was as if Marcus were reading a script.

Marcus continued. 'The bottle hit her across the side of her head. I tried to do mouth-to-mouth – anything – but she was dead before she hit the ground. I didn't know what to do. I panicked, left her body there and went back to our tent. You know the rest.'

'You're lying,' Sam said, searching his friend's face for an explanation of why he was doing this. 'I know who murdered Cathy.'

'I killed her, Sam, don't you understand?' This time there was some emotion, something like frustration. 'I'm admitting it, here, face-to-face.'

'I know who killed Cathy,' Sam repeated. 'The guy from the campsite, in the clubhouse. Vincent McGuire. The one you warned off in the toilets. He murdered my sister, Marcus, not you.'

Marcus listened. He looked worried. Sam could see his chest rise and fall with each breath.

Sam continued. 'I don't know why he did it – maybe revenge against you for challenging him, maybe revenge against Cathy because she rejected him. Maybe it was just fun for him, a sick game that he's still playing.'

'You're wrong,' Marcus said, but this time the words were clearly forced, staged, as if he himself didn't believe them.

'I'm right. This person, this sick individual, he's set up everything. The train crash, Richard Friedman – everything. He's been doing this to play with us all, Marcus. He's been in control for the past fifteen years. You, me and Louisa. It's all been about the three of us. Everyone else – the Ainsley family, Anna, Richard Friedman – they've been used by him to get at us. And now he's using you, isn't he?'

Marcus blinked.

'Is he watching us now?' Sam asked. 'For kicks?' He looked around the small room, finding what he was looking for in the top right-hand corner.

A camera.

'This is all part of the same sick game,' Sam said, looking at the camera.

'You don't know what you're doing, Sam.' Marcus lifted his sleeve to reveal a tattoo: a black wolf. 'I'm one of them, Sam. I killed Cathy, and I'm part of this, don't you see? Those men who beat you – I'm with them.'

'No,' Sam replied. 'I don't believe you.' Again he looked at the camera. He felt empowered. He had worked this out. 'It's time to end this.'

'Here, Sam.' Marcus pulled out an object from his pocket and tried to hand it to him. It was a small handgun.

Sam recoiled. 'I don't want it.'

Marcus tried again. 'It's loaded. Do it. Point the gun right at me and pull the trigger.'

'No.'

'Whether you believe me or not, Sam, it's the only way to save Anna.'

Now he was telling the truth, Sam could see. 'He wants this, doesn't he? He wants me to kill you, while he's watching. I'll never do it.' He looked once again at the camera. 'Do what you want with me, but please don't hurt my wife.'

Suddenly Marcus looked defeated, the gun falling limply to his side. 'Why believe me now, Sam? All those years you believed I murdered Cathy, but now you don't?'

'Like you said in the snooker hall, I know you well, Marcus. I can see it now when I look at you. You didn't kill Cathy. At the trial, if I'd really looked, I would have known then too.'

Marcus put a hand to his head, resigned horror across his face. 'He's going to kill us all now, Sam. The game's over. And it's all my fault.'

'Why is it your fault?'

Marcus ran a hand across his face. 'This is all for me, Sam. Not you or Louisa. It's all for me.'

'What do you mean?'

'He murdered Cathy and set me up as a punishment for challenging him, just for daring to tell him to leave her alone. I never knew, but he had friends in the prison – the gang in there, they called themselves the Black Wolves; they were with him. He had people watching me all this time. And when I was released, he came after me, using you, Louisa and the others.'

Sam stared at the gun, then back up at the camera, still thinking of a way out of this situation. 'When did you know that this was all about you?'

'Today. Richard Friedman's drawing in the Tate. I saw their image, the black wolf, in the background of the picture. I knew then it was all connected, so I went to contact them, to see if I could do something, maybe exchange myself for Anna.'

'But they got to you first,' Sam finished.

Marcus nodded, suddenly looking utterly defeated. 'He'd killed before, Sam, before Cathy. He told me. If I'd known what kind of person he was, I'd never have gone in there after him. Then none of this would have happened. Cathy would still be alive.'

'You can't blame yourself. You only did what I wanted to do.'

'Sam, killing me is the only way to save Anna.' He gestured at the gun. 'I'm ready for it. I'm prepared.'

Sam ignored Marcus's sacrificial offering. There was no way in the world he would do that, even if he thought it would make a difference. For fifteen years, as Marcus had languished in jail and he'd progressed in his medical career, this sick individual had climbed the criminal ladder of loan sharking, pimping and violence, maintaining this grudge. No, Vincent wasn't going to give them a happy ending, and there would be no plea bargains. Their only chance was to stick together and try to overcome him. 'Is Anna still okay?'

'I haven't seen her, but I've heard them talking. She's in this building.'

Sam stood up and moved towards the door.

Marcus reached out to pull him back. 'Sam, don't. He said he'd kill her if we tried to do anything.'

The door was open. Sam turned back to Marcus. 'I've got to do this. Is that gun really loaded?'

'Yes.'

Sam took the weapon from him and moved out into the corridor. The gun felt so alien in his hand, and he didn't even know whether he'd be able to fire it. But he needed something. Marcus followed close behind, looking out at their rear. 'Sam, it might be too late.' But Sam continued, undaunted, hoping to God that Vincent McGuire hadn't carried out his horrific threat. They moved nervously from room to room but saw no one.

And then, with one more door open, there she was, facing them, tied to a chair. She tried to smile through the gag. 'Anna, thank God.' Sam quickly untied her as Marcus guarded the door. Sam gently cupped her face. He had never felt so overjoyed. The emotion was intoxicating. 'Are you okay?'

Anna nodded. She looked exhausted but smiled again. 'I am now.'

'I don't understand,' Marcus said from the door. 'It looks like everybody's left.'

'They said something about a fire,' Anna said. 'About starting a fire.'

Sam turned to Anna. 'What?' Vincent intended to kill them all as the final act in his vendetta. But he wasn't going to succeed. He looked across at Marcus. 'Let's get out of here, now.'

The three of them fled the room and headed for the stairs. But as they neared the bottom, they realised that something was very wrong. They could feel the heat, radiating from along the downstairs corridor.

Marcus stopped and threw back a look of horror. 'The place is already on fire. They're trying to burn us alive in here.'

Sam smelt the air. 'Petrol.'

He stepped past Marcus and reached the bottom of the stairs. As he turned the corner, he was hit with a volcanic blast of hot air, and smoke billowed from further down the corridor. Behind it he could see the glow of the fire, which had already taken hold.

'Back up the stairs,' Sam ordered, shepherding everyone higher. 'There's no way out down there.'

Back on the original level, he searched the rooms for an opening window. Most of the rooms were windowless or had no opening, but he finally found one. Moving to the window's edge, he peered out at the ground below. They were too high up to escape this way.

He tried the window. It wasn't locked, so he thrust it open as far as it could go and leant out. 'Help! Someone help!'

But the side road below was deserted, and no one responded.

'What now?' Marcus said.

'You follow me,' a voice said from behind them.

All three turned to see the teenage girl standing by the entrance to the room.

'Come on, what are you waiting for? I know a way out.'

Without question they followed her along the corridor and into what looked like a storeroom. Passing piles of laundry, they exited through a door at the back and down a metal stairwell.

'He was going to use this route to get out,' she said as they descended. 'So it's clear.'

They reached the bottom and emerged onto the street, gulping in fresh air at the very moment that a fleet of emergency vehicles screamed into view, sirens wailing. Within seconds, the scene was transformed. Fire engines began tackling the blaze while paramedics and police swarmed around. Sam made sure he stayed close to Anna as she was checked over by one of the paramedics. Marcus was talking to a uniformed officer. And then Cullen appeared at a distance, exchanging a nod with Sam. He must have got his message and raised the alarm.

But in the melee, the girl had disappeared.

⌣

Immediately after leading them out the building, Jody retreated to her vantage point and watched the scene. Everyone looked to be okay. She spoke into her mobile and then waited for the van to arrive.

Locky smiled as he pulled up alongside and stuck his head through the open window. 'Hello, young lady. Locky's emergency taxi service. Where d'ya want to go?'

'Home,' Jody smiled. 'I want to go home to my family.'

Locky glanced back nervously. 'What about McGuire? Aren't you worried what he might do?'

Jody shook her head, toying with the lighter in her pocket. 'It's over. He can't hurt anyone now.'

Epilogue

Sam stood in the theatre, his world spinning around him. In all the years of his medical career, and the few months as a newly appointed consultant, he had never felt so powerless. He did the only thing that seemed useful and squeezed Anna's hand as the maternity team continued their work.

'Almost there, Anna,' the midwife encouraged, 'almost there.'

Anna smiled at Sam through the pain, and he returned the gesture, although in truth he felt sick to the stomach, hoping that everything would go well. They were so close now. Marcus and Louisa, the godparents-to-be, were waiting outside.

'If it's a girl, we'll call her Catherine,' Anna said, grimacing as she pushed again, her hair slicked back with sweat.

'But you wanted Elizabeth, after your grandmother. You always wanted—'

'The baby's here,' the midwife announced. 'Just about to come out.'

Anna smiled nervously, and Sam squeezed her hand that bit harder. He turned just as their baby daughter emerged into the world. A quick check, and Sam was handed the little girl, wrapped in white. She felt like the most precious, fragile and beautiful thing in the world.

'Elizabeth Catherine Becker,' Sam whispered into her ear, bringing her over to the bedside and into the arms of her mother.

Anna nodded, transfixed at the new arrival who had now revealed a pair of stunning, searching blue eyes. She placed her little finger into the baby's tiny palm. 'Elizabeth Catherine. I like it.'

Sam leant in to his family and wallowed in the joy of the moment.

Everything was going to be all right.

THE END

About the Author

Photo © 2014 Rebecca Millar

Paul Pilkington is a British writer from the North West of England. He is the author of the Emma Holden suspense mystery trilogy, the first of which, *The One You Love* (2011), was #1 in the *Bookseller* Official Fiction Heat Seekers Chart. The second in the series, *The One You Fear* (2013), was named as one of the Best Kindle Books of 2013 (UK Kindle Store Editor's Choice). The final instalment, *The One You Trust* (2014), has helped the series to achieve over 2,000 five-star reviews on Amazon. He is also the author of *Be Careful What You Hear* (2015), a standalone mystery novella.

Paul's work has been translated into several languages, and his novels have been e-book bestsellers in a number of countries. He has sold over 300,000 e-books.

Paul loves hearing from his readers. You can find him online at www.paulpilkington.com, chat with him at www.facebook.com /paulpilkingtonauthor or tweet him at www.twitter.com/paulpilkington.

About the Author